The Steering Group

By

M. J. Laurence

Grosvenor House
Publishing Limited

This book is published by
Grosvenor House Publishing Ltd
Link House
140 The Broadway, Tolworth, Surrey, KT6 7HT.
www.grosvenorhousepublishing.co.uk

A CIP record for this book
is available from the British Library

ISBN 978-1-83975-206-3

For my wife, who has always stood by me.

For my dad, who stared death and cancer in the eyes and simply said, "Have you got a smoke?"

The bravest man I ever knew.

Disclaimer

The Steering Group is a semi-autobiographical novel told in the first person. It is a work of fiction, inspired by some real events. There are no guarantees of fidelity regarding actual places or events. All places, dates, people's identities other than those clearly in the public domain have been manufactured or altered, and any resemblance to actual events or individuals (alive or dead) is completely coincidental and a product of the author's imagination.

The Steering Group

Index

The Steering Group

Prologue

We all make choices, lots of them, and from those choices we make a lot of mistakes – that's life. I was given a couple of choices to make when I was about 13 years old and then my life changed forever. I didn't plan any of it, life just took over and transformed a lonely, quiet, stupid and cocky boy into an intelligence operative working for a group of people known only as the 'Steering Group'.

How did it all start? We all buy a ticket in life but it's the question of where to? Why does life take us to the places we don't understand, or where we didn't want to go, even to the places we didn't even know existed in the beginning. Life is a mystery of challenges, surprises, pain, success and disappointment, but often somewhere along the way we are given a choice that could lead us somewhere very different. We can dramatically change our entire life's direction with one single decision, enabling us to go off grid, to dangerous places we never thought were achievable, or we can do nothing and stay on the rails that have been laid out for us – it's all a choice.

I went off the rails at about aged 12. From a truanting misunderstood boy (today you would probably label me as having ADHD) to a Naval Intelligence operative – how the heck does that happen? Well, I got into a lot of trouble as a boy because life was way too slow and boring for me. I didn't attend school much; and that, coupled with a few other bad choices I made, saw me taken from my home and put into a correctional facility. About two years into that stretch of hell I was given an unexpected choice by an outsider. To me it was a no-brainer of a decision: to continue along the path where no one understood me (or even bothered to find out why I was so frustrated and angry) and go into the prison system; OR join the military. It was in that split second when life chose me. A guy named Commander Brown took one look at me and saw something no one else did. He saw a rejected unwanted human being with an undiscovered and unusual skill set and offered me a family that really wanted me.

By accident, sheer luck, I had been interested enough to learn a language at school and gained a penfriend in Russia. It wasn't long before that friendship grew. That friendship, unbeknown to me at the time, was to be the door into a family that was incredibly well connected behind the iron curtain, and Cdr Brown knew it. This family was linked with the underworld of arms dealing, and later, through my Russian penfriend, the trading of science and nuclear technology to the Middle East. After a string of painful personal lessons that needed to be learnt, and endless training with people who understood me, my abilities began to shine and I was soon on my way to getting under the covers of the intelligence world. A battle of friendship over loyalty ensued, eventually leading to the loss of my friend Anatoly.

It wasn't all excitement – many months and even years were spent waiting patiently, long-sufferingly, sometimes endlessly, to uncover England's enemies. Waiting, gathering, learning, deceiving and delving deeper into the places and communities that hide the truth that your liberty is under threat. It's constantly being eroded by those seeking to supply arms to terrorists, those who hide behind corrupt government officials, trade drugs for weapons and fight for the ability to have a nuclear weapon.

I know now that in the beginning I was probably expendable; but because I was hell-bent on pleasing those who had chosen me, there was no way I was ever going to fail them or myself again. That one chance I had been afforded was all I needed. There is nothing quite like the feeling of belonging. You may find it in a church, a community, the local pub, with work colleagues or even in a street gang, but my family was closer, more powerful, tighter knit, more influential and more resourceful than any other. My new family and friends were rocks, and they never ever let me down, never betrayed me or hung me out to dry, and that is something I had never had before and so it was reciprocated. They put that to the test many times. Initially I worked alone, quietly and untraceable – that's the proving ground before the blinkers are removed and your rite of passage is granted into a wider world and you meet your brothers in arms who you will never forget or replace.

Let me just say, life in the intelligence world can be boring. For months or even years I wouldn't even be attached to the Steering Group, just simply hidden out of sight within the safety of the navy and the British military machine, awaiting orders or further instruction. I underwent endless training in things I could never quite understand, grasp the relevance of or see any need for at the time, and on many occasions I was simply doing some other job to keep busy whilst the powers that be figured out the next move on the world's chessboard. It's all about staying quiet, doing the long sleep, hibernating before being allowed to come out from behind the veil to undertake your task, releasing your skill set without anyone ever knowing where it came from, and only then for the briefest of moments. At first, I found it fun, it was almost a game, but in the end it became a fight for survival, not just in the field but in the mind.

Finally, amongst the train wreckage of all that I have been involved with, I found love – a special woman who remains with me today. Love; now, there's a thing that can really change your life. I don't think I held onto this treasure very well at times, but when losing it was threatened by my own hand or otherwise I knew the right choice without exception. Anna must now come first above all things. She stood by me when no one else would, was the only person to come to meet me when I returned from places we never talk about. She stood firm through the trauma of suicide threats, mood swings and everything PTSD can throw at a confused mind, and finally my departure from the Steering Group. God bless you, Anna.

The Steering Group

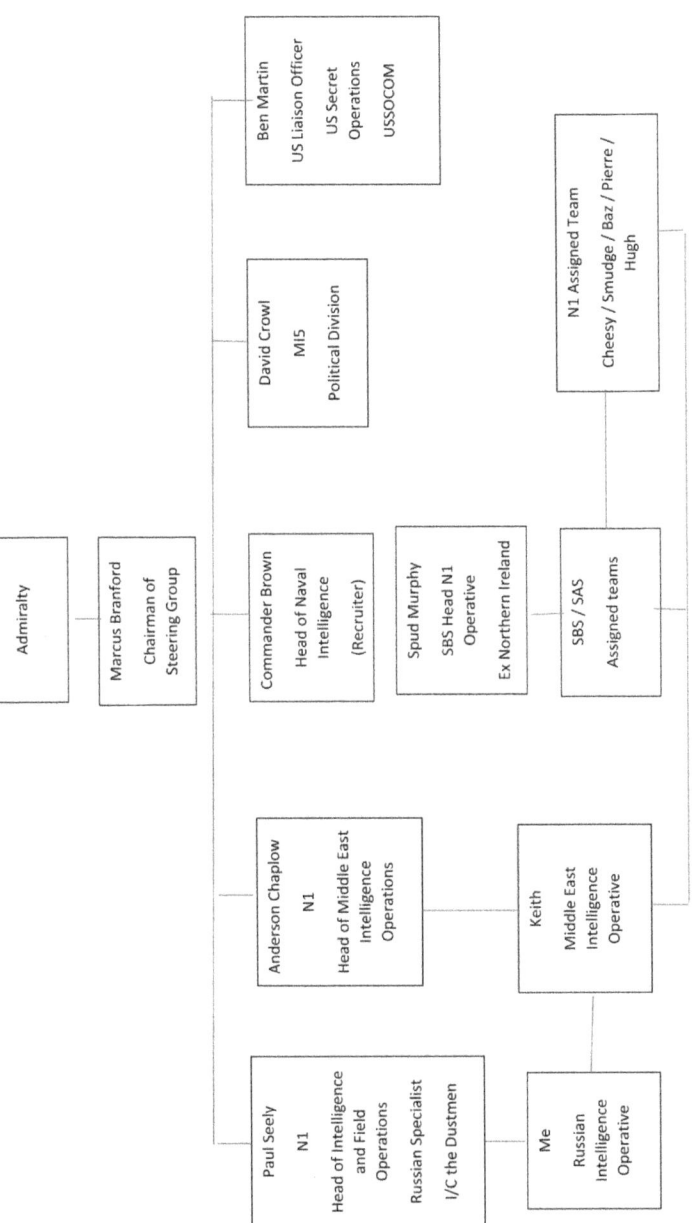

The Other Side

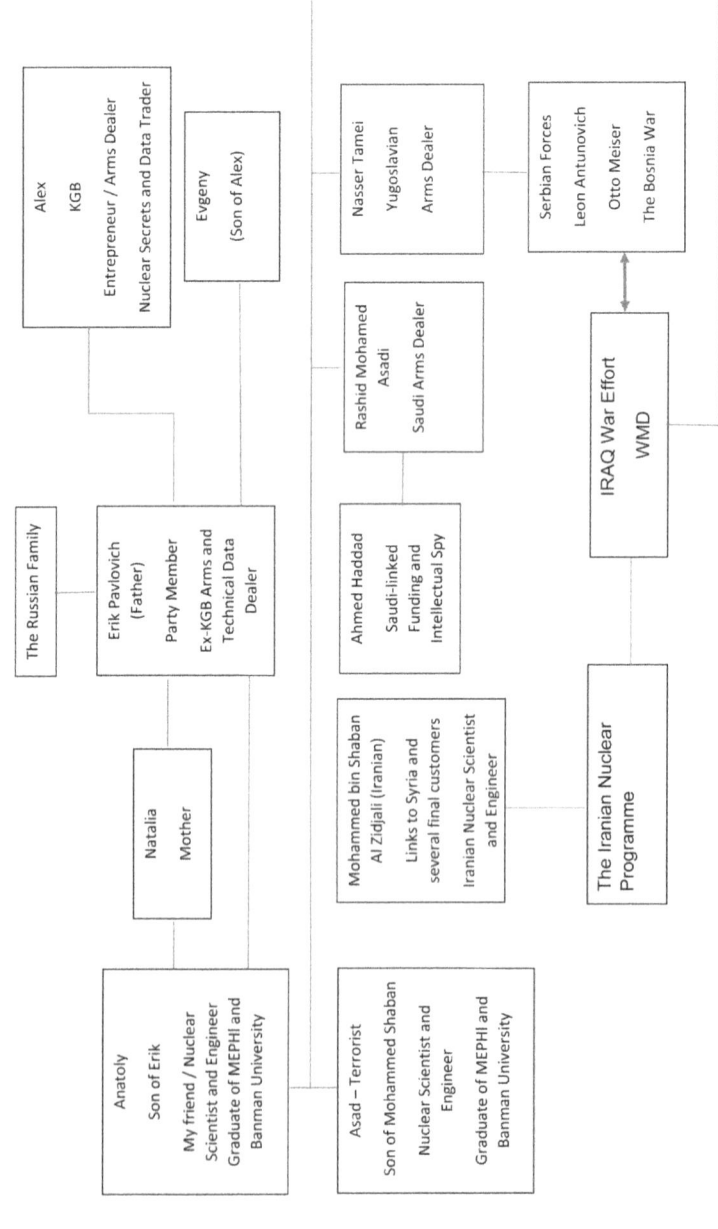

The Russian Family

Alex
KGB
Entrepreneur / Arms Dealer
Nuclear Secrets and Data Trader

Evgeny
(Son of Alex)

Erik Pavlovich
(Father)
Party Member
Ex-KGB Arms and
Technical Data
Dealer

Natalia
Mother

Anatoly
Son of Erik
My friend / Nuclear
Scientist and Engineer
Graduate of MEPHI and
Banman University

Asad – Terrorist
Son of Mohammed Shaban
Nuclear Scientist and
Engineer
Graduate of MEPHI and
Banman University

Mohammed bin Shaban
Al Zidjali (Iranian)
Links to Syria and
several final customers
Iranian Nuclear Scientist
and Engineer

Ahmed Haddad
Saudi-linked
Funding and
Intellectual Spy

Rashid Mohamed
Asadi
Saudi Arms Dealer

Nasser Tamei
Yugoslavian
Arms Dealer

Serbian Forces
Leon Antunovich
Otto Meiser
The Bosnia War

IRAQ War Effort
WMD

The Iranian Nuclear
Programme

The Steering Group

Chapter 1

First Secrets

It all started at the age of about six – that's over 40 years ago now. I'm from what may be described as a normal family and my parents were just amazing. I'll just say that again: my parents were amazing. People tend to blame their parents or childhood events for everything. My life has been an incredible journey and that started with a great mum and dad. I attended normal school (initially) and was involved in all the usual shit that is associated with anyone who is considered to be part of normal society. My dad worked at Pye in the beginning – yeah, what's that? They used to make TVs and radios and the like. Turned out that the Pye workshops were a great place to meet influential people, and this is where I first learnt from my dad, who was a great bullshit artist, how to get just about anything you wanted by talking to people, which usually gets them doing things they wouldn't normally do. My dad was short, of slim build, always wore a tie (a cravat in the early days) and had a well-trimmed moustache coupled with the usual side parting reminiscent of the post-war era. Dad was always very calm and collected, it was very hard to get him upset, but I'd never recommend that you push that boundary or find out where that line is, as I did on occasion.

I remember him telling me how he had met Harry Trent. Dad was working in the workshop at Pye doing a few jobs as a radio telecommunications engineer; it was just an ordinary day like every other day, I guess. Now, my dad always said it's not what you know it's *who* you know, and I've always remembered that because it was sound advice. So, there was my dad in the workshop when this Harry guy comes in; everyone ignores him cos Harry looks like a pikey. Harry doesn't give a shit what he looks like and that's because Harry doesn't have to, because he's loaded. Harry had the kind of money that made any business presentation bullshit unnecessary, the kind of money where the cost of a night out would have covered your mortgage for a year. Well anyway, Dad goes over and asks what he can do to help. Harry responds that he wants one of these new in-car radio telephone jobs. (Now, remember this is before the mobile phone even got started so it's new technology and very expensive.) Everyone in the workshop is pissing themselves laughing, but Dad plays the game and says, "Okay, mate, let's go have a look." Now, outside is a fucking brand-new Bentley V8 T series convertible. No fucker is laughing when the workshop doors are opened and Dad drives it in for the new radio telephone installation. Yeah, no fucker is laughing now, and I'm sure Harry loved that moment, and every time that he'd pulled that stunt.

Dad went on to do many jobs for Harry and they were good friends. Harry owned a nightclub beneath an undertakers in Newcastle out towards Jesmond, and it was mainly a blue light club. He also owned a golf course in Bermuda but that's an entirely different story. My dad would often go to do the wiring and lighting in the club to earn a few extra quid on those exclusive evenings Harry seemed to arrange so often. He kept Mum happy with a few flowers and a box of those chocolates... Oh yeah, Dairy Box – mustn't be any other make – and no one is allowed the coffee chocolate, not even the one on the second layer. Harry had a few girls who would do favours and that kept all the awkward customers happy, I guess. Nice girls, and I'm sure my dad never touched them because he was a true gentleman. But who knows what went on between all the other customers after a full night at the club. Harry was a big bastard and liked the beer and the women. He was genuinely a nice guy, always there to sort out any shit that came along, always there to smooth out the unexpected bumps in the road of life, a really good friend to my dad. As a kid I often met Harry in a pub in Newcastle for lunch with my dad; I'm guessing he and my dad did more than have lunch there – maybe a few dodgy deals were done over those pub lunches, who the fuck knows – it was a place where such deals could be conducted without needing to worry who might be overhearing your conversation.

Mum was a stay-at-home housewife, which sadly ended up being her prison some years later. Mum was a big-hearted lady who loved her family, it was her little flock, but I think she secretly yearned for that fast-paced London life she had once enjoyed in her twenties. Mum only mentioned that previous life once or twice to me when she revealed her abilities and how she could have gone to university and attained a degree. That was saying something, as back then it would have been an achievement rather than something to do because everyone else is doing it, like some of today's graduates who don't know what the fuck else to do except go to uni, get drunk and attend some sort of course leading to nothing. My mum should have been a career girl but ended up with us four kids and a life which became cemented between anxiety and agoraphobia, to which the only and very rare relief was a plate of plaice and chips at the nearby A1 Little Chef restaurant. The whole family used to pile into Dad's little work Fiesta and zoom down the A1 for lunch, six of us, and we were all allowed to order what we wanted. That was a real treat indeed for us kids, ordering what the fuck we wanted from a menu and not having to share any of it with anyone; a treat we all looked forward to but rarely enjoyed. Mum always looked after us all in her own way, and by putting her family first she never had much of her own, such is the sacrifice a good parent makes. I think she became very weight conscious after having her first two kids. I never saw an issue in this personally but I think it destroys a woman, this obsessive weight thing, but they are all the same: diet after diet and endless weight loss plans. Me, I couldn't give a shit, never stopped me, and I've been real fat and real thin more times than I can remember. For me it's what season I'm in, I think, but it tends to be the fat one seven out of ten times; and besides, I'm a bloke so no one cares.

Mum always did well with the meagre allowance she had and made meals from nothing. At one point I remember the family having only 10 pounds a week to live off when my dad was briefly out of work. I've no idea how that translates into six breakfasts, lunches and dinners for six hungry people but it always did. Shit, that woman could bake as well – always had a cake tin full of cakes whether you wanted them or not; and if you didn't eat a cake you'd requested, the whole fucking family would be having that shit with custard the following week. Poor old Dad liked Madeira cake, but could never eat it all before it became stale, so he would take some serious grief over the fact he hadn't gobbled it all up in the first week, and then we would all have to eat our way through it with pints of that Birds custard mix, and God forbid the custard turned out lumpy.

School was a boring uninteresting place that never interested me in the slightest. I guess most kids feel like that, even today. I remember those early days up in Newcastle, I had a fascination with stealing all the shiny stuff from the classrooms, and right from the age of five finding new and interesting ways and excuses for how not to attend lessons. I think I managed to steal just about everything out of the school stationery store and stockpiled it in my den at home, which was an over-the-stair's cupboard in my bedroom where I would often sit alone with the door closed amongst my hoard with a torch. I always thought if there was a subject you weren't interested in or it was your birthday, you shouldn't have to go to school; turned out me and my mum fell out about that thought process on a great many occasions. If I was forced to attend school, I'd just fuck off out the back gates when my mum had gone back home. She was great – walked me to school and picked me up every day; how rare is that nowadays? I loved my mum. This skiving off from school was the best introduction or training I could ever have had at learning the art of deception and lies, I think.

As with all things in life we can trace the source of a fuck-up right back to a dumb decision or action we took some years previously, and heck I've made more than my fair share of them and continue to do so. I didn't expect to get into anything other than a bit of fun in my little adventures skiving off from school but it was all destined to become something more through a labyrinth of semi realities and circumstances that took me along a path to a life that would show me the world – the very best and finest to the very worst places and people on the planet.

Well, as it turned out, me and my dad loved to go down to the docks in Newcastle and he would bullshit his way on to any ship that happened to be in port. He was just brilliant at talking his way on to ships so he could show me around and dream of going to sea. Dad loved ships and from the very first day I knew him as a boy he built beautiful model ships. I have two in my office today. Getting into the docks was easy back then as it was way before the days of ISPS and all those international security requirements we have today. There was nothing more to do than share a fag with the gate staff security or gangway watch officer to get a great day out and maybe a free lunch or a few drinks on board a ship or two. It was always a great day out with my dad down the docks, and I think he loved it so much because of the fact he was never allowed to be a merchant mariner.

He was never in the navy or the merchant navy but was signed up for the Royal Air Force, just for his two-year stint for national service, which was mostly in Kenya. Being a fly boy, as it turned out, was not of his choosing but his father's. Dad wanted to be in the merchant navy, just never happened. Fucked if that was gonna happen to me; and my dad sowed that seed in my little mind right from the very beginning. Do what you want to do, son, and fuck the world. Good advice; just that sometimes the world didn't want to turn in the same direction as me, making my future destined to be so out of control that had I of known what lay ahead I might have been a little more careful in my choices.

I couldn't have been much more than six or seven years old when my dad and I were down the docks and were in luck as some warships and coasters were alongside. We would get all excited and of course spend far too much time looking over these fine war canoes and coastal traders, inevitably making us lose track of time and arrive late home for dinner leading to a right old bollocking from Mum. My dad would always put on the bullshit charm with ships' staff, and we would somehow manage to get down to the engine room which was just fascinating for us both. But I never wanted to become an engineer, always wanted to be the captain, a boy's dream. Life or fate, however, would use engineering through me to help me find a different path in life. On this one occasion we had managed to get on a Type 12 frigate, and I remember being down in the mess deck with my dad whilst he was smoking a cigarette and sharing a can of beer with one of the crew, whilst I was fascinated, just staring at some guy who was box stitching an anchor for a keyring. He gave it to me and I was just made up. That was it – I was gonna go to sea and see the world.

Newcastle was, for me at least, innocence, beautifully delivered in a cotton wool fantasy of happy families. I attended school for what it was worth, my dad did the nine-to-five and

I remember our first colour TV. Mum even had a few friends and worked part-time as a checkout girl in a supermarket for a short while. Shit, it makes me feel old to say we had a black and white TV – most people now wouldn't know that they existed – but I genuinely remember watching the snooker in colour just because we could. Heck, to think it only had three buttons – one each for BBC1, BBC2 and ITV – and no remote; well, the remote would be one of us kids! Life went on, a life which was just normal, nothing to get excited about. Good memories, family Christmases with piles of presents – it just seemed like back then we would get tons and tons of presents. It would be fair to say I was really lucky to be in such a great family. Mum and Dad never had any money so I have no idea how they ever afforded Christmas from the day I came on the scene until they tragically opted out. Funny how as life goes on, the fewer gifts you get, the fewer people keep in touch and the more you want to just forget the whole issue and get drunk. I think Christmas is mostly a depressing time of year, both for me and for the wider population who don't have wads of cash to waste on unwanted gifts and other shite we all seem so desperate to buy in the big build-up.

I dodged school one day to go with my dad to the Pye workshops for a day out of school. I rode shotgun in the van, one of those real old Ford Transits with the curvy bonnet and the double windows in the back doors, and we went off and did some off-site work before going into the workshops. I think my dad and I did this maybe a dozen times together, so he's as much to blame for my schooling as me, I think. For lunch Dad took me to a spit-and-sawdust pub in central Newcastle called The Albion, where I would always have sausage and mash with tinned veg. The sausages were fucking awesome and the mash was served like ice-cream scoops, which for me made it all taste great for some reason. Harry would sometimes meet me and my dad at this pub and let me have a pint, and if I behaved I'd sometimes get to ride back to the workshops in his Bentley – damn, that was fun. My mum always found out about the pub visits and it drove her mad that I would eat veg at the pub but not at home. This sometimes ended up with me and Mum having massive fights over such ridiculous things as not liking spinach or cauliflower, pointless arguments that always seemed to happen after a good day out.

I suffered badly from hay fever in childhood, not so much now. Not just the odd sneeze, hell no, I'd become almost completely blind as my eyes swelled up and became all crusty with all the gunk I had to use to help treat it and the never-ending watering eyes. Fucking doctors were shit; I had the multi-jab thing and no end of injections, all to no avail. I was always off school in the summer and even played on it a bit for more time away from school. I guess I just never liked people, or too many of them at once. I still find people generally annoying to this day unless they have something to actually say or share that is genuinely interesting. I used to spend hours and hours playing marbles with a kid called Johnathan in the street; he had some really bad fucked-up disease as I remember, and I think he was grateful for some friendship as he was always off school. He was an okay kid. I always stole the odd marble from him for my collection but I don't think he noticed or even minded because he enjoyed our time together. Often us kids would disappear down the local quarry to play war or cowboys and Indians; it was a great place – we used to sink no end of stuff in the lake, shopping trolleys and stuff we had stolen from the Blaydon Estate. My brother and I spent many days building tree houses and dens in that quarry. We made great bows and arrows that really did fucking hurt if you got shot. Phil (my older brother) managed to drop a huge lump of wood on my hand one day whilst we were building a tree house, and I remember coming home screaming like a crazed lunatic. I still have the scar on my finger from that accident. In retaliation I split his head open with a spade a week later.

Newcastle holds my fondest memories of childhood; I had cool friends and things to do. I still think of it as home.

Occasionally my older brother and I were sent off to our grandparents on my dad's side who lived near London. This was always sold to us as a great holiday but was most likely to get rid of us both so our parents could get some peace and quiet. Heck, it was traumatic; don't get me wrong, my brother and I would be just as good as gold until we got there. Our grandfather, a short-ass dapper gent, would allow us to work in his shed; the old guy was quite a clever chap in making models and stuff, model railway engines mostly, and I guess that's where my dad's model boat building talent came from. Phil and I would learn many new skills down that shed, and of course I would learn how best to use a chisel to draw blood from my brother in one way or another. We occasionally joined forces and sabotaged all manner of things in the shed, including Grandad's whisky supply. He would have bottles stashed just about everywhere. Our grandmother would innocently think that her husband was down the shed making models and steam engines, when actually he was slowly drinking himself into oblivion. From what I can remember he never got on with my mum's parents as he never saw action during the war so he was never part of the club. Bill was considered a war dodger in Grumps' household from what I gathered from my mum. (He was called Grumps because he really was a miserable bastard.)

I got a taste for whisky during those visits to London, and I would be held to ransom by my older brother, but I always had more dirt on him than he had on me, and if I didn't I would make shit up. I just love the memory of Phil and I sinking many of our grandad's plant pots in a water butt at the end of the garden that collected all the rainwater off the garage and shed roofs for watering his plants in the greenhouse. Grandad had heaps of plant pots in the shed and greenhouse, stacks and stacks of those nice terracotta pots, in all shapes and sizes. Shit, that was funny; the old guy couldn't figure out where all his plant pots had fucked off to! There were probably only a few inches of water left in that water butt, the rest displaced by all his pots!

Grandma would be in the kitchen making the worst rock cakes known to man (or were they grenades for the army?) and the most disgusting lumpy mashed potatoes to go with some carefully prepared nightmare dinner on a plate. For fuck sake, when you make mash it's supposed to be mash or it would be called 'lumps'. Heck, she had all the best intentions, but both Phil and I would delight in finding innovative methods of getting rid of this shit during mealtimes. Of course, Grandad was too pissed to notice what we got up to; and well, we were too young to care. They were really good people but we were young, and getting into trouble was much more fun. Later, when we would get back home, we would tell Mum how bad Grandma's cooking was and have a real laugh about it. I guess it made Mum feel more appreciated when we returned home from our holidays.

One night we were made to dress up and go to some OAP event at the local community hall where our grandparents showed us how skilful they were at ballroom dancing. It was a young boy's nightmare, ballroom fucking dancing! Turned out to be a pretty cool evening as I would minesweep as much beer as I could, and most of those old guys would let me have a drag on a cigarette or even give me a sip of whisky or rum after telling me some old war story or other tale from their past. However, typically, I just had to brighten that one night up, so decided that I would help out with the tombola thing and fixed it so my brother Phil won first prize. We never got invited back after that. Funny old thing. Oh well, shit happens, I guess.

My dad's father eventually died, God rest his soul, after many years drinking whisky which led to a progressive decline in his health to the point where he literally shit his pants on a holiday bus trip, which finally made my grandmother realise the guy was on his way out. Although it really isn't funny, I still chuckle at the fact that the old boy enjoyed his drink and just casually shit his pants in front of everyone. I guess he must have been pissed, and I know what it's like to try to hold in a crap when you're pissed; you're gonna lose so you might as well just smile. Gran died shortly afterwards and, if my memory serves me right, my poor father never really got to mourn their deaths because of the geographical distance, and time away wasn't easy.

After my younger brother had been born in Newcastle, a happy accident by all accounts, we moved to a small town in Nottinghamshire and to a much larger house because Dad had landed himself a good job, a manager's position at some big radio telecommunications firm called Air Comms, if I remember correctly. The move would take us closer to Mum's parents. What a joy, we would see more of Grandad Grumps – he was a seriously miserable bastard. He was 6ft plus and a real live war hero and survivor of Belsen concentration camp during the Second World War. He had a chest full of medals and, when we went round to visit him, he would let each of us boys have a coin out of this big old ammo box where he kept tons of war memorabilia that fascinated both my older brother and me. The old war horse had fucking everything in that old ammo box – coins, medals, German SS knives and spent ammunition cartridges – no idea what happened to all that. They had moved out to South Africa to be with Mum's sister for a few years and later returned to England, ending up in a council house. They had had servants and all that shit out in South Africa but I guess the money must have run out or something so they ended up back in sunny old England.

It was a one-horse town, sold to the unsuspecting house-hunter as a historic market town; translated, that means shithole with nothing going for it except a market in a town square where we used to love going to see the hunt set off. I remember seeing those tall horses with the red-jacketed riders and all the dogs; seemed like real England, a scene perhaps from the magazine *This England*. With a river and a canal flowing through it, it was somewhat interesting to me as a boy as both waterways presented some adventure to my young enquiring mind. But it basically consisted of cheap housing, a town hall, a collection of cheap shit shops, too many banks and building societies, a good butcher called Hogg & Son which is still there today (they do great pork pies and awesome cream cakes), Cooplands the baker, a cinema and about half a dozen pubs. If you go there today, you'll think I am lying because it's actually a really nice place. It has become very desirable, with great shops and restaurants all adding to the café culture. It's clean, well-kept and, heck, I'd probably move back it's changed that much!

My grandmother on my mother's side was fucking awesome. You could see where my mum came from – just the most caring selfless person in the world. Grandma Bramworth was 5ft and a fag paper and weighed in around the half ton mark. She was just the greatest person on earth. I suppose she had to be to put up with that miserable bastard Grumps. Never had any nice outfits, or anything special, just old crap clothes that stank of cigarettes, and she always wore one of those awful 'pinnies' old people wear to do the housework in. On countless afternoons I would sneak out of school, steal some fags and go play backgammon with her whilst drinking Grumps' supply of brown ale. Black and Tan was her drink and she would have no problem sitting smoking and drinking away those many afternoons with me knowing that I should be at school but would rather I be safe with her than out and up to no good. Clever old bird. When Grumps came home Gran would let me escape out the back door which backed on to the railway line, which covered my escape from Grumps quite nicely. I really, really loved my grandmother.

Moving meant a new school, friends and enemies, and of course having a Geordie accent was the perfect excuse for all the other boys to pick a fight with me despite me trying to avoid it at all costs. Let's just say I continued to skive off quite a lot. I started to learn a few good swear words in the playground, often repeated to the teachers to my downfall, and I soon learned how to throw a punch. I wasn't hard or anything, just a skinny kid who preferred to bunk off than go to singing or recorder lessons! Yeah, music lessons where boys are expected to get up and sing or play the recorder are just a no-no in my book. I can remember Mrs Callington's music lessons; we each had to stand and sing solo and play the recorder to the rest of the class – what a load of bollocks. I went down the river instead and gradually learned new ways of how to steal cigarettes and other assorted goodies from the local shop without being caught on my way. I would go on my own, with a friend or with my brother, but he was at a different school soon after we arrived because he is two years older than me so it wasn't often we got into trouble together.

The river was great. I remember taking our inflatable dinghy down there after filling it up with air at a local petrol station; I'm sure the staff there grassed me up a few times for not being at school, and they hated me using the air supply for the dinghy. I loved riding the dinghy down the river, which was fast-flowing, and towards the edge of town it plummeted though a weir; you had to be careful not to get trapped in the weir's sluice gates and not to spin too fast or tip over before hitting the big wave at the bottom which we called 'the muncher'. From the weir we would go onwards, collecting old bottles and shit from the riverbed, finally getting to an old firing range the TA used. This turned out to be an awesome discovery; we would find live rounds on the range which had been abandoned in exercises and we collected them. I later introduced a few friends to the firing range, and we later learned together how to put unspent rounds on the railway tracks in order to try shooting each other across the tracks, pretending we were in the trenches like in the stories Grumps had told me about. Being in the 'trenches' was where teams took up position either side of the tracks, which we thought was awesome, not realising just what we were playing with. I can't believe no one actually got shot playing that game. I think only one train stopped after passing over about a dozen rounds, which resulted in a number of ricochets against the trains wheels. We didn't hang around to find out the result of our handiwork.

We later moved into an older house near the town centre, which was great, and I had just the biggest bedroom ever. All the rooms had servant bells that rang down in the kitchen. Everything felt like it was gonna be okay. The house was totally unmodernised but to compensate had great big coal fires to keep us warm, and they were in the bedrooms too. No carpets or central heating for the first few years but it never mattered much to us; it must have been a major headache for my dad, getting all the earache from Mum to get on and do all the DIY shit. I liked that big old house; it was kind of a mess but at the same time a really nice home. I think because it wasn't perfect and not a show home it felt more of a home, even if the mess drove my mother insane.

The next-door neighbours introduced themselves quite early on. Curly, as he was affectionately known, was in the demolition business, but only of his own home. This guy was into DIY on a biblical scale. Just about every night this fucktard would start banging, demolishing one of the interior walls or some other destructive process in his home. The banging and crashing would sometimes go on all night and it simply drove my mother mad. On and on this went for a few years, almost to the point of my mum having a nervous breakdown. I guess it was this chapter in her life that made her so anxious and paranoid. You had to see the funny side of all of this too because Curly was a brilliant entertainer as well as being a total idiot.

He brilliantly decided to knock down the wall between the living area and the kitchen – or was it the living room and the dining room?; I can't remember – but he unintentionally took the stairs out at the same time. Kids were stranded upstairs and the fucking debris had blocked the way out to the yard so he couldn't get the ladders to get to the kids or his dogs! It was Billy Smart's Circus on some nights, and we would watch in awe from the bedroom windows at his DIY show. Curly wasn't the brightest bulb in the shop but he had everyone else's lights on all night on many occasions. It all came to a head one night after the endless noise, crashing and banging forced my dad to go round and confront him. He was married to Marie, who had no teeth and was mother to his six boys. They all looked the same: really short-shaved skinheads, home-knitted jumpers and ripped jeans. I guess they were just trying to make ends meet like the other 90% of the population. Anyway, Dad went round there, all 5ft of him, half Curly's size, and offered him out. Of course, after that incident the banging and the piss-taking got worse and Mum and Dad eventually moved on to a bungalow the other side of town, but that was way after I had left home.

I started secondary school and was just not into any of it. My friends and I eventually gave the French teacher a nervous breakdown pretty early on by clowning around at the back of the class. I later took up playing the trombone to get out of doing French altogether. Schoolmates were pretty okay, I guess. I was in the top stream for all subjects but I never applied myself to any of the subjects initially. Couldn't care less really. It was all a waste of time. What was the fucking point of learning that a+b = fucking x? But what suddenly became interesting to me was the fact that my school taught Russian. I was fascinated immediately by the language and its new crazy alphabet, and I was actually genuinely interested in something for the first time in my life. My tutor was Mr Richards, funny looking fucker but strict; I didn't mind his authority for some strange reason. He had a full black Russian beard like one of those woolly hats they wear in Moscow and NHS black-rimmed glasses, but he was sort of smart and composed with his black doctor-style briefcase, very shiny black shoes and heavy overcoat. It was like he was stuck in a winter's scene from Moscow, and he had squinted ice-blue eyes which didn't miss a trick. You could almost imagine him in Stalingrad during the siege as a commissary officer or something equally as sinister behind the Iron Curtain. I always expected him to have a hip flask of vodka or something but never saw one, to my disappointment.

I spent just two years learning Russian in school with Mr Richards and learnt it obsessively for some reason. I don't know why I was obsessed, but I soon became absolutely fluent, taking extra time to do additional learning at home and in school, including asking for those language cassettes for Christmas. I listened to those cassettes every day. My older brother would be recording *Top of the Pops* and I would be learning how to speak Russian. I just wanted to be a Russian I guess, in a childish way. It was still mysterious in the '70s, and the Cold War remained very real and on the news every week. I guess you could go as far as to say Mr Richards and I got on really well, as well as a student and teacher possibly could. I gained pen pals and personal friends in Moscow through him and later wrote regularly with families all over the country as far east as Vladivostok. I probably took too much time to impress Mr Richards and to show my desire to learn, but at the time he would be obliging enough and even take the time to hold a conversation in the school corridor in Russian to see how much I really knew. I guess you could say I admired him in some strange way.

Not only was I learning to speak Russian but I was learning to write it and pick up all the slang that would be common in Moscow at the time from all my pen pals. I also got to hear of how they lived, the hardships and the crazy systems that were in place for common Muscovites. For example, they had to queue three times for meat: once to choose it, once to pay and then again to collect, because you were not allowed to handle food and money at the same time or some bullshit like that. I gathered quite a collection of souvenirs and trinkets from my penfriends, including Russian hats and badges. It was cool and interesting. I became popular at school because I excelled in this subject, and Russian homework was just easy so I ended up doing all my friends' homework for them. I studied maps of the Soviet Union, the CCCP, its history, its wildlife, its size, its military might, the love of vodka and mushrooms, and the simple delights of the common people, with music, simple food and the ability to play chess. I still often sing that annoying song 'Kalinka' in my head. It's totally fucking annoying.

My favourite pen pal, Anatoly, wrote to me and explained that now he was 18 (some years older than me) he was about to go to an academy of science within a Moscow university and they had to wear a uniform. He had been forced to have his head shaved and was so upset about it because he had loved his long blond mane. He was elegantly Russian, like a young Nikolai Romanov, very handsome and very Russian. I wrote back immediately and promised I would shave my head like his and send him a photo. My mum was horrified when I came back from town one afternoon with a very short crew cut; I think it was a zero all over, bald to look at. I remember that episode in the barber shop – the barber was so unsure about my request but I think he enjoyed doing it as much as I liked seeing it all fall to the floor. He did a reverse Mohawk down the middle, and heck it was short. There was that 'oh shit, what the fuck am I doing?' moment but actually I thought it was so cool. I sent a Polaroid immediately to Moscow, much to Anatoly's delight. Anatoly was to study nuclear physics and chemistry and would later become a huge success in the Soviet nuclear programme.

Now, if I was a child today, you'd have me labelled with ADHD or some other exotic excuse for bad behaviour. Apart from my interest in learning everything about Russia and its language and customs, I was a bored teenager who simply yearned for travel and adventure. In my mind I simply had to go to Moscow; it had become a fascination, an obsession. I had to get out of England and see the world. I spent the next year or so mostly bored. I enjoyed cycling, becoming an expert shoplifter, learning my Russian and taking long afternoons off school to go down the river with my friends and sometimes my older brother. I spent days on the firing range, fucking around on the railway tracks, and I remember seeing the first ever HST train arrive at the railway station; the stationmaster was horrified to see us kids on the track talking to the driver, who was happy to open the cab door and let us climb in for a look. We later tried firing a couple of rounds in the general direction of the stationmaster, and then spent an entire afternoon on the run from the transport police. Life went on like this for a while, until I took an interest in the local antiques shop, with a view to stealing a few nice silver pieces from it.

Now, the local antiques shop was owned and run by the local vicar, a guy called Carl who was the quintessential wolf in sheep's clothing. He was a rogue; he would be my Fagin and I the Artful Dodger. Quite simply, Carl was a bigger thief than I would ever be. Behind the dog collar was the dodgy dealer who could charm the knickers off any nun – and, as it turned out, he had the ability to take advantage of my innocence to sexually abuse me.

He befriended my father after offering me work at the church shop after he caught me shoplifting, instead of getting any police involved. He did a deal for an antique camera with my dad to cement their relationship and the arrangement between my parents, him and me. He soon had the confidence of my parents who thought I would be well looked after in his company and pick up some good habits – have a good mentor, so to speak (they had no idea what was actually going on). I was to attend church and listen to classical music with Carl to keep me out of trouble at night. Carl held me to ransom over all my thefts from the church and his shop, and extracted sexual favours from me for about a year, a trade-off so that I wouldn't blow it all wide open and destroy my family. There were many threats of calling the police or social services because I continued to steal from the church and his shop. Eventually, threats of being taken away would come my way if I didn't conform to all his demands. That's the thing with most secrets, they always fuck the innocent as well as the bastards who made them necessary in the first place. However, bizarrely and unconsciously I think it was attending that church that allowed faith into my life, if you could call it that. Couldn't ever explain it, just that this was the entry point of religion into my life, which was then buried for the next 25 years.

I eventually came across a lad at school who saw that I was trapped like him; he had seen me with Carl and just knew what was going on. We compared stories of our encounters and became good friends very quickly. We spent many days away from school and did some life together. Robert was in a foster home and explained how he had also been sexually abused by carers and was trapped in so much as he couldn't break out of the system. He had seen the same issues in me that were troubling him: a loner, afraid to talk and mix with the other kids. He had been all alone throughout his short life. I think I understood him entirely. He moved away (or was moved by social services, I'm not sure) and committed suicide not long after I had got to know him. I was the one who got the suicide note. I lost my first friend at just 13 years old. I attended the burial, secretly hiding in the background waiting for everyone to leave. No one knew anything of what had actually happened or the reason for Robert's suicide. In fact, the very opposite. All the social bullshit niceties were displayed, as one would expect at any funeral. But it was all a lie, a great big coverup, and one that I learnt a great deal from. Secrets do go to the grave sometimes, and I put the note on his coffin before the gravediggers covered him up. Crazy, isn't it? They covered over the letter, which then covered up the reason for his death, which covered up the whole deal. This was my first real secret.

I took a bit of a downward spiral but continued to work with Carl and we made a lot of money together in those strange days. We would often get drunk in the vestry on wine afterwards, together with his other boys, before he had his way with me alone. We would go to old folks' houses and Carl would offer money to take 'awkward' pieces of furniture away for a good price; of course, they were all sold on in no time for a profit. I guess it sort of felt normal after a while. It was all done very politely over a nice cup of tea, and the poor old buggers thought they could trust him. We had a good turnover in the shop, and if there wasn't anything in the till the money collection from the church could always be utilised. Funerals and weddings were great; I actually enjoyed working with Carl on these occasions and sometimes forgot what he was and what he had done to me. Fucking made a fortune. The money collections at church services, plus my wage working for the church and the shop, saw to it that I had more money than I could spend. It was only a few years later when Carl went safely to his grave that his secrets that had been kept safe with me became redundant. How it must have eaten at his mind knowing I could have ruined his entire life at any time when he was alive. I forgive you, Carl.

I ran away a few times after some of the sessions with Carl; the best trip was to Aberdeen where I managed to stow away on board an oil rig supply ship bound for the North Sea oil and gas fields. I ended up working as a cabin boy for just under two weeks. I hitchhiked up to Aberdeen, which only took a day as back then hitchhiking was commonplace and safer than it is today. It wasn't hard to get on board a ship – my dad had taught me well. I had my dad's bullshit on my side, and I put it all to good use as I casually joined the workforce in the morning rush onto the docks and chose a ship that looked pretty interesting and blended into the busy dockside. The *Atlantic Star* was a chance of adventure to my young eyes – a huge supply and anchor shifting ship with a beautiful flared bow, lovely lines, freshly painted and looking in fine fettle, it had great big anchors the size of the Eiffel Tower and a bulbous bow that looked like it was meant to be on an ancient Greek trireme or 'ramming' ship in the Aegean Sea.

When you're doing something wrong you just have to look like you're meant to be doing it, my dad had told me. So, I'd pick up a crate of bread and follow the crew up the accommodation ladder, then I simply didn't follow them off again – that's all there was to it. I remember going onto that ship like it was yesterday – it's the smell. A ship smells like nothing else, it's hard to describe: a mixture of oil, exhaust fumes, paint, the galley and that blue shit they use to clean the decks with (that shit really stinks), and inside it was really nice and warm, comforting and welcoming. I soon found a plenum chamber in which to hide before I felt the ship moving as she left the berth. After being discovered I ended up washing pots, cleaning up, my own sick mostly, and got to use lots of that blue shit. I was so seasick but still managed to have the most amazing experience. I was just simply having the best adventure of my life. Captain Melton, or Captain Pies as he was affectionately known, was a top man; he obviously had to call it in when I was discovered but he didn't let on to me, and he looked after me like a real Sea Dad should. I was allocated my own cabin, bunk and shower. I was free to roam around the ship and sit on the bridge as we ploughed the North Sea out to the rigs. From the calm of the harbour we ventured around the gentle coast and then, before you know it, you're out of sight of land and into the full force of the North Sea and those big North Atlantic rollers.

The first time you see a rough sea is the best. It makes you feel so small, so vulnerable and insignificant to the power of the weather, and you start to believe in God. I should imagine many poets have tried to capture how it feels and many artists have tried to paint it. It really is an animal that you can't tame, a beast that lunges and tries to knock you over with all its weight, as well as a calm tame friend upon a leash. But there is no leash strong enough for the dog of the sea when Neptune opens his storm gates.

One morning I remember clinging on to Captain Pies' arm while he was secured in his chair on the bridge as that ship buried her beautiful flared bow in one huge wall of a wave after another. The ocean was crowded with white horses jumping off the tops of the crests like it was race day at St Leger. It was like being in a car wash: every time we ploughed deep into an oncoming wave all the windows would turn green as we were pulled almost completely underwater on the bridge. The ship would shudder and twist to one side and gently pull herself up to meet the sky again. Gentle creaking of the wooden fixtures and Formica bulkhead coverings, the occasional bilge alarms and the odd mug falling on the deck, coupled with the gentle vibration of the engines and the smell of the ship, all played a part in the beautiful orchestra of this ship at sea. There really is a mystique to the sea. I loved to go out on deck and have that spray in my face and the cold wind cut through to my soul as I'd tighten the straps of my lifejacket and hold on so very tightly to the rails. The whip of the spray over those guardrails into your face is like the sting of a wasp that comes again and again. Just beautiful.

It was my fear and excitement, the raised tempo of the ship's orchestra and the sea battling for harmony with a kid's mind who's run away from home on an adventure that made the world seem like a great place to be. This, coupled with buckets of adrenalin, excitement, fear and joy, was any boy's dream and it set the foundation of what I wanted, in fact now expected, from life. None of this was in school! It's like having heroin for the first time but legally, and it was free for the taking. Captain Pies went to great lengths to explain to me the ways of a ship, and how each ship was a lady of the ocean and how we should respect her and her ways at sea. Every ship sails differently, every ship handles differently, like every woman in the world; every old salt will tell you the same story in many different ways, I guess. I learnt about radar, navigation, charts, tides and the moon, engine operations, ship's maintenance, horsepower, bollard pull, the whole deal, and why a+b = fucking x is actually worth learning about at school. I was hooked on every word he said. I slept the best I'd ever sleep in my entire life those two weeks at sea.

As soon as I'd turned that bunk light out at night, I was away dreaming about tomorrow's adventure at sea and eager to be up real early the next day. You'd have to strap yourself in with a kind of seat belt but for a bunk, or you'd risk being tossed out on to the cabin deck unexpectedly. I'd sometimes think of Robert and what it must be like to be in a coffin, as the bunks on that ship were really small – not enough room to sit up and certainly not enough room to really stretch out. It was like a coffin because you had a personal little curtain to pull across the entire length of the bunk, which left you all alone in the dark. Yeah, I was frightened a few times lying in that bunk, unusual sounds waking me up and always wondering what was on the other side of that thin sheet of steel separating me from the big ocean just 10mm away from where I lay.

It all had to end and I was eventually met at the dock by the police and my parents when we returned to port. No brass band or welcoming party, just a bleak wet and windy jetty with very upset, angry parents waiting with the police who delighted in quoting the law every two fucking minutes and any excuse to offer insult to any part of my most amazing first experience at sea – not once asking to hear about the sheer delight and joy that was bottled up within me from such a great adventure. Why, oh why, couldn't they just have seen that I had been out into the world, brave and alone, to see a life, like they all wanted to but would never have dared to even imagine. I had had more fun in my short life at this point than most people get in a lifetime, and I just wanted to get back out into the world and do it some more in whatever form it might take and wherever it might take me.

Eventually it all got really messy and I was in trouble with everyone for truancy and for a few other trips I had managed to disappear on. In the end, there was no choice: boys' correctional school was on the agenda. My parents, knowing that I needed taming, had me set to leave for a boys' correctional school up in the north of the country where I would learn all about what one boy could do to another and take the leap from boyhood to manhood in one very short step. Looking back, I was about to join the school of life; no nice long childhood of growing my hair long and dating girls and getting drunk down the local pub. No, I was to be hurled straight into the British equivalent of a Spartan military school for fuck-ups and undesirables. Fucking nightmare.

Just to add to the boxing ring of life, my grandmother died at about this time, and at 65 it was such a fucking shame; she was such a great person. Isn't that always the way though? The great people in your life are like a flash of light in the void of time in which we are given, whilst the dull and arduous tend to linger and fester even after they've left your life. I remember getting the news, and for once I was in school and was called for by the head teacher. Thinking I was in the shit for something else, I prepared my excuses, not ever dreaming that I would hear the news that my nana had died. I was utterly devastated and wailed the whole way through the funeral. It took eight pall-bearers to carry the old girl. A fucking great big box of love wasted. I loved her because she saw what was important in life and didn't let all the other shit get in the way. She saw through me, into my soul, beyond all my failures, and above all she knew all my secrets and kept them safe right up to the day she passed. She lived simply and modestly; even when there were servants at her beck and call in South Africa, she jumped in to help, washing, cooking, ironing, and even eating with the servants. Never did she see herself above any other; she was a real friend and so old school, loyal and loving to a fault.

I often wonder now what a normal upbringing would have been like, in so much as staying on at school till I was 16 and having lots of sex with girls and going on school trips or to concerts. Or maybe even going to university to do one of those worthless degrees and having a blast getting high and working in bars and, who knows, maybe even getting a qualification early on that meant something perhaps. Today I see my nieces doing rather well in this and think it's just marvellous. I took a very, very different path, one that was probably a little more exciting but definitely more reckless. I had bigger dreams and wanted to explore this amazing world in which we live. I had too many questions and a thirst for all things new that couldn't be quenched.

Poem for Philis, my grandmother, God rest her soul

She stepped softly off crisp autumn leaves on to winter hills,
Death waiting on jagged rock, soaked wet with mists of tears.
Hard to climb the rock laden with all life's tragedy.

She stepped softly out of cancer's grip on to soft spring fields.
No false summits to this horizon, white shores free of fears.
Hard to focus a mind that wants to falter; no looking back at
*   all life's majesty.*

She stepped softly out of life, on to the summer shores,
Her heart not attacked but relieved, awash with love as she
*   nears,*
Hard now for the lives left to wonder, soaked wet with mists
*   of tears.*

The Steering Group

Chapter 2

The Preparatory

And so it began… I left home to be taken to a detention and disciplinary school just south of the Scottish border. I was 13 years old. It took all fucking day to reach this place. It was raining, very cold and an incredibly long day. I remember, after we had left the motorway, there being long parts of the drive with no civilisation, just open countryside. There were drystone walls for miles that crawled along the roadsides and up the hills into the mist, with sheep desperately clinging together under isolated trees for a little shelter from the persistent downpour. It was pretty bleak and already I was trying to dream up some sort of escape plan. I was desperately trying to memorise landmarks of one type or another throughout the journey so I could possibly backtrack and find my way back to civilisation, not knowing how important all this would become. I drifted in and out of daydreaming but my thoughts kept returning to me heading back to Aberdeen again sometime soon for another shot at being a merchant sailor – well, a stowaway again at least. I found some comfort in this daydreaming as I sat patiently as far over to the window as possible, breathing on the glass as I tried to make a tune out of the sound of the windscreen wipers scraping over the glass, fighting the weather just like those on the bridge of the *Atlantic Star* in the North Sea in a storm.

Eventually the transport arrived at a gatehouse that opened up from the main road that took me over a railway bridge and into the main compound. No greeting party, just an empty arched stone doorway through which I would pass and then be left alone to the mercy of all its occupants. My arrival was simply greeted by what appeared to be an abandoned dark castle-like building. It was late afternoon now and the light was fading quickly. A tall, masculine building, built of stone, with one turret-like structure holding on to a flagpole at its summit that looked down over the entire complex. The flag, whose cloth was soaked from the rain, slapped itself together in the wind, making for a cracking sound like a whip, as if to suggest to me that I would be subjected to a regime of a similar nature upon entering this place. This turret and flag dominated the rest of the assembly of add-on structures that clung to the more masculine-looking stonework, as if for protection from something, or claiming to be part of the older building because their modern construction made them feel out of place or somewhat inadequate.

The main structure disappeared behind a compound wall shadowed further by skeletal trees desperately trying to hold on to their few remaining leaves in the howling wind, as if they were the last layers of clothing keeping their bark warm. The flood lighting made great efforts to penetrate the rain to reach the trees but simply illuminated the sheets of rain as they pelted past the beams of light, creating a weird and wonderful flashing light show. An Alcatraz for kids, I put to myself. There was not much lighting from within that I could see – a few silhouettes passing the tall windows – but mostly just a dark shell that was perhaps a little overwhelming for a 13-year-old boy, away from home and all things familiar. Welcome to DECAF (Defiant Disorder Educational and Assessment Facility). Defiant Disorder or Oppositional Defiant Disorder can be translated to ADHD, not that I was ever seen by any medical professional to officially label me with that disorder;

I think just the fact that everyone thought I was out of control was enough.

I remember the induction process: I was greeted at the main entrance by a correctional officer (CO). (I don't remember him because you just don't, and besides I was trying to stay unnoticed as much as possible, not wanting to stand out or for my name to become too well known in this early stage.) I remember walking down this huge long corridor, as long as the eye could see almost, with large solid oak doors to the right and huge Victorian-like windows to the left which were barred, caged on the outside and half blacked-out by weatherboards or shutters. The floor was polished teak, similar to a ship's decking; all floors from this point onwards would be referred to as decks, even though they would never see a storm at sea.

The walk took us past some young lads buffing this deck with hard wax blocks that stuck to their hands. I could see them attempting to wipe the wax off on their trousers, to no avail, just simply adding to the build-up of stains from previous floor polishing days. They were busily swinging industrial-sized heavy buffers backwards and forwards in a pendulum motion over the waxed floor, totally ignoring me as if I were to be avoided until I'd been fully inducted. They had half the corridor blocked off using buckets and brushes as bollards, like roadworks, so you couldn't walk on the wax they had laid. You could smell the wax; it smelt old and disciplined like a longstanding police station, town hall or the old law courts I had so often attended. There was no mistaking that this whole place was kept painfully clean and in immaculate order. I remember thinking, *There's no way I'm polishing fucking floors*, but in time I would be proven very wrong. Those boys looked lean, and they weren't playing at polishing that floor, you could see the sweat under their arms as they buffed that floor to a high sheen, and the warning in their eyes to stay low was transmitted almost telepathically as I caught them glancing up before I passed by, careful not to tread on their hard work. Then a familiar smell – they had that blue cleaning shit, like on the *Atlantic Star*; it's like paint stripper and works good on removing your skin too; there's no mistaking that shit. There were other boys wiping down the overheads and cleaning windowsills with cloths soaked in that blue cleaning fluid, hands red raw with the chemical, but satisfied that their work would not be criticised or, worse, rescrubbed (slang for made to do it all again following a failed inspection).

It's an interesting feeling and one that I suspect any inmate feels at a real prison – feelings of dread, loneliness, isolation, being targeted, fear, expectation, excitement, all entwined and confused with the unknown and the future. Where will I sleep? Do we eat tonight? Will it be shit or will they have a good kitchen? Will I make friends? I hope no one picks on me first and, of course, why the fuck am I here? How the hell did this happen to me? Followed by a million other unexplained feelings and questions that only time can answer in such places.

That feeling comes from your stomach; it's not a light thought in your head or a passing *Oh shit, I've forgotten my coat*, it's a feeling that consumes your body and mind, and you are literally sick from the inside out. Your mind goes into a kind of reduced readiness state, focusing only on what is the here and now. Your mind descends from multitasking transmissions and wavelengths to a kind of binary code or survival mode, only processing the most important information you need to survive and do what is necessary in the here and now. I know this place wasn't a prison but it was probably close to it, and I was only guessing that it wasn't as well controlled. Being just boys, I think the organisation thought we couldn't get up to much more than the odd fight or other such minor misdemeanour and we would all be too scared to fall out of line with the correctional officers. What a crock of shit – this place truly was a bumble fuck and its control measures were non-existent.

After walking almost the length of the main hall, every boy would be told to stand in front of a huge noticeboard. You were then instructed by the correctional officer escorting you regarding the contents of this main noticeboard, the most important thing apparently being the station bill; fuck knows what that meant at the time. There were timetables, classroom allocations, division lists, laundry duties, dormitory allocations, work duties, punishment programmes etc., etc. – everything that you apparently needed to know, where to be, when to do it and with whom. You only had about 30 seconds to absorb all the information given to you. If any of the information at all went into your brain you were doing well, as listening to the instructions whilst at the same time trying to find your fucking name amongst all the other names and the plethora of other notices covering up parts of this all-important station bill was an impossibility.

No time to linger before we passed the dining hall and kitchen, then I remember descending a stone stairwell into the main hall where there were stalls for uniform, other clothing, bedding, toiletries, and a depository for everything you'd brought with you. The main hall was huge and cavern-like. It was transposed into what looked like a Sunday market but with all the stalls numbered. You received a small card with 15 numbers on it, to which you needed the corresponding stall stamp to show you had been round all the stalls, and your induction would then be complete.

You were systematically stripped of all your clothing and belongings and transformed into one of them, an inmate or member. For me it was like preparing for special treatment at Auschwitz: stripped of all identity before being cast into the furnaces or herded into a gas chamber. At just 13 years old it was the most crazy and frightening experience ever and one not easily forgotten. It wasn't meant to be happening or would be over just as soon as I'd had the standard bollocking from my mum, or something similar, which then usually allowed me and everything around me to return to normality. But this shit wasn't short-term, this was for the long haul – well, two years at least. As you removed clothing you felt stripped of all defences; left standing in only your pants, nakedness and self-embarrassment ensued, wishing you had some sort of trendy pants on or something to look cool in front of the other lads. Or wishing you'd spent more time building up your biceps and six pack at the gym, not that anyone really gave a shit at the time. But then, as you got to the end of the lines, you were rebuilt into an inmate, a clone just like all the other boys in their uniforms. We were all transformed from individual little hooligans into members of a semi self-disciplined organisation, or perhaps this was more a disorganised mustering of the unwanted youth safely excommunicated from society, nicely out of the way, and out of sight from those nice people in society.

Getting a haircut when you're near bald is fucking stupid, but there were no exceptions. But bizarrely you weren't allowed a crew cut, just a short back and sides, so I was in the shit straight away; the little skinhead from Nottinghamshire was in for trouble. There were cool 'az' boys with trendy blond streaky hairdos who cried when it all hit the floor, and others who fought it and were disciplined immediately. To me it was a free haircut and I couldn't understand the fuss. In the end it just made us all less like individuals and more robotic and conforming. It's a simple trick to get everyone into a single way of thinking or a way of life.

I guess, looking back, it was all just boys being boys and all that. However, when you mix around four hundred young, all male idiots with a lot to prove, gallons of spunk and testosterone, no parental influence, deliberate correctional officer absence, laced with a blind-eye attitude, crammed into a confined space with a survival of the fittest mentality, some real tough bullies and a side order of homesickness, you get absolute chaos. This was a regime that will undoubtedly turn fuckwit wimps into some nasty young cunts, a place where boys became young men really quickly regardless of who you thought you were and where you'd come from. No telling Mum to fuck off here.

I had a two-year term; most had longer and weren't they the lucky ones. I had arrived on a large intake day along with a whole year's worth of other kids from just about every background and corner of the country, as well as some lads from overseas. I think it was important to try and look hard even if like me you were a complete fucking mummy's boy who'd never really had a good kicking. Fortunately, or unfortunately, my skinhead haircut which I had kept in honour of Anatoly had caught the attention of some of the more experienced inmates, or BUL's as they were known. Immediately I was marked as a hard fucking little skinhead who needed a good kicking, trouble that needed to be sorted out on the first night. Great, my first kicking was already in the post.

As soon as I'd been kitted out, I was assigned a wing. All the new guys were assembling in their wings, with a 'BUL' (as far as I remember this was Boys Unlimited, meaning they could do anything) taking charge of the welcoming speech. He, Trent No. 1165 (everyone wore a number and surname on their shirt), was very clear about it; the regime was really simple: if you were in your last year you were a 'BUL', if you were new you were a Kilk (Kids I'd like to kill). BULs and Kilks! If you were really young you'd be a Sprog, but there weren't many real young kids – I'm talking under 13. BULs had total rule and could kick the shit out of anyone, and Kilks had to do as they were ordered by the BULs and take all the shit. It was an absolute. If you didn't do as a BUL wanted, you were fucking dog meat and were gonna be taken care of and disciplined. BULs were untouchable, protected and used by the COs. Oh, fucking great, who made this shit up and how the fuck was I gonna survive two years of this? We all received a copy of the DECAF rulebook on completion of this little speech and told to hold on to it at all times. It was the Stanford Prison Experiment reinvented for kids, with no one monitoring its progress, and this experiment of reality was set to last for two years not two weeks. The supposed oversight had been completely handed over to the inmates.

Next, we were assigned lockers for our kit, followed by a stampede to the locker rooms to claim them. There was only one locker room, a labyrinth next to the ablutions block. It was one of those huge spaces with only small windows at head height that barely let enough light in to see what the fuck you were doing as the fluorescent lighting was all but fucked. The lockers were in long rows and all battered and dented, with some unable to be properly closed or locked. The locker itself consisted of two metal shelves, one drawer with the lock removed and a hanging space wide enough for about three items. I was reasonably lucky, I had my locker in sight of the exit and reasonably intact. So, here I was, No. 1127, next to my tiny locker with a bag full of kit surrounded by all the noise and confusion of about one hundred and 50 half-terrified young lads, wondering what the fuck they or I should be doing. Or what to do after attempting to squash everything we owned into these poxy lockers we had all been allocated. So, to avoid any unwanted encounters, I remember deciding to go back into the main drag to find the big seat in the corridor I'd seen when I was escorted in. Now, this was commonly called the hot seat, a wooden bench arrangement that was placed over about four radiators at just the right height. You could probably get 15 kids on this seat. It was awesome; I was freezing cold and this did the job beautifully at warming you up through your ass, or you could even lie down and get real toasty.

I guess that was to be fuck-up number one. This seat was for BULs only, of course! How stupid of me. I was soon dragged out the back doors by three lads and properly fucked over. It was pretty quick. I tried throwing a few punches as I was being dragged out, but I couldn't hit target, just a spasm of fists in all directions – splitting pain, bloodied nose and after a few punches to my head and a heap of kickings just about everywhere else I was released. Word spread quickly and it wasn't hard to see the blood trail into the shithouse where I found myself cowering in a corner. A crowd soon gathered, I guess excited and relieved they weren't part of this first test of the BUL's rule and their sheer will to enforce it, all there to see what *could* happen to them. Fear would now enter their minds and always be there to torment them, remind them of what awaited them in the dark places they would have to tread.

This is when I met Owen 1149. A fucking American whose parents (expats from the UK, I think) had gotten rid of him for a few years for whatever reason. Owen was from a Middle Eastern background and had missed school for the last few years so he was kinda here to catch up on both schooling and life I guess. So that made him the most targeted boy in the establishment. Owen was too tall for his own good, spoke way too much and was generally annoying to most of the BULs. I think he felt, as he was American, he should be allowed BUL privileges, or perhaps the American male supremacy thing was kicking in and he felt superior in some way. At times I thought he was a dickhead but he really was an okay guy and we hit it off straight away.

So, here we were in the shithouse getting acquainted with the BUL and Kilk regime; he had been dragged in behind me and held by his throat as I lay on the floor holding my face together. I staggered onto my feet and decided to smack one of the boys holding Owen in the side of his head. It was my first good fight, I think. We lost, of course, rather badly, and Owen ended up getting an orange shower in the urinals after he and I were completely done in (pissed on by the BULs). Funny, but that cemented a really cool friendship that little scrap. I think those early fights helped us in some weird way to gain a kind of favour with the BULs. In the end I think we maybe even earned a little respect.

I remember dinner was to be a few hours after that fight and we were all left to our own devices between organised activities. Time to get cleaned up before more shit came our way. Shit usually comes on a train with many carriages, I had found in my short experience of life, so best get ready for the next carriage was my philosophy. I had spent nearly an hour in the ablutions trying to get cleaned up. No showers, just 20 rows of sinks with those annoying push-down taps that only turn the water on for a few seconds unless you permanently hold them down, often burning your hand on the hot water tap. The ablutions were a separate block connected to the main building by only a covered walkway consisting of three separate areas: washrooms, shithouses and showers, all at the most basic level.

The washrooms were simply rows and rows of sinks over a red-painted concrete floor which was peeling off by the sheet. The sink drains simply poured out of open-ended pipes over the open floor (or your feet if you were unawares) and never quite made it to the central drainage system. No windows just dim lighting, a mangle for squeezing out your clothes after washing them by hand, and long benches built over the lakes of water that never seemed to drain away – ever. The whole place stank of dirty drains and stagnant water, adding to the smell of old soapy water and toothpaste stuck in the clogged pipework and blocked sinks creating a distinct aroma that really was a horrid musty acidic stench.

The showers were kept locked and only opened from 0600 to 0700 and 1900 to 2000. There were about 40 shower heads lining the half-tiled walls of a two-zoned shower area which were turned on at a separate locked stopcock only by a correctional officer at the allotted times. This worked out at about 10 boys per shower, which if no one messed about meant six minutes per shower per boy in the allotted time. The floors were super slippery and there was a pecking order to who showered where and how. BULs had the use of the left-hand side showers, which obviously had high pressure and fully functioning shower heads; and the right side had dribbling shower heads and poor pressure, ideal for us newcomers or Kilks. So, privacy was non-existent and you'd stand there in front of everyone in all your glory, hoping to get six minutes under a dripping shower head, which often didn't happen, and sometimes you would have to finish yourself off in the bird bath that was the sink. Often boys would sit in a sink naked, feet in the next sink, with a mug to get a bath that way. It certainly helped you get over any shyness you may have had, and forgetting about home comforts happened quickly. Kilks often had to give baths to BULs in the washrooms. I remember the BULs had a lad called Danny 1195 who was the bath boy. Fucking sick. He would have to wash some of the BULs as they sat in the sinks; I think it usually included a hand job. Sick.

The shithouses were just as accommodating: two rows of shitters and a full-length urinal ideal for sliding young Kilks down and giving them a golden shower at the far end, as Owen had found out early on. The pans were aluminium, with no seat, just two bolted-on half horseshoe plastic ridges which made for a quick shit, all hidden behind broken doors that were only half height. They were generally used for smoking in when it was too fucking cold outside, and wanking competitions to please some of the sexually sick BULs on too frequent an occasion.

I remember trying to wash my uniform, covered in piss, blood and mud, and trying to get my face back together. It wasn't gonna happen and I looked like shit. I looked like I had just had a real good kicking and had made a fucked-up attempt to clean it all up, but there was no hiding it. It was one of those moments in life when you know you're fucked but you look up to see if there's anyone else as equally as fucked as you in order to have a laugh. Owen and I were in stitches for 10 minutes or more in the washrooms just laughing at each other; at that point we couldn't care less about drawing further attention to ourselves, although I'm sure it was just as much on his mind as it was on mine that we should try and be quiet.

Now, it was fucked up how things worked in DECAF but one thing was very, very clear: no one 'dobs' anyone in to the COs – one of the many unwritten rules that must be common in all such establishments, I guess. Although we looked like absolute shit there was no way this first scrap was gonna be allowed to be exposed to the COs. The BULs who had given us the kicking came back around and as cool as ice said we were gonna be eating with them. I wasn't too keen on that idea but I guess we had to go along with it.

Everything in DECAF was announced by military bugle, and the bugle was sounding for dinner. Now, as a Kilk I had no way of knowing where to go or what to do, or the fact that different instructors had different rules. Owen and I were taken under the BULs' wing for dinner, not for our benefit you understand but for insurance that they wouldn't be implicated in what had just occurred. They would simply hide us from the instructors. We went into the dining hall the back way. So, we were dragged out of the ablution walkway over a courtyard and up some stairs into the dining room. We had to go; it was a headcount so no getting out of it. I guess for the other newbies it was just a case of following the crowd every time the bugle sounded.

The regime revealed itself just a little more as each time the daily routine was slowly unwrapped: the BUL's had a head boy and NCOs just like the military, and they ran the place following orders from the correctional officers. The boys did the headcount under the supervision of the COs and reported to them. It all started to make sense – I think! It was all run from within, a military regime run by the boys for the boys with minimal input from the COs, which allowed the BULs to basically run the place on their behalf to their own satisfaction, which included bullying, rape, abuse, extortion, theft and racketeering, to name but a few things. It was all corrupt and open to exploitation, making my first thoughts turn to what it would take for me to bribe a BUL to lie on a headcount. Time would tell.

The supervising CO on that very first night was a Mr Tyrell. He was like an English version of Mr Miyagi from *The Karate Kid* movie – a little poisoned dwarf motherfucker with small-man syndrome but hard as a coffin nail. He stood maybe 5ft tall, had rotten teeth, a beard which was sort of patchy and incomplete, slicked-back black greased hair strands (he was going bald), dark eyes and tattoos that were faded blue and almost unrecognisable, except for the naked woman on his right forearm, a Japanese lady with a sun umbrella. Yep, Mr Tyrell looked like the devil personified; all he needed was a pitchfork and his act would be complete. Mr Tyrell, as it turned out, was the PT instructor; and his gym, as I would later find out, was really a beating house.

Mr Tyrell stood at the front of the dining hall, which was built above four classrooms on a lower level and had 180-degree views out into the darkness and the freedom that lay beyond, with lots of old metal-framed locked windows with cages over them. The main entrance was via double swinging doors, mirrored the same by the exit. There was a strict in and out policy in force which any fool could see but which was often forgotten to the detriment of any perpetrator. The dining room was pretty bright and airy, with huge tables with that crap Formica-type top covering. They were sticky and smeared by a poor attempt to clean them with dirty cloths; you could almost write your name in the greasy surface, which ran contrary to the other cleaning regimes I had witnessed. Bizarrely, each table had salt and pepper pots and those super-crap plastic red and brown squeezy sauce bottles that you'd find in a lorry café on an A road or layby somewhere. The blue and white chequered tiles on the floor were scratched and scuffed by the overly heavy bench seats, giving the whole place that nice cheapo, worn, lived-in feeling.

I was hidden at the back by an overpopulated table of BULs. Absolute silence was required under Mr Tyrell's watch. It was almost unnerving to be in a room with almost four hundred people in absolute silence. There was the occasional cough or splutter, the scrape of a chair, but it was a long silence that beckoned any sound to enter its vacuum and relieve it of its own torment. I remember one of the BULs whispering to me, asking, "Are you a skinhead?" Back in the late '70s and early '80s it was all about mods, rockers and skinheads. Skinheads were sort of an extremist British youth culture that liked to beat up any ethnic minority and anyone else who wasn't a true Englishman, so I guess I looked the part, and it was kind of intriguing for the BULs who wanted to know more. I guess I played along with this fantasy for a short while to make gains for my own advantage.

Hundreds of kids had poured into the hall and had taken to the benches as per their allocated wings. Fuck, we weren't in our allocated wing. I had been in this place less than four hours, had had a couple of fights, looked like shit and was about to get into another darker shade of shit. I remember panicking at this point. It must have been obvious that there was something drastically wrong with us two; still blood-soaked and filthy, we two unlikely characters sitting amongst all these BULs must have really stood out. However, the headcount went off without a hitch; obviously the BUL and Kilk network was working and our whereabouts had been approved to the leaders and everything was covered up nicely, without a fuss.

So, there we were, four hundred boys all totally silent, patiently waiting for dinner and savouring the meal to come like wolves gathered for a hunting trip, silenced by hunger. It was also kind of cool as so many of the boys knew what was going on and kept looking our way in the silence. But many were left wondering and guessing why we were with the BULs on their table and why we were beaten and bloodstained. It was an ingenious vehicle to spread the fear, spread the rumour, spread the message that the BULs were most definitely in control. I was there in the middle of it all, learning to keep my fucking mouth shut, playing along, learning a lesson I took on board wholeheartedly.

There were a few announcements and a shit-arse sarcastic type welcome to us new boys from Mr Tyrell, and then the food counter shutters went up to reveal the meal for the evening. One lad let out: "About time." Bad move. Holy shit, you'd have thought he'd committed murder. You could feel a vacuum as the whole room took in a deep breath. The culprit was immediately identified and hauled out in front of Mr Miyagi. Interesting punishment: the little prick had a chain with some big-ass keys on the end; basically, it was a caning with a set of keys – forced on top of a table, bent over and whipped. Fuck me, no one spoke for the rest of the meal. It was somewhat unbelievable that this was even permitted in any way, but there I was just a few hours into my two-year term and it was a fucking big education already. There was no getting away with shit there, not like at home. I think I had met my match and then some at this point.

This meal, and every meal thereafter, was conducted in orderly fashion, by allocated wing and by table. Not a word was spoken, just eager boys waiting for the nod from Mr Tyrell which indicated they could stand and proceed to the counter. There was never more than one table queuing up at the counter for food at any one time. We were nodded to about halfway through the proceedings as a signal to head off in the direction of the food counters. I was pleased to be shown what the fuck to do and where everything was by the BULs, and of course the order in which to do it all. I remember hiding behind one of the bigger lads to avoid the attention of Mr Tyrell as we trotted off down the dining hall past all the glares from the other lads to the counters which were across from the exit doors. First you had to grab a tray, a plate and a bowl, and they had to be in the right places on the trays as the trays were marked as to where items must be placed, although faded in some cases. The plates were green plastic and about the size of your standard side plate at home. This was accompanied by a green plastic bowl, suitable for a small dog or cat, and a plastic glass which was stained orange by your juice; they only ever served orange cordial, and when it ran out the boys at the back just got water.

I waited patiently in line, eager to catch a glimpse of the meal, my first in this place, and one I'll never forget. The food was served by boys on 'duty week'. Each wing would have a class that would be assigned to domestic tasks all week on a roster basis; I too would get this task in good time. So, there I was, standing there wondering if the boy behind the counter would give me a decent lump of that pie which I was hoping was steak and kidney. I wasn't disappointed. The mash and veg were served just like at the pub in Newcastle so that was cool, and for a moment I remember my mind being free of the current surroundings, just for the briefest of moments, as I was transported back to Newcastle. The lads were very generous, as everyone had to be because, sooner or later, you'd be on the receiving end as the rotation of boys on duty week moved around, so it wasn't in anyone's interest to short-change any boy at the food counter. It wasn't shit, it was okay actually; I don't remember ever not eating at this place. There was always a sponge pudding and custard, or even sometimes ice cream and tinned peaches for afters. The breakfasts were always full English, so happy days I guess, especially for those who hadn't had a good family like mine and had probably never enjoyed three squares a day. Some days there would even be second helpings and that was always well received; the simplest of privileges made a huge impact on the daily life of all the boys trying to get through the two or three years they faced.

Mealtimes ended just as orderly as they had begun, with a structured process for each wing and tables standing up and clearing the table and taking all the crap to the scullery which was just around from the serving hatches. The scullery was outside of domestic duties and normally reserved for those on punishment. From there everyone proceeded to the main hall where a film would be watched most evenings, but on this first night, or intake day as it was known, we were to be allotted our sleeping billets which were assigned according to which wing you were in. There were four wings each with one hundred or so lads, give or take. They were named Churchill, Wilson, Pitt and Balfour. We were all allotted a dormitory and bed number within the segregation of each wing. There was a great excitement which swept through the entire establishment like a Mexican wave as everyone was eager to learn who they would be sharing a dorm with. This process was as terrifying as it was exciting, as both BULs and Kilks shared the dorms together as equals. So, as it turned out, the BULs were learning who was gonna be in their dorms, who would be their slaves and servants for the night.

Name, number, dorm wing and bunk number, then off we went back to the ablutions for a six-minute shower, then upstairs into locked dorms with our little bed blocks consisting of two sheets, an itchy blanket, a thin-as-fuck pillow and a pillow case. Everyone needed to be behind locked doors by 2100 except the duty watch who patrolled with the duty COs – a kind of fire watch who occasionally needed to raise the alarm if things got out of hand, things that had nothing to do with fires. There were a lot of alarms, especially in that first year.

The dorms were on level 4; a main staircase took you to an upper hall where there were two corridors leading away to two sets of dorms and an additional two half staircases up to two other dorm complexes, each protected by a fire door and lockable inner doors. The hospital or medical centre was on this first landing also. My allocation was immediately at the top of the main staircase, up a further short staircase and down a long corridor. I remember my dorm only had 12 of us in it, but most were a lot larger. I had to pass through two other dorms to get to my bunk space, which served as a kind of buffer between my dorm and all the nightly shenanigans. The rooms were Victorian-like, cold and airy but certainly not welcoming. The floors were all polished wood with not a stitch of carpet in sight, very high ceilings, and everything was painted a light grey. Above all I remember it being fucking cold.

Most lads only had shorts to wear to bed; some of the BULs had dressing gowns and even slippers. However, there seemed to be a significant percentage who only had their pants on and ran barefooted up to the dorms. Obviously mummy and daddy, wherever the fuck they were, had failed to provide anything for those boys, just an additional helping of humiliation. Often the BULs would target these boys for what was called a 'wedgy'. Two BULs would grab the victim, one from the front and one from behind, grabbing the pants and lifting the victim up by said pants until they split, or the boy had screamed enough to appease the attackers.

Bedtime, if you could call it that, was really quite something else. I remember on that first night the BULs were in a panic to get all us Kilks together and demonstrate how the beds needed to be made. We were all in bunkbeds (except the NCO BUL's who had their own rooms), the typical steel-framed military beds with metal battens pulled over the frame by about 40 springs, covered by a rather narrow mattress. The sheet had to be pulled really tight and have hospital corners. Dalton demonstrated the methodology of how to stretch the sheet by pulling it over a bent-up mattress, which when released would pull the sheet completely taught – tight enough to bounce a coin on, fucking brilliant! This would come in handy later on. The blanket had to be folded exactly twice the size of the DECAF rulebook, which you had to carry at all times, and the pillow placed neatly on top with the crease in the pillowcase athwart the bed. Fuck me, when do you get to sleep? I remember thinking.

At 2130 a bugle would sound and the duty CO would conduct rounds of the dormitories, which usually took about an hour, and then it was lights out. Even numbers must be standing up on even days, and odd numbers lying to attention in their beds, and 'vicky-verky' on odd days. The dormitory would be called to attention when the CO came in, and upon being told to stand easy the standing boys were to immediately get into bed and lie to attention. Funny as fuck. I remember Bradley 1129 opposite me jumping up onto his bed and the whole thing collapsing through to the bunk below as nearly all the springs had been removed. He slept on the floor that night, not that there was much sleeping to be done. It was funny to see that bed collapse, and I smile to this day as it was the first of many practical jokes that I was either a part of or a victim of in my many years that followed in the military.

After the duty CO had left, all manner of shit started to happen, as if the bugle were the starting gun for the night's events. It was like zombies coming out after sunset. All the BULs went around the dorms seeking out who was new in their wing and where they all were, looking for an excuse for a fight or to flex their muscles as the guys in charge. Haunting, hollow, distant echoes of boys crying out or screaming from distant dorms pierced any silence, but like a storm approaching they soon became closer and more audible, before any conversations were soon overpowered by lads being beaten in their beds close to us on our wing. And then the storm would pass. There were some fucked-up lads in there and I guess we just lay there hoping it wouldn't come our way. Many nights passed like this, waiting, cowering in fear, but over time we would talk till the early hours, and the 12 boys in my dorm all looked out for each other.

Occasionally we would fight back and have a scrap if the fight came to our dorm. I like to think we took our fair share that first year but looking back I think we were pretty lucky actually. Not everyone had the bottle to fight back; it attracted attention and further fights. Bradley was the weak one in our group and was always sought out by a few of the headcases from other dorms to give him a hard time; it was very regular. Poor little fucker took some shit and we couldn't defend him all the time; the BULs would come in force and take me and Owen on whilst Bradley was dragged away kicking and screaming like a girl. Often, we would spend long nights trying to console him after he came back to our dorm. He would often cry himself to sleep.

However, it wasn't all bad. I remember many nights we all just sat talking and trying to have a laugh about our day. We would spend hours telling each other stories about what we did back home, how we ended up at DECAF; and my stories about going to sea were a hit. We made plans to escape and all go to Aberdeen together. It was on one such night we found out that Owen spoke Arabic and was able to write in various dialects. Soon a trade was reached where I would teach him and the others Russian in return for Arabic lessons. Over time it fell to just me and Owen to teach each other, and it lasted pretty much the whole two years, both of us promising to take the other to the Middle East and Moscow respectively. I think we were pretty fluent in the three languages of English, Russian and Arabic by the time we left DECAF. One of the few great advantages of a life hidden from the masses is that there's always plenty of time on your hands.

We were always woken to the sound of the bugle – reveille – and it was loud as fuck; this was the signal to join the rush to the ablutions and my first introduction to the phrase 'shit, shower and shave'. You had to shave every morning even if you had a face of pure soft baby skin. I know young Bradley took the blade out of his razor and simply scraped foam off his face with the plastic to keep everyone happy. Then after that it was straight into breakfast. I have always liked a cooked breakfast, and I guess we were lucky to have one each morning. My favourite still remains crap cheapo overcooked sausages in a butty made with cheap nasty white bread, too much butter melted by the sausages so it dribbles out and then dipped in egg and baked bean sauce. Not all the meals were in silence and we got to know the slack officers who would allow a little conversation. A few of the lads would then sneak out the ablutions block and have a crafty fag over by the roadside hidden by some trees. Then every morning there would be crowds looking at the noticeboard to check the timetables for lessons and instruction and all manner of other notices before morning parade; there was always some sneaky change to catch out the stupid or simple amongst us. It was done deliberately to keep us sharp, I think.

Morning parade and headcount was the start of each and every day, except Thursdays which was parade in PT kit. On Thursdays the whole establishment would run around the perimeter of the establishment as a wing, in step and at pace. It was about five miles each time. Rain or shine the establishment all mustered on the parade ground for headcount and inspection. Normal parade was conducted full military style and you were inspected for a clean shave, ironed uniform, shiny shoes and smart haircut. It was all bullshit but I guess it instilled the need to be on time, and on time every time. This is where I was to pick up probably the most annoying habit of my life, which is to always be early. Five minutes early is on time, and it's a discipline that has served me well but can be just the most annoying thing to friends and family, and now I just hate anyone who is late. I'm the guy who is 15 or even 30 minutes early for everything, and I expect everyone else to be early too. To be late for parade could mean anything from extra PT to scullery work or extra cleaning duties or simply a good caning. Or if you fell foul of Mr Tyrell, you'd probably be keyed, and most likely be invited to accompany him to the gym for a beasting. After parade it was off to normal school lessons, with some minor differences to what you might encounter at a normal school.

This was my life for two years. I undertook all the normal lessons of maths, English and the like, endured the separation from family, whilst accepting the intense disciplinary regime coupled with all the bullying on that first year. It was simple reveille, shit shower and shave, iron your uniform or PT kit, breakfast, noticeboard, parade, morning lessons, dinner, afternoon lessons, a few hours free, evening meal, shower, often a film in the main hall and then up to the dorms – a rigid timetable that never really changed and was all announced by the bugle. Once a month you had to attend church, and as the roster rotated you'd pick up the domestic duties. It was straightforward, and so long as you kept your head down and took a few kickings without making a fuss or making any noise about it, time would pass by relatively quickly.

Of course, a lot more went on because we were all there for a reason and not because we wanted to be. I don't think it is possible to ever fully know what a person is capable of until his or her surroundings are changed so much that it becomes inevitable that a behavioural switch is absolutely necessary in order to meet the appetite of the most basic of human instincts: the need to survive and to endure. We humans are despicable creatures really. We pretend to be civilised, caring and educated, but deep down inside each of us is a beast hiding quietly, waiting for an opportunity, waiting for a meal, and this was demonstrated often by both the staff and the boys. The staff savoured the plentiful opportunities to live out their perverted desires within a leaderless herd which was often forced to turn inwards on itself to satisfy the hunger of the beast within. The beast in you is a skin-changer, a chameleon that will adapt to your surroundings and pretend to be your ally but in truth is the mirror image of the darkest fears hiding your true self within.

Institutions such as the one I found myself in were intentionally built and manned to be the trellis of juvenile discipline. Upon this trellis it was intended that compromised, lost, discarded or confused young boys would be reattached, grown and groomed in some way back into the fabric of society. This is the desire of the populous, a deliberate intention to somehow re-grow difficult or unmanageable boys into worthy citizens deserving of a place on their precious trellis. It was all a paradox; the very place that society had constructed for this metamorphosis of reshaping the future of us boys actually in many cases had the adverse effect. All the boys craved the social lives they had once had; but they had been given such an absurd society in which to live, the trellis simply highlighted the tragedy into which so many boys had now fallen and indeed was pushing others in the same direction.

This place was so unlike the many good groups or institutions parents and society desire their offspring to attend. DECAF offered an education in a more abrupt and immediate fashion. The topics learned here were not just of mathematics, English and science but of life itself. But in this place many of the pupils were already well into completing their masters in violence, perversion and extortion taught by the choicest professionals in whose propensity the darkest of subjects were covered in great detail and included the very best practical lessons.

I think this environment pulled me in many different ways, and I found myself keen to make some decent money again, by whatever means possible. The BULs had the right ideas and ingredients to be successful. They had set up small underground cottage industries or businesses to make some significant financial gains, which included such things as selling tobacco, alcohol; a café, which sold toasted sandwiches and real coffee and tea; a laundry service to have your uniform washed and ironed perfectly; a shoe shining business; and a 'steal to order' for those more difficult-to-get items. It was fucking brilliant! Each business relied on an entrepreneurial BUL at the helm orchestrating the smuggling of goods into the establishment, or having some boys escape the compound to steal such goods or use contacts on the outside to complete the supply chain. The boys who were the runners were always Kilks. Runners would go and meet contacts on the outside or be tasked to steal from local shops in order to meet the demands of the businesses on the inside. Failure to return or attempt to escape usually ended in the runner receiving severe punishment from the COs, possibly having your time extended into a further correctional facility depending on your age. Some correctional facilities were run by the HM Prison Service and could keep you up to the age of 23; they were not where you wanted to end up. This was the main deterrent in the runner recruitment process, not to mention the kickings from the BULs for a failed excursion, in payment for the loss of their initial investments. So, I guess there was significant risk.

I immediately put myself forward to be a runner.

The boys in my dorm thought I was utterly mad, but I wanted to escape. Fuck this shit. And working for the BULs gave you several additional hours' head start on a genuine escape attempt as you'd be able to dodge one or even two headcounts. Additionally, of course, it bought favour amongst those in power. I reminded Owen about our talks of escaping and going to Aberdeen and the fact we could actually make a serious run for it. After a lot of deliberation, the lads agreed that it was actually a good idea, but this was after I promised to steal some shit just for them. The issue I really faced was to make a run for it first time and go all out, or build up some trust with the BULs which would also allow me to make some cash on the side. I had no intention of just running for them; I wanted to have a few scams on the side for me and my dorm mates too. I had done the maths: I needed £150 to make it all work just for me, so I had to do some running before I made it out for the big escape.

Stealing cigarettes was a big earner: a pack of 20 cost about £1.20 at the time and the going rate was 20p to 25p a cigarette. Max. profit from a pack of fags was £3.80. So, I if stole 100 fags, a few loaves of bread and some cheese for the sandwich-making business, per run, that worked out at about £60 in profit to the BULs of which I would get 30%, which gave me £18 a run, which meant I'd have to do 8.3 runs to get my £150, which would probably get confiscated! Fuck that! I would have to steal extra fags, some spirits and do personal requests. I planned on two runs then the big one, to properly finance my permanent escape plan.

I wasn't the only runner, there were a few lads doing it with contacts on the outside for legitimate deals where cash was exchanged from all the running and stealing for high-quality goods such as alcohol. After signing up for the runner job the BULs got me a meet with one of the other runners. I had to attend what can only be described as an interview with him and the BULs in which I had to explain my ability to shoplift and break into people's homes. I think I mainly bullshitted my way in. They knew I was a good runner as I played wing for the DECAF rugby team and no fucker could catch me once I had the ball. It was heart-pumping fucking excitement. I was finally getting involved in the inner machine.

There were various methods for getting out of the establishment's fence line but getting back was bizarrely harder, and I was given a few ideas by a lad called Sticky. He was a good runner but had been caught once and given a real beating by the security staff and the BULs, as well as being extended by six months. He was called Sticky because he was a little thieving bastard, and not just from outside DECAF – he'd just fucking steal off everyone, all the time. But he was respected as he delivered pretty regularly. I think he was a prick to keep coming back in to DECAF with so many opportunities to make a final departure, but he supplied me with valuable information on the surrounding area: road maps, locations of easy hit shops and petrol stations, etc., etc.

My first run was a blast. I remember it well. I sat up with the lads in the dorm until maybe 1am with the plan to jump the fence near the railway line at about 5am, allowing me a clear run of about an hour into town avoiding the trains. The nearest town was a shithole but only a few miles' run along the railway tracks. I was reliably informed that the station and surrounding shops were an easy knock-off. I didn't sleep but was still given a shake at about 4.30am by the BULs who were sponsoring the run and very eager to get me away. I was given £50 to pay for some exotics, a name of who to meet, a big list of shit to steal and some civvy clothing. Awesome.

It was like I had suddenly become a popular kid; all the fuss and support from everyone to get me out the dorm fully kitted up to do the run was surprisingly well organised and enthusiastic. The BULs had stolen a few come-in-handy tools to get the cage off one of the dorm windows, which allowed me to run across the rooftop to the dining hall and jump down onto the ablutions block's covered walkway. Then it was off the walkway and across the road into the trees before hitting the fence running parallel to the railway line. It was a real scramble and struggle to get over the fence here but it was the lowest point and it only had barbed wire instead of the usual razor wire at the top, plus the fence was angled over the wrong way, removing any need to go up and under. One of the trees offered a branch close enough to put a foot on and give me a leg up whilst I negotiated the barbed wire section at the top of the fence. I was cut to fucking ribbons but was too excited to give a shit, oblivious to any pain because the adrenaline release was overwhelming now – increased heart rate, lung capacity at 110%, all set for the hour's run to town; my mind was set and my legs were in auto. Typically, the track ran in a gully with high sides and was well hidden by trees and bushes. I had to pass under the entrance bridge to the establishment with the guardhouse above, which I noticed wasn't occupied. I later learned the motherfuckers locked the gates and always headed into the complex for a free early breakfast, making early mornings an ideal time to head out on any future escape plan.

I was running like mad now along the tracks, laughing and drunk on the excitement that I'd successfully made it out of the compound. I tried to run faster by stretching out over two sleepers at a time, tripping and falling into the gravel on more than one occasion; it was an anxious half marathon that saw me gasping for breath most of the way. Fortunately, it was a cool morning, not yet light but with enough illumination from the moon to light the path ahead. There was a really cold breeze blowing down that railway track like the surge of wind you feel when you open a door into one of those walk-in fridges at the off licence for a case of beer. Really welcoming at first but only enjoyed for a short time whilst you collected your desires. It was attempting to keep me cool as it cut through the cheap jumper I was wearing to my sweat-soaked body. Now, I've always sweated like a defendant on a rape charge and that night was no exception; I was wet through, the nerves driving me on and the excitement and anticipation fuelling the ever-increasing pace. I remember seeing the lights of the station platform coming into view, a warm light that drew me to it like a moth. Glittering dew on the ice-cold steel rails stretching away to freedom was a tempting thought that was a distraction to my already troubled mind.

My rendezvous was waiting at the south end of the platform with the magics and a special order of vodka. There's no way of describing your first pick-up or exchange but it was kind of boring. Didn't have a name, just met this guy at the end of the platform who simply said, "Order for 1127," like I was in McDonald's or something, to which I replied, "Yep," and money was exchanged for the goods and alcohol. Easy. Nothing exciting, no big trade-off or guns or threats, just a very simple exchange with no questions. It was all a bit flat to be honest.

I decided to stash it under the tracks back towards DECAF; I had some shopping to do now. The station was deserted, so harder to pull any jobs, but there was a café and a mini supermarket with an off licence over the road. I'd have to wait till it got busier. I had till the lunch headcount to get back. I needed to steal fags – as many as I could get my hands on. Then basically take as much shit off the shelves as possible that would add to my reputation when I got back. Now, back then it wasn't all CCTV cameras everywhere and impossible to steal stuff, it was just a case of being cocky and a little bit clever. The off licence was an easy hit: they had all the fags laid out on a sloping counter in front of the cashier's till, not locked behind the cashier in a cabinet. Simple distractions allowed for multiple packs to disappear, along with Rizlas and a few pouches of tobacco and other random stuff. Being so young it was easy to pretend to be interested in football cards and other shite which the shop attendant was really watching. The supermarket was harder. I fucking hit the fire alarm to allow me access behind the counter, grabbed as much as I could, legged it out in the rush and made it casually as fuck straight over the road and into someone's garden and out of sight. In total I got away with 260 fags, two pouches of tobacco, five packs of Rizlas, two loaves of bread, 2lb of cheese, bags of confectionary, a small bottle of gin, a bottle of whisky, three dirty mags and two wallets. I was up £45 before the cash in the wallets! I needed to get a rucksack for the next hit cos the fucking bin bag split and made for a nightmare run back to DECAF.

In the small world of DECAF I guess I became a little fucking hero, if only for a short while. I had made a good run which bought off a few BULs, which in turn made life more bearable for me and all the guys in my dorm. I guess they were sort of protected now by me. It was cool. It felt cool and I guess I was 'in' so to speak. Plans needed to be made for the next run and it needed to be bigger, and I suggested two boys should go together and work the town centre in a team effort. The Scottish shopkeepers were a little bit tougher to distract or steal from than their English counterparts. Life started to revolve around planning the next run, and the next run and the next, whilst for each subsequent run the orders got a little more ambitious, a little more difficult, which was to be expected I suppose, but I had to bring it back to reality. In truth I'd just been a lucky bastard on my first run, and stealing on an increased scale brought increased risk, plus who the fuck was I to trust to work with me? Planning was fun and infectious and it really had gotten me into the engine room of DECAF, albeit on the wrong side!

I remember selling some of the extra fags I'd nicked, and as a kind of celebration Owen and I decided, as non-smokers, that we should give smoking a try over a gin. I don't remember much more about that afternoon apart from being violently sick. But for some strange unexplainable reason I tried it again and eventually became a smoker. What can I say, it was good for business. I did two more runs. My third run met with an abrupt ending when I came face to face with the security staff on the railway track below the guardhouse at around 5.30am when they usually sneaked off for their free breakfast.

Fuck.

Panting and out of breath, and startled by the appearance of the three security devils stopping me in my tracks – literally the promise of Mammon fulfilled – I looked up to the night sky, watching my warm breath vaporise into clouds and up further into the cold of the night and started to laugh. I knew I was fucked. Mr Buchanan was a hard bastard, with a reputation; he was a bit perplexed by my laughing. He stroked his beard before saying something like, "Go on, run, you little prick." He wanted the chase and the fun of fucking me over on the tracks, which would lead to a definite extension of time and punishment. He needed the excuse to kick the granny out of me with his two henchmen.

"Nah, I'll stand and fight this one out, mate," I replied. I remember there being some polite conversation, an exchange of threats and then eventually an invitation to the gym. Accepting an invitation to the gym was a topic of great conversation amongst all the boys, both the BULs and the Kilks; it was like a myth, stories told by people who had only ever heard the tale second or third hand. No one who spoke about it had ever actually witnessed 'The Gym' in person; it was spoken about like it was some kind of movie or a comic book story that must be seen. The most frequent outcome of any boy or any idiot who accepted such an invitation mentioned in these stories was always a trip to hospital. The invitation usually had two options, and as per the myths at DECAF I was offered three rounds in the boxing ring, or take a beating and just three months' additional time, no questions asked. There was no way I was gonna be taking extra time.

The gym was an older outbuilding, set away from the main complex up a steep single-track road and surrounded by dark trees filled with thick undergrowth. It was always wet and damp up that road for some reason and the gym was sort of like a large stone barn with moss-covered roof tiles. Inside was open, two-storeys to the rafters, with high beams and small annex for an office and toilet at the near end. Always damp and cold inside, it stank just like your laundry basket and worse. A stinging perfume of vomit, floor polish and sweat made for an unforgettable smell. All gyms today remind me of this place, the smell of sweat and its disgusting bacterial metabolism of body odour emitting from every contaminated object in the building.

The gym consisted of three main areas: the boxing ring, large deck area for deck hockey, gymnastics and murderball, and a weights area, all overlooked by high wires and ropes for leopard crawls and rope climbing and of course the rings. The walls were lined by wood panelling with ladders, scramble nets and climbing frames just about all the way around, a few hobby horses and equipment boxes and about a dozen of those fucking medicine balls. Everything was well used, patched up, worn and outdated, as though it had all been donated some years previously. One common punishment was to clean the gym windows which were only accessible by leopard crawling up in the rafters; often boys would fall and break an arm or a leg. Nothing was ever said. In some cases I think boys fell deliberately to get time away from it all.

When we attended gym lessons we were usually split into opposing teams and, as sure as eggs is eggs, you would be pitched either against your best friend or someone who really had a vendetta and wanted to take revenge 'legally', so to speak. Teams were always Skins and Tops, and in winter Skins would freeze their asses off no matter how hard the workout. The workouts were brutal and the usual sessions lasted two or four hours depending on if you were lucky enough to pull a double session. I still have the stretch marks on my biceps from the weights and presses, which were nothing short of brutal; these are stretch marks from too much exercise and not being a fat bastard. Being too young to take the physical punishments so frequently often caused the boys a lot of distress and injury.

In a typical session, boys were subjected to grids and weights – so your arms were fucked for the ropes – a game of deck hockey and then a run, after which there wasn't much left to offer in the boxing ring or for murderball. Murderball was a knockout game utilising a medicine ball used to throw at each other, a bit like tag, but the last one standing got to go for a shower and then the game was repeated. Basically, there was simply nothing left at the end and lads would get punishment if they couldn't compete or complete. I always enjoyed the deck hockey as it was fucking easy to foul the shit out your opponent's shins. It was a brutal game, and if you were smart you'd take out the big guys prior to murderball.

So here I was with Mr Buchanan about to get in the ring for a bit of reality show and tell. One of the BULs was on punishment and was cleaning the shithouse. I remember the look of absolute horror on his face as he stood gawping, mouth ajar, with a *you're fucked* look on his boat race. He stood statue-like, holding his mop and bucket and waiting for his brain to catch up with the situation unfolding right before him. His expression, coupled with my almost sudden realisation of what was happening, made for a very unnerving and extended few seconds. I think there was total disbelief at what was about to unfold in all three camps. Looking back, I don't think I really knew how much shit I was in at all. But I had pulled from the archives a thought that made me smile: my mum always said to me, "Whenever you fall into a bucket of shit you come up smelling of roses." I was hoping for proof after this event.

Mr Buchanan was changing; he was calm and expectant, savouring the moment as if it were routine, as if this sort of behaviour were acceptable and beating on a 13-year-old kid in some way made him a hard man. The gym was warm, the temperature rising at the same pace as my heart rate. But I was strangely controlled, almost resigned to the outcome, but very determined to hit this cunt, just once. So I thought I would piss him off, get the heat into the fight from the start, say a few worthless words. He fucking laughed as I called to him, "Come on, you cunt," and he lunged towards me, but I side-stepped and got a punch in right there. "You fucking dancer!"

Now, anyone who has ever been in a boxing ring will tell you there are rules – yeah right, that shit's for the television. This was Gypsy rules. It wasn't over as quick as I'd expected or even dared to hope. I think he wanted to tease me, see what I had to offer before I gave up. I took a few blows to the head, shin scrapes to the legs; he was a dirty bastard. Being punched was like a pillow fight but with footballs – try smashing yourself in the face with a hard football a few times; you sort of get numb to it but at the same time disorientated. The gloves were old brown leather, cracked and hard, not soft or subtle, and the laces were too long, and each time I caught a punch I'd get the whip of a lace in my eye or across my face. It was all very amateur and I did my best to try and get a few punches in. I had a cut in my cheek from his glove and a fat eye, no corner to run to, and was holding up but not for long.

Seconds feel like fucking hours in a ring against an opponent who is clearly way out of your league.

Now, the BUL, a guy called Chris, had gone out back and somehow convinced the other two guards to fuck off, and he returned with a deck hockey stick. He ran over toward the ring; and as I looked up thinking, *What the heck?*, Mr Buchanan takes the opportunity and fucking floors me. It's a weird sickening feeling and stars in your eyes isn't a myth – they're like little white dots that glide all over your tunnelled vision after a direct hit. They're smooth little lights that like to cut through the haze into the green and black of your now closed eyelids. I was on the deck but soon conscious enough to see the hook of the deck hockey stick come under the ropes and pull Mr Buchanan off his feet and on to the canvas.

Fuck. Chris is in the ring now and kicking his head in. Dazed and disoriented I'm up on my feet and on the attack. Chris has the hockey stick over his throat now and we're trying to hold this cunt down, Chris at his throat and me holding on to his legs, which was like holding on to a giant caterpillar contracting and expanding, moving me backwards and forwards as I held on to his legs for my life. Remember, Chris is older than me and isn't a little kid; we had him. Yeah, we had him but it was like catching an alligator – that's great but what the fuck do you do once you've gotten hold of it? Lots of swearing, struggling, kicking, violent twisting and epileptic movements until Mr Buchanan calmed down. Chris was cool, explained to Mr Buchanan that the whole event didn't happen and all the beatings of boys was gonna stop. Shit, I didn't know what to do. I looked at Chris as he pushed harder on the deck hockey stick, choking him further. I remember watching his eyes bulge. Fucking awesome seeing his eyes bulge out like that, looked like they could pop or something. I almost wanted to pull them out.

Chris whispered something about drinking whilst on duty and leaving the gates unlocked whilst fighting other boys; he had been beaten by this guy years ago and had a photo in his hand – it was game over, the perfect bribe... or was it? I don't know what was in that photo. The COs had drawn a blank as to some boys' injuries and the continued disappearance of staff from the security points and missing boys from headcounts. The security guards had dropped themselves right in the shit. I guess they never had anyone stand up to them before, and Chris had something on them that was more than rumour.

Now, this was an interesting scenario, we had entered uncharted waters. We didn't know if we had it under control, if the bribe would last, if the photo would be taken from Chris in a dorm raid or locker search, plus we didn't know if we could hold out against an officer's word in an internal investigation, if it ever came to that. I guess being young we thought we had pulled it off – only time would tell. On top of this we also had the BULs to deal with; a failed run was not gonna pass without a kicking. I hoped Chris would help us out there. We would need to re-organise and bullshit our way out of the situation.

Going back into the main buildings and getting breakfast was nothing short of interesting. No one said a thing; I think the bruising and injuries said it all and it's best not to ask too many questions. I remember casually walking into the dining hall and sitting down in amongst my wing and calmly waiting for my table to be called forward to the food counter. The pain was kicking in now and I just needed to get something to eat, get cleaned up and go to the dorm. Wasn't gonna happen: had a slip of paper handed to me at the food counter. The BULs wanted a meet on the hot seat.

Summoned to the hot seat, I wasn't fully conscious I don't think, sort of drifting in and out of reality, or was it even consciousness, not sure. There was a crowd gathering, and the BULs had arranged a tunnel of death. I thought it was for me and really thought I wouldn't make it. I had resigned myself to the possibility of my running days coming to an abrupt end. Yeah, I guess I had given up or just accepted this as the end of it all, but the punishment was for another lad who had grassed up a BUL who had gotten extra time. Word had spread and Owen and I were nothing short of untouchables now following the gym incident with our new friend Chris.

Tunnels of death had to happen in the morning or at shower time so that the crowds in the locker room would look normal, I guess. All the boys had gathered. I can't remember this boy's name, only his nickname, Horse. Yeah, those sorts of things get noticed in communal showers and any difference that is noticed is an excuse to make fun or a cause for bullying. I was held back to watch. Everyone was lined up around the locker room with the idea he had to make it round, with everyone, BULs and Kilks alike, ordered to kick the shit out of him; no way this poor bastard was gonna make it all the way round. He made a good effort. Halfway, I think. I'd passed out a few times and everything was a blur accompanied by screaming static.

I don't remember too much of the conversation that followed between me and the BULs following the tunnel episode, except waking up in the urinals worse off than I was before. It was just a mild concussion I think, cuts and bruises, the norm, but I ended up not leaving the infirmary for a while. I didn't do another run. I dreamt of it, dreamt of escaping so bad. I only had a few months until I became an BUL as I'd been there a year. I remember spending many hours talking to Chris in the infirmary trying to find out how he got the photo and what he had on the security guards. He never did tell me, nor where he kept it. What really mattered was that we had pulled off the impossible, in so much as the heat wasn't on us and life had gotten a little easier. Owen came to visit every day and brought news of the latest scams and goings-on. He also brought my schoolwork, which I didn't have so much interest for. He was becoming a real close friend.

I got to know Horse, who had just come back from A&E during that time in the infirmary. He was a really nice kid. He was real fucked up after the tunnel of death, so we compared notes and injuries and promised when we became BULs we would stop the whole regime of bullying and just have boys and the correctional officers – no more bullying, beatings or abuse of any kind and that's what we would enforce, and we fucking did. It was to be an enforcement that would be more painful for the ones who had endured the worst of it all, not the new boys.

When I left the infirmary, I took time out, kept myself to myself and even became a bit of a recluse. I kept to the routine and only spent time with Owen, Bradley and Horse. We spent time together, talking and sharing our dreams and our regrets – mostly our dreams – smoking cigarettes and trying to make time pass. We had to decide what exams we would sit so I guess a bit of reality kicked in for us all and we tried to study and learn some stuff in class but it was all half-hearted by both the tutors and by us boys. An opportunity missed, I think. Looking back, I think if I knew what I know now I would have studied and gone to university. That opportunity wasn't very realistic for me back then, neither mentally nor physically.

Then it was discharge and intake day, but before that happened the new SNCOs (senior non-commissioned officers) would be announced. I fucking became an NCO! Fuck. In the little world of DECAF it was like being made in the Mafia, becoming part of the Gambino family or something. Well, I was just turning 15 and, becoming a BUL as well, big changes were gonna happen, and Horse was to be the big cheese and become the head BUL – what a great new start. My group was on domestic duties that day and I remember supervising the floor buffering in the main drag and seeing a new intake looking on in horror; yeah, it was funny, especially when they walked past the galley and the fucking place was near on fire because I had put those fucking green plastic plates, bowls and cups in the oven to get warmed up… well, to melt the fucking things so we could demand some fucking proper crockery!

There's not much to say about the next year, except we did try to change everything and it was really great to see the life come back into some of the boys I had seen pushed to the edge and some beyond it. The correctional officers weren't sure what to make of it all as there really wasn't much trouble to deal with except the odd crazy kid, who didn't know how fucking lucky they were, kicking off for all the wrong reasons. I guess they needed a lesson and reminding on occasion what had been sacrificed to allow them to live in relative safety and comfort.

Horse, and I became the new regime with the help of two great lads called Mike and Sam, and the one thing we wanted to continue doing was to make money and trade on the outside. Now, it wasn't quite like the previous year: we had agreed we wanted to stop the drugs and focus on cigarettes, the toasted sandwich business, alcohol, and the running of a sort of tuck shop – remember, we were kids. It was because of the resilience and the sacrifices of Horse that life became bearable in that institution. He was a true hero, and because of him I also managed to get the video library up and running for a small cinema that we would run out of the dorms at night. It was a good plan as it helped calm the nights and changed some of the mentality about what went on in the dorms. Although it turned out to be a bad idea to play kung fu films as on those nights all the lads would become Bruce fucking Lee and try kicking the shit out of each other. It was much more for fun than out of hate or spite, and laughter was heard for the first time in years in those dorms. The boys could actually go to sleep without fear of being beaten up or anything else. I'm sure like me many boys still had nightmares for many months. Thanks, Horse, you saved us all.

Life went on.

I think I had about three months to go and there was a military recruitment drive coming to the establishment. I put down to have an interview. It was just after the Falklands War and there was a lot of drive from the MOD for recruiting. Now, the housemaster came to see me just before that day. He took me to one side and very calmly explained how it was gonna be, after pulling out my file and reading it to me. The atmosphere remained calm up until the point where the recommendation was for a transfer after the age of 16 to another detention centre, or recruitment into the military. I remember just thinking the military was an easy option, plus you get paid, so I don't think they quite got what they were hoping for. I wasn't in the least bit concerned. I think that fucked them off royally, and I left by simply saying we all had enough to make them all inmates someplace soon too. He fucking knew his threats were empty and mine had substance but he kept trying to assert his authority over me and give some weight to his pathetic rank in this establishment of misfits.

I had my interview with two Royal Navy officers. One was a great big fat cunt and the other was as skinny as a butcher's dog There was a two and a half ringer, or lieutenant com-mander, depending on the currency you want to use, and a two ringer lieutenant who was the fat cunt; it was like a Laurel and Hardy double act. I was fascinated by the medals and the gold bars with the pleated gold ring above them, so I guess I wasn't paying too much attention at first. Now, I had a grandioso plan to be a navigating officer. No idea why, but that's what I put to them. I think I had seen a photo in a magazine or something, or maybe the time I had spent with Captain Pies had inspired me. After a raised eyebrow, a shuffle of my file and a big drag on a cigarette, the fat cunt simply said, "You don't have any qualifications, son." So I calmly as fuck pulled out some Benny Hedgehogs (Benson & Hedges cigarettes), lit up and said, "Okay, how about I become a naval architect?" There was little reaction to that, except the skinny fucker looked at my file and asking if I spoke Russian. I remember replying in Arabic and then in Russian just to show off. They both sat up. There was a lot of interest in me now, then a serious conversation that I think lasted maybe two hours or so.

The conversation went around and around for ages, and eventually the fat one went and made a phone call. He came back looking very pleased with himself. He invited the lieutenant commander to step outside for a moment, then they both returned and sat down with a coffee. Lt Cdr Brown put his feet up and explained what he wanted to happen. I would be offered a chance to become an engineer and ship's diver to get a trade and get me into the RN with no qualifications. They would prep me once I had passed basic, and get me educationally acceptable for possibly becoming a translator. Of course, I would have to pass the Russian exams after basic or I would remain in the service for two and a half years as an engineer. I wasn't that keen, to be honest. Sounded like a big scam that was getting everyone off the hook except me.

Now, Mr Brown, or Lt Cdr Brown, seemed like the good cop in the 'good cop bad cop' game that was being played. I just warmed to the spell-like trance that he gently put over me. He was immaculate, not like the fat bastard who clearly was in the dead end of his career. Brown was well decorated, just back from the Falklands, seen some shit, I guess – perfect uniform, razor sharp creases, immaculate well-groomed naval officer side-parted haircut – looked like he'd got brown boot polish holding it in place – and deep brown eyes that sat under half-raised eyebrows. I think he had a motor tic – his eyebrows kept on raising up all the time. But he had one of those taut faces like stretched wet canvas over a rigid metal frame.

To give him his dues Lt Cdr Brown invited me for a walk. We went out onto the exercise ground where we walked around in zigzags like a pair of minesweepers whilst he explained further what he was trying to offer me. There were no guarantees, no certainties, but he did promise me it was a genuine offer and he would meet me at Raleigh to ensure that I got the next interview and the language tests done ASAP after arrival.

I signed up that afternoon. He was the first fucker ever to really live up to a promise; as for the fat fucker, who cares?

The Steering Group

Chapter 3

An Introduction

I had a weekend at home with my parents before I got the train to Plymouth. Phil had joined the army whilst I was at DECAF so I didn't get to see him, which was unfortunate as I really wanted to get the inside track on what basic training was actually gonna throw at me. It was a real nice time at home I guess, and I enjoyed having some time with Mum and Dad but was so keen to just get started. I had a new life opening up ahead of me now and I was becoming impatient. The weekend passed okay, except my mother was fucking insisting I wore a suit to Plymouth. I eventually agreed and kept the peace for the sake of my dad. I think he was pleased that I was joining the navy – "sort you out," I remember him saying – but secretly jealous as he had always wanted to go to sea in the merchant navy. We spent an afternoon in the shed together, smoking fags and dreaming of owning a boat. He was building me a model WW1 battlecruiser, HMS *Scimitar*. It was always fucking freezing in the shed so we ended up in the garage smoking Marlboro cigarettes and looking at porn mags in the car after Sunday lunch.

I enjoyed the privacy of a hot bath that evening and a shit without any interruptions, despite my mother insisting on the window being wide open; she always had the window open even in the very depths of winter. Privacy is a thing no one really appreciates if they've always enjoyed it. Nor do such people have the slightest understanding of those who demand it after being denied it for so long. It's absolutely sacred, just to be alone now and again. You've seriously got to have been incarcerated or have been in the forces to understand what a privilege privacy really is.

The train journey took about 12 months... well, eight hours actually, as it was slow as fuck, stopping at what felt like every tree and station en route. I was excited. I had left DECAF and got a way forward, a job no less, and I was keen to experience being at sea again as soon as possible. I would write to all the crew on the *Atlantic Star* and let them know just as soon as I got my first pay packet. I had changed out of my suit in the carriage toilet shortly after boarding the train and sat down with a can of beer from the buffet car, one of those delightful warm Stellas, or wife-beater beers (they were known as wife-beaters due to the fact that if you drank too many you'd go home and beat up your wife, or something like that). Later in the journey I overheard a few others who were talking about joining HMS Raleigh. I went over to join them. They were my age. It was like talking to a bunch of kids; I'd grown up all too quickly for my own good, the precious gift of innocence and childhood already lost to time. These young things were in for a far bigger shock than me.

I think it is fair to say that after DECAF no one seemed to measure up to the lads I had known. All very immature, mummy's boys and the like. I played along for a while but I think I was out of place right from the start. DECAF had changed me into a young man, my childhood had already passed, and I think looking back that that's what really changed me, and I guess it's a bit of a shame too, to lose all the freedom of childhood so early in life. All that time can never be recovered; no playing games or fucking around with girlfriends, no family holidays, just hard labour, beatings and living in endless fear of what might happen to you next. What a bummer.

Arrival in Plymouth was amazing. Sun was shining – it was June so the weather would be good for basic training. Finally got to dip in for a change. (Dip in – get lucky, dip out – be unlucky.) We all got off the train and there was a meeting place for new recruits out on the roadside where a very happy petty officer waited to greet us and tick our names off on his clipboard, then guided us to a 4.5t truck that was waiting to transport us over the River Tamar to HMS Raleigh. It was one of those typical 4.5-ton Bedfords, almost like the ones you'd see in *Dad's Army*! All the other kids were excited. I thought it was all quite ridiculous, all the shouting and the giggling. As sure as eggs is eggs, all that shit stopped once we arrived at the main gate. Training started immediately. To me it was just like my first day at DECAF all over again and I didn't bat an eyelid. All that confusion and shouting was just background noise to me now, all just normal. It fucking freaked the others out something terrible.

Unbelievably some guys quit that first day! They would PVR, which is premature voluntary release. What the fuck? RN (Royal Navy) basic training even back then wasn't nails. But some kids couldn't cope with the petty officers shouting orders, or the continual abuse and punishment of press-ups and the like. To me it was just funny. The first day passed quickly: haircut, kit issue, bunk allocation, etc., etc., just like DECAF – been there done that. Easy. It was soon noticed I had a lead on all the others and my leadership was being noticed. Ironing the uniform, polishing shoes and boots – I taught a few how to iron their boots to get that parade gloss look, and started a little cottage industry on my first day; old habits and tricks coming in handy already. All that domestic shit, including ironing and folding stuff the size of a book, was piss easy to me. I soon became platoon leader and everyone's friend to help them through. I think I lied a little as to how exactly I had acquired all my skills but bluffed along with the bullshit that I'd learnt it all in the Sea Cadets. It was almost like being taught how to suck eggs in the beginning, but I played along quite happily, riding the wave while I could.

However, it does take years to get used to all the terminology and acronyms they use for everything in the MOB. There's even a book that's been published called *Jack Speak*, for those who need to translate how matelots actually speak. The first issue I faced was the ranking system, and it's real hard not to call everyone sir. Call a chief sir and you're in for some abuse; call a sir chief and you're on extra duties and punishment – fucking headache – plus you have to remember all the uniforms: No. 1 uniform; No. 2 uniform, No. 8s; No. 4s; half blues; pirate rig; rig of the day; PT rig; mess undress; raincoat; windcheater; and many more I've simply forgotten.

Raleigh was a huge establishment, with all the classrooms and accommodations looking very new and almost space age. It hadn't long taken over from HMS Ganges. The buildings were made of new brick in the lower half and sort of white space-station type upper floors with big windows; there were no bars or cages over them which was secretly a nice change for me. Lots of roadways with signs like 'Keep off the grass' and 'Men Marching' all fascinated me. The only resemblance to DECAF was the perimeter which was well fenced with barbed wire, well patrolled and security cameras were evident everywhere. But this fence was to keep people out, not us in. Felt just like home again. I did enjoy looking out of the window from my barracks room as it looked out over the Tamar and open countryside. The accommodations were simply five-star compared with what I'd been used to. All the showers worked, ablutions block was fully tiled and in great condition, and the shithouses were immaculate with full-length doors. I thought it was fucking great. I guess the other kids had that struggle to deal with for the first time being away from home and there was some crying in the night that first few days; fucking weird after DECAF but I understood. I really understood. My locker was the same size as at DECAF but was fully functional and even had a lock. What was there to complain about?

I remember the first week or two, it was all cool and all a bit of a laugh, but I remember one lad saying it was all going to change as the pressure came on. Yeah, he was right. A lot of tension is created when you are with a group of lads; it gets competitive and rightfully so in my opinion. But if you were the slowest or someone with substandard kit you attracted punishment for the group. It was old news to me but these lads hadn't had the BULs and Kilks experience so I guess they needed to be brought up to speed on how to keep up and look out for each other, not fuck each other over. Lucky for me, turns out that's exactly what the navy wanted and I was already there and leading the pack. I fucking hated the log runs up to the fire school when some fuckwit or 'gash hand' messed up at kit inspection or some other easy as task they had been set. Then the whole squad had to do the run up to the fire school with the telegraph pole and get an ink stamp on their hand from the duty guy to prove they'd been all the way.

It was only eight weeks' training. I won't go through all the details because you can read about that shit just about anywhere, and it wasn't too different to DECAF except that had been two years. It was simple RN basic training, nothing to get too excited about. They taught you how to have a shower, get a shave, wash and iron your clothes, turn up on time, fit everything you own into the smallest fucking locker ever and be transformed from a complete fuckwit into someone they could teach to be a sailor, learn a trade and above all take orders.

We were taught how to be robots (and it worked), how to get a very short haircut, how to be competitive, how to work as a team, how to march, march with a 303 rifle, march in step, about turn, left incline, right incline, salute, how to stand still, how to stand still for a long time, how to hold a rifle until you had gorilla-like arms, scraping your knuckles along the deck, how to hate the drill instructor, how to get along in a team and how to treasure any privacy you were ever afforded even if it meant five minutes in the shithouse reading a porn mag. Then you'd learn how to eat your scran like a fucking pig because they never gave you time to eat it – no time to sit and eat a meal properly and maybe have a chat. That shit is with me today; I always eat everything in two fucking minutes flat and I'm always half an hour early for everything. It annoys the shit out of everyone who crosses my path, including me. Of course, eventually we were taught how to drink as well. Alcohol was the reward from the gods to the ordinary ranks. Failure to be able to consume copious amounts of alcohol with the boys was seen as a weakness; it was like an entrance exam into the military family. No doubt that's all changed now – for the worse, in my opinion.

The parade ground at Raleigh and all parade grounds in the navy, as I'm sure they are in the army and RAF too, are just a fucking nightmare – you're not allowed to walk across it (you have to double – military term for run); in fact, as far as I remember you had to double everywhere as a new recruit. For some reason every man with small-person syndrome reaches the rank of parade commander and is transformed into the wanker who just loves to scream and shout at every mother-fucker who walks across the most precious pieces of tarmac in the world. This tarmac is pristine in all military bases, immaculately swept and perfectly painted, allowing for perfect divisions of men to be aligned upon the painted markers and then be shouted at to the point of utter humiliation. I never understood how a man's voice could change so much when he had to shout orders on a parade ground. Fucking amazing what can come out of your cakehole when you want it to. 'Attention' was verbally deformed by screaming – from Attention to Shun to simply Haggg! So, you'd get something like "Squad ha!" followed by "Stand still"; then on the march, left and right would become "Luf rah luf rah luf rah luf rah": all very fucking comical.

There's a sketch by Monty Python that sums it up, where John Cleese ends up shouting at himself as the sergeant major marching up and down the parade ground on his own. As a recruit you'd spend hours on this sacred ground being inspected and yelled at before marching round and round and round the fucking thing until you were all in step, all in a straight line and all totally fucked off with it! Often, you'd see lads running around the perimeter of the parade ground with their rifle above their head because they had fucked up royally, often shouting out something stupid like, "I must not smile at the drill instructor," or some such bullshit.

Then there were the uniform inspections or kit musters. Now, at the time it all seemed very pointless but I guess I wasn't to know then how important it is to keep your kit clean and in great condition. For example, there's a need to keep all the sand out of your weapon in the desert and for it to be well cleaned & oiled for action; and dirt can damage clothing or equipment meant to protect you from chemical attack. I think, looking back, if they had explained the purpose of why they shouted or why they wanted everything immaculate we wouldn't have complained so much, but I'm sure they were just working hard to get rid of the recruits you simply didn't want by your side in such situations. White dubbing on your trousers from your gaiters seems innocent enough (although almost a cause for hanging on a parade ground) but is easily compared with breaching the guidelines from the IATG (International Ammunition Technical Guidelines) where such careless mixing of substances could lead to premature initiation of an explosive. When put like that it gets you thinking more.

Sure, there was lots of fitness, all done with those fuckwit PTIs (physical training instructors) who had basically failed at a trade earlier in their career and ended up in little white outfits and white pumps, pissed with power and ready to try and make you fail at any one of the assessed 5-, 10- and 15-mile runs, obstacle courses, log runs, fitness tests, rope climbs, grid workouts and BFTs (battle fitness tests). Lots of guys failed – they couldn't do the runs or some other shit because they had spent their entire childhood indoors on a computer, and that was back in the '80s. The trick was not to end up on a remedial of any description; if you had to go back in the evening for additional training, you'd get behind with your kit prep for the next day then you'd be in the shit again. Vicious circle, it always snowballed when you fucked up. Gradually the classes got smaller and you became good friends with those who remained as the weeks wore on. Basic training wasn't too hard for me; what I was thinking more about what was on the other side of basic. I wanted to go see the world, have a girl in every port. I felt like a captive animal in a zoo.

Basic training did have some purposeful components to it, like basic firefighting, sea survival, damage control, seamanship skills, leadership training, problem-solving, learning the terminology, the firing range, learning about different weapons, lessons in ship and aircraft recognition, and naval history and traditions. All standard stuff I guess, nothing to get excited about, but it was better than being in detention. I think my only memory of the fireground at Raleigh was all us recruits standing outside in the pissing rain during a NAAFI break, or 'stand easy', getting a hot coffee and an oggie from the van that came around at lunchtimes. It was sort of built into your DNA that during coffee break, or your 15-minute stand easy as it was called, it was almost compulsory to have a smoke, a coffee and a Cornish pasty – that shit lasted for about 10 years of my time in the military. It wasn't like smoking was expensive in any way, as you were given 600 cigarettes a month, affectionately known as Blue Liners. Pusser's fags or Blue Liners came in silver foil wrapping and were definitely cancer sticks made up of all the trash other cigarette manufacturers would throw away after sweeping the floor. I still call coffee break 'stand easy' today.

Then there was the gas chamber.

The gas chamber was awesome. I think it's banned now but back then it was a full day out, learning about chemical warfare, getting sized up for a respirator and then putting on a full NBCD (nuclear, biological & chemical defence) suit and going into the chamber itself. The gas chamber was a small building out in an open space away from the main accommodation blocks, dark, cold and empty, except for all the unsuspecting sailors who lined the walls in single file. About 15 recruits at a time all marched in after the instructors lit the CS gas (tear gas) tablets (probably half a dozen too many because they really did get a laugh out of gassing the recruits), then we were all ordered to take off our gas masks, take a deep breath then blow out hard three times with the mask back on and recite the rainbow poem. I think the poem was actually written by someone who must have worked in the gas chambers in WW2 or something. The idea was to try to teach everyone how to expel any gas and then seal the mask properly and clear it. If you didn't then any little hole that might be in the mask would let the gas inside and you'd be brown bread within nine seconds, apparently. Then at the end you had to take your mask off again, say your name and number and tell a joke. Everyone nearly died! Except we had an Irish guy who had been hit so many times with CS gas in Northern Ireland he stood chatting away to the instructors for about 10 minutes with not so much as a cough! The rest of us lay outside on the grass dying of mad cow disease or some other similar-looking horrible death – well, that's what it probably looked like. Makes all your wet parts itch like fuck, eyes puff up and produce so much snot you could drown in it – and for fuck's sake don't scratch your balls; it would be like rubbing chillies on your jap's eye.

I think we were about six weeks in when I got a message to report to the education centre. So off I trotted, not expecting anything untoward. Lt Cdr Brown, now Cdr Brown, was waiting for me in interview room 3. I remember marching in, saluting and taking a seat in front of a panel of four officers and a civilian. Cdr Brown asked me how training was going and I simply remember informing him how fucking easy it was; some of the others laughed but not the civilian. I remember Cdr Brown being pleased to see me and he made a comment about his visit to DECAF and how he was looking forward to my passing out parade in two weeks. I congratulated him on his promotion; he smirked and pretended not to be impressed. I think looking back we had a special relationship after DECAF, and my following up on his recommended path made room for an unofficial friendship of sorts. I don't think it was quite normal for such easy conversations between a senior officer and a new recruit to take place as they did, but there we were like old friends, with respect keeping me chained to his every word. He would later become my handler, and as such respect needed to flow in both directions.

The room was very well organised and resembled a board-room type arrangement. All the seats were those annoying pusser's officer chairs, which wore those gopping (naval slang for disgusting) cream seat covers with the green floral arrangement that furnished every wardroom in the fleet. (Someone obviously took a backhander to allow such a pro-curement.) Mine was one of those annoying wooden seats that creaked every time you shuffled, making it all too obvious I was a little nervous. A long table centrally located with a green cloth covering like that of a snooker table dominated the best part of the room. I sat at the door end with the far quarter commandeered by way of a semi-circle of all the interviewing officers. The walls were lined with light fake wood panelling and various ship's crests and paintings were hung between the panelling arrangements. Each painting had a dedicated wall light and green shade; I always liked that arrangement for some reason. There was a loud ticking clock that was 40 minutes late and a number of badly marked and dented filing cabinets at the far end of the room that seemed to be overflowing with obsolete documents that no one knew what to do with.

I was clocking the various characters who were all hiding behind their glasses and notebooks. I had guessed there was some assessment to be done but at the time I didn't know they were simultaneously assessing me personally. There was a bit of brass in the room, which made me a little uneasy I have to admit, their ranks given away by the fact that a few of the hats had egg yolk on the peaks hanging on the coat hooks above the coffee station. I hadn't become completely familiar with naval ranks at that time but it was easy to guess that these officers weren't straight from Dartmouth. I smiled as one of the hats had the perfect coffee ring in the middle – fucking punishable by death on the parade ground to be sure. Each of the officers took it in turn to write something and then looked up and gave me a stare. I was focused on the civilian who seemed to be the one they all wanted to impress or assist, especially my man Brown. He was a tall guy, sat very upright, dressed in a plain dark suit that was too big for his body; he was so incredibly thin, he was skeletal in build. I was fascinated by his eyes set in cave-like sockets which were piercing ice-blue and almost continually obscured by overactive, fluttering, almost lash-free eyelids. He sported very proud cheekbones which exacerbated the obvious skin issue he had, as there were bright white blotches to his face, cheeks and forehead, as if the pigmentation in his skin was failing in some way. His hair was dyed black and looked overloaded with some hair tonic or cream which reflected the fluorescent lighting above. He could almost be related to Cdr Brown, who sat calmly opposite him.

Now, I remember the actual interview was really quite something. I was handed a series of documents to fill in and immediately the civilian started to speak in Russian, asking if I understood him, what I thought of the interview, did I know anyone in the Soviet Union, if so what contacts did I have and what did I think the purpose of the interview was. I replied calmly in Russian to all of the questions and then asked if the other officers were able to understand the conversation or just what the two of us were saying. He replied simply that I had 10 minutes to give an answer to that question myself and complete the initial assessment documents simultaneously. The challenge wasn't too difficult as I simply stood up, approached each officer, swore and gave an insult in Russian to get a reaction of some description; this was met with a mixed reaction that left me nervous as hell and wondering if I'd indeed overstepped the mark. I passed back the documents to the civilian, who smiled and looked to the others in an approving manner as I delivered verdicts on them all in Russian and Arabic. The most interesting thing that followed was that I remember him saying with a little chuckle in his voice and in Gulf Arabian that I was brave to offer insults to such high-ranking officers. The prick had a sense of humour at least.

It was all smiles and then the civilian simply looked at the attending officers and said, "Recommended for further language assessment and, if successful, practical training and possible career progression." Brown was obviously happy and quite prepared for this outcome as he had all the paperwork ready to go. I remember that making me feel quite special, that this guy believed in me and my potential even before this interview. I guess he could just see raw potential. I don't know, maybe it was a huge gamble. I later heard that Brown was a recruiter of special talents; it was either that or he was a fucking unicorn and I was getting all my wishes at once. Or maybe the friends I'd made in Moscow were indeed of interest to the military. The civilian stood up and shook my hand; I wasn't sure what the fuck to make of that. I think I'd actually pleased someone for the first time in my life, so it was coffee all round and a smoke. I was invited to complete the paperwork.

Brown and the civilian wanted to go over my contacts or penfriends in Moscow. We sat smoking cigarettes and they were really keen to hear about all my correspondence and who I was or had been writing to. I said I would pop some photos round for them to see the family I was writing to and sarcastically suggested I get each of them a Russian souvenir or something. It was made pretty clear right then how all future correspondence was going to take place. But Brown softened the order in so much that they wanted me to continue writing but not to mention I was in the services now.

Brown and the civilian (he never gave me his actual name at the time) played tag in the delivery of the process I would go through. I would sit three two-hour verbal tests followed by a six-hour written test at the weekend. I'd be excused church and ceremonies. This would be passed to my division petty officer as I was now a rating required for special duties. I was NOT permitted to discuss anything with anyone outside of the group that sat before me. I was to complete basic and engineering training at the Royal School of Military Engineering. (I had to have a trade or speciality, that was part of the deal, because I could always be RTUd (returned to unit).) Then on completion join a warship – name to be passed by draft order – for eight weeks to test my abilities and then report back to Plymouth and the office of CINCNAVHOME (Commander-in-Chief, Naval Home Command) and Admiral Roger Fell. I don't think any of what was said went into my brain, not a thing. I was very excited, nervous, bewildered, unsure, a whole plethora of confusing feelings and emotions. All brought back to earth on return to my division – just a pleb again, cleaning corridors and polishing shit for the next inspection, muster or parade.

The tests on Sunday went okay. I was suddenly very unpopular as I remember everyone was getting their No1 uniforms ready for church and I just put on some 8s and bimbled (bimbling is a slow walk in naval speak) off to the education centre. I was met by a pretty little Wren who took me into one of the classrooms. She asked me if I was learning a language, to which I just smiled and said yeah. It was a small classroom with maybe 12 desks, but individual soundproofed booths and high-sided partitions all fitted with headsets and microphones. The headsets were old, heavy and uncomfortable, and the 'press to speak' button in my allocated booth was all but worn out. The room was bare brick walls, well-lit but no windows and it all smelt damp, a bit like an old bomb shelter or something.

Sitting at my work station I remember being presented with a simple page of instructions. Basically, the first three tests would be to listen and answer the questions, either on the paper or, if asked, respond verbally through the microphone. Simple enough. There was a pause button and when pressed you could request a bathroom break, or between tests a smoke and coffee break. My first two were as simple as 1, 2, 3. The third test was a surprise – it was a test of my memory to exactly what fittings, fixtures, paintings, etc. were in the interview room earlier in the week. The questions were very fast and in both Arabic and Russian, which was totally unexpected, so I had to switch between three languages quickly, and I don't think the Russian speaker was that great to be honest, certainly wasn't a native Russian that was for sure. Some questions asked in Arabic needed to be answered verbally in Russian and vice versa, with written responses required in English. I think in total it was maybe over 200 verbal questions. One of the questions was to describe the interview room and I took great delight in mentioning the coffee ring stain on an officer's hat. It's a great thing about the navy, they don't wait around, and I got my results the next day: 100%. It was a simple call from the education centre to my divisional officer. I guess this was my introduction to the wider world of the navy – simple, no fuss sort of shit I guess. It was a bit deflating, almost a disappointment, as there was no celebration or recognition.

That was the end of it for a while. I had to get on with the basic training and pass the final tests and evaluations. Nothing too heavy. It was like the whole episode and encounter in the education centre hadn't happened. But I guess doing the training with the lads made for a good laugh. You don't have too many things to worry about in basic as everything is organised for you. All I had to do was to simply follow orders, and so it continued up until passing out. There were just a few final kit musters to pass and, if successful, we could all take shore leave and go to a local pub. It's the same for every class that passes out – you were all loaded into a bus and taken to the Crown & Anchor pub in Torpoint with the instructors. I guess it was a controlled piss-up and a way of saying well done unofficially, and an introduction to alcohol for those underage recruits, which was the most common reward given in the MOB. No enforcement of the underage rule back then, no one gave a shit, and it was a guaranteed income for the landlord. Everyone was happy.

The first and last time my mother ever came to see me away from home was my passing out parade. It was a great day as both Mum, Dad and my younger brother attended with my dad's parents. It was cool as they all saw me pass out before they passed away. How little we realise how short our time is. It's a shame looking back as I had no one to be proud of my many achievements made throughout my career that followed. All successes were celebrated in isolated loneliness. I won an award for the best sailor and still have the official photographs. Cdr Brown presented the award in front of the whole establishment and all the families. He even took the time to speak to my parents after the parade in the NAAFI. Fucking awesome.

On completion we had weekend leave and my parents had booked a hotel in Cawsand, a place I would later take my wife and eventually live close to for some 10 years. Cornwall is a great part of the country and I would recommend it to anyone; I have so many good memories of our times there. It was a great weekend, all very nice and relaxed, good food, even my mum had a few brandies and Babychams so a very rare weekend indeed. I really enjoyed seeing her so happy. The weekend soon passed and I was on the train headed for the military engineering school.

I think at the time the Royal School of Military Engineering was probably the biggest military engineering establishment in Europe. I think it used to be an aerodrome during WW2 but all the hangars had now been converted into workshops and training facilities. I remember turning up late at night and fucking around trying to get a pass to get in, and being directed to the other side of the camp. The accommodation and the technical buildings were split into two sort of separate camps and my accommodation wasn't anywhere near where I had turned up, so it was a hike to find the accommodation main gate. There were always fucking NPs (naval provosts) on the gate, both here and at every other establishment I attended, who would love to drop you in the shit for anything they could the next day with the master-at-arms. Wankers, the lot of them.

However, engineering training was significantly more relaxed than Raleigh and I was allowed to travel in civvies and had most weekends free. The accommodation felt like it dated back to WW1: shitty accommodation that was cold, made worse by ill-fitting sash windows, open-plan draughty dormitories in a decaying brick building. It was all very depressing and tired. Pussers' steel-framed beds and lockers lined the dorms that were all definitely in need of replacement, or could possibly be sold on to DECAF! Only three showers and a cracked bath were provided for ablutions and the whole thing was duplicated upstairs for another class. Nothing new here, standard crap military accommodation that we all needed to get used to. The only difference being that after I had bought a portable TV with my next wage I had something to do other than study and get pissed.

Getting paid in the navy back then was a real drama that beggars belief. Usually the whole division would line up outside the regulating office and be called in one at a time by name and number to receive pay. You had to march in, salute, state your name and number followed by sir or the appropriate address of the issuing officer and then hold out your left hand. Sounds dead simple but if you were to fuck up any component of this precious and precise sequence you would have to wait and try again the next day at mis-musters in order to receive your pay. What a fucking drama that was; if it wasn't for the money, I don't think anyone would have bothered going back at all.

We had spare time on our hands for the first time in months and that generally led to boredom which in turn led to skylarking or drinking. Most of our spare time as recruits was spent at the NAAFI desperately trying to avoid the ID checks for underage drinking. They all knew it went on and generally turned a blind eye but occasionally there would be raids on the NAAFI in order to try and catch someone. If caught you would then be found on punishment, polishing the cannons outside the admin offices or the ship's bell, the next day and for a week thereafter.

I think it was tolerated to such an extent because there was still the IRA threat, and terrorism was active toward servicemen, so keeping us boys on camp was easier than herding cats on the outside should there be a heightened security alert or something. The most popular drink at the time was Newcastle Brown Ale, none of those fancy Italian lagers everyone raves about nowadays. Most lads were smashed two or three nights a week, and I guess it was because part two of training was mostly boring study and revision for exams. Which, let's face it, is what we had all failed at before joining up and was why we were all there in the first place. We all just wanted to be on board a ship and get away to sea to see the world. 'Join the Navy, see the world' as the old adverts portrayed. Usually a night in the NAAFI meant a takeaway and we'd get the duty bod to go get it for us.

Everyone paid regular visits to the drafting officer and filled out preference cards, all hoping for a ship that would take them on a global trip. It was known as a dream chit – you'd write down all your preferences as to what type of ship, what port you'd like to be based in, even names of ships after you had researched what ships were deploying where, and of course areas to avoid. But it was all a pointless exercise really because as a new recruit you were destined for the first available billet on the ships that needed you most.

There were occasional scraps between classes and a punch-up when the blocks had an inspection. Inevitably one class would sabotage the other's accommodation to try and look good and divert attention to secure weekend leave or the like. To be honest, cleaning those old buildings was like trying to polish a turd, fucking pointless, but a clean ship is a happy ship, so I was told. The navy really did love cleaning and painting for no other reason than it kept us all busy and gave the officers something to pick fault with when there really wasn't anything else to do.

We had to march everywhere in a platoon wearing green gaiters to show we were still trainees, so you'd get the odd officer screaming out of an office window if you were out of step who'd report you to the parade commander, who was no doubt related to the tosser in Raleigh. Same rules applied; the parade ground was sacred. We did remove the gaiters on occasion to avoid all the attention and just 'bimble' around the base with the other crowds of engineers who were there doing additional engineering training relating to their trade specialisations and ranks.

I never wanted to be an engineer. However, it was a ticket to the big wide world from a place I would always try to forget. I remember it all being very interesting, even fascinating in some parts, and actually relevant to the world we occupy. For theory I studied basic maths, physics, engineering theory, thermodynamics, ship's systems, HVAC, power generation including turbo alternators, gas turbines, Y100 boilers, super-heated steam systems, SW systems, FW systems, power and distribution, hydraulics and ship's husbandry.

Ship's husbandry to me was the biggest waste of space in the known universe. The instructors were obviously deficient in the brains department, and I remember the whole class being subjected to a week of theory on how to clean a floor, a tiled floor or a wooden deck, and what colour bucket and cloths to use. They even had the amazing blue cleaning shit! Now, in the navy it was affectionately known as pusser's blue, which was without doubt the cornerstone of all naval and quite possibly all cleaning organisations throughout the world. Who knows where this shit came from but it seemed to me like every ship on the planet used it. You were only supposed to use a capful per 10 litres or something, but we all learned using it neat was a lot fucking quicker. After endless lectures on how to clean we were then subjected to how to chip and paint, what brush to use and how to clean them. Now, looking back the navy could have saved itself a whole heap of time and money on this subject, because in the real world at the time no fucker did anything like how we were instructed. All cleaning equipment was kept in cleaning lockers on board ship, which inevitably ended up having only one bucket, three filthy cloths, gallons of pusser's blue and an equivalent amount of deck polish, this being despite the endless resupplying of such lockers. This was due to the fact that the whole lot would be thrown over the side on completion of any cleaning periods. MARPOL (the International Convention for the Prevention of Pollution From Ships) wasn't even known about back then. As for upper-deck maintenance, all rust was painted over with generous amounts of grey-white or black paint slapped on by the bucket load whilst having a fag and trying to sunbathe if at all possible.

Workshop technology was interesting and eventful with everyone getting to know a lump of mild steel and a file very intimately. We had a trade test where this lump of metal had to be rubbed to death to form a clamp to exact measurements and within tight tolerances. Only when this was completed were you allowed to progress to lathe and milling machine work. To be fair, at the beginning I don't think anyone knew the difference between an open-ended or ring spanner, let alone being able to manufacture everything from a gasket to an engine part. So I guess it was pretty sound training. The workshops were really cool but possibly the hardest part of the training, as you really did need to pass the trade tests. However, the instructors, all old boys, were actually very helpful, patient and informative so it was a useful time of learning. You were allowed to smoke as much as you wanted and take breaks whenever, but failure to complete the test pieces or the diesel engine overhauls and have a successful running machine at the end of the allotted times meant you'd be either back-classed (start the course over) or SNLR (Services no longer required; in other words, fired – dismissed from the RN). All manufactured parts, engine strip downs, overhauls and rebuilds were examined and tested for tolerance, torque settings procedure and completeness, in addition to our theoretical and practical abilities being continuously assessed. I must have done okay as I won the Best Engineer award at passing out. I still have it in my office today.

The day before we passed out from the engineering school the issuance of draft orders was made, detailing what ship and where we would be going. There were lots of screams for joy but more disappointments amongst us than anything else – not many global trips going on at the time. Some were drafted to go on to further training and become electricians, and others to the submarine service which was very short of engineers. No one wanted to join the 'sludge mariner' brigade. I was drafted to HMS *Gainsborough* for eight weeks' special drafting and instructed to join her in Portland two days after passing out.

The *Gainsborough* was a guided missile destroyer and, at 5,400 tons, a sleek grey messenger of death, and fuck she looked awesome to my young eyes. She had just finished a work-up and what was called BOST, which is Basic Operational Sea Training. She was sailing at 4pm for the fjords of Norway and then up to the Arctic Circle. Joining the *Gainsborough* was just weird – my first ship. I was joining as a junior mechanic. I remember trying to clamber up the gangway with all the stores going on board by way of human chain and then hordes of people coming off in what appeared to be an uncontrolled and chaotic fashion, all part of an organised plan to get the ship ready for sea. It was just incredible how much activity was going on all around the ship and her berth. It was like watching swarms of bees in a hive, busy looking after the queen and preparing her for something remarkable and exciting – a hive of activity, so to speak. I introduced myself to the quartermaster, who piped (made a broadcast) for another young lad to escort me to my DO.

My divisional officer was the DMEO, a Lt Dent, who was a very calm, polite and nice kind of chap, nothing of significance, probably a uni graduate, so all brains and no common dog. I had an interview with him in his cabin almost immediately. An officer's cabin on a warship isn't much to write home about – there's a settee, which in fact is the upturned bunk, a foldaway chair and a cabin door curtain, all made with the very same gopping ('gopping' is naval slang for disgusting) cream and green floral material seen throughout the fleet and as I had seen in Raleigh, a small fold-down writing desk and a foldaway sink. Despite the draft order instructions and any expectations I may have had, I was to be berthed in the bear pit, or stokers' mess. I was to be assigned marine engineering duties and allocated a part of the ship where I would be expected to work on a daily basis. However, I'd be called upon by the ops officer for special duties as and when required and given further instructions when appropriate. My divisional officer encouraged me to follow the engineering watch bill as much as possible to get my task book signed off quickly. Failure to complete my language or other special assignments meant I'd probably be forced to remain on board as an engineer because the fleet was so undermanned after the Falklands War. I think many matelots had left the service after the Falklands War, causing huge manpower shortages and fuelling the mega recruitment drive that had saved my ass.

He informed me that he knew why I was on board and then simply offered me a cigarette; inhaling deeply, he was almost at pains to tell me this was going to be a difficult eight weeks for me. To achieve and maintain confidentiality of my secondary tasking whilst living aboard as an engineer would be a bigger test than the one planned for me when we reached our theatre of operations, but apparently it was an assignment that was meant to be a test not only of my engineering and language skills but of my ability to fit in to new surroundings and be a team player. I remember watching the blue smoke from his cigarette spiral upwards and then get sucked up into the extractor as I looked up searching for some sort of divine inspiration or confirmation to continue with what I had got myself into. He was super-overprotective of me I think and he wanted me to know that Cdr Brown was hoping to hear good news and that I could come to him at any time for help or advice. He wanted promotion, I remember thinking. Fortunately, there was to be a group of trainee engineers joining before we sailed who were specially selected for fast advancement and this would help my blending in with the whole shebang. He wished me good luck, signed my joining instructions form, pulled back the cabin curtain and released me into the Andrew proper fashion.

I'm not sure I was ready or even properly briefed as to the double life that was implied and that I needed to adopt for the coming weeks or indeed for my entire future. Looking back, if I'd fucked up it wouldn't have mattered as I wasn't anything other than a baby engineer at this time, and if it had all gone pear-shaped I would remain on board and no one would be any the wiser or even give a shit. Maybe that was the idea, and a bit of an insurance policy for the organ grinders, whoever they might have been. The challenge of adopting and embracing this opportunity to run parallel careers at such an embryonic stage in my service was no doubt a mindfuck but hugely attractive for some reason. I guess being different is exciting and it certainly made me feel valued, which is something I had craved above all things since DECAF.

The whole ship was alive and buzzing with action – all too much for me to take in really. I wandered the passageways wide-eyed and lost, trying to find my way around the labyrinth of compartments and decks. A whole new bigger orchestra than that I had experienced on board the *Atlantic Star*, everywhere was just manic with activity. I had just a few hours to get all my kit on board, new safety kit issued, my joining routine completed and get all my shit unpacked in the mess. All the smells and noises were very familiar and exciting, just like the *Atlantic Star*, but she was different in so much as she was packed with so much equipment and so many crew, leaving very little room to manoeuvre through this steel maze built on iron decks and weapon systems. It was overwhelming.

The bear pit, or stokers' mess, really was a fucking amazing place. I think that I was billeted in 3Q mess, which translated means three decks down and reasonably far aft. I had my kit bag and pusser's suitcase to unpack and stow away before we sailed. Now, there were about 40 guys down that mess deck and enough room for about 10. Mess decks are like catacombs, dark and full of bodies; half of the entire mess deck was in darkness, as watchkeepers who had worked through various times in the previous night slept in bunks that were three high, very narrow, all with curtains or blankets hung to afford some privacy to the occupant. As many as three rows of bunks lined each side of a 'gulch' (a gulch being a bedroom or bunk space within the mess deck, with the exception of the mess square bunks that were folded down to form a settee arrangement to afford some kind of living space). Of course, all these settee beds would be assigned to the sprogs or newcomers to the mess, with the senior guys and leading hands living in the deepest darkest gulches where there would be no disturbance to their sleep from noise or light pollution. The higher you were in the pecking order the better sleeping arrangement you could command.

Bunks were very narrow, about the width of your forearm, with approximately 30cm of headroom when lying down, fitted with a seatbelt or bunk strap (for rough weather) and a bed bag into which you'd zip up the mattress and all the bedding once you vacated it. You had a bunk ventilator and a bunk light, which initially you were made to believe you had to pay the chief electrician a usage fee for. Under each bunk space were three drawers for your footwear, and a good tip was never to get a bottom bunk, as you'd either get stood on as someone tried to climb in the bunks above you, pissed on (drunkenness or just bed-wetting) or have the drawers underneath you opened and shut so often it would drive you simply insane due to additional sleep loss. The deck was tiled and obviously a fucking nightmare to keep clean. The place stank of cigarette smoke, half empty trays of food and heaps of empty beer tins from the previous night's piss-up, which no doubt added to the suffocating atmosphere which was to be home for the next two months. It was cold as the ventilators blasted fresh air in from the world above. No windows or views except the odd poster of a naked woman on a beach someplace exotic which all matelots seem to dream and talk of endlessly in the boredom of a life at sea. I stowed my shit and went up top to sneak a look outside as we sailed.

My daywork assignment was to work in the shipwright's workshop, which was on the upper deck. I went up top to find it. I remember listening to the gas turbines spin up, a high-pitched whistle that grew in intensity as the turbines each passed self-sustaining speed, and then waited patiently for further orders. Increased vibrations through the deck and into my boots gave an indication that the *Gainsborough* was being released from her ropes holding her alongside. As the ship's props gripped the water to push her ahead, the harmonics changed, the turbines wheeze became a roar and the ship slowly moved ahead. Ropes were tossed from ashore and hauled in by seamen in No. 2s, there was lots of shouting from the deck petty officers and a blast or two from the ship's siren as if to confirm the conductor, the captain of all the goings-on, was in agreement or approval.

We had left the wall and were making our way out into the Channel all looking very smart, with the berthing crew at harbour stations in No. 2 uniforms lining the waists, forecastle and flight deck. Off to sea. The sea air in our nostrils and excitement in our hearts. It's not to be underestimated or simply laughed off; it's an experience to be on a British ship of the line, the sheer history demands your respect; 'England expects' is upon you as you imagine being aboard with Lord Nelson but with more firepower than the entire Spanish Armada beneath your feet. Only now, instead of the bosun calling us to beat to quarters, it would be a siren and a call to action stations as tradition was again replaced by technology.

The *Gainsborough* had both gas turbines and a steam plant, the operation of which remained a complete fucking mystery to me. I was initially satisfied by simply learning how to find the engine rooms, gear room, boiler room, generators or other machinery spaces around the ship. I learnt how to conduct machinery rounds with a mentor; I wasn't allowed to do anything on my own as I wasn't qualified at the time and needed to double bank and then pass AMC (auxiliary machinery operator) certificates and an oral board before being allowed to become a 'watchkeeper'! Wow, no fucking thanks, that would have meant more work on top of the endless cleaning and all the exercises that never seemed to end. There were watchkeepers and dayworkers. The watchkeepers would have the privilege of keeping the ship running at night and through the silent hours, whilst the dayworkers worked a normal day with the exception of the compulsory attendance at all the exercises and drills. It was hard work, long hours and relentless. I don't think many of the crew really wanted to be at sea, but instead all wanted to reach new and exciting ports of call where they could spend all their money on booze and women, including prostitutes, it mattered not to most.

Life at sea is routine, routine and more routine, but with lots of little surprises like fire exercises, flood exercises, machinery drills, weapon drills and a whole plethora of other drills to keep every day interesting, but then even this becomes routine, routine, routine, routine, sometimes made more difficult by the changing of the watertight condition ordered by HQ1. All ship's doors and hatches are assigned a flood risk of X-ray, Yankee and Zulu. X-ray identifies those hatches lower down in the ship, and Zulu is every fucking door and hatch from the bottom to the top, making moving around the ship really difficult. State 1 was war, State 2 was ready for war or defence watches, and State 3 was peace time – it changed every day as we exercised continually, which is what the navy did and probably still does when it's not cleaning ready to conduct exercises.

Meals were breakfast, lunch and dinner, same time every day and with a strict pecking order to who went through to eat first. There was always some sort of additional snack at 4pm which I still affectionately remember as 'four o'clockers', which became 'nine o'clockers' when the ship was alongside. This was often a boiled egg, bread and spreads, cheese and corn dog or some other light 'snackage'. Food was good or bad depending on the chef or the mood of the chef. However, to this day it amazes me how a chef could engineer a potato to be completely incinerated on the outside with nothing but fresh air on the inside, like a hollow piece of coal. Maybe the fluffy inside was extracted for the officers and used to make mash potatoes... Chefs, hmm... I think mostly they were just people who tried to prepare food, albeit sometimes in horrific conditions especially as the weather deteriorated the further north we steamed.

The galley was always awash as they tipped the broilers onto the floor or were scrubbing out after trying to cook something. I always liked the cooked breakfast. Doesn't matter how much they fucked up everything else, a bit of crispy bacon or burnt sausage in a cheap slice of white bread is just fine. That is until you were on ship's bread – that meant one swipe of a knife with butter over your bread resulted in it all rolling itself up into a ball of fucked-up bread and butter that looked like a dough ball and became absolutely fucking useless. Back then supplies ran out quickly and the first to go would always be the milk, after which the chefs made up great big churns of 'millak' which was white watery shit that you'd only give to someone if they were your worst enemy. It goes without saying the NAAFI (Navy, Army and Air Force Institutes – a shop), which was commonly referred to by all those at sea as the 'Colonel' or 'Colonel Gaddafi', did a roaring trade about a week after sailing on just about every pussers' grey I sailed on.

You lived in darkness most of the time; your bunk space never saw light because there was always someone sleeping, except for evening rounds when an officer would walk around the ship inspecting heads, bathrooms, passageways and mess decks for cleanliness. Fuck, the navy loves to clean, every fucking day you would be cleaning something, and when you'd scrubbed it to death you had the joy of painting it and then cleaning it again. Being at sea is generally boring and it drives everyone to seek something fun to do in order to cope with the mundane routine that becomes your life. Thank fuck for alcohol. As ratings we were allowed to be issued with three cans of beer per man per day. This was issued, paid and signed for at the Gaddafi. This usually got stockpiled for party nights and hidden in all manner of places, like vent trunking, in the A/C space or plumber block space until the appropriate evening, sanctioned by the mess leading hand, for a party night.

The first night out at sea proved to be such a night and it was to initiate all us newcomers to the navy and to our mess deck. Let's face it, it's just plain old bullying by today's standards but I still believe that it had its place and should be allowed to continue to this day. The choice of poison was very limited: CSB, Red Death – or McEwan's – and golden cans of cider.

Initiation takes a boy and makes him part of a family and a team that will, in the event of war, fucking fight for each other all the way. It's not PC anymore, but it's what gangs seek to achieve in cities around the world, what churches cry out to their congregations to put together in the way of fellowship groups. Initiation, coupled with pride, honour, tradition and all the other bollocks civilians don't understand, despite all its faults, bonds men into that band of brothers which breeds a loyalty and respect that no other country in the world could fucking understand or emulate. Yes, alcohol is bad, and bullying is bad, but what I'm describing was the foundation of what made us different, made us better than the rest, made us the best. This shit happened in all the units I joined throughout my career and made me and all my military brothers become so fiercely proud and protective of why we defended Great Britain, this green and pleasant land. Proud to stand and drink toasts to Her Majesty at dinners, functions and events, that's what the fucking terrorists hate – our pride, our history and our traditions. Fuck them! This was just a taste of the initiations and bonding that I experienced, but I know that those who later served with me and later saved my life did it because they belonged to the same gang as me. It's that simple. We belonged to the best gang, HM Forces UK.

Sheepishly after dinner that first night, and dressed in my half blues, I was welcomed to the mess, the Andrew (The Royal Navy) and the family. I wasn't alone, there were eight other new lads. We were well looked after initially as things needed to get warmed up. We each faced a pyramid of beer in front of us to drink. A can of beer from each mess deck member, given as a welcoming present and stacked in front of you like a pyramid. Of course, we were all pissed as fuck after a few hours and struggling to make a dent in the pyramid which seemed to regrow after you'd made an attempt to drink it. Eventually the drinking games began, from shooting tins to the game of spoons that led to an ironing board being bashed over one lad's head! In a game of spoons you're supposed to hold a spoon in your mouth and bash your opponent over the head as hard as you can until he gives up, all done blindfolded so as to make you believe you have a chance you may miss getting hit. However, as it turned out only the new guy keeps the blindfold on and the instrument which is used to hit him over the head grows in size each time until it become ridiculously obvious what's happening.

The endgame for myself and each of the new boys in turn was to be humiliated and punished in some barbaric way. I was to be tarred and feathered and then crucified over the A/C hatch. There was a brief courtroom hearing before sentence was passed. This, translated, meant I was stripped of all clothing and then lashed and masking-taped naked to the mess deck table. I was shaved with a Bic razor from head to toe, so ending up absolutely hair free, with anyone and everyone joining in, and occasionally being pissed on before being covered in what was called at the time 'niggers' grease' (Clydspin grease, a very black grease) and my pillows torn and then emptied out all over me. I guess it was fucking hilarious to see a guy running around half covered in grease and feathers. After what felt like hours of struggling, I was then put into overalls and a pole of wood was pushed through the arms and hung over the aft hatch, crucified for the rest of the evening. Fucking unreal, but brilliant in many ways. It was quite hard to explain the next day why I was bald to passing officers and senior ranks in the ship's passageways. They all knew what had happened, ignored it and had a laugh at my expense. Now, some of the lads did go too far, there were a few tears and a few fists that night, but we all ended up with new nicknames and were soon at home with the worst of them. Everyone became part of the family, no exceptions. It didn't matter if you were a weirdo or quiet or loud or had big ears, none of that shit mattered, you became a mess member and proud of it.

We patrolled off the coast of Norway for two weeks solid and the weather soon deteriorated. Seasickness took a hold of me. There's no place you can go, nothing you can do to relieve it, no stopping the symptoms and no break from it, not even for a moment. Doesn't matter how long you look at the horizon, or how long you lie on your bunk, if you're seasick you're just no good to anyone. I guess I got it bad that trip, spewing all day, five-finger spread, feeling hot, cold, sweaty, tired, exhausted. You feel dizzy yet very alert to all the movement, especially your brain sloshing around in your head. Smells make it worse; engine room odours, galley smells and any normally offensive smell is magnified in intensity by about a million per cent to present you with a whole new toolbox of reasons that will take you to the shithouse or the guardrail to release in a projectile fashion anything that may be left in your stomach. Pre-death is the bursting of every last blood vessel in your eyes as the retching near kills you trying to expel every last drop of bile. The only place to go was your bunk to try and die quietly, which is less annoying for the others around you.

It's not just the nausea, the simplest of things became mammoth tasks, like getting dressed was a major issue and there was no way to avoid it, putting socks on was problematic, let alone taking a shower. Standing in a shower cubical whilst holding on for your life as all the water races from one side of the washroom to the other like a miniature tsunami laden with washbags, soap, shampoo bottles and any other non-secured item was incredibly unpleasant, and this, added to the vomiting, made the whole idea of getting cleaned up seem like a pointless waste of time and energy.

One lasting memory of this whole nasty episode of my first attempt to gaining some sea legs was about four weeks into the deployment when we had to go into one of the Norwegian fjords to conduct a boat transfer for mail and some urgent parts. It was planned to take place at around 1pm, which would allow me to grab some lunch for the first time in days and maybe, just maybe, survive the whole experience. The ship was behind schedule and special sea duty men weren't called until 1.15pm, just as the ship approached the entrance to the calm waters of the fjord. I remember feeling so excited as I went to the galley counter to get something to eat, dreaming of succulent steak, chips, anything to fill my painfully empty stomach. I was met with an almost empty counter with the last piece of chicken going to an equally sick shipmate in front of me. Asking the chef for more was totally the wrong thing to do, and I received a raw chicken, thrown at me from behind the serving counter. A lot of abuse followed, together with a stern reminding of mealtimes before the counter shutters were pulled down abruptly, ending any hope of a proper meal. I think I settled for bread and butter with some crisps from the Colonel Gaddafi. I did eventually get some sea legs but I have never been much other than a fair-weather sailor.

Work really started for me as the ship passed up through the Norwegian Sea towards the Arctic Circle and into the Lofoten Basin. The Lofoten Basin was where new ships and subs coming out of the Soviet Northern Fleet base in Severomorsk on the Kola Peninsula usually started trials or began a deployment. It can be a busy seaway, with the Arctic Bridge and Northern Sea Route starting or ending in this area depending on the voyage direction, which is the ideal starting point for a sub to submerge and get lost in the noise of surface traffic before trying to disappear.

It's daylight all day and all fucking night that far north in summer, and I remember spending almost three whole weeks in a dark cupboard in the operations room. I basically lived in an anteroom which was probably only 6ft by 3ft, one bulkhead completely lined with communications equipment that I didn't touch, all painted in that blue-grey pussers' paint that did its best to hide all the nicotine staining. The floor space was about four tiles long covered in ash from the overflowing ashtrays that balanced precariously next to the two badly worn-out chairs that were firmly secured to the deck not allowing any adjustment for comfort. I spent my time writing down and recording transmissions between Soviet surface ships, shore establishments and Soviet ballistic missile boats conducting trials and manoeuvres alongside and under the merchant shipping. I occasionally got to go out on deck, usually at some obscure time like 3am, and was always greeted by daylight.

I don't remember enjoying much of it except to say that good food and iced Fanta orange (my favourite at the time) was brought to me constantly, as though what I was doing was indeed important in some way. Everything I wrote was typed up and sealed in HM Service envelopes then stamped 'Secret' in big red bold letters across the seal and never seen again. The content of the messages and forms I completed, I'm disappointed to write, were quite boring except for the occasional target simulation drill sequences, names of naval officers and civilian contractors and a whole new language I actually struggled with regarding nuclear reactor parts and system bugs and problems they were encountering. My intelligence gathering extended to working with other NATO units and British submarines in the taping of submarine communication cables and surface communication intercepts, which were encrypted but decoded by my contact, only known as Uniform Oscar, who would also provide live communications from within the Soviet submarines which included everything from what was for supper to detailed briefs for upcoming deployment passage routes. This was of course all continually interrupted by our friendly shadowing spy ship pretending to be a fishing boat. I remember even waving to her one night whilst I was having a cigarette outside the chippy's shop with a cup of tea. A friendly war, you could say. We were watching them watching us.

The Cold War game of cat and mouse went on for another five or so years, and I remember reading about the Americans fucking it all up with the incident of the USS *Baton Rouge* colliding with the *Kostroma* in 1992. There were many operations around this time, some I don't even know if I was involved in or not, but they were all just intel gathering missions; I have to say that even when I was involved as a young interpreter in the mid-'80s things got a little close, with the ship being brought to action stations a few times with an unknowing crew as to the real reasons why, and no idea how close we came to an incident ourselves. It was on one such occasion I was involved in when we had a Soviet sub under our hull, but what was exciting for me was that I was one of only a few aboard aware of the British S boat under the Russians talking directly to me. Us watching them watching us watching them!

I guess that was the one thing I had to play along with back then; the crew would be complaining about the endless exercises and drills, then going to defence watches, moaning and complaining tirelessly but they never really knew why. It kind of made me feel at least more involved and connected to the whole purpose of sitting out at sea for weeks at a time. No wonder the lads got so smashed when the ship finally got alongside and leave was granted.

Eight weeks had passed quickly and I had packed up my kit ready to leave the *Gainsborough* in Portsmouth and return to Plymouth as ordered. What a relief to be getting off the ship; my trip had been nothing short of exhausting and I was actually hoping to slip away quietly. I had a leaving routine to conduct which included an interview with my divisional officer. I was really looking forward to a weekend at home maybe. Lt Dent was excited to see me at my leaving interview and passed me a new draft order. On arrival at Portsmouth I was to report to HMS Raleigh by 0800 Thurs and meet Cdr Brown and attend GCHQ over the weekend to brief the JTLS team (Joint Technical Language Service) on the content of my interceptions. No fucking weekend off. Shit train ride over to Guz, meet Cdr Brown and then drive up to Cheltenham, in his car. I wasn't keen on spending that amount of time with a naval officer after the eight weeks I'd just had.

The Government Communications Headquarters (GCHQ) is an intelligence and security organisation responsible for providing signals intelligence (SIGINT) and sensitive information to the government and armed forces of the United Kingdom. I had never heard of it nor that it was based in Cheltenham. I remember arriving there after over two hours of light conversation with Commander Brown in his amazing Ford Sierra. It truly was amazing as I'm sure he had explained how amazing it was at least 20 times on the journey. It hadn't been too painful, we had a laugh about seasickness and cramped living conditions at sea, but he was more focused on seeing how I had enjoyed it and my opinions of the work I had undertaken. But he let slip how interested everyone had been at my penfriend family in Moscow and how there was a growing interest in them. I didn't think too much of it other than that the system was keeping an eye on me. We set a game plan for the briefings, planned a delivery, which went over my head I think, but I remember him being very relaxed about the whole affair and quite reassuring. My work at sea had been very well received apparently by the Admiralty, which had passed the whole thing along the food chain, including all my private correspondence with Moscow.

Arrival in Cheltenham was met with a level of security and sensitivity I hadn't yet seen in my short time in the service. Sure, I had a military ID, but to get into the base required a signal of invitation, or SOI, military ID, car pass and area passes for the sections we would be visiting. GCHQ is a circular building surrounded by orange segment-like car parks and outer buildings almost like an airport terminal, giving suitable distance from the fence line security to the actual building, which was and still is referred to as the 'doughnut'. There were a number of out-of-perimeter security stations and a QRF, or quick reaction force teams, for any security breach or attempt; there are probably more cameras in GCHQ than in the whole of Hollywood! For me as a young recruit it was simply overwhelmingly exciting.

This place is a fortress. It is the security agencies' safe house and the ultimate conduit into the hidden world of global operations, counter-espionage, secret services, NSA, CIA, special operations, all the MI. Of course, there are other groups of people walking these corridors – men and women who work there in silence and behind limited-access doors, whose real purpose is hidden and who should not be interrupted in any way. The heightened security states and the interests in Russian elements were possibly due to the recent capture in America of a former Naval Intelligence analyst, Jonathan Pollard, which is very well documented. His work involved passing over 800 documents, including intel from the US Navy's 6th Fleet on Soviet shipping and submarines to Israel. This made for a biblical breach of security which the UK had become very aware of.

Of note: Pollard was a former US Naval Intelligence official and was used as an example many times later in my training for positive and negative effect.

I was totally out of my depth in the briefings and had to rely on Cdr Brown to coax me through, all in front of a plethora of intelligence agencies. The briefing room was like a mini amphitheatre with two small podiums at the front with a drop-down white screen behind them which was fed from a projector outside the room. The room was soundproofed, black soft cloth seating, each with foldout desk arrangements, and microphones for the occupants to speak into. It wasn't a big room but it was a very formal arrangement, with cameras in every corner of what felt like a hollow room. There was just one window into the central courtyard that had been blacked out. No phones allowed, no cameras, no bags, just the 20 or so guys who had had their weekend fucked up to listen to me and all the shit I had translated on my first trip away with the Royal Navy. That's what I was thinking at the time anyway.

I'm guessing many agencies were present to listen to my interpretations of the intercepts, which had been coupled up with a slide show of the units and people I had been listening to. It was actually great to see what I had been doing. So, there I was, looking like a scared rabbit in the intelligence community headlights, ready to be shot. I gripped the microphone stem like it was a lifeline as I described all the conversations in turn, their tone, the excitement of those communicating, the technical issues that the submarines or the shoreside personnel had been facing at the time, as well as all the destinations, routes and speeds that had been discussed. I think I managed to get it all across and with only minimum swear words which seemed to pass unnoticed.

There were some interruptions as various participants added confirmations or supporting information as they saw fit throughout the presentation, but there was not a great deal of discussion or argument, just lots of paper shuffling and deep sighs. There were some interesting questions, like what accents or locations did I think certain speakers had, did I think any of the conversations implied a state of emergency or shock or anything out of the ordinary? Did any of the conversations appear to me to make little sense, be false or be in code of any description? Did I know or recognise the names of any of those persons speaking or mentioned in the conversations? Yes, I did actually. Some of the names I had heard in the communications I had also read about in letters from Anatoly (which they obviously knew as all my mail was intercepted). It was like there had been a death in the room, utter silence, then lots of whispering, and then a louder conversation grew until the questions changed away from the presentation and more towards my knowledge of any of the persons in the presentations, my abilities and future commitments and ambitions. What I really remember was how polite and courteous they all were with me, how genuinely interested they were, and how fucking great I was feeling. To be in a position of knowledge that the security services seemed to be devoid of was somewhat of a cool feeling. I felt needed.

I was politely dismissed from the meeting and escorted down through some brightly lit corridors by some civilians to break for a coffee and asked to simply wait in the rest room, which allowed for some fresh air outside in the huge atrium-like courtyard, the eye of the doughnut so to speak. Nothing happened for about three hours, and there's only so much Nescafé Gold Blend one can drink before going insane with boredom. I had read or scanned all the out-of-date papers and magazines when a young guy by the name of Simon said I would be needed again tomorrow and he asked if I had an overnight bag in order to stay. It was like staying at one of those boring Holiday Inns or Novotels without any of the services. Fucking boring as hell. I had been allocated a room with nothing to do apart from sleep or stare at the one painting on the wall that was a reproduction of a five-year-old's attempt at a landscape. I wasn't allowed off the base and had to be ready to go again in the morning for a second round of talks.

Delivering the news the next day was a group of six plainly dressed guys all in light grey or blue suits and naff ties, with pussers' white-lapelled shirts that were clearly over starched and done in a laundry, not by a stay-at-home wife or girlfriend. I was invited into an overly casual discussion about the outcomes of the previous night's talks that had occurred in my absence following the presentations and the revelation that I had contacts, albeit simply friends, in the Soviet Union who were, let's say, known to the security services and of particular interest. They were all very keen to see the whole thing progress. My correspondence and photos from Moscow were of further interest and I was politely asked if I had any other photographs. I had a photo in my wallet. There were smiles and gasps all at the same time. I was invited to talk through my whole relationship with the Moscow family. I think Brown knew most of what had been going on between myself and the family but wanted to allow the revelation to the wider audience to be leaked out gently by myself, maybe giving Brown the points for finding me in the first instance.

It was all done in a much more relaxed setting than I was expecting or had been used to up to this point, with the coffee and cigarettes readily available and flowing freely. Calm tones in the questions being asked were building into an intensifying atmosphere of expectation within the room. Basically, a job interview similar to that I had had in Raleigh but all in very simple English and ending in an offer to work for the intelligence services and formally become a sort of Naval Intelligence operative. We were on first-name terms now and the conversation had become littered with idiomatic expressions, allowing slingshot ideas to be passed on how I would integrate into the programme of espionage that N1 wanted to pursue whilst maintaining the camouflage of innocence that I currently had in place. I can only say that my excitement and anticipation had reached its zenith that day when I signed up for my first assignment to Moscow. I had yet to realise it would be two years of my life that I had just signed away.

I went home a few hours later with a week's leave pass in my pocket and never said a word the whole time I was at home. I digested that day's events and the preceding eight weeks over and over in my mind for the full seven days and seven nights. The beginning of insomnia had sown its first tiny seed, which I wouldn't come to realise fully for many years to come. I listened to the nonsense that the everyday life of a family brings and thought how fucked up the world must be for someone like me to be voluntarily entering into a confusing mismatch of complacency toward my supposedly true and unassuming life as a sailor and ex correctional facility attendee and the complexity of reality and true essence of who I actually was about to become. It was a total mindfuck. But nothing like the mindfuck training that was about to follow.

It was a relatively quiet week, my last innocent one, but I know now that the weeks and months of pre-insertion training were a very busy time for the security services as they investigated and background re-checked my whole family, their past and every soul I and they had ever met. I was oblivious to all this background checking and somehow managed to put all my focus on passing my driving test. I bought an old T reg Ford Escort that would hit 85mph when I zoomed down the M1 with the choke out! I had gone out and bought it from a local dealer before taking my driving test, recklessly taking out a bank loan to get the car, insurance and a full tank of petrol at the same time. My dad taught me how to drive and we would go out together at the weekends in my car (usually to a pub), smoke about 20 cigarettes and come home needing a drink as my driving wasn't exactly a calming trip out into the countryside. It was a bit of fun and I passed the test first time on a Saturday, allowing me to drive south on the Sunday night all packed up with soup and sandwiches by my mum who must have thought it was a three-day trip or something. God bless her, she was such a good mother really.

I never made it as far south as Plymouth. My real destination was to a very unassuming training facility in South Wales where my identity was cloned into two of me, laying the foundations for the dual life ahead, including building my new background identity for life in Moscow. I was on my way into a more interesting life.

Chapter 4

Moscow
First Deployment

My specialist training and preparation was an intense eight months, learning a whole new variety of skill sets, some of which just stay with you for life. It wasn't for combat or for frontline military personnel, this was a tailored suite of modules designed for intelligence operatives in civilian arenas, simply a foundation course that secondary and tertiary training modules could be built upon, and eventually used to integrate or dovetail into more intense or specialised training programmes at a later date. Sometimes this would pave the way for the intelligence operative to work alongside their SF counterparts or support teams to achieve a common goal. This more intense training was to enable an intelligence operative to operate in theatre or in a war zone should the need arise, which I guess was the plan for me from the outset. I really should have asked more questions, but it all felt like a great opportunity rather than a dangerous occupational choice I was making.

The facility in which I undertook training was a complex group of small buildings in an isolated location in Wales and run by the 'Steering Group', which I had yet to meet. I'd only heard of them through reading my orders, which were always signed by the 'Steering Group', but not yet had the privilege of meeting these unseen masters of my destiny. I had heard them mentioned in conversation a few times during my visit to GCHQ but I still really didn't seem to have a grasp on the chain of command I was subject to, and it seemed very ad hoc, especially who I reported to and where. Perhaps it was meant to be like this. I was only given one point of contact: a civilian at an address in London, a contact that should only be utilised on return from my assignment during leave and on completion, or if I had intelligence or information that would necessitate an immediate RTU (return to unit). The guidelines for this were very carefully written. My contact was a guy called Paul Seely, who was always very quiet and unpretentious. Calm and very monotone, he communicated within a very limited or controlled response dialect that was usually kept to between 5 and 15 words max.

There were a few others on the course, if you could call it a course, or attending the training facility, as it was mainly one on one and I assumed that each individual had a tailored programme much like my own. We were all ordinary people. 'Grey men' is the phrase that is commonly used today. You have to be a grey man I suppose to be selected for any sort of intelligence work or service. I am, and will always look for the grey man in every situation, place, meeting or encounter. He's the guy who will have the answer, the authority, the training or will simply be the man in control. I think I can spot them today without trying; they're not who you first think they are, it's like a double mindfuck. They're always the quietest, or the noisiest, but always remain unobvious, the ones you don't even notice, or think are the least likely to be anything interesting, hiding yet obvious in and amongst the crowd.

I found that undertaking intelligence functions even at the lowest levels requires the ability to switch personality and character for sustained periods with no visible or detectable flaws. It's a required sin and is a skill and a profession in itself.

It has to stand up to interrogation and the test of time under the most onerous of circumstances. There is no comparison to be drawn between this ability and the absolute loyalty to the service, the Crown and those with whom you serve. There is nothing that I wouldn't have done for those standing next to me in the hellholes of the world; they were my brothers, my family, held in the deepest and most sacred part of my heart. Let's be clear, the progression of my service into military combat teams carried an ethos that demanded the utmost loyalty, respect, honesty and commitment which went beyond anything that can be delivered in any form of training. This training was simply to deliver the ability to create a masquerade, a diversion to the truth, to allow an operative to maximise his chances of evading detection or, in the worst-case scenario, avoid giving up the truth under capture.

Training here under the regime of the Steering Group was designed simply for the individual, the lone operative, learning the architecture of espionage that needed to be understood in a world where relationship building, networking and integration was an art and a key into some of the darkest corners of terrorism, arms dealing, government secrets, and terrorist funding by rogue governments. I was not being trained as a team member of an elite fighting unit, my function was to be able to operate in isolation, go undetected and totally immerse myself into the local surroundings. Teams and brotherhood would come later on. For now, I needed to be a maverick. The training was perfected for the young mind; it's easier to brainwash and train a young mind. (And twice as hard to un-fuck it later). The Steering Group needed young eager minds, not old warhorses, in order to have control and clarity in the kind of roles it needed potential recruits to fulfil. It needed to breed a remarkable new strain of young operatives who would fly well under the radar and then grow into a more lethal asset in more direct combat situations. It's not brute force that wins a war, brings down a terrorist cell or overthrows a government, it's just hard clean confirmed intelligence from a reliable source which is then translated into a very discreet kill order or something more subtle to fuck up the opposition's plans by absolute stealth.

Before undertaking my assigned modules allocated by the Steering Group, I was subjected to a week of aptitude, personality and skill tests. This included multiple Criteria Cognitive Aptitude Tests (CCAT) which determined my ability to solve problems and digest and apply relative information whilst discarding false leads. I quickly learnt the new skills required of me to complete the tests, especially thinking quickly and critically – under pressure. This process was tied into rapid-fire MiniCog Rapid Assessment Batteries (MRAB), a series of six scenarios each consisting of nine short tests that measured my 'information processing' functions, which were thrown into the other longer tests at random intervals during the week, to apply pressure in the most unexpected ways.

Of course, all this was entwined with trainee personality profiling tests that measured 12 personality traits. These results would need to be analysed and understood by the team and me in order to overcome them (like some kind of obstacle). Basically, it was a way to identify your weaknesses and learn how to transpose or cloak them into positive attributes for your future assignment. To me at the time it was all a psychobabbling experience in order for the MOB to tick boxes to cover their asses should it all go to shit in the field. I don't think I took it all too seriously and doubt I would pass any of those tests today. I guess it's that untarnished young mind that's so devoid of twisted opinions that they were looking for, because life undoubtedly slowly burdens the mind over the years, and in the world of intelligence gathering that can be dangerous. Of course, there's nothing like real field experience, that's why you start off conducting missions that are low risk and can almost be unproductive to a fault. But the operative is deliberately never truly made aware of the entire picture or its risks, to retain focus, unless the situation becomes critical in some way. You have to look at the average age of spies globally – generally operatives are in their mid-twenties or younger and started early in life.

Module 2 of initial training was based upon dissociative identity disorder (DID), also known as multiple personality disorder, which is a mental disorder characterised by at least two distinct and relatively enduring personality states. The training teaches you to be two very different people. (Later I would learn to become three.) So, I had to learn and be fluent in 36 individual personality traits and then re-sit the personality profiling tests from Module 1 for each person's personality. This gave a distinct advantage during interrogation training which even at this level was a huge four-week module. Later, this foundation would be the cornerstone to surviving and out-thinking any future interrogation training techniques, as the groundwork for RTI (resistance to interrogation) would already be embedded, almost implanted. Looking back, this may have been the mustard seed to my developing the embryonic stages of paranoia and even insomnia. It's a real mindfuck to jump in and out of character at the depths I needed to go. I guess hiding my real personality was a hidden bonus for me initially as it helped me escape some of my childhood past.

Those first modules and the subsequent training I undertook made very clear that the absolutely vital ability to lie was of paramount importance. The learning of all the pantomimes, all the body languages, how to fake them, how to turn any mistake into a success by leaving scenarios open, incomplete or just unfinished became second nature. I learned how to intertwine some truth into a lie to protect the team or the mission, and to allow for other unforeseen developments, giving room for mental manoeuvres. I was taught how to cry, laugh, grimace and hide emotion when confronted with unexpected news or outcomes. I truly believe that this kind of training really messes with your mind and your ability to communicate and make friends in later life. Everything becomes a clouded conspiracy if you don't take a firm hold of the game you're playing and the real realities of life.

Often interrogation was reversed into sympathetic confrontations, with different people utilising situations that were not real – an example being perhaps your mum has been hit by a car and you brother has had a plane crash, or your blood tests have come back and you have an incurable disease – to get a reaction, trick your mind into a carefully controlled mismanagement of realities in multiple layers to test your ability to switch characters, remember the lies and settings under pressure and give the correct or the right controlled response, protecting the truth but simultaneously and continually appeasing the interrogator. I learned in depth about control questions and how to give non-committal responses, to be personal and friendly in responses and how to divert questions and directional leads.

It goes deeper and deeper until there is almost no truth left in the character you have morphed into. The methods employed included micromanaged sleep deprivation to the point of hallucination, mental exhaustion through psychological interrogation techniques, noise, mental tests, confusion and misdirection, including manipulating personal realities into plausible future encounters or disappointments, such as food deprivation, cancelled leave passes, being ignored for long periods, a simulation of failing the course and exploitation of any exposed weakness or known family issues. I think, looking back, this was a far more demanding route than the simple physical exhaustion which is the main military vehicle to 'breaking' someone in order to realise their capacity to succeed. The only truth that needs to be hidden is the mission, which is buried, in your subconscious by the polished ability of character assimilation taught through the adaptation and study of a mental illness. Yes, mental patients were used for such study to great effect in the development of field operatives. However serious it all sounds, the training was fun, it was a game, encouraged by fascinating tutors ready to pull you back if you truly fell in.

This ability or new skill to lie and to live the lie, to be all the mission wants you to be, believe in the mission all the way to where all the lies become the truth in your mind is a labyrinth of mental organisation. Careful mental mapping needs to be mastered before you are able to paperclip the lies of the mission to one of your formed identities, completely separating it from the other characters you need to be in order to be the mission. Paper-clipping is another vital mental skill as it helps the mind organise the lies into chronological order and attachment to characters, places, times and events. It builds scenarios (a map – similar to brain dumps and mind mapping) that the mind can tap into and become truly deceived into believing itself that the lie is the truth by choice and supported by the evidence of the paperclips, which themselves are lies or sometimes half-truths with additional paperclips etc., etc. The deeper you go the harder it gets to see the surface; it can be like disappearing into an abyss on an endless oxygen tank of half-truths. But if you truly believe that you are who you need to be, then under interrogation, buried in your subconscious, is the escape, the utter deception to regain your freedom. It's a fucking weapon, a really dangerous weapon if you can wield it.

The training goes further, enabling you to switch characters and become the second or third character, which may be a phasmid to give the mind a rest or to deceive different people or situations in quick succession. This can be for 10 minutes, a day or a week in order to simply relax or decompress for however long is needed. Decompression sessions after a mission or assignment were always mandatory and could be for several weeks or even months of stand down; in the early days that translated into a lot of drinking on base behind closed doors, reverting yourself back to the real you, or disappearing away to sea in order to unscramble in a safe controlled environment. This became the ultimate challenge after any assignment and why I always tried to keep character number four a secret – he was a nobody, someone I could collapse into, my true phasmid companion, that was the real me no one really knew; he was just for me and I wasn't going to share him.

I think, looking back now, all the training confused even my soul, leaving all real emotions and feelings in disarray. Now, watching a film makes me cry and laugh for no reason. Overreacting emotionally within the world I'm now trying to occupy is just normal. I get upset easily, I can't watch the news, and I get all soppy when I watch vet programmes and the like. I'm now learning how to untangle my mind into a reality that exists in the here and now.

Endless memory tests were conducted throughout the courses and modules. I needed to develop an almost photo-graphic memory of rooms, places, people and all the details that they carried, utilising a scanning methodology every time my surroundings changed. It was mental barcoding: a car would become a make, model, colour, reg number, passenger numbers, left-hand drive or right-hand drive, distinguishing marks, badges or stickers, speed, position, lights, leather or cloth, number of exhaust outlets, etc., etc., etc., etc., etc. It could be as simple as a person coming into a room whilst I was under tuition and the lesson changing immediately on that person's departure to me writing down every detail of the person I had just seen. It became more and more complex with more and more detail required.

I had to learn the art of 'ninjutsu', and not in some ridiculous getting dressed in black Hollywood silly way, but to understand invisibility, to be seen but not be noticeable. I spent many hours practising to be evident but insignificant, seen and quickly forgotten, like a tree in a forest of exactly the same trees, always there but ultimately never actually seen. My studies included carefully examining clothing and appearances, mannerisms and characters of natives in chosen destinations, which could be as simple as a market town in England, a market in St Petersburg or an elders meeting in Kabul. The local customs and the greetings, the way people moved and behaved. Training sessions were conducted on base and in local towns. It is a discipline of human stealth that involves misdirection, diversion, disguise, stealth, camouflage and very simple behavioural applications, enabling you to walk unobserved, penetrating forbidden areas unseen, departing at will without leaving a trace. It is the expertise and strategy of guerrilla warfare. This part of the training was actually quite fun and made for some interesting days out, upsetting local authorities and the general public on occasion. It would take time to perfect as with every discipline in life.

Thieves inadvertently employ this methodology – if you get dressed up as an engineer and go to a site and steal a works van and then take on the pretence of an engineer to gain access to a property in order to steal from it then you've succeeded in the art of deception. I once witnessed a team of thieves who turned up at a marina in a marine engineers van; they set about removing the outboard engines from a flash speedboat on one of the finger jetties; they engaged with other boat owners in polite conversation; and then casually walked away with over 10 grands' worth of Suzuki outboards. They looked like they were meant to be there, that's the trick.

I only had a brief introduction to self-defence and small arms this first encounter; after all, I was just training to be an

English student studying Russian, making me feel the whole training was a massive overkill. There was extensive language training, no English spoken, all interviews and instruction given in Russian, including the whole mission package, targets, points of interest, people to observe, places to go, where to eat, what to observe, where to get money, when I would take leave and how I would travel home, how to report. My entry documentation to the universities and supporting certificates for the education all had to be carefully prepared and applied for by the team. I wrote regularly, with the assistance of the training staff, to Anatoly, working together to build the picture that I wanted to come and study Russian in Moscow. His excitement was plain to see in the letters sent to my home address that were intercepted and brought to the facility. I still have the photographs of me wearing the Russian hats he sent me, sitting on the sofa at home with all my family when I was on leave. They had no idea. I was sitting there with my whole family amidst an intelligence operation as though nothing of the sort was happening – it was great. The deception was easy; the truth had already been paperclipped, manufactured and deposited in all the right places. The entry point was established, the correspondence lined up and accommodation arranged. I'd live with Anatoly and take up a student's life in Moscow. The organisation made all the necessary arrangements with the universities, and the dates all confirmed flights were booked, bank accounts opened and passports arranged.

I had to be Andrey throughout module 4 of the training, simulating family dinners, answering awkward questions about what I had been doing over the last few years, describing a false background and false family stories, events and holidays on my side, carefully avoiding any names of towns places, etc. that would give direction to my real family. Then we conducted interpersonal conversations with mock individual family members and with a number of hopeful targeted individuals it was hoped Anatoly would lead me to. My life had to be re-scripted and paperclipped into my character ready for the real event. Switching characters in this build-up was very hard as I still looked at Anatoly as a personal friend. There was no doubt betrayal would take place in this friendship and I was prepared for that by a seemingly endless timetable of interviews explaining the importance of what was being undertaken, and then hours spent with what must have been specialist councillors whose goal was to depersonalise everything in my mind and focus me on my training and my objectives. Then towards the end of the course I was introduced to the world of non-official cover – this, in simplistic terms, is intelligence work undertaken under assumed identities in private sector industry and how to access money etc. More of that later.

I guess this is where a compromise may have occurred; this is where to look in counter-espionage, at the innocents who must be removed to protect the Crown. I was now Andrey the Russian language student, and Andrew the junior mechanic in the Royal Navy, and Andrew the N1 operative, but always Andrew the boy who was now out from behind bars, chain free and living a new life. I was already adding my own paperclips, facts, lies, places, names and memories, true and false, lies and camouflage. Brilliant. I was actually in my element; it was an open invitation to reinvent myself which satisfied my desire for acceptance into a bigger life, into a new organisation, and to do it well to the best of my ability.

I left training and joined HMS *Deptford* bound for the States. I had some great runs ashore in Plymouth with the lads before the ship deployed, going to nightclubs and pubs, drinking all day. DTS (dinner time sessions) followed by drunken nights in The Two Trees, The Long Bar, The Malthouse, Boobs and The Tube, all finished off by a shit burger at Cap'n Jaspers, the local fast-food outlet in a mobile unit in the Barbican. I'm sure I was being watched; didn't think of that at the time but the more I fitted in to a character the better, including getting into trouble and being drunk and disorderly. The very ability to be unnoticed, normal, totally encrypted with a chameleon characteristic to adapt and be unnoticed, but if seen to be totally in harmony with the surroundings – I was adapting. The training ground was within the safety of the second character. It's a very clever programme because you can practise your skills with people you trust within the military; it's a safe testing ground and a place to run back to and become invisible. It's easier and safer to hide within the military and disappear off the grid when the need arises by sometimes simply disappearing to sea whilst hot scenarios or situations blow themselves out. It's like a safe house that's well hidden in a secure city, that city being any ship, establishment or base of the UK military – globally.

It was a great trip. I worked hard as a marine engineer for a number of months and sent the postcards, wrote the letters and got the souvenirs as were needed. I needed to be serving time out of the country to clear the snail trail of my 'real' life before making the switch. I continued to work at passing exams and boards for the engineering trade, which was a necessity and one I didn't fully understand at the time as career grooming hadn't crossed my mind at this point. It was all a repeat of the *Gainsborough*, I guess. A couple of things that I remember well of that trip included my first crossing of the Atlantic Ocean. We had hit a huge storm and I remember going up to the bridge and asking permission of the captain to come on to the bridge and observe.

Never have I seen an ocean like the one on that first trip – beautiful blue skies, deep blue almost black mountainous waves, building up to fluorescent green curls before the white horses were blown from the tops of these mighty ocean skyscrapers that then came crashing down as if by controlled slow motion demolition. It really is something to watch a warship plough through such a storm; it's not a violent affair with the sea, it's just magnificent. It's humbling to witness the power of the ocean in all its fury and to be at its mercy. I remember standing next to the captain, who was strapped into his chair smoking his pipe, seeing the sky disappear, looking at the bottom of the darkest troughs before seeing the 4.5 inch gun gently disappear beneath the water and the bridge go dark, illuminated only by the sun's rays through the green water against the bridge windows – a very intense car wash experience. I have always loved being at sea. It feels safe, you're detached, a satellite that can communicate if you want to but generally just be alone away from the world and all the shit that goes on in it.

We had encountered storm damage and the ship had pulled into Halifax, Nova Scotia in Canada. It was winter and there were snow drifts up to 10 feet deep everywhere. We had to conduct a boiler clean, so all the engineers would be working flat out for the first few days. Only fuck-up was we decided stupidly to blow soot during the night before the boiler clean, and the morning light revealed the extent of our pollution to the world. To everyone's horror all the snow for miles was tainted by our soot and there was no hiding the fact it was the Royal Navy that had committed the offence. I'm sure there was a lot of explaining to do, but that wasn't my concern.

A boiler clean is a really manpower-intensive job and I loved the whole experience of going inside the boiler and firing bullets from the Elliott tube cleaning kits through the boiler pipes, climbing into the cathedral and steam tubes. We all looked like the Black and White Minstrels, working long shifts in the hope to get a night ashore and get as pissed as farts. I made some great friends doing real shitty work. Isn't that just always the case in life, where the worst or hardest times bring the best friendships? At the end of the clean the furnaces were wallpapered with newspaper, and maybe 20 crates of beer were brought into the furnace through a tiny unbricked entry point and through which the whole engineering department would enter for a furnace party. Fucking awesome. These were happy days. I remember waking up to the sound of the inspection glass cover being lifted and the Lucas torch ignitor being inserted into the furnace, indicating they were about to light the furnace. Screaming at the top of my voice thinking they were not aware I was still in the furnace, my screams were met with a quick blast of the ignitor to shit me up properly, before many smiling and laughing faces appeared at the inspection window! Bastards.

I left the ship and flew back on a MAC flight (Military Airlift Command) to Brize Norton, no airline ticket, no traceable travel, just fond memories of my crew mates whom I'd left with a compassionate cover story. I needed to change passports and luggage at Brize before travelling to Heathrow. Moscow was waiting and Andrey had an appointment with old friends and to start his course at Moscow State University and the language faculty. Flying Aeroflot was scary as shit and probably still is, but I enjoyed the rest and set about changing into a student mentality. I flew the day after my birthday on an Ilyushin Il-86, which is a four-engine jet airliner. Moscow, holy shit, it felt like I was on a holiday, an excursion or something, anything but a serious trip, a fucking mission or an intelligence assignment. I guess, looking back, that was a good thing as it helped with the whole experience and to keep my nerves in check. The lie felt real, it felt right, it felt normal. It was easy. I was probably expendable and didn't know and didn't care at that point in time. I'm not sure I was taking it all as seriously as I should have been; I was young and it was a great adventure, a trip of a lifetime. Actually it was a great laugh and an amazing adventure.

I arrived at Sheremetyevo International Airport Moscow, which is about a 35-minute drive outside central Moscow. Flight, immigration and customs were no problem, and I had to get a bus into the city. It was all a big step into a wider world. In no way did I feel anything other than I was there to undertake a language course. Fucking bizarre now, looking back; the Admiralty and the Steering Group, whoever the fuck they were, had just paid for me to have the greatest holiday experience ever. The weather was typically cold and around 18 degrees Fahrenheit, or -7 Centigrade, which does take some getting used to. I think I was always cold in Russia. It's very, very cold, just plain freezing, and you talk about the cold all the time, not as cold as last year but colder than the year before, and then the old folks talk about the cold of 1938 which was really cold, and on it goes on and on and all the hardships are eventually lost to the past.

I needed to get city bus N851 to Rechnoy Vokzal (Речной вокзал) Metro station on green line 2 to get into the city. The fares are really cheap and luckily travel time is 40-50 minutes, which is the quickest time available to passengers during the working day. I bought my ticket in the ticket box for 50 roubles. I was headed for Patriarch Ponds (Патриаршие пруды). Little did I know it was, and I believe still is, an affluent residential area in the downtown Presnensky District of Moscow. To put it into perspective, it's like living just inside the North Circular road in London which in turn is surrounded by the outer belt of the M25, to which the Moscow equivalent is the Third Ring Road, so I was very central. There's a new campus accommodation building near there today that didn't exist whilst I was there, and if it had I wouldn't have had the same experiences or opportunities I enjoyed and encountered whilst staying with Anatoly.

I remember arriving at the park or the pond and Anatoly was waiting for me. It was so very emotional and exciting. Anatoly embraced me like a Siberian bear through his amazingly thick long black heavy coat fitted with deep dense soft brown fur around the neck. A bear hug from my dear friend. I remember just holding his arms and admiring his Russian ushanka black hat that sat upon his very thin white cold face, with his blue lips and frozen cheeks stretched into the biggest smile ever. He pulled off my hat and swapped it for his. He had grown his hair again and looked just as he had done in the photographs he had sent when we'd first communicated; he so looked like Nikolai Romanov but even more so now he had a moustache. I made fun of him, before he begged me to walk with him awhile before he lost me to everyone who would be waiting to greet me at home later after work. We dropped my case off at the lobby to his apartment and set out in the snow, my heart pounding with excitement to be in Moscow. I guess it's the same feeling that is experienced by those who go on a gap year or go travelling today. That shit wasn't really available in my time; joining the army or working down the pit were the real options that faced most school leavers of my era.

We walked together for what seemed like hours and hours, just busting with excitement and joy that we were finally together and how amazing it was I was here to study Russian in his home town. The streets were shining white with snow and ice, making each individual person look like a dark matchstick silhouette against this dynamic typical Russian backdrop. Any photograph would have most certainly resembled a Russian winter version of a Lowry painting. Clouds of snow blew around like dust clouds in this cold white ice desert, with caravans of Lada cars and Trabants and many other unusual looking cars racing to work through the snow- and ice-filled roads. My breath was almost ice before it left my mouth and my nostrils exhaled clouds of steam. Breathing in was like inhaling fire it was so cold, and I could feel my extremities painfully freezing up. We walked around the streets and the pond, lost in conversation as if we had been together for years already. The pond is about 9,900 square metres, with the depth about two metres, making it a great ice-skating rink when it is frozen. It was almost a cool cliché to be in Moscow and see children skating on the ice all wrapped up in thick coats and scarfs. Tverskaya Street, known at the time as Gorky Street, was close by and very busy, a mixture of modern buildings amongst the more imposing and more traditional older buildings, some of which were proudly flying the Russian flag from their upper balconies. Tverskaya Street led all the way to Red Square and the Kremlin and made for a breathtaking first walk in the capital.

We talked and walked aimlessly for hours, both for fun and secretly for me to deliberately negotiate the area, to familiarise myself with our location, what was close, my routes to college, perhaps taking in short detours. Mental details being taken, planning routes to cover objective observation points that I would build into a daily commute to a metro station at Kropotkinskaya, from which I may have the opportunity to observe two target persons on my list before taking the Metro to Lomonosovsky Prospekt in the academic district where my campus was located. Anatoly was eager to show me around and have me to himself so there was no rush, so it was easy to get started photographing the whole area like a tourist.

We stopped for brunch in true Russian style; we were like comrades standing in line for cafeteria service as we waited ever so patiently for my first authentic Russian breakfast of wheat and potato pancakes and Karamazov omelette (with chicken livers, sour cream and caviar) for me and the Siberian omelette (Russian sausage, cheese, sour cream, pepper, tomato, onion and caviar) for Anatoly. I ordered in perfect Russian, joined the second queue to pay, then we sat patiently on creaky little wooden seats at a table in the window watching Moscow go by as we discussed such things as the latest UK pop music, CD players, Nike trainers, and many other brands that drew such an interest from young Russians of that time. We also chatted about our letters, my old school, hard times and good times, and Mr Richards who had coordinated the pen-pal scheme so long ago now. We were building our friendship and our trust which I would use, and use to my advantage; and although it pains me to think of how I used Anatoly, he was a vital portal and conduit into the Russian elite and was beyond any possible cover story that could have ever been manufactured by the security services. I guess everyone was using everyone else; who knows, maybe Anatoly was using me.

That evening was a very special one. Although I had suspected Anatoly was from a, let's say, privileged background, I hadn't expected the reception that I received back at the apartment block. We made our way back to the apartment that overlooked the pond at around 4.30pm; it was already dark, the interior lighting in the foyer making for a warm welcome that was surpassed by the whole family that was awaiting my arrival. The lift was out of order so we scrambled up a spiralling staircase to the 5th floor. Anatoly burst through the door and thrust me into the middle of the waiting crowd. I was stripped of my hat and coat and quickly made to sit in the middle of the room so everyone could see me and ask questions about my travel and welcome me to Moscow. It was a very warm welcome full of excited faces that seemed in shock to see an Englishman in their home. Of course, they all wanted to practise their English, which I have to say was better pronounced and with a more expansive vocabulary than my own, making me ask them to repeat as if I didn't understand. I passed out gifts of CDs, chocolate and English souvenirs, but I had brought some Levi jeans and some Nike trainers for Anatoly (all nicely funded by the UK taxpayer); there was almost silence as everyone was taken in by such a gift. Back then there wasn't the influx of Western goods so this was indeed a big gesture to have made. Anatoly was overcome with emotion as we were fast tracked into a close friendship beyond that of just mere pen pals.

The whole family had turned out to meet me: mother, father, grandparents, four brothers and two sisters, together with uncles and aunts, nephews and nieces. I would struggle to remember so many faces let alone names – with the exception of Anatoly's uncle, Alexander Markoff, a name I had in my top three to report on if I heard anything of him or by chance saw him in Moscow. He had also just returned from London on business. Alexander was KGB (FSB in new money). I didn't speak to him, I played the part and enjoyed the evening, deliberately trying to stay with Anatoly, laughing, drinking, playing cards and chess. However, Evgeny, Alex's son, was absolutely glued to me everywhere I went in the room. Alex and Evgeny were, to all intended purposes, like brothers because the family often looked after Evgeny when Alex was busy with work, which was almost all the time. I knew what I had stumbled into but the gravity of this encounter and the intel I would extract would not be fully realised until 1992 and the Bosnian conflict and later again in the Middle East.

Don't be mistaken in thinking Anatoly and his family lived in a mansion. On the contrary, the apartment boasted only four rooms. The main room was a quite a large living room/diner with a small kitchenette in the corner of the room; it had obviously been part of a bigger home as it was a huge room that accommodated three settees, a piano and various other antique-like furniture. There were three large floor-to-ceiling arched windows that opened onto the balcony, encased in thick blackout curtains that had survived many occupations of the building. This was the heart of the apartment, where everyone gathered, ate, sang, spoke, read to each other and shared life. It was always kept warm by an open fire which was the only heat source. There was a small bathroom and two bedrooms which led away from the main room, one of which always reverted to an office during the day and was often used for meetings. Everyone slept together in the other bedroom, which could be up to eight of us, with Anatoly's parents taking sole occupancy of the second bedroom or office. I think at the time this was good living, and I enjoyed the whole family thing immensely.

The building itself was of a grander era most certainly. I think all the apartments had once been part of a very grand Moscow residence now divided up, with some of the apartments offering a glimpse back into grander days. We were soon ushered back downstairs to the ground floor where food had been laid out ostentatiously in what can only be described as a huge reception room, like an old ballroom or hall. The banquet was fabulous, and the room was significantly warmer with huge fires at the far end and two further fires mirroring each other in the central area slowly radiating heat that was melting the ice sculptures the children had made from outside. Huge windows looked out onto the street, framed in the heaviest of rich red curtains, all illuminated by chandeliers that were simply the most impressive constellation like chandeliers hanging from the beautifully painted ceiling.

However grand it felt that first night, the daylight later revealed just how worn and tired the place actually was. I think the hall was seldom used, maybe only for special occasions, official party meetings or drink receptions, when it was required in order to impress or show where the family sat in society. But for that first night it felt like a grand ball that had been arranged for the Tsar himself. I think all the buildings' occupants made a visit to the party and partook of the festivities, or possibly just took advantage of the free food and drink. It was like a very warm family gathering on the grandest of scales and the warmest of welcomes anyone could possibly have hoped for. It made for an easy first night away from home, the navy and all the suffocation of the recent training and conditioning supplied by the Steering Group. It was like being released back into the wild and I felt completely free of all the bullshit and able to actually relax. I do confess, I remember thinking I'd just enjoy the uni course and ignore all the other shit as if it wasn't what I was being paid for and have nearly two years of fun – who was to know anyway? I don't think there was much expectation that I would have any success on this first solo mission. I was of the mind that the whole thing would just be some sort of confidence test or lesser assignment.

Anatoly's father had been a former party member in the Communist Party of the Soviet Union, or CPSU. This was before the time of Yeltsin and all the reforms that would soon follow in the early 1990s. At the time I knew him, he remained a close friend of the party and those who served in the Kremlin's inner circles of the Central Committee and former politburo – all good communists, but supporters who were leading a directional change that led to Mikhail Gorbachev entering into talks with the US. There were many visits to the Kremlin Senate Building and the Lubyanka, which I documented and reported on, not just by Erik (Anatoly's father), Alex and other Russians but by our friends from the Middle East, Jordan, Syria and Iraq and many characters from the Balkans. There were, on occasions, visits to the apartment and meetings held in the office in the apartment that were easily eavesdropped upon and that usually involved some heavy drinking that sometimes spilled out into the living area. My list of interesting persons grew exponentially as each month passed and visitors came and went, but mostly they were insignificant or had become just too drunk to be of any coherent interest to me or my controller.

I had a really great routine in Moscow that allowed me to enjoy my time as a student and live amongst an incredibly interesting Russian family. There was time for fun and good living, sightseeing, and all manner of tourist attractions were visited and photographed in detail. Special focus and attention to detail was given to the background to those photographs and the people in the background, the best ploy being simply to get other tourists or Anatoly to take photographs of me at appropriate times and at different angles. It wasn't complex at first, but sometimes I had my film ripped out of my camera by local guards as I pushed the boundaries too hard. No digital cameras back then! It meant a continual repeat of attempts to capture the right photos of the right people or groups of people together in the right places. I always remembered my dad saying do it as if you were meant to be there, and that was what I was doing. The building of a jigsaw of characters, places, meetings and timings was slowly assembled, and this raw intel would need to be digested and sifted to give focus and meaning back in the UK. I was working semi-blind with little objective other than my bottom-line directive, which was to observe and seek out certain people and places, which was a little frustrating and too obtuse for me to draw any real substance from.

This was to change after my first leave period in the UK which saw the operation gather pace and focus. Returning to the UK for Easter, summer and Christmas holidays made for some interesting turnarounds – Aeroflot flight to London, met and immediately transferred to Brize and then taken for debrief, sometimes in Cheltenham at the doughnut and sometimes at the training site in Wales. Easter was spent entirely in debrief with no leave, going over every detail of every photograph and every person I had met or observed. It was exhausting. After my first long summer leave I had to meet the wider support team in the zoo, a name that had come to me – slang for the Welsh facilities – before conducting the return journey. Intel had my contacts, Erik Pavlovich, Anatoly's father, and Alex Markoff, linked to increased Soviet arms trades to the Balkans via the Middle East utilising funds originating from Saudi Arabia and the UK hidden by other trade deals from an unknown source, that source quickly identified by my intel as Alexander. It was suspected he was also supporting a movement against Muslims in Yugoslavia and managing the trade of munitions through various countries to support a possible war in the Balkans.

My directive was to make the link between Alexander, the Middle East and Yugoslavia. The start of the collapse of communism in the Soviet Union was giving rise to a worsening situation in Yugoslavia. As communism in Yugoslavia began to disintegrate, Yugoslavia began over the coming years to break into religiously nationalistic regions, of which the most prominent were Croatia and Serbia. The Steering Group wanted direct intel from Russia as to who was supporting the communists in Serbia or Kosovo and any contacts relating to Slobodan Milosevic, Radovan Karadzic or any other unidentified source. I headed back to Moscow feeling quite serious and for the first time not exactly looking forward to getting back. Shit was getting very real now and the pantomime needed to be rehearsed and become theatre worthy.

I arrived home in Moscow and set about rebuilding my relationships within the family and set myself goals for the next full term at university. I slipped back into a routine of school, observation, study and socialising. I decided to confide in Anatoly's mother and used several paper-clip half-truths – that I was stressed at the prospect of sitting my final exams later that year in England and the cost of my education. She received me, well, like a mother; she always sat on the outside of all things non-domestic, and I think she was secretly pleased that I had sought her counsel. I laboured weekly on these issues through gaining her support and trust, looking to draw her in with the 'son in need' paperclip, a young man faced with much expectation, pressure and study; I think she took me under her wing as a second son next to Anatoly. The pressure wasn't hard to fake as I was feeling it, not only from making the university assignments on time but also the needs of the Steering Group were now very real.

Natalia was very elegant, with long thin black hair, and was always well presented. She always wore pink, and looked very attractive in her grey furs and pink scarfs whenever she left the apartment. Natalia decided she would assist me further in my studies and we secretly used Erik's office (their bedroom) during the day whenever he was away so that we had some peace and quiet. It was interesting as the office was arranged so it could be converted back into a bedroom very easily, and the furniture was surprisingly quite modern. There were many fascinating pictures on the walls of all the family and some more interesting pictures of Erik with various officials attending functions and conferences. I was caught looking deeply at a photograph of Erik and Alex hunting together. It was quickly taken from me and placed back on the wall. They were better days I was informed.

Alex was a frequent visitor to the apartment and I really needed to make contact or connect with him in some way, and the picture was my way in. I think he scared me a little at first, he was the real deal after all, a KGB operative working across all the lines and into the UK working well as a businessman, and he had a keen interest in construction, apartment blocks in London, football clubs and stadiums and anything financial or technical. He loved spending time with Anatoly who was now pursuing engineering and scientific studies at both the National Research Nuclear University MEPhI and the Bauman University, the oldest and most prestigious in Russia where Anatoly was enrolled in one of the military sub departments. My limited engineering knowledge was truly exposed during such technical discussions at night which covered everything from nuclear medicine applications to enhanced applications for chemical defence and all manner of things that were nuclear related. I needed to become more able to engage during such conversations to better understand Alex's interests here.

It was during one very cold evening, when Anatoly and I were both studying together in the living room in front of the fire, when it was announced that Alex would be coming over for dinner with all the family. Natalia prepared a banquet from nothing as usual, and there was a great atmosphere building in anticipation of the gathering. It was especially fun when Evgeny, Anatoly and I were together because it was like we were brothers, and both Erik and Alex found amusement in how well us three young men got along together. I think I felt closer to Evgeny and Anatoly than my very own brothers at that time. Although very cold outside the family made for a very warm evening in every respect when such gatherings were arranged. We all sat around the table talking freely about our days and weeks at work or school, our struggles and our highlights and lowlights since the last time we had gathered. We ate well: salads, which were very rare, lots of black bread, beef and potatoes, all slow cooked and without doubt very delicious. It was always washed down with what seemed like gallons of Kvass, a very low-strength alcoholic drink made from rye bread I think, but always followed by too much vodka. The dishes were passed around and everyone glowed with warmth towards each other. It was quite amazing to feel part of this family, and after a year with them here in Moscow I felt right at home. I mean really at home.

Later after one such meal, Erik and Alex invited us all for a vodka in the office, usually reserved for special occasions or private meetings: Nostrovia! – a toast to the family after a great meal. All the men took the vodka in one hit, big smiles and handshakes. I took the opportunity to point out the photo of Alex and Erik hunting.

"Ahhhhhhh..." said Alex, and took the picture from the wall and sat us all down to tell a story. "Let me tell you of friendship and the party," he said.

I remember this story because it was like he knew – he didn't of course but it felt like he knew who I really was, the real Andrew looking for a place in the world. The story touched my heart; he told it passionately, with feeling and depth, and after each paragraph he paused and looked deeply into Erik's eyes and the photograph.

We all sat around in the dimly lit room fixed upon his every word.

"Once upon a time, there was a pack of wolves that lived in the deepest darkest woods of Siberia. Their leader was very old. One day, when the pack was going out hunting, the leader told the young pack he was not capable of leading them. A young strong wolf approached the leader and asked him to allow him to lead the pack on this hunt. The old wolf agreed, and the pack went out to seek food.

"In a day the wolves returned with prey. The young wolf told the leader that they had attacked the seven hunters and easily killed the men. The pack ate well.

"Soon the time came for the pack to go hunting again, and the young wolf took the lead as before with the blessing of the older wolf. The wolves did not return for a long time, and then the wounded young wolf came home alone. He told the leader that the pack attacked the three men and only one young wolf survived.

"The old wolf exclaimed in surprise, 'But during the first hunt you killed the seven hunters, and they did you no harm!'

"The young wolf replied, 'There were seven hunters at our first hunt, but this time there were three best friends.'"

Alex looked at us boys, stood up and held up his glass, paused then loudly declared, "To three best friends!" A toast to Evgeny, Anatoly and me.

Absolute honour and pride were in everyone's eyes. I hugged Anatoly and Evgeny and we laughed uncontrollably together in the joy of the moment. We drank some more and asked to hear more stories of the hunt in the photograph, and who their third friend was. We heard great tales of older days and family gatherings in the forests that were not so far outside Moscow, of the family cabin that still stood but unvisited for so long, of second- and third-hand stories of the great wars from past ancestors. We heard stories from long ago all spoken with a deep desire to live the older times again in honour and glory. We drank too much but, before those lights went out, we stood in a circle, saluted the party and promised to go hunting before winter, visit the family cabin and be like a family of wolves. We all slept together in the bedroom that night under handmade Russian patch quilts, with the door ajar to gain some heat from the fire. As I was about to close my eyes I looked at Anatoly, whose face was glowing from the flickering light of the fire, and said, "Goodnight, my wolf." He smiled and howled out loud like a wolf; loud laughing could be heard from each and every one of us. I closed my eyes and wondered who Alex's third wolf was.

Time passed slowly for a while as everyone went about their daily and weekly routines. Breakfast, rush to the university, photographs along the way, detours to pass the right places and seek those on my list. Nothing new, endless monotony, some homesickness as things felt a bit bleak, attend lectures, do assignments, travel home, dinner, sit in front of the fire and try to keep warm. The Russian way of life seemed quite slow and almost sad. It was an endless battle to make ends meet and just keep warm. However, I think it was my relationship with the family, and in particular my time spent alone with Anatoly, that kept me truly warm. I had so many long periods where I simply didn't do anything other than be a friend and son to the family. I think it's a very special part of being in intelligence as you've just got to get on with being who you're pretending to be for extended periods. I was actually enjoying the whole experience as though I was with real extended family members, like distant cousins or uncles.

There were very few things to look forward to except being together, which looking back wasn't such a bad thing. To be alone is death, and the Russian ethos simply revolved around family. I kept the discipline to keep on point, remembering the reasons for my placement. I spent endless time and effort seeking new friends and new acquaintances through uni and those who attended the apartment. My quest was always to be looking for a reason to get closer to anyone political or in the military who may unveil a path to the list. My searching usually ended in dead ends, drinking tea in an apartment block full of freezing young Russians just seeking to hear my stories of England. Some of those I met were nothing short of living in poverty. However, I enjoyed the time I spent with ordinary Russians who would give you anything and were so very grounded in everything they did. Moscow can be a lonely place and its buildings can be like heavy clouds that block the sun's rays, stopping you from seeing anything remotely positive, the way ahead or what good things the future may bring.

It's always a chance meeting, it's never planned and always catches you unprepared. Rashid Mohamed Asadi, my No. 1, was on the Metro in the same carriage as me, obviously lost having arrived in Moscow by air and changed onto the wrong line. He was dressed totally inappropriately for the weather but was unmistakably trying to appear as a lost tourist, fumbling with a map. He had asked several people to help with directions, but his pidgin English was too mixed up with Arabic to make sense. My stop was the next one which would take me along my route past the Lubyanka. I stood up and asked him in English if he needed help. He was surprised but relieved and asked for directions to Lubyanka Square in the Meshchansky District. I took the opportunity and invited him to walk with me to a café near the square where I was meeting fellow students and from which he could get a warm drink and then make his own way. He agreed and looked to his friend, who nodded in approval, so we got off the tube and chatted all the way to the café. Just tourist stuff but enough to learn that his friend was from Sarajevo and was called Nasser Tamei.

After a very quick coffee, I watched them go towards the main entrance of the Lubyanka, the KGB building (later reorganised FSK, then FSB in 2003), but they were directed to a side door, where Alex met them to take them inside. I really needed a photo which necessitated me to stay at the café. It didn't happen. I remember waiting almost till midnight pretending to study in that café. I limped home to the apartment just in time for a hot drink before bed. I couldn't sleep. I now had three from the list all in the same place – seen together the link was made – but nothing to substantiate any activity that would be of any use. It was a long night and then a whole wasted week looking in vain trying to get anything more. Fucking so close but I'd lost the trail, let it go cold. Alex meeting with Rashid Asadi and Nasser Tamei was priceless intel. This was the KGB meeting with the frontman of finance, possibly the Saudi regime (which was suspected of funding arms to numerous groups, watched by London and the US), with a known arms dealer, Nasser Tamei from Eastern Europe, possibly Yugoslavia. Alex was sure to be the middle man here, setting up the transaction with Russian interests at heart. I had to call this one in soon but knew there had to be more information to make any risk worth taking.

The rest of the week was slow, no movement and nothing to substantiate any theories I may have made up in my head. It was eating me alive that I could be so close to establishing a direct link to the funding and supply of weapons with 'on one' direct intel. I was bound by my brief and continued as normal attending class and following a normal routine. It paid off as I bumped into Anatoly on my way home and he introduced me to Asad, a friend who had just started studying nuclear science with Anatoly at the Nuclear Research University. He had just arrived with his father earlier this week and they were really excited as we were all to be going hunting at the weekend with the whole family, friends and guests. Anatoly took great delight in explaining the wolf story Erik had told us three boys before his arrival. We were all very excited and talked about how good we all were at hunting, none of us ever actually having any idea what to expect or any experience of a hunting weekend. Coincidence doesn't exist in the real world and there was without doubt a gathering of the families; the whole cartel was in town and I had a front row seat to the show.

We arrived home and there was great excitement and joy in the apartment. The whole family was gathered and packing for the weekend; we would leave Friday morning just as soon as we had finished attending our studies. We were bound for a small settlement outside of Yaroslavl, a small town in the heart of Russia, between Moscow and the Ural Mountains. Yaroslavl is around 300km north-east of Moscow where the landscape is reasonably hilly and predominantly covered by forest, occasionally interrupted by large meadows and fields, making it an ideal habitat for game and bear. Heck, the excitement was infectious, and I think Natalia was packing up the whole flat. We had each been given chores to do, and Evgeny, Asad, Anatoly and I were given a pile of money and a very extravagant food shopping list to get that night and tomorrow before we departed.

Friday morning was a true test of my nerve and upfront engaging abilities as I met Rashid and Nasser when they arrived at the apartment with Alex. Looking very surprised when it became quickly apparent I had met his friends already, he was quick to ask how I had met Rashid as this was his first visit to Moscow. I had to give him the whole story of our meeting on the Metro by accident on my way home from university and how I had seen Rashid struggling with a map and thought he was a lost tourist. It was an easy deception as I was dealing in truth and the Metro line was my everyday commute to school. The awkward moment I was expecting didn't materialise as it was probably too much of a coincidence for Alex to flag as anything other than good fortune that we had met in such a way. I can't say if Alex ever suspected anything because he was probably much more skilled than anyone I have ever met at hiding his true feelings or thoughts. His pantomime, if indeed he had one, was a polished act and one I would come to admire and later try to emulate.

A true Russian holiday experience, a hunting trip to Yaroslavl for moose and bear – seriously, this was a dream come true, a trip not to be missed. It was easy to get sucked into the excitement and the whole family thing. I felt like I was family, one of the young wolves, accepted and incorporated by everyone into the family. Alex was keen to keep us all on side for this trip; it was to be a true show of Russian hospitality. I never felt that Alex had any reason to watch me or to suspect anything after the whole meeting of Rashid on the train episode but I had stepped up my own game in my mind none the less. He was actually becoming quite close to me and Anatoly. I don't know if this was truly genuine or if he wanted to get through Anatoly to the real me in some way. This is the paranoia of espionage, double guessing and adding layers to the already implanted layers and paper-clippings that have an already established grip on your life. Cognitive dissonance and insomnia make homes in such places of the mind if you let them in when working with what could have potentially been a serious if not dangerous situation of possible discovery.

Being with the whole family was like nothing I could compare with, belonging to such an intense close nit family, I was almost proud to be a part of it all, they felt like my family and it was a pleasant distraction away from my actual reality. I think I fell into the role very well as it was like having part of my childhood back, being in a family that was accepting and even loving towards me, as we prepared to go on holiday together. It was like I had been adopted like Moses into the Royal family and Anatoly was my Rameses; I don't think the Steering Group would have approved of my way of thinking. Anatoly shared everything with me, confided in me and trusted me. I remember seeing Alex and Erik standing back laughing and watching all the family dash around in a state of euphoria. Friday lunchtime everyone had gathered with all the luggage in the downstairs hall, the family as usual – Alex, Evgeny, Nasser, Rashid Asadi and Asad and his father Mohammed bin Shaban Al Zidjali. We were all set and piled out of the apartment block into the pouring rain under a very heavy grey sky to a waiting convoy of Mercedes cars for the 300km trip north. It was obvious the cars had been funded or authorised by someone in authority, someone Alex was working with; the state was clearly onside.

I travelled with Anatoly, his new friend Asad and his father Mohammed Al Zidjali, and Alex. We had just over a five-hour journey ahead of us as conditions weren't exactly great for the drive north. We talked about killing a bear and eating moose that night or at least tomorrow, lots of bravado and boyish laughing, until conversation eventually subsided and gave way to the sound of the rain banging on the thin metal roof of the car as we boys fell asleep. I awoke to overhear some conversation in Arabic between Alex and Mohammed Al Zidjali, a bit broken but all to do with finance and the expectations of a guy called Ahmed Haddad from Saudi Arabia who apparently was growing impatient with the progress Nasser was making. I deliberately sank back and tried to listen into the conversation as much as possible. Nothing entirely convicting or damning, but general requirements that necessitated a change in the movement of goods before payments from Ahmed would be made. There was discontent from some generals that I hadn't heard of, Leon Antunovich and Otto Meiser; fucking had no idea who they were but needed to make some notes mentally and make sure I got it all down for a possible transmission. It was as if the whole purpose of my being there was interfering with my new family life. I loved being with the family; I guess it made things easy in some respects.

We arrived later than expected at the log hut, which was about 30 miles outside of Yaroslavl, a comfortable distance for everyone to relax and be at one with nature and to make as much noise as we wanted. The house was deep in the woods near Lyubim (Yaroslavl Oblast). We were greeted by paid housekeepers, local peasants if you like, who had been paid to prepare the house. The fires were lit and the stacks of firewood made inside and outside, as convenient as possible for us the guests. Lanterns hung from the overhanging veranda, guiding us to the front door that led us into a main living space where riverbed stone fireplaces roared with welcoming dancing flames and a warm light to draw us in closer. The log cabin was exactly that, great big logs formed into a timeless home away from home. Big wooden floors and handmade wooden furniture, including all the kitchen cabinets, showed off a local carpenter's skill of hand as we explored all the rooms. There were five bedrooms upstairs and a huge living space and dining area downstairs. The living space was littered with odd chairs and sofas that didn't match but were befitting of the house. Everything was a little worn and ragged but it gave a nice at-home feel. This, together with two bathrooms and a separate toilet, was very lavish compared to the Moscow apartment. Our guests would have the spare bedrooms to themselves whilst we young wolves shared a bedroom together with the family.

The evening meal was simply nothing short of phenomenal. We had all gathered for drinks prior to dinner, wearing our best shirts and dresses. The meal was prepared by the local staff who had dressed in local costume and awaited Erik's every instruction. The local costume was very elegant and beautifully bright in colour. The ladies' dresses resembled something from India, like a wedding outfit but heavier and more robust, lots of bright blue, all part of what is called an Olenka, added to which all the ladies wore a tiara-like hat. The men had open coloured shirts in the style of a matryoshka (Russian doll) and big baggy black trousers and boots. I think the occasion presented itself as almost a little formal because of all the attention the waiting staff were displaying, yet the atmosphere remained relaxed as everyone was a little tired after the drive but eager to eat and drink.

The conversation was electric, with all the new faces amongst the family eager to meet each other and become quickly acquainted. Alex and Erik wanted Evgeny and me to look after Asad as Anatoly was fully engaged with Mohammed Al Zidjali in some very technical conversation regarding something to do with centrifuges. I tried as best as I could to pick up as much of the conversation as possible, deliberately trying to move closer with Asad and Evgeny, but not really succeeding too well at understanding or getting close enough to engage in the conversation in any way.

For me the main aim was to piece together the diaspora of individuals and all the family in the assemblage and figure out how that made up any sort of organisation or cell group within or under a wider umbrella of the Russian Government, then to try and establish if any such organisation was or was not funded from the Middle East in support of the 'whos' and 'wheres' that had the UK in a state of almost controlled but obvious panic. There would be more questions than answers to come out of this hunting holiday for the Steering Group back in the UK and I knew this wouldn't be the last time I would have dealings with all those present on this seemingly innocent hunting trip.

We drank some local beer before sitting at our places, set beautifully upon a handmade tablecloth. Very old place mats, each with an image of a Russian city, were symmetrically placed around the table upon which stood china plates and bowls ready for the meal to come. We were served several courses: soup, a fish dish, lamb, pheasant and then ice cream. I think the whole meal took over four hours and the conversation didn't slowed its pace at any point. Attention drew away from the food to the spectacular finale of the evening where we all sat together to watch the locals perform some local dance accompanied by the balalaikas and domras played by the male locals who had been serving us dinner. The evening was called to an end quite early after that as we were assigned quite formally our hunting groups for the next day.

We were up at 5am and I was with Alex, Anatoly and Mohammed, who were super keen to get up into the hills. We had dressed in heavy coats and hats accompanied by long boots bound to our legs by long green gaiters. We met Vadim, a local man who was simply as big as a bear himself, unshaven and of very heavy build, slow but powerful and laden with four rifles, a backpack and four fully laden leather bullet belts. He gave a very short and to the point introduction and showed us where he had laid bait for the bears on a map. Then he showed us all how to load and fire the weapon, make it safe and how to hold it, then passed out the supplies and we set off in our different groups. We walked for maybe four hours in complete silence and in the dark through a light frosty mist that hung around us as we made our way through forest and up into some hills. Nothing so strenuous that we struggled but enough to know we had walked a few miles, and our stomachs cried out for breakfast.

We eventually stopped and Alex said he would take me on alone as it would be better to hunt in smaller groups. I was nervous for the first time since I had arrived in Russia. My mind was working overtime. We both had loaded rifles and were totally in the middle of nowhere. Was this a test of nerve or just a friendly gesture from a man who enjoyed my company? It was hard to separate all my thoughts from the situation at hand. Calmly we climbed together further and further into the hills. Daybreak had released the forest from the dark of night and we came to rest at the top of a rocky outcrop. Alex signalled me to sit with him behind a large boulder. We could see an open field below amongst the trees, an open space half enveloped in the remaining morning mist. He pulled out a flask of water and explained we needed to drink cold water as he didn't want our breath to be seen in the cold air, that we needed to breathe slowly and calmly and await the bear. The field below was evidently where Vadim had laid the bait. I could almost hear my heart in my chest as I sat with Alex sipping water, waiting for something to happen, and not from the field below.

He whispered to me to lie down and rest and as he laid next to me showed me how to hold the rifle. It was an old bolt-action un-scoped Mosin-Nagant M91/30 – a weighty, nearly indestructible bolt-action battle rifle capable of carrying five 7.62x54mm rounds. It would be easy to bring a bear down with such a rifle. We waited and, as we did, he started explaining to me how happy he was that Evgeny had found a friend in me, how he had been bullied and hadn't made many friends, and how I had become his best friend, a friend that Evgeny loved as a brother. He explained his regret as a father for being away from home so many times when Evgeny had needed him. Evgeny was a happy boy now, and Alex wanted me to know he was grateful. It was sincere and I was half able to breathe a sigh of relief but scared to release a cloud of hot breath into the air. It was true, Evgeny and I had connected. Bullying and rough times had struck a chord between us and we had shared many intimate moments together revealing our pain, building our friendship and helping each other do life together in Moscow, both of us missing a true family life.

Now, Alex switched into concentration mode – a tree was waving, you had to look at the treetops, a bear was close. He whispered in my ear, like a father to his son, ready for the moment I would squeeze the trigger and release the powerful cartridge and feel the kick of the mule inside the rifle against my shoulder. Patiently we waited, the cold ground pushing up against my chest, his warm breath whispering in my ear as the bear came out of the mist, sniffing the air, scanning for danger – the moment had come to become part of the Khanty. The Khanty was an old Russian indigenous group who lived in Siberia and believed the bear to be the son of Torum, master of the most sacred part of heaven. According to legend, the bear lived in heaven and was allowed to move to earth only after he promised to leave the Khanty. To shoot a bear here would mean the locals would accept me as a member. It had to be a clean shot. I gently released the bullet from the rifle and simultaneously moved into a whole new world, a world with Alex as a new member of the Khanty and as an accepted friend and guardian of his son who simply loved me so very much. I think it was because of my time at DECAF that I found listening and understanding simple. I knew what it was to need a friend and to be treated well, be able to trust and not be afraid. At that time in Russia I don't think there was too much room for sympathy or understanding, just a cane to drive you to success despite all other human needs, as failure was not an option in a fast-changing and sometimes harsh country.

There was much celebration that night at the log cabin, with all the locals coming to the house. I think everyone was drunk. In a state of drunkenness alliances and friends were unveiled, and Alex's third wolf was without doubt Mohammed Al Zidjali, meaning I had no further work to do in Moscow

– my jigsaw was all but finished. The puzzle was complete. I was able to enjoy the family holiday without further distraction, relaxed and content in every way, a feeling that I think has escaped me now for over 30 years. I think that night was very special – it was safe, it was family, it was freedom and warmth, and above all I slept with no fear or thought interrupting my peace that night.

I enjoyed my remaining time in Moscow – it was free from all the worries of my deployment, there was no need to panic or transmit anything with only a few months to go. I would go back with all the photographs and information needed by the Steering Group to keep them busy for probably years. The finale of my time in Moscow culminated in the witnessing of the Moscow Summit, a meeting between US Pres. Ronald Reagan and the then General Secretary of the Communist Party of the Soviet Union Mikhail Gorbachev. This saw a treaty for intermediate nuclear weapons finalised between the two countries.

All this news and other gentle press releases interlinked and confirmed all my intel and two years of observations, bringing together Rashid Asadi, Nasser Tamei and Alexander. Asadi, wanted by the West's security organisations as an arms procurement frontman for Middle Eastern supported terrorist organisations, was now firmly linked to Nasser, his mirror from Yugoslavia – both seen meeting Alex at the Lubyanka to discuss arms deals to the Middle East and Yugoslavia, all confirmed first-hand at the Pavlovich household in overheard private meetings, discussions and occasional drunken parties. This was clean intel and first-hand, all following that simple innocent meet on the Metro, which then later witnessed Mohammed Al Zidjali, a nuclear scientist and engineer for Syria and Iran, attend the family holiday with Asadi and Nasser before attending the summit unofficially, but officially confirming there was a link to both nuclear technology trading and arms trading, with all the funding coming from the Middle East and all carefully arranged and orchestrated through the family and approved through the side entrances of the Soviet regime.

I returned to the UK that summer. It was a very emotional departure for me and Anatoly. It was simply amazing to have had my two years at DECAF given back to me in a way that I couldn't possibly have imagined. Family, friends, fun, adventure and brotherhood. I miss them all to this day, the love they showed, the memories and times we shared.

I took leave before being summoned back to the Steering Group. I had some time to reflect on the two years of being a Russian student in Moscow. It would be a hard adjustment going back to the MOB. What the fuck was I going back to? The urge to go back to Moscow was huge. I hated the idea of going back into the navy, back into the circus of the Steering Group and that fucked-up training camp in Wales. Life was to change again after that summer, my fun was over, the game at an end, back to reality and one I wasn't too bothered about returning to.

The Steering Group

Chapter 5

Metamorphosis

Returning from Moscow had me severely depressed and that soon became very obvious to the training teams in Wales. My decompression and debriefing were scheduled over the early summer of my return and it hadn't gotten off to a good start by any stretch of the imagination. I had found leave boring and had become disconnected with home, feeling anything but part of the family, my real family that is. I think the adrenaline, the excitement and the adventure of being an operative away from a normal home at such an early stage in my life gave me a hunger that couldn't be satisfied by anything other than being actively deployed. Being someone else for a long time and living the tightrope of deception in order to avoid discovery is a major rush, a drug, and it's addictive no matter how significant or insignificant my role may or may not have been.

Looking back of course, it had all inevitably spilled over into my private life. My mind has gradually become like an endless water feature with the thoughts and memories of the years of deception pouring back into the source pool of my mind, then mixed up with part realities and brought back to life by being pumped endlessly back into the everyday of here and now, devouring and twisting my real life into a distorted reality. It did and still continues to slowly eat away at my sanity and tolerance of those who are pleasantly oblivious to my previous hidden life and the torment it brings with each drop my memory feeds me. Every smell, noise, sight and feeling can be linked back to an event or time in Moscow.

The past realities of those situations I faced and the memories I continue to live with are all-consuming in every way. It can take days, even weeks, to convince myself no one is coming, no one is watching, there is no mirror agent watching me. The madness, the paranoia, will go with me all the way to the grave, occasionally stopping for visits with alcohol, depression, anger, insomnia, or any combination. The mixed cocktail of PTSD from live ops and false or induced hysteria becomes a hell in which your mind is imprisoned and tricked into a delusional nightmare which becomes a battlefield of the mind on a daily basis, always fighting to make it through back to a stable reality. I had yet to find a solid link back to my reality.

Of course, some of the memories I tried to either forget or re-live were mostly good memories spent amongst 'friends' to whom I had perhaps allowed myself to become too attached, which I hadn't anticipated. What a mindfuck. I guess in the early days it was all too easy to think I could get away scar free, but this beast waits until it's all but over, the actual events long passed into history, and then creeps back into your mind just when you thought it was safe, and like a time machine transports you back just to fuck you up. The path of the operative always crosses the path of time, memories like oil always float to the surface and the results are incredibly hard to disguise or hide from those closest to you. Indeed, it is only those precious few who get pushed away never knowing the reasons that sit behind your irrational behaviour.

I was between HMS *Deptford* and Wales with no firm affiliation to either for some time, travelling home sometimes at the weekends. Alcohol played its part, which pissed my mother off no end whilst I was on leave, and I'd come home with both my mum and dad waiting up to see if I returned okay as if I were some out-of-control teenager still at school. Being pissed out of my face all the time on leave didn't help much to ease any of the situations that developed at home, and my mother and I argued bitterly each and every time I came home, usually over nothing. Each time I left home to go back to the circus meant leaving my father to pick up the mess after the usual whirlwind 48-hour visit. All this shit after two years away in Moscow working and living a fast-paced and adrenaline-fuelled double life of uni and being a Moscow operative to now dealing with this domestic crap – what had gone wrong? It wasn't working and each weekend presented new challenges that made me even more frustrated and angry. The visits became less frequent over time as I sought to become more detached from life in order to pursue the challenges of the service.

My parents were actually amazing and of course they had no idea what I was involved with and so never understood my situation. How could they?! I was never able to tell them what an amazing job I had been doing. I guess I wanted some recognition from someone, but couldn't get it where I needed it most. It felt like I had received a lot more support from my surrogate family in Moscow when I was supposedly studying. How fucked up it all seems now that the enemy was providing the support for me to achieve my goals. It was a twisted wreckage of loyalties and truths. But I craved and needed more of the adrenaline, the drug of all drugs, back into my life to straighten some or all this shit out, and soon. Being out of Russia made me feel empty.

I continued, persevered and tried to lead a normal life, if there is such a thing. I continued to travel home over leave, and on the weekends I had to conclude my draft to the *Deptford*, decompress and get off the grid, out of the way, a safehouse to ensure no tail had grown. I spent a short while day-running out of Plymouth, which was easy shit. I was enjoying being back with the lads, going out at night doing the same old routine of getting pissed, taking a curry back to the ship and then nursing a baggy head till lunchtime before a few pints and an oggy (Cornish pasty) in the all-ranks bar in the dockyard. Breathe and repeat. It was a good distraction. I had used the compassionate paperclip for the lads and no one fucking cared really, life goes on I guess, and the lads just accepted me back into the fold as though nothing had happened. We spent some time away at sea and this allowed me to further adjust and get a disconnection from everything and realign my thoughts. Looking back, the safe house of the navy was a real retreat and a place to be truly lost from the world of the Steering Group; it's like being in a safe deposit box within a vault hidden behind an allegory of combinations, locks and walls. The service knew how to hide its operatives and keep them well looked after and, probably more importantly, on a leash whilst readjustments were allowed to be unveiled and managed in a controlled environment. I remember throwing myself back into the whole navy thing and enjoying the simplicity immensely. It's the routine that brings balance back to the mind, and the navy loves routine.

Life on board was always routine and I had some good downtime away from all the complexities of the Steering Group and Wales, albeit sometimes interrupted by the occasional communiqué from London via the captain direct. Routine is boring but it's reliable and safe, and that's the key and answer to it all. I would have the same day at sea again and again like groundhog day, all contained within a cold grey steel box. It's like a self-functioning independent satellite that is completely free except from the orbital path around the parent planet which occasionally reminds you there is a god and he gives orders. I worked a watch routine that made the routine more routine, and I conducted the ritual well and had fun with the other lads who had chosen this ridiculous life at sea away from anything green or solid.

I lost my first life at sea on the *Deptford*. We had been 'working up' and exercising in the Atlantic in the North West Approaches, and the ship had to conduct a RAS (replenishment at sea) for fuel and stores. I had volunteered to help out and was assigned as dump party on the heavy jackstay to receive the supplies from the RFA (Royal Fleet Auxiliary). I think we were on the edge of the weather envelope, a force 6 gusting 7, but needed the fuel and supplies so there wasn't much of an option for the old man but to go ahead and take the risk. The sequence of events was simple: the *Deptford*, being the receiving ship, came alongside the RFA at a distance of approximately 30 yards. A gunline was fired from the RFA, which was then used to pull across a messenger line, distance line, phone line and the transfer rig lines to facilitate the RAS. All was going well until the ships hit an awkward wave whilst making a coordinated 10-degree turn to starboard, increasing the distance between the ships quickly and considerably, stretching the wires to breaking point and then literally pulling the securing points out of the ship's structure. Needless to say it sounded like an explosion followed by the screaming of twisting metal and gasps of the upper-deck crews. It's true, wires do sing at a high pitch just before they snap, and they whip like a snake made of chainsaw blades.

As with all fuck-ups it all ran in slow motion. The RAS mast on the forecastle collapsed, and I remember simply standing and watching the mast whip across the deck then crushing three of the crew against the bridge screen. The wires zipped around the deck and grabbed hold of me, dragging me to the guardrail. It was nothing short of bizarre as I went over the rail. I was pulling like fuck on the inflation toggle for my lifejacket, to inflate it well before hitting the water. I remember the faces of the guys on the RFA looking down at me as I descended into the cold black sea; it would have been great to have waved or shouted something cool, but no time to think. I just had that an *Oh fuck, this isn't good* thought in my mind as I entered what can only be described as liquid ice. If you've ever watched *Titanic*, the description Leonardo DiCaprio gives of a thousand knives stabbing you all over is a pretty good likeness to what it's actually like when you hit the freezing waters of the North Atlantic. I couldn't breathe and was being dragged deeper by the wires. The craziest thing I remember was hearing the propeller blades of both the ships as I raced aft between the two ships wondering if I was gonna drown or be chopped into mincemeat. It's a really loud thrashing sound, and I felt as though I were in the world's biggest washing machine as I was tossed and turned, inverted and eventually spat out. What felt like an hour later (probably only 40 seconds) I surfaced, free from the wires, and watched the two ships sailing away into the horizon. It was just good luck that I had been separated from the wires in some way. The only reason I survived is because the ship's helicopter was already airborne (doing VERTREP operations) and lowered its cargo net into the water for me to swim into. I had a nice bath in the captain's quarters for my trouble, read some instructions from the Steering Group given to me by the captain, whilst later coping with some mild hypothermia and had a day off work in my bunk. Never went up top to see a RAS ever again after that.

Families Day would conclude my time on board the *Deptford* and I was excited as my brothers and my dad would be coming to Plymouth to go out to sea for the day and play navy. Dad loved ships, always wanted to be at sea, and so it was to be an awesome day out and one I would remember forever. The navy always liked to take the families of all crew members out to sea and do the whole PR thing, wine and dine all the families. It was a cool thing to do and it was great to share the experience of being at sea with my dad. The ship would show off its manoeuvrability, give free helicopter flights and allow families to have a go on the upper-deck guns and let off a few rounds. It was like a naval theme park but just for the families. Naturally the catering department would demonstrate its true abilities and cook up a great meal for all to enjoy, and the beer was basically on tap in every mess deck. Families Day showcased the navy to all those who came along and actually made parents and the like proud of those who wore the uniform. I would get to do it only one more time before my father died.

Bizarrely, prior to Families Day I learnt that Harry owed my dad a favour following a few jobs done on the side, and as my dad turned down the offer of a free night with two of his girls from the club Harry had agreed to send a couple of his best girls down from his club the night before Families Day as a gift to me! I was instantly popular with the lads that night and remember us all hitting the strip in Guz, going the whole nine yards, the Barbican, Two Twigs, Long Bar, Malthouse, and of course Boobs. It was a crazy night out and the girls played along beautifully with the story that they were both my girlfriends from up north. Thanks, Harry, wherever you are – it was a real cool thing to do and got me a great rep throughout the MOB as a ladies' man, if only for a short time.

The fun ended too quickly and I found myself back at the training camp, and I managed to get myself into a position of argument with all the team in Wales within the first week. The relationships from Moscow had distorted the reality of the assignment, fouling up the decompression and debrief process simply because it was all too hard to forget all the great people I had spent so much time with, who were not friends, which is how I saw them, but the enemy in the eyes of the Steering Group. This and the *Deptford* incident had an almost pro-found effect on my repatriation back into the MOB and its future plans. It was all cocked hat in my mind after such a suc-cessful mission, and I found it hard to accept the criticism I was receiving regarding the methodologies I had employed in order to get the results that I believed had been so successful.

We had a clear family tree of the organisation operating under Russian, Middle Eastern and European governments, with all the connections to funding and arms trading that were clearly being sanctioned by those governments to achieve political or military advantage. I was never happy being told there was other intel or other avenues of interest that took priority over the evidence I had gathered confirming the involvement of established individuals in clear actions being undertaken that were without doubt in my mind a prelude to war.

It all came to a head I guess after two weeks, and I had been pushing hard against the machine to steer it my way when warnings were issued. I had overstepped the mark; my temper was out of control and I guess it was because I was sick of the team psychobabbling the heck out of everything I did and said. It drove me mad as everything was questioned and re-examined literally to death, making it simply impossible in my mind to reach any sort of logical conclusion to the whole process and move forward. We would go over the same details endlessly day after day after day after day. All the relationships I had built were dismantled and rebuilt into some sort of collage on the briefing boards, photographed and then stored electronically. Then all my photographs were destroyed and every document removed from my possession as though I had never had anything to do with it. It felt as though I was now the enemy, as though I hadn't spent two years of my life gathering information for the group. I remember starting to feel a sick resentment toward the team.

It all turned a corner after a guy called Timothy Murphy (Spud to his friends because he was Irish) was assigned to me. Spud was fucking awesome, a short, bearded calm guy who had worked for the Steering Group in Northern Ireland for three years as an IRA member, both as a sole operative and then with UKSF. We hit it off immediately. He was my lifeline back to a normality, back to a mental even keel. He totally understood the whole fucked-up second family attachment issues, the anger of betrayal to those I had lived and worked with and the trough of depression that follows extended periods in theatre. This, coupled with my absolute frustration that the Steering Group didn't see my work as a priority, and their fixation on disassembling everything I had put together was just normal, old ground to Spud.

Spud had all the answers, he understood, he knew where I was at this point in time; I was young and relatively inexperienced but clay ready for the potter's wheel. He also knew I was very dangerous. I had a lot of intel that was raw, new, and an incredible skill set which had the Steering Group nervous, especially as I was so young and possibly reckless in their eyes. I had made a huge dive into an ocean they originally thought was a little goldfish bowl, and they didn't want their little goldfish getting swallowed up by all the sharks – not just yet at least. Spud explained everything beautifully; he had all the same stories and experiences but all set in Ireland instead of Russia. It was just a tonic to know there was someone else the same and the whole process was real, it was necessary and my work wasn't being dismantled but cut into jigsaw pieces that needed to be placed on the playing board at a higher level and the full picture accurately realised. However, I forced a meeting with the Steering Group in London to sit and go through the Russian trip and my future within the group. I was and still am far too headstrong and determined for my own good. Spud agreed to ride shotgun and come along as my sidekick. I'm sure Spud had a special relationship with the group and our connection was no coincidence. We became friends immediately; and if that was manufactured, I don't care, Spud saved my ass, I think.

I can remember it was at this point in time when the team in Wales, Spud and I discovered that I had a devil inside, a temper and an anger that needed to be harnessed but not tamed. It needed to be trained and disciplined in order for it to be focused and released when the occasion demanded it or when the Steering Group ordered it. It's not all bad to have emotions and anger but learning to control them better would and always will be a challenge especially for a very focused mind set on getting a result no matter what the cost, personally or professionally. It is an asset to have this demon in the intelligence business, but as liked as it was in the end for getting results it has always needed a leash that has always been missing in my civilian life. You can train a tiger to jump through a few hoops but it will fucking bite you as soon as you lower the whip. I don't think I have ever caged my tiger completely; the cage door of my mind is sometimes left open and the innocent who want to stroke or pet me sometimes get a nip from the animal that hides inside, and this is more often than not when I'm bored or not fully immersed in a project, task or mission. But in the end it all became a protection mechanism as I waited and still await my own downfall left by the fear of my successes.

The trip to London was beautifully organised, with all the transport and domestic shit properly taken care of. I finally got to meet the gods in their white temple. Whitehall, home to the Ministry of Defence, or the MOB as we called it, housed the Steering Group under the watchful eye of the Chief of Defence Staff and the Lord of the Admiralty. The only way to describe the feeling of walking into this place is to try and compare it to, say, a roman soldier going before Caesar himself, or attending the Roman Senate with bad news in the *Curia Julia*. I remember walking the echoing halls enclosed by beautiful smooth stone walls leading through atrium-like passageways with floor-to-ceiling glass partitions and pillars that reached up to an open glass sky. There were green rays of light reaching out from behind the glass partitions, gently calming the atmosphere for all those busy people walking swiftly over polished floors carrying dispatches or documents to briefings or secret meetings. No one spoke, just the echoing of footsteps or the clacking of high heels as well-dressed ladies rushed to their appointments and masters. We passed many empty bench seats carefully placed outside closed doors before reaching the big polished oaken doors of our designated meeting room. A tall dark-suited man with a sidearm checked our ID and another guy did a pat down and bag search before letting us in. I think this was probably our fourth security check within 10 minutes.

We assembled in what looked like a fine dining room with a large oval antique walnut table, with simple water jugs and glasses placed at convenient points between the 16 chairs that surrounded this antique centrepiece. The walls were plain, no pictures, but with extensive ornate architraves and a huge ceiling rose from which hung an oversized chandelier arrange-ment directly over the centre of the table. There were three highly polished doors to the rear of the room and a huge TV and video arrangement that dominated the far wall, in front of which was Cdr Brown making himself a coffee from a little hostess trolley. My eyes lit up and I walked straight over to Brown, passing the other occupants, and to his initial shock and horror grabbed and shook his hand whilst making some bullshit comment that he was looking well or something.

I think it was all meant to go a little more seriously than I had opened it up to be, but what the hell. Brown and I entered into polite conversation and laughter broke out about my attempts to piss everyone off in Wales, then he beckoned me to grab a coffee and sit down and meet the team. I recognised Marcus (Capt. Branford), Paul Seely, my contact on the outside for my deployment into Moscow, and the civilian from the initial interview at Raleigh. Additionally, there were two other officers who looked less than impressed with my somewhat informal entrance but were finding it hard not to smile as casual conversation generated some laughter in the room, with

Spud just sitting there in amazement with a big grin on his face, relieved that all was going so well. Cdr Brown pulled the meeting together by formally addressing the Steering Group and the recently returned Russian field operative (me) to take note of the agenda that had been prepared in front of each of us, an agenda that was loosely followed to say the least.

Cdr Brown opened by asking each person to introduce themselves and their role. I remember being very eager to learn who everyone was; it had been plaguing my mind for some considerable time who indeed made up the Steering Group. Despite my intrigue and outward enthusiasm, I remember actually being quite nervous now back under the complete supervision and control of the group, under military control in the centre of the MOB's lair, the circus, or the zoo as it was known. The civilian introduced himself first: Anderson Chaplow, MI6 DI (Defence Intelligence), Head of Intelligence Operations Middle East and links with the former Soviet Union; Marcus Branford, Head of Naval Intelligence, Joint Military Operations and DI (Defence Intelligence); Paul Seely, UKSF Field Operations, Coordinator and I/C (In Charge) of the dustmen (a specialist group which cleaned up any mess physically or politically created by field ops) – Paul had been the man in the background during my time in Moscow, and if it had come to it Paul would have led the extraction if I had needed to pull the plug at any time; David Crowle, MI5, Political Division; and Ben Martin, American, Joint Special Forces Operations, United States Special Operations Command (USSOCOM). This was the Steering Group – well, the guys in charge. Fuck, it was quite something to sit in that room and chew the fat that first time with these guys; it was as if we had known each other for a lot longer than we actually had. I was probably more comfortable than I had expected to be and was soon making conversation easily and openly with everyone. I wasn't being evaluated, just spoken to like a guy on the same side for the first time in what felt like years, and that made us a team in my mind – I had a family again. We all had common purpose.

There was a good half hour of chit-chat before Cdr Brown stated that as the meeting had been called by the Wales team, with concern as to the progress of debriefing and decompressing of the operative returning from Moscow, he would like me to speak regarding the issues I had faced and give a full brief to the group of the intel I had compiled and where I saw the programme going from here. I remember the wink from Marcus; it really was time to get serious. It took me six hours to go through the details of the mission to Moscow. We didn't stop for lunch or allow anything to interrupt me as I systematically built, on a pair of whiteboards, the family tree of all those I had met in Moscow, for the group to see and understand – the involvement in arms trading, political links to both the Middle East and the Balkans, as well as nuclear technology trading and funding pathways coming from Saudi Arabia, and distribution networks to governments and possible terrorist cells.

I made clear that I had provided a comprehensive portfolio of photographs and documents to the team in Wales that supported the dossiers set before them. The room was in silence for some time. I had poured my heart into the detail of the evidence of what I saw as irrefutable links and relationships that I had been involved with or witnessed and the stink trail came all the way back to London, with Alex a member of the KGB's higher-level directorates doing regular business here on their doorstep, right under their noses, including using British export licences to export arms 'legally' to Iraq. David didn't even raise an eyebrow. My concluding synopsis was to plan an eradication of all the key players over time so as not to raise immediate suspicion of the sudden intelligence gain we had made and then to remove the facilities associated with those key personnel in disassociated campaigns or missions.

Anderson, who had been pacing the room for about an hour, becoming more and more irritated by what he was hearing, came to the table and agreed that the links needed to be explored further and in detail, but then when fully realised broken down into specific possible targets with timings that didn't compromise other missions, operations or political interests. He explained that the programme needed to be kept alive long enough to get new teams in place to conduct the termination of the human target's ability to conduct business, but the bigger issue would be the disruption and eventual destruction of the facilities supporting the nuclear technology and arms trading. This would be a huge transatlantic commitment and one that would take up a significant amount of time from the group, possibly over several years. There was then a lot of heavy and loud discussion regarding other issues, the Middle East, Libya, Yugoslavia, North Korea, China; the jigsaw was without doubt bigger than I had ever imagined, but it was not one for me to piece together. I sat back and just listened to the complexities of what each member of the group had to consider, who was tied in with what, and other operations and surveillance that couldn't be compromised despite the new information unfolding before them. It felt like I had just made the whole world unsafe in one afternoon. The penny had dropped as to why all the delay, and I was in awe at the labyrinth that had to be worked through to get any progression.

Paul Seely, who was the first to break the cycle, stood up and enquired, "Where to for our young Russian operative now?" There was some discussion as to how the fuck our little goldfish had come back with such a bag of whales for the group to deal with, and a great deal of talk about security, my age, future deployments and the issues I had caused in Wales. However, a plan had been hatched by Paul and Ben, which was for me to RTU, get off the bus and disappear for a while whilst the teams did the sift of all the intel before them and feed it all into the bigger machine. All the agencies needed to deepen their awareness of the new revealed links by exploring individuals, locations, homes, workplaces, building the bigger jigsaw picture prior to any plan of action being developed for integration into the wider military programme and existing operations. It was going to take time, not to mention the need for political support. Paul asked Cdr Brown for his thoughts. Brown stood up and, walking around the table, explained that I would RTU, get off the bus, as Paul had indicated. I needed to get off the grid whilst things were worked out; this was not for me to get involved with. My safety was paramount and the deception needed to continue whilst delicately maintaining a live but somewhat less active communication programme with Russia, and then allow it all to fade into a gentle controlled semi-separation from me and those I had made contact with in Moscow, if that were possible. More conversation regarding the underlying issues of relationship management so as not to raise suspicion and a need to maintaining some contact in order to track the unknowns was obviously causing the group a headache.

My instructions were to join HMS *Flamborough*, planned for her decommission, then return with 42 Commando and undertake all arms training with the Royal Marines, get my head into the right space, get the animal trained and the temper restrained. If I successfully completed the All Arms Commando Course, I would join the next warship destined for the Middle East and be on standby for insertion into Jordan, Saudi and Iraq to translate and observe. I needed to complete my engineering training, to progress my career at sea in order to attend the Naval Nuclear School so that I could gain a better understanding of the nuclear issues I had raised regarding the purification processes for uranium and pluto-nium without raising any attention to why I was attending the school. I had to get back into the navy, disappear safely for a while where I could be kept close but not easily found from the outside. Then Cdr Brown looked at me and I remember him being very sincere when he said to me and the wider group, above the chit-chat, "What a mess all this has made, but when you've done all that, we will get you back, assign you to Paul and get you working to finish what you've started. You belong to the group now and there's no going back."

After joining the *Flamborough* I was sent almost immediately for 'commando training' – not really commando training, the All Arms Commando Course was a lesser course, something to make you more interesting, and in my case more compliant. All arms training was a nightmare and something I don't wish to repeat. It's just a beasting for the sake of it in my opinion. It's designed to be the backbone of British military training for those who need to get up close and personal with the enemy in more of a support role, 'where the metal meets the meat', to coin a phrase, but not actually become a Royal Marines Commando. For me I think they were instructed to focus deliberately on developing my temperament, mental resolve, physical robustness and core military skills so that I could go back in to the field in a more robust manner but safely within the intelligence framework.

I didn't do the mandatory PCC (Pre-Commando Course), I was just slotted into the course at short notice by those with such powers. This made it all too easy for me to be the target for as much abuse as the training staff could muster over the bad-tempered last-minute entrant. I'm not sure how the Steering Group got me a place on that course – it wasn't me really, and it must have shown. I'm just not into all the fitness they threw at me, I couldn't see the point of it all. Basic fitness test, battle fitness test, bleep test, swimming tests and endless runs and endurance tests that, to me, didn't prove a fucking thing except that I fucking hated it and I learned I really don't like being wet and cold, hungry or especially being deprived of sleep. My weapon-handling tests were a breeze and somehow amazingly I scored high enough to be awarded sniper status, a skill that was no doubt smiled upon.

I guess the Steering Group must have enjoyed the reports that would have been sent back detailing my failures, anger outbursts and all the remedial training that saw me pull many 24-hr days trying to make the grade. Three hits and you're out, and I think they all worked pretty hard to get me to quit, but in the back of my mind I was always wondering what would they would do if I failed. Go round again, or would that really be the end of my career under the Steering Group? Or were they instructed to make me pass? Fuck knows, all I knew was I didn't really want to pass the fucking course but wanted to get back working in the intelligence sector again and soon. So I guess that drove my fat ass over Dartmoor a few times carrying far too much attitude, which outweighed the kit I was carrying by about 10 to 1. It's bizarre because later, at 40 years old (quite some time later), I enjoyed nothing more than going out onto Dartmoor for fun and running 20 to 30 miles over the hills just because I could, and I often ran past the new boys struggling to do eight miles and offering them lame encouragement to quit before it was too late.

The Marines fucking hate part-time 'green lids' and they always made it known they were the real deal and all us 'lids' or crap hats were just plastic soldiers to them. I guess they were right, I get it, and thank fuck they are as hard as coffin nails because I was on my way to working with the hammers who, like me, always found it easier to out-think an enemy rather than fight him. The Marines are fucking awesome at getting into trouble and getting others out of it, and they're scary as fuck when they're doing the business. I never wore a green beret, never thought I'd earned it like those boys; I think it was all a bit plastic like they said. But I've got to say thanks for showing me how crap I was during those weeks and months training me.

I remember lots of jokes I had with the marines once I was deployed, and my favourites would be shit like "How do you scare a marine? Give him a spelling test!"

OR

Three guys, one navy, one army and one Royal Marine, are taking the test to join the SAS. They have all passed the mental and physical sections and are down to the final interview.

Guy from the navy walks in to be confronted by the SAS staff who gives him a gun and says, "There are six bullets in that and your wife is upstairs – go up and kill her."

The guy disappears but comes back two minutes later to say, "Sorry, I really want to be in the SAS but she's my wife and I love her."

"Sorry," says staff, "but if you can't take orders we don't want you."

Guy from the army walks in and the same thing happens; he gets the gun and is told to go upstairs and kill his wife, but also can't do it, so is told to thin out as well.

The marine walks in and is given the gun. Off he goes and suddenly six shots ring out from upstairs, followed by an almighty commotion, and 10 minutes later he walks back into the room drenched in sweat.

He looks at the SAS staff and chucks the gun at him saying, "You wanker, they were blanks. I had to strangle the fucking bitch!!!"

The serious side of this is: be careful what you ask marines to do because they don't fuck around in my experience and usually see shit through to the end no matter how crazy or how much you think they won't do it and that includes stupid bets and dares made down the pub.

I passed the fucking training and picked up my orders for HMS *Berwick* destined for Gulf patrol. The *Berwick* was a destroyer based in Portsmouth, a great upgrade from the old steamships, the *Gainsborough* and the *Deptford*. I joined the *Berwick* in the winter of 1988, older and wiser than my previous two drafts, and there were no initiation ceremonies or skylarking at my expense this time. But it was cool to see new boys down the stokers' mess getting their introduction to the Andrew. I was moving up just ever so slightly in the world of the navy and I found some great friends in the mess to see out the deployment with and indeed the next two years.

I managed to secure a bunk down a quiet gulch away from the mess square with a deployed group of six SBS who were on board for the ride and no doubt anything else that came along. I soon found out I was to be their interpreter if needed and, yeah, I guess their plaything after a fashion. They just kept themselves to themselves really. They never complained about the noise of all the piss-ups that happen very regularly at sea and they never really joined in. I can remember spending many late nights lying in my bunk just talking shit with these guys when they were on board, teaching them Arabic and Russian. I think it went down well to pass the time with them in this way and as we made our transits from one zone to another. A mutual respect was to develop between us and it was just cool I guess to be with other guys who probably had more secrets than me and just didn't feel the need to talk about any of it, so it was just sort of understood in both camps. I didn't ask their names and we just called each other 'mate'. Like with any military acquaintance you recognise the person but can't remember the name so you just call them mate.

I remember going to my assigned part of ship to see my section chief upon joining and, fuck me, knock me down, there was Spud. This was gonna be an interesting trip. I was beginning to believe it was all pre-planned – too many nice little coincidences. Spud had grown a beard and was looking older. Spud was a ginger, but I won't hold that against him; he wasn't a big guy, just sort of insignificant really. He was always well presented, but it was so obvious to me that all his navy kit had just been issued to him about a week ago, and probably in a hurry as this was a late-notice assignment and so his uniforms looked like cardboard nailed to a beanpole. Very polite and kind-hearted, he always had time for me and I appreciated him as my mentor. He was actually there as close protection in the first instance (following the Moscow trip) which was quite strange, as I never had felt threatened or in danger in any way, but the whole deal had the Steering Group a little nervous for a while and I suppose they just liked having Spud keep an eye on me.

Prior to sailing for the Gulf from Portsmouth, the *Berwick* undertook sea trials, shakedown and Basic Operational Sea Training. It's the navy's way to train up a crew prior to an operational deployment. Starting with basic safety and readiness training, progressing through single-threat and multi-threat scenarios to advanced tactical training out at sea and all achieved through a structured system of relevant and focused operational training, with an emphasis throughout on realism, including battle-damage simulation and all aspects of war fighting. And of course, every Thursday was all-out war where Blue and Orange forces (some foreign navies were trained in the UK) would conduct the Thursday War, which inevitably meant lots of onboard fire and flooding drills, machinery breakdowns, gunnery exercises and all manner of naval skulduggery orchestrated by the FOST teams (Flag Operational Sea Training).

For the crew of the *Berwick* it meant a long six weeks of training and exercises day and night that eventually becomes routine. I think everyone who has done shakedown and OST will always remember the days spent at Portland Bill doing the disaster exercises that do a fine job of simulating a hurricane-stricken island or some other similar disaster that leaves everything on fire, damaged and all the inhabitants displaced and injured but just well enough to give the crew a hard day out, screaming and pretending to be everything from pregnant to half mad. I think they had a hardcore of locals who just loved to act and come along for a big day out to give the matelots a hard time. It was the DISTEX (Disaster Relief Exercise) that concluded your time at Portland and, looking back, it was a great theme park they put on for the training – everything, including helicopter rides, burning vehicles and the best disaster movie sets found this side of Hollywood. Spud and I took every opportunity to explore all the scenarios and delve in deep where he thought it would benefit me. The engineers did really well under Spud's leadership as he was just a born leader.

The great thing about Portland was that it was an 'away from home' port; both the Guz crews and the Pompey crews were too far away from home to do the daily commute, so everyone lived on board at night and those with families didn't disappear home when some random exercise was sprung on the duty watch. But more importantly, it meant everyone would be out on the piss in Weymouth or Portland every fucking night. I think it was part of the training as the hangovers we gave ourselves were the best way to simulate battle fatigue, and all the lads made sure they were all fully fatigued every morning.

A typical night out would involve shooting a few cans of beer on board before jumping in a 'Joe Baxi' (taxi) bound for Weymouth. I was okay in Weymouth as I knew a few of the Booties (Royal Marines) from my previous training and steered the boys away from 'Green Beret only' pubs to avoid any punch-ups, and when we did run into them it wasn't hard for me to talk us out of any bother, knowing a few of the lads from 45 Cdo or 42 Cdo. It was a great night out, usually starting at The Black Dog and then I can't remember all the names of the pubs, but we all drank Newquay Steam beer washed down with gin or vodka chasers before heading back to the green shutters in Portland. All piss-ups were followed up with what was known as 'BIG EATS', which translates into anything greasy and fulfilling in the food department for a pisshead, which usually meant getting a chicken on your fist (literally) from the hole in the wall, or a burger from the greasy spoon, as you made your way back on board smashed out of your face at about 2am, always remembering not to take a shortcut across the local graveyard to take a piss on any of the headstones as that was where the local provost (military police) liked to hide in order to catch us pissed, fucked-up matelots and put us in a cell for the night. This would ultimately ruin the rest of the month, with extra duties and a fine for our troubles.

It was on one such night out in Weymouth that I met Pierre, a guy from the hard at RM Poole just up the road. He was sitting in a bar on his own nursing a pint when Seth, Happy, George, myself and Spud poured into the otherwise deserted battlecruiser (boozer/pub). I bought him a pint for his sorrows as he was at the bar alone, whilst we played pool, fed the jukebox for an hour and entertained the barmaids. Never did think much of that meeting with Pierre until much later on in life. He was and remains an amazing guy. This is when I first met Keith, who had tagged along as a baby stoker with the lads on his first real piss-up off the ship. A strange cockney geezer that to look at you'd have thought had gotten lost on his way home from school. Keith and Pierre had just become two threads entwined into the hawsers of my life's tapestry without me even acknowledging it at the time. The encounter was nothing other than part of a piss-up but a meeting that was of special significance in my life. I know now that Spud and Keith were also in the embryonic stages of something bigger for Keith, but that wasn't to be realised for some time by me. Nevertheless, Keith ended up working for me and Spud on the *Berwick* for a short while. I thought he was fucking useless to be honest but he would later prove my initial assessment to be utter bollocks, becoming after training an invaluable member of the Steering Group toolbox.

So, there we were, all assembled incognito on board the *Berwick* headed for the NAG (Northern Arabian Gulf), me, Spud and an SBS section aboard. I had been taken under Spud's wing for my first attempt at going live into the Middle East. Over that six months Spud and I grew quite close and I think he did everything possible to keep my mind active, keep me sharp, but at the same time open my eyes to what life was to become and how to process everything, and more importantly keep it all in perspective. His temperament was just great and his teaching skills simply exemplary. It was so easy to get all the instruction I needed, both in engineering and in the hidden skills and methodologies of the hidden espionage operative – how to be all you can be without yourself or anyone else noticing. Spud was reporting directly to the Steering Group and was above the bullshit of the RN. It was obvious because he was absolutely carefree about his RN role, and the captain always came to Spud for a cigarette and a chat at about 4pm, which was always preceded by the captain's steward bringing fresh cakes and nibbles at about 3.45pm. Spud always made out to everyone it was because he was doing some work in the wardroom but, trust me when I say, he never went to do any navy work on his visits to 'the wardrobe' as we called it.

I received many letters from Anatoly (intercepted and analysed of course) which were passed on by the Steering

Group whilst I was fucking around in Portland and in the early weeks and months of the deployment. They needed a personal response and were quite out of date before the Steering Group finally released them and the replies. Things had been going well for Anatoly and he wrote with such compassion and heartfelt sorrow at my absence. Evgeny wanted to know when I would return so we could go hunting together again with Anatoly and his father Alex. He had missed my comradeship and yearned for the three best friends to be back together like in the wolfpack story Alex had told us so many times after the boys had become like brothers. My mind wandered back to Moscow and I could almost hear the laughter above the sound of crap music in the apartment as everyone sat down for dinner. I wrote my letters and posted them to Wales. Fuck, I missed Moscow and I missed my friend Anatoly.

Bound for the NAG and escort duties for merchant shipping down through the Strait of Hormuz, we had left Pompey on a Friday of all days. Our transit took us across the Bay of Biscuits (Biscay) and into Gibraltar for a run ashore before heading to Suez and then the Red Sea. It was the time just after the tanker wars, and the Iranians had threatened a blockade of the Strait of Hormuz and we had to sail through the Iranian silkworm envelope each time we took up patrol. We dropped off the SBS boys at Suez, not to be seen again for a while, and then I guess for the most part it was a very quiet deployment. I guess boring for the most part.

I continued working hard at getting promotion and picked up my next rank shortly after getting into theatre. I was preparing myself for further engineering qualifications, to secure a place on an engineering qualifying course – submariner – which would give me the basic understandings of a nuclear power plant and all the theory that I needed in order to possibly engage and understand a conversation around those involved in nuclear technology trading between the Soviets and the Middle East. It was all just mad science to me at this point in my career. I hadn't figured out the connections, hadn't joined all the dots why the Steering Group kept me in training on things I thought irrelevant. Spud kept me on track and focused on the bigger picture and the real promotions that I sought outside of the Andrew. The engineering was of course of significant importance to the group, a skill they wanted me to have. All operatives have at least two separate skills. Mine were language and engineering, Spud's were engineering and ordnance. I was keen to pick up his skills and knowledge in the ordnance world, and it was an inevitable rub off.

Gulf patrol is generally boring and no different around the time of the first Gulf War and Desert Shield, so don't let anyone tell you any different. We were up and down the Gulf following merchant ships and occasionally observing a Russian escort doing the same as us, mirror imaging. I usually got called up to the EW office (electrical warfare) or to the operations room to translate or listen in, but it was usually very boring shit. Occasionally I was part of the boarding parties and went aboard merchant ships to say hi and all that bollocks but also to familiarise myself with merchant ship layouts and systems. I would always face in-depth questioning from Spud on my return from any such outings – everything from machinery layout to number of crew, nationalities, languages, ship's particulars, and he always wanted a ship's manifest. It was training beneath the training. I remember spending many nights drawing detailed deck plans from memory for Spud to examine in-depth and then interrogate my knowledge, or lack of, about everything I had seen and who I had talked to.

On one such boarding operation I remember meeting the captain of the *Maersk Navigator* on that trip who I later bumped into on port state control (PSC) duties. It's funny how the cloth of life is woven together. There was a lot of traffic from the NAG oil platforms, but the serious threat was still the Iranian terminals and further possible attacks from Iraq. Nothing really materialised. I remember spending Christmas at sea, as well as my 21st birthday, without a drop of alcohol – that's how fucking boring it all was. Some nights the captain would take us into offshore waters to allow us to have a flight-deck BBQ and three beers but it just didn't cut it. The runs ashore when they happened were mayhem and it always ended badly with one or more of the crew in trouble for drinking too much and getting lifted on the streets of Dubai, which was never a smart move.

It was after Christmas, around February, when the ship was planning advanced leave which would allow approximately 30% of the crew to fly home so that the rest of the crew could take leave on arrival in Pompey. Spud had put my name on the list. But I wasn't going home. A more carefully constructed departure from the ship had already been engineered and I guess I had been waiting for something more interesting to come into my circle for months as we were so close to all the piss-holes of the world.

I was going ashore with Spud and the team to a compound in Jeddah, Saudi Arabia as intel had suggested that Rashid Asadi was staying in Saudi and was expected to have some other possibly familiar friends joining him for a business trip into Jordan or possibly Israel. It was an easy switch: pack everything up and store it at a US airbase in Jeddah before taking a trip into the sand with the team. I had a few nights in Dubai to get pissed up and sell the story that I was flying to Australia to be with family, hence why I wasn't on the transport back to the UK with all the lads. It was a quick and welcome mental switch to get back into the intelligence role.

It was a cool start to the day; it's always the best temperature at around 6am in my opinion, and I remember as we prepared to leave for the airport the amount of equipment coming with us. Spud, the team and I went to Dubai Airport separately in a minibus and were taken over to a military apron for boarding a USAF flight to Riyadh on a simple C130 transport aircraft, nothing special. After a short flight sitting in cargo nets, we arrived unannounced but were later met by the American representative, a tall skinny guy who seemed a little flustered and unsure what to say to us except "Welcome, and how was your flight?" How was the flight? Seriously? It was a fucking C130 transport – there wasn't any in-flight entertainment, refreshments or movie! He messed about asking for transport documents, to which we just smiled and Spud simply retorted, "Don't be ridiculous," and showed him an ID badge, at which time he quickly got on his radio. We were then quickly transferred and billeted in Eskan Village, about 20 miles south of the airbase. It was originally built for the local tribesmen but they never took up the offer by the Saudi Government, but the Yanks did. We were allocated a villa away from all the traffic, so to speak; it almost felt like we were on R&R or something. The villa had four en-suite rooms off a main lounge, all with sectioned sleeping areas. Two to a room and I was in with Spud. There was an expectant silent atmosphere, laced perhaps with some detailed preparation and nervous anticipation on my part. No one said much. I just copied Spud.

Once we had settled into our temporary accommodation Spud called a meeting in the common room. We needed to break the ice. It was a weird first meeting with a brief introduction by Spud of the entire team. Spud introduced himself as our group combat commander and then introduced the six SBS guys as 'Guns', 'Bombs', 'Tricks', 'Meds', 'Engines' and 'Chaos'. I let out a sarcastic laugh that was met with louder laughing. It broke the ice, and it was obvious that Spud and the team had worked together before. Spud made a grand gesture that I, the new fish, had been given promotion to NCO Intelligence. There was a round of applause and more sarcastic laughing, and comments like "Good luck with that, mate" and "Fuck working with you". I'm sure the team was just happy to have a new plaything I guess. Spud beckoned me over and, after inhaling deeply on his cigarette, was gracious enough to fill me in that this was his team and I was his guest. I was then invited to invent a name for myself. 'Thumper' was unanimously agreed by the team as I was known for my temper but it was more to do with some other joke about future jungle training. We poured more coffee and lit cigarettes. We had all sort of got to know each other quite well over the previous months on board even though we hadn't worked together until now. Weird. I guessed that's how things would roll from now on.

Spud then proceeded to give a more serious brief received from the Steering Group. They had issued a kill list. It's hard to hear those words when they're said out loud for the first time, and I remember there not being any reaction to those piercing words from the other guys, just me looking at their faces hoping I wasn't the only one with a 'what the fuck?' look on my face. We didn't have the complete list but the Steering Group had activated Spud's squad to infiltrate known and suspected arms deals that were taking place within the Middle East originating in Saudi Arabia and supplying the Iraqi Army in the prelude to the possible invasion of Kuwait. This was news to most of the team; we had been aware that Kuwait had been seriously pissing off the Iraqis as it was out pumping its quota by OPEC, preventing an increase in crude oil prices thus preserving its own downstream refining businesses. Plus, according to the former Iraqi foreign minister Tariq Aziz, every US$1 drop in the price of a barrel of oil caused a US$1 billion drop in Iraq's annual crude income, forcing a massive financial crisis in Iraq. Between 1985 and 1989, Iraq lost somewhere in the region of US$14 billion a year due to Kuwait's oil price strategy. So, behind the news were all the familiar (to the team) undercurrents to change the Middle East map once again.

Kuwait's refusal to decrease its oil production was viewed by Iraq as an act of aggression against it, and now Iraq had employed our man Ahmed Haddad and his frontman Rashid Asadi to help arrange/finance arms from the Soviet Union through Yugoslavia to then be shipped to Syria or Lebanon, the complexities of which seemed to be interlinked with further deals made with Leon Antunovich and Otto Meiser for the safe transit of arms through Yugoslavia in return for a percentage of the arms being retained by Serbian generals. Ahmed Haddad was the central bank for all the transactions but his right-hand man Rashid Mohamed Asadi was the frontman in both the Soviet Union and in Yugoslavia. We would go across country, track Rashid and remove the threat either in Jordan or Israel but using Saudi Arabia as our springboard and first-choice escape route. Saudi was and remains a solid ally in such matters but had to deal with internal issues flying under their own radar. My task was simply to positively ID Rashid Asadi, then eliminate him utilising the support team under Spud's command. David Crowle had got the all-clear from Saudi so we had 'white cards' (it's a phrase used to indicate we had carte blanche to do what was required but/and is an actual engagement card) sanctioned by the Saudis for insertion and travel as they were just as nervous about the threat from Iraq given the recent intel regarding chemical weapons being positioned near their borders in the form of Soviet-built Scud missile assemblies, possibly from the same source.

That took some time to sink in, two days to be exact, and I had time to think it through as we hiked it overland in Land Cruisers down to Medina, a rotten seven-hour drive, and then on to Tubuk. I don't know what we looked like – a cross between tourists, a piss-take at looking like an Arab with one of those fucking Arab black and white checked scarfs, baseball cap, combat trousers with hidden webbing for a sidearm and other shit. I had grown a beard, which had been good advice as it helps keep the sunburn down. I guess with all the fancy dress we must have looked almost like real sand people. We all had either an HK G36 assault rifle made by Heckler & Koch or an M203, which is basically a standard M16 adapted to accept an underslung M203 40mm grenade launcher, and of course the old favourite, a Browning 9mm sidearm.

However, 'Guns' had an L119A1 or CQB fitted with a sound suppressor, laser pointer/illuminators, fore grips and Trijicon ACOG scope topped with mini red dot reflex sight as backup to his main sniper rifle which was undoubtedly the widow-maker of the entire arsenal – an A3, or long range sniper rifle featuring a detachable sound suppressor, all-weather day sights with improved magnification, with an 'aim and forget' reputation in the right hands. Yes, you could say we were well equipped for the trip. I've no fucking idea why we were given rat packs but there you go; in my backpack was a NATO B ration pack which I ripped apart and reorganised with my escape pack, which consisted of 200 cigarettes, my No.2 passport, a sign in Arabic that simply stated 'I am not an American' and a change of clothes should it all go tits up.

I think it's desert sickness or something but looking at sand, rocks and brown shit all day makes you fucking miserable, tired and, yeah, want to shoot some cunt. It's just tediously boring and very tiring on the eyes. It's like being on Mars or something, the ultimate moonscape, rocks, rocks, more rocks and sand. I think the reason why there is so much conflict in the Middle East is due to the fact that everything is so damn difficult. There is nothing green for the most part and everyone is irritable, hot, tired and fucking thirsty, and everything gets covered in dust and sand. It's an instant childhood reminder for me, all that sand; after playing on the beach you'd have to have your feet rubbed down with a towel by your mum, which made it like sandpaper, before you were allowed back in the car to go home. The whole experience is painful. It's like being in hell. No one gives a fuck about the place really, it's all about the oil – there's nothing else out in the Middle East worth a damn, including human life – everyone is fighting over every last drop of the black stuff. However, I always took time to soak in the sights as we drove through the oil fields, just miles and miles of pipework simply disappearing into the brown burnt horizon, with the skeletal steel horse like silhouettes of the pumpjacks littering the desert like lost herds of wild steel horses endlessly bowing up and down to slurp up the oil from beneath the sand.

Another five hours of miserable tedious desert driving and Tubuk was on the horizon. Tubuk is a weird as fuck place and stands alone in the middle of nowhere like most Arabian towns. Don't be fooled; although it can get pretty warm in Tubuk it can also fucking snow. It's not a bad place, and to be fair there's even some grass and an abundance of water. There was some modern architecture and it seemed like a reasonably well-kept place, with Western hotels and shopping areas. It had a huge air base and I guess that's because of its proximity to the nearby borders of Iraq, Israel and Jordan. So, I guess it's what you'd call strategic. We were supposed to pick up the stench trails of our friends Rashid and possibly Ahmed here. I don't remember being anything other than tired. I wasn't excited or nervous, just preparing myself mentally, I guess.

We stayed in a hotel and acted like tourists for two nights. Now, Saudi may be dry but it's the biggest importer of Jack Daniel's in the world. It's all horseshit – every fucking dry country I have been to I've found a bar and it's full of Arabs. The SF guys had already been and done the reconnaissance of the whole border crossing area into Jordan and the route back before we had made our transit of the Suez Canal six months earlier so they were real relaxed about the whole deal – just a clean insertion, quick delivery and invisible extraction were required. It was anticipated that our friends would be exiting Saudi and we would engage in Israel rather than Saudi as it would be less politically sensitive. The guys seemed unperturbed, that is until they saw me talking to some businessmen in the hotel lounge. I was asking if they knew where to get a cold beer. They were Arabic businessmen from over the border who happened to be waiting for a beer train – this is an organised trip out into the desert in 4x4 SUVs beyond the sight of civilisation into the dunes to consume some alcohol away from prying eyes. I agreed to go and join in the fun, jumping into a van, with Guns leaping in behind.

I got the evil stares all the way but the whole thing was innocent enough, and after an hour we arrived at a camp amongst the dunes. It was well lit, with Western music coming from the main tent arrangement. US$100 to get in and it was well worth it. Inside there was a full BBQ at the far end, no restrictions, plenty of beef, pork sausages, anything you wanted, with the tent opening out to a collapsible pool with a few well-placed girls in bikinis. The bar ran the length of the tent, with Arabian-style seating forming booths around the entire internal perimeter. I casually parked myself at the food end of the bar and was greeted by a very American-sounding Arabic barman. It was Owen from DECAF! Fuck me, it was gonna be a good night. Guns was displaced and didn't know whether to have a drink or shoot me. I explained who Owen was and Guns and I both lied that we were working for an oil company.

Owen was making it rich selling illegal alcohol to the Arabs and anyone they invited along. I remember it being a fucking good night but don't really remember getting back to the hotel or saying goodbye to Owen, although my hangover was reminder enough of the entire evening. It had been good to see Owen, and I had got hold of his address and phone number in Saudi. Spud was fucking furious about our little excursion but Guns brought it all under control by stepping in and claiming it had been his idea, which somehow made the whole thing more acceptable, especially after he revealed that Owen had told us they had closed the eastern access road to the Jordanian border. He only knew this because Owen was smuggling in alcohol from Jordan. Guns had seen Ahmed and Rashid's names on the guest list for the two previous nights so the chance meeting had proven to be quite worthwhile in more than one respect. The other guys were pissed that Guns and I hadn't invited them along for a night out so it was all sort of diffused into a bit of a joke.

It was nothing special. The scene was set in a peaceful hotel just south of Eilat Harbour in Israel, just over the Jordanian border. I had checked in for one night, with Spud in the room next to me. It hadn't been hard to follow Rashid Asadi and Ahmed Haddad; their scent was soon picked up by utilising simple tracking methods, access into some satellite activity, telephone and internet usage, and some banking activity that UK intelligence had kindly passed on to us. We pinpointed Rashid using a credit card for a hire car from Tubuk and then the hotel into which we had booked a few days ahead of him to do our prep work. The boys camped out in the desert and Guns set himself up in the confines of the harbour, utilising a vantage point from on top of a warehouse. The coverage was excellent to the front and side of the hotel.

Spud and I went to the restaurant in the evening and enjoyed a dinner waiting patiently as we systematically recorded all the staff movements, access and egress routes and security cameras. We were keenly aware that the other guests might be involved in the arms deals that were planned for tomorrow's scheduled meeting with Ahmed. Everyone was photographed.

The one great thing about mid- to high-end Middle Eastern hotels is the food. There is always an endless selection of hot dishes displayed in a kind of mini food court where you can walk around aimlessly trying to choose a dish. There are happy-to-help smiling chefs on hand to serve and to cook up speciality orders. There was a cold buffet that included crab and lobster, with mountains of greens and other cold meats. Of course, the dessert counter would have any woman weak-kneed at the endless opportunity to satisfy any chocolate or sweet craving they may have. Inevitably, such meals always ended up being a five or six course affair – eats and treats before business, however legitimate or sinister that turned out to be.

We kept checking in with Guns to see where the best positions were for clear lines of sight not interfering with blast routes and casualty minimisation issues. It was about 9pm local time before we finished our dinner, and then Spud briefed Tricks and Bombs who were already in the grounds to set up the diversions and the explosives that would be initiated at kill + five seconds. Spud and I then disappeared into our hotel accommodation for the evening, but that wasn't to sleep. We were attaching detonators to an explosive string on the camera network, recording and cabling feeds before calmly checking out at 7am after enjoying Arabian coffee and dates in the lobby. We then calmly sat waiting for our ride out of there, which was facilitated by Engines in the Toyota Land Cruiser freshly embellished with oil company logos. He even helped us with our bags, nice and calm like a well-organised business trip.

I was on top of the warehouse now at about 10am with Guns. I had a spotter scope scouring the hotel, waiting, waiting, waiting as if time had slowed like some kind of space-time continuum. The temperature was rising now and it's just fucking inconvenient when your target package is running late. We just had to lie calmly and wait for him to show. There was no movement now on our part, but the harbour was fully awake and alive with activity. I caught a glimpse of Guns out my left eye, absolute concentration through the scope, eyes like lasers, a bead of sweat running down from his temple and a fly desperately trying to get his attention but to no avail. I could hear the seconds ticking, no wind or breeze just the heat and the time to accompany us. Just as I was starting to feel the first drops of sweat rolling down the small of my back, a car passed the warehouse on the way to the hotel – nice ride, Mercedes, black AMG – Arab, business suit, well dressed, possibly Ahmed, couldn't confirm, photographed.

False alarm.

Waiting, time ticking.

Waiting, breathing.

Waiting, time ticking.

Hot, cramps.

Concentrating.

The heat was rising unbearably, really hot now, uncom-fortable, and we just lay there under a canvas peering through our scopes through the heat haze toward the hotel foyer drop-off area. A sea of heatwaves rose up to meet me and my expectant heartbeat as we waited on our warehouse roof, patiently waiting, expectant, hungry for the kill. The radio earpiece crackled into life: "ETA 15 mins" – this meant the package was now on Route 90 south of Eilat, headed in our direction. I allowed myself a small shuffle of my legs. Guns was just stone. Then he handed me the rifle in exchange for the spotter scope. Total composure, no conversation, no eye contact, it was clear to me this was my sign-off. It was all my responsibility now. I calmly changed the sights to my settings and relocated the target area. I had a solid team behind me, nothing to worry about, all in position to take it all down if I fucked up. *Don't fuck up. For fuck's sake, don't fuck this up.* A split second of thought about getting captured, then silence. I was zoned in now. The noise from the harbour muted, my eyes focused and my mind was totally clear. It's just like just dipping your head under the surface of the water in a swimming pool. No sound, but perfect vision from your goggles, and no distractions.

The Range Rover pulled up to the lobby and there he was, clear as day, Rashid Asadi, long, pristine, sharply pressed white Arab thobe and headdress, holding a soft tan leather suitcase. He had three companions – one I think I recognised and two unknowns, not Mohammed or Ahmed. Looking into his face through the scope now, I recalled the Russian hunting holiday briefly, the cars waiting to take us on holiday. A brief moment of pause. Then Rashid was out of the car, well-groomed, ready for business, perfect Arabian beard, could almost smell the barber's aftershave, confident for a business deal but unaware of the business at hand, finger on the trigger, safety off. Permission to engage. Execute.

Then he was gone, sharp recoil, then reload and that was that. The target area was now engulfed by the timed explosions. I was in the Land Cruiser heading for the border in under five minutes, chaos in the other direction. It was a two-part elimination: sniper shot x 3, followed immediately by controlled explosions. There was nothing left of the target and nothing to see; a clean finish and nothing to come back to. A confirmed kill. And later the photograph of the Arab emerging from the Mercedes was confirmed as Ahmed Haddad.

We then had to rendezvous with Spud in Eilat and then change immediately into new cars – a new plan switched at the last minute by Spud for security purposes – and we were pretty much silent all the way to Haifa, a long drive. Spud had the binmen arranged but I don't think anything came of the mess; all they had to do was clear away the equipment from a drop point in the desert, just a grid ref nothing more, and get the hire cars back. I was back home within 24 hours as if nothing had happened. I flew out of Tel Aviv airport as a tourist, and I guess all the boys were happy with the result. No goodbyes or anything emotional, just a handshake that meant so much more. It was a confidence mission for the Steering Group. I had seen it through under the watchful eyes of Spud and his SBS (Special Boat Service) support team and made the metamorphosis from intelligence agency student to active SIS (Special Intelligence Service) field operative for the Steering Group. I guess this assignment was relatively low risk, but a success nonetheless, and the first is the fucking hardest despite having Spud and his team with me all the way. I still can't separate the picture of Rashid in Israel next to the Range Rover from the picture in my mind of him in Moscow, outside, ready to get in that car for a hunting trip with the family.

I had late leave at home and did nothing except feel the pointlessness of civilian life. The walls in my mind just closed in an inch more on my little life before I was once again released and flew out to the USA to join the *Berwick* in the Caribbean with Spud and a few others from the crew of the *Berwick*. We were now on a Standing Naval Force Atlantic deployment, which translated into a very carefully orchestrated safe and controlled decompression for us. This included an unforgettable tour of all the islands in the Caribbean, including Antigua, Tortola, St Thomas, Cuba, Jamaica, St Lucia and of course Bermuda, with stops in mainland North and South America. It all ended with a trip to Disney World in Florida which was just the most ridiculous place to be after a Middle East op. Spud and I drank a lot and talked a lot on those long five months in the sun away from the circus and where it would take us next. It was perfect decompression, perfectly safe, with Spud carefully watching me process that first kill, conversations not allowed to spin out of control, just Spud's uncompromising positivity to keep me on balance and ready to go do it all again when the time came.

I managed to take some station leave in the States and met a girl call Vicky from Estonia. She was a fat cow really but great fun. Downtime is rare and we drove her Mustang all the way from Baltimore to Key West with a couple of friends, Wally and Buster. Shagged all the way and stayed in shit hotels and drank way too much Yank beer and took in the sights. Life was great; it was like I had it all worked out and managed to erase Israel from my mind. I spent all my wages and then some on ensuring that I had enough good regrets to try and outweigh any future mission regrets, or something like that. I needed a justification for life, and pulling that trigger with a familiar face in the crosshairs makes you see life differently – there's no going back and you can't tell a single soul.

It was whilst we were deployed across the Atlantic that Operation Desert Shield commenced and then quickly developed into Desert Storm in January '91. The ship, myself, Spud and the support team were all on standby for possible deployments, but I wasn't fully trained at that point to go it all alone, so to speak. I remember Spud and I watching the invasion of Kuwait later in August 1991 on CNN from the safety of HMS *Berwick* now steaming full speed back across the Atlantic. I think I was beginning to see the picture side of the jigsaw pieces come together as the arms build-up in Iraq seemed to then gather pace and intensity as intel from the Steering Group went viral. However, it wouldn't be until the Iraq War in 2003 with the invasion of Iraq by a United States-led coalition that overthrew the government of Saddam Hussein that the sheer size of what I had become involved in trying to stop in the Middle East became apparent, not to mention the transfer of arms to Serbia prior to the Bosnian War between 1992 and 1995; it was all much bigger than any individual could have possibly identified at the time.

I think, looking back, if I had been in possession of the Steering Group's wider picture of world developments and all the intelligence showing arms trading and political buy-offs and their inevitable progression into conflict, I'm not sure how well I would have been able to function as an operative keyed into some of the main suppliers of arms. The whole jigsaw remains a puzzle as you never get to see the entire picture, for reasons of security and personal safety, I guess. Spud and I discussed it all and decided it was probably best not to know too much. His time in Ireland had proved that, with some targets now legitimate politicians – how fucked up is the world we live in?

I left the *Berwick* a year or so later and never saw Spud again. Well, not for a long time anyway.

The Steering Group

Chapter 6

Prelude

I made my way across London from King's Cross on a particularly wet and miserable day to make the day's briefing. The London underground is everything I hate about England. A tiny cigar tube overfilled with wet miserable people going to jobs they hate and half of them dying of a cold or flu. It's the rat race personified. I was dressed plainly and needed to be in the Steering Group's briefing room in the old MI5/NIO building on time. Strange to be meeting somewhere different other than Whitehall, which I had nicknamed the oval office as the room allocated to the Steering Group resembled something out of the White House, which Ben had found amusing. I was met outside by David who wanted a coffee off site before we started the day's meetings.

David seemed a little on edge and keen to talk just to me alone. Sometimes only having half the jigsaw puzzle is a blessing and I could see in David what the whole picture looked like. Disturbing, very disturbing. The mission success in Israel was old news now and I think he wanted to bring me up to speed with all the events and developments that had been building since Israel, before the meeting with the other members of the Steering Group. I think, looking back, being a Steering Group operative or agent is like being a clairvoyant, half in, half out; you sort of know where hell is and are allowed a kind of semi-safe passage into the underworld where there's an invitation to do something people would rather not discuss over dinner or in church. It's like being half dead, in that you're either bored to death waiting for the rush of an adrenaline-fuelled mission, or are running the risk of being caught on a mission and facing death if you fuck up. I think David was in the 'bored to death' category that day and was ready to stir shit up.

If the truth be known there was without doubt some serious rivalry and inter-departmental shenanigans between MI5 and the SIS or MI6. The lines between all the services, including Naval Intelligence, or N1, melting into the Steering Group operations were blurred and a little ambiguous to say the least. I don't think the Steering Group gave a fuck; it just wanted everyone to get the results it demanded and all be fucking 'purple' – a new phrase that had crept into the military which actually meant Joint Forces, not blue for navy or green for army; if you worked together you were now all just purple. Someone somewhere was being paid a lot of money to come up with bullshit like that. We worked across all the forces all the time so it wasn't a new concept by any stretch of the imagination. David took me to an old café down a back street a few minutes' walk from the offices. We ordered coffee and sat in the window on a pair of old stools looking out into the street. It reminded me of Moscow and my first brunch with Anatoly in the café window looking out on a snow-covered Moscow. I guess my mind wandered for a while before David managed to voice what he was thinking. I didn't know David too well but I sensed he was really nervous about something. My instincts proved right as he muttered between sips of coffee that the list was out now and the group would issue it today. Asking how I felt and making small talk all seemed a little ridiculous to me but no doubt he had seen the masterpiece that needed to be painted before anyone had been issued their orders. Of course, I would only see my jigsaw-size piece of the puzzle and the colour would without doubt be black. At least black ops were still black ops, I guess, not dark purple or anything crazy. Things had changed so much in my short time working for the group it was as though we all had to learn a new language. It was no longer 'shoot to kill' – this became 'sweep and clear'; 'eliminate the target' became 'removing the problem', etc., etc. It was all becoming politically correct in a world where nothing could ever be remotely related or linked back to such a government department.

We arrived back just in time for our meeting, which was surprisingly very formal. We were in a bland room with overzealous air conditioning; the room was freezing, as if they were trying to preserve something that had died. Cdr Brown, as always, was keen to sit with me and share a cigarette and welcome me back into the fold, asking about my 'holiday' in the States and Caribbean. I'm sure the teams in London were a little jealous of the amount of 'off duty' time field agents appeared to get when they were decompressing or simply off the grid following an op. A lot of water had passed under the bridge since Israel and I was needed again, back on the books. We wasted so much time I think in those meetings; it was as if no one really wanted to say what needed to be said up front but would rather spend three hours trying to make things sound nice or more palatable.

The entire Steering Group was present, plus a few other operatives who had been out gathering or confirming intel from just about every corner of the globe to put the list together and to build the bridge from intelligence whiteboard dream lists to hardcore operations. Anderson, Marcus and Paul all looked exhausted and almost welcomed the lunch break. The briefings were all bulked out with way too much historical shit and irrelevant (in my opinion) background information on those who had been raised up in importance to make it onto the list. Ben was the only one who looked like he had had a night's sleep that month despite flying in from the States late the previous night. We all caught up over lunch and it all seemed very pleasant, eating and drinking as if we were some sort of civilian business team out for a free lunch on the company, all pretending the whole thing was just a business transaction or something more 'normal'.

The afternoon session was short. David brought up the list on the screen, which was followed by mugshots and latest known whereabouts of the 10 most wanted from the Steering Group's Russian-linked intel, now confirmed and identified by three separate sources, including cooperating governments, as being involved in over 16 separate trading routes and illegal international arms and intelligence trading. The web spinning out of Moscow was way bigger than I could have imagined despite any legal statements that had been made from the Kremlin, and my little slice of the cake was only the crumbs from the cake compared to what had been going on elsewhere. Moscow was ground zero, the source; it was the nerve centre for all the other transactions, deals, shipments, arrangements and alliances. Kill the cancer at the source and everything else becomes 'gravy'. Silence had gripped the room as we all sat and contemplated the list.

The List

1. Mohammed bin Shaban Al Zidjali and son Asad in Moscow (Iranian nuclear scientists linked with Syria)
2. Ahmed Haddad (the financier – Saudi Arabian – and wanted by his own government)
3. Alexander Markoff (KGB), organiser and main supplier of all Soviet military arms at the highest levels, both legal and illegal, and through the UK. Linked with Iran, Syria, Eastern Europe and Africa, and of course supported by Erik Pavlovich.

4. Erik Pavlovich (Russian official linked with supplying illegal arms to Iraqi and Serbian generals and Rashid Asadi), party member and linked with the development of the Iranian nuclear programme.
5. Anatoly Pavlovich, nuclear weapons development scientist, Sarov (linked to trading secrets to the nuclear programme in Iran) (also linked with Serbian arms dealing)
6. Evgeny Pavlovich, arms dealer and linked to Serbian and Iraqi WOMD biological
7. Nasser Tamei, Yugoslav arms dealer trading through the USSR with Iraqi and Serbian generals
8. Leon Antunovich – Serbian – warehousing of arms and onward trading to Iraq, Syria and Iran
9. Otto Meiser – Serbian – arms build-up in Eastern Europe and onward supply to the Middle East
10. Dlip Mehrotra – Indian transporter of illegal arms
11. Rolando Hernandez – S. American dealer and funding for arms to the Middle East and Serbia

I don't remember there being much more discussion after the list had been revealed. Marcus simply announced that the list was legitimate and we were authorised (multinationally) to complete all mission assignments in order to eliminate the threat. Each of us was given our orders in plain envelopes and requested to leave all the documents in the room prior to departure for destruction. There was no problem discussing the list with each other prior to departing or asking each member about their role and instructions, but it didn't really happen; we all just shook hands and departed to go our own way. I suppose we all sort of just wanted to get outside and take a breath of London's polluted air to contemplate what had just happened. We all needed to let the information we had just received permeate into our minds and souls and soak up the reality of the tasks ahead. We all had to stay calm and look like it was no big deal, look professional and undisturbed in front of each other as if to offer inner strength by telepathy; but the telepathy was more like: *Fuck, this is BIG shit*. Besides, cigarettes tasted better in the fresh air after such a meeting.

I don't really recall how it felt to see familiar names and faces on the kill list. It was surreal and almost ridiculous to my mind at the time. I even remember making attempts to say or try to convince myself how stupid it was to think that Anatoly, Erik and the family were involved, a rash and passing thought that contradicted the very fact that I was the main source of information that had put their names on the list in the first place. It's all too easy to forget that my role as an operative for the Steering Group wasn't part of the armed forces as such, I was a NOC, non-official cover operative, conducting intel and government work under assumed identities, simply utilising military support as required. I was part of the team but simultaneously alone. I guess that's what made me all the more interesting to the SF guys in so much as I was supposed to be a lone operator with my own agenda but was reliant on their support and tactical abilities. I read my instructions and orders and within the hour was on my way to RM Poole to start my familiarisation and integration with an appointed SF support team which would ensure that the implementation of Operation SEGMEnT (Steering Group Middle East) was a success.

Royal Marines Poole. I have very fond memories of the place and all the guys I teamed up with. It was definitely the real starting point for military operations that were more complex, intense and without doubt carried much higher risk. I was definitely treated differently than I had ever been up to this point. I remember arriving in my new Ford Granada 2.9i Scorpio; it had been fitted with a tracking device and bulletproof glass by friends in the transport division after I had bought it. It was a year old but, fuck me, it was fast as fuck – an armchair ideal for cruising between the south coast, Wales, London and home. The transport division had been granted a sizeable budget to have my personal car upgraded, including the 2.8i V6 chipped engine, and the suspension modified for evasive driving. It was just awesome to drive and without doubt would get me out of any situation that might present itself, however unlikely that may be. The budget stretched, allowing for a few additional toys including an in-car radio telephone that was state of the art at the time and pretty cool as this was before mobile phones had really taken off.

Security was tight on the main gate but without too much of a fuss I was soon shown to my own room which was the best accommodation I had ever been allocated. I hadn't been used to anything quite so comfortable and had only been allocated shared accommodation up until this point. I was met by Paul, who had been waiting; he had come down from London to introduce me to the team I would be working with. He was the real bridge between the Steering Group, UKSF and the 'N1' intelligence operatives such as myself. He had been my backstop for Moscow but I hadn't realised his full role up until now. He was complex in every way but made quick and accurate summaries and directives when chaos consumed others around him. His very presence instilled a confidence that changed the atmosphere instantly. He was deeply into all aspects of the business and had an overview even senior members of the Steering Group envied. Paul knew the difference between a wish list and a reality show, and because Paul adapted to the realities of all assignments he was able to deliver without compromise. It was explained I might not have the same support team all the time but Paul was keen to try and keep me with familiar faces. Intel gathering, infiltration and execution of orders in the Middle East (even with my Russian friends) was proven to be very difficult and needed a good support unit and an extraction team that was very experienced when the shit hit. To be honest I was hoping to avoid any close encounters and do any necessary trigger work from a comfortable distance, like in Israel.

I was introduced to the guys in the hangar in the upper camp in Poole. There were two camps: an upper camp comprising accommodations, offices and hangars; and the lower camp, known as the 'Hard', where the boats section was situated. There was the main fleet of landing craft (LCU – Landing Craft Utility, and LCVP – Landing Craft Vehicle Personnel), together with the SBS patrol, LRIC (Long Range Interceptor Craft) and the FB-Mil-50P engagement craft, with all the associated workshops and naval engineering support staff, etc. Pierre was in the team and I was so pleased to have a familiar face. It was all low-key and it was clear right from the start we were gonna be having a lot of fun together.

So, here I was with the guys from C Squadron, Pierre, Smudge, Cheesy, Phil, Hugh and Baz, all Special Boats, and what a collection of hard bastards who had been brought together to see the job done. The guys were very gracious to welcome me into their world and we spent the whole day just sitting in the hangar on deckchairs, chatting and getting to know each other; nothing about the mission was discussed, come to think of it no one mentioned work at all. Occasionally a few of the guys would kick a ball about or throw a few hoops. Lunch was brought in, muck on a truck delivered by the SNCOs' mess. Sizing me up as a deadweight or as an asset they would go all the way with – who knows what people think of you when you first meet. I'm pretty sure now that this had been their opportunity to accept or reject both me and my accompanying mission package. I don't know what they thought of a young guy like me entering their world; maybe they thought I was a problem waiting to happen, another assignment they had to babysit or endure. The bottom line, however, was that the Steering Group was in such a position to pass requests down the line that couldn't really be refused, such was their influence and position in the halls of power.

From what I learned, despite being specialists in CT (counter terrorism), MTC (maritime counter terrorism), SR (special reconnaissance), OA (offensive action) and all the standard SBS stuff, the guys had other sub specialities or defined skills in which they were considered experts. This could be as many as four sub specialities but was normally one or two. Cheesy was young, thin, blond hair, very clean cut and was always wearing a bright welcoming American-style smile. But underneath that smile was something a little more sinister, and he was a little pugnacious at times; he was our 'chaos' man and our medic (weapons, target acquisition, medic and chaos) with fuck knows how many other ops under his belt. He was sort of a loose cannon, unpredictable in a great way, but I was pleased he was on my side. We got along real well right from the word go and he was joined at the hip with Baz (formerly X Squadron, weapons, demolition and ordnance), a big cunt, greasy black hair and hands like fucking shovels, and without doubt the clever one amongst us. Baz was our bomb building expert. He was always very quiet and well-spoken but could probably crush your skull with one of those shovel-like hands. Baz was a true killer, perfected by practice, a very calm and deadly weapon. Pierre was fun, a sniper, black-role specialist, sabotage and intel-gathering expert. He was French, which always attracted all the piss-taking, but he took it well and was the meat in the whole sandwich and was our guns man. Hugh, an amphibious boats expert, was a fellow linguist and only spoke to me in Arabic; he looked very Middle Eastern but was born and bred in the UK. He had the whole terrorist look weighed off and simply didn't look like he should be with us on a UK military base. Hugh was our trickster and comms man. That left Smudge, who was a short-ass with curly black hair and he was a Scouser, and there was no way he could ever lie his way out of that accent! He was our most talented engineer, with an electrical bias, and he liked to remind us all of his skills on a regular basis, in jest of course. Sniper, medic and submarine expert, he was always interfering with the electrics on Baz's bomb-making efforts. What a team. We now fell under the wing of C Squadron as a sort of specialist unit.

I enjoyed that first day despite being nervous; after all, I was the new boy and an outsider coming into the shadows that would support my work. It was like a marriage of experts. We were being spliced together for the long haul in joint operations. These guys were assigned by the Steering Group to be my protectors and support team in order to ensure that the assignments I had been given were seen through to the bitter end no matter what that end looked like. I spent a few hours with Cheesy that night in the cages going through all the kit that had absolutely no meaning to me whatsoever. It was like a religious ritual – each day the guys would go into the cages, prep their kit, check and re-check. I'm sure I wasn't the only thing on their agenda and it became obvious I needed a lot of training if they were going to take me on in any way.

Just the very fucking next day, day two and 4am, I'm being dragged out of my sky chariot (bed) by Baz and Cheesy, up the stairwell and all the way onto the roof four floors up. Pierre handed me a jumpsuit, hazardous duty life jacket, helmet, knee pads and just smiled at me. Chinook inbound, heavy thudding mechanical thunder growing louder from the twin rotors, back door down and we're boarding the fucking thing off the rooftop of the accommodation. Complete disorientation as the door closed and the cargo bay switched to red light as the Chinook took a series of heavy turns and ascended for a good 20 minutes before levelling out. The guys were all just sitting in the cargo netting as if it were all fucking normal at this time of the morning. They were all just sitting, happily applying cam cream to their faces and blacking themselves out, whilst I'm sitting there still with a *Fuck off, you've got to be kidding* look on my boat race. The guys settled down to eating, smoking and generally messing about. We must have been airborne for over an hour, all the guys pretending to be sleeping now, when the yellow light went on at the back of the cargo bay and the helo ('helo' is the military way of saying helicopter) descended rapidly whilst simultaneously opening the rear door. The noise and wind was as crazy as a Caribbean hurricane, forcing the engine exhaust fumes into the cargo bay as the Chinook manoeuvred and then levelled off. Green light on.

Bastards. Baz and Smudge interlocked arms either side of me as we ran towards the rear door in a threesome, the Chinook doing about 60mph over the water at about 50ft, and out we fucking went. No parachute, no training, just me screaming, in fear and in excitement, the downdraft of the rear rotor blade firing us all down into the water like vertical torpedoes. I was gonna fucking drown. I hit the water like a bullet and went under for about an hour... well, maybe 30 seconds I suppose, my life jacket auto inflated after a short delay (saltwater activated), and bingo, I'm floating in the fucking sea with no idea where the fuck I am and half near dead from all the seawater I had just ingested, coughing my guts up in a half panicked girly state. No idea where the guys are, can't hear anything. Then I can hear a powerboat, RIB (rigid inflatable boat) maybe. Can't see anything, just hear that shit getting closer. All I'm thinking is I'm gonna be a fucking death statistic in a boating accident report.

No time to get upset, the RIB pulls up right on top of me, no lights, dark, cold, wet and totally fucking bewildered, I'm then dragged out of the water. I'm on the floor of the RIB as we accelerate max chat away from the drop point and I'm like a sack of shit on the deck. Can't see the guys' faces, so I'm just holding on for the ride, body bouncing and crashing on the floor of the boat as it navigates the sea swell. Helicopter flies overhead, no lights or fuck all, then I see it land in the water with the back door down, strobe light guiding us in as we fucking drive the RIB right inside the fucking back of the helo. We just went under those rotor blades with inches to spare; I reckon if anyone had stood up they'd have been decapitated, brown bread for sure. A few seconds later and we are all out of the RIB, into the cargo nets, RIB disappears and we are airborne again. White light goes on and every cunt is laughing their tits off at me. So I stood up, took a bow and just collapsed on the deck like a sack of shit. We were all cleaned up and eating breakfast in the mess by 8am. Yep, the fun had started alright.

That had been my first wet jump – and no fucking training at all. Baz told me it was sometimes better not to know what I was gonna be doing or what they had planned for me; besides, they wanted to surprise me. We practised these kinds of manoeuvres of insertion and extraction frequently and it was a fucking blast every time, the guys always wanting to push the boundaries and extend my operating envelope with every exercise whilst raising the risk or fun factor depending on the point of view. The training progressed from jumping out of a Hercules or Chinook over water to a full HALO (high altitude low opening) skydive into Belize, which I have to say was an amazing yet terrifying experience. I'm not sure if some of the training was necessary or even relevant, but I am sure the guys enjoyed taking me out and scaring the shit out of me every time. I guess the fact that I enjoyed it all, embraced their challenges and didn't complain may have gone some way to my being somewhat accepted into their world, if only as a temporary member of the club.

My time at Poole was brilliant. I was a free agent. I had a mission package with timeframes that weren't suffocating, plenty of prep and integration time with the team. The mission was just kept on standby, on the back burner, waiting for the green light to intercept and remove target items 1 & 2, our top-tier targets. Let there be no doubt there was plenty of detailed and careful planning and collaborative work being undertaken by the Steering Group in coordinating the re-introduction of me into the fold with Alex, who had been operating between London, Moscow and Dubai. It wasn't clear if he had been meeting with Mohammed bin Shaban Al Zidjali or Ahmed Haddad in Dubai or if any such meeting had taken place outside of the UAE. There were obviously other jigsaw pieces that needed to be in place before the team and I were put into play.

Correspondence between myself and the Pavlovich family started to ramp up and there was intense pressure and interest from the Steering Group, which aided the wording of all my correspondence, or should I say vetted the wording of my correspondence to get things moving in the right direction. It was obvious the group was looking for a way in. I was communicating fluidly with Anatoly for about four to six months before we had the break I needed. I had been communicating, by snail mail and email, that I had taken a gap year and was travelling seeing the Far East and hoped to extend my travels as much as possible and maybe come back home via Moscow to see my friends and the family.

I had hinted in my correspondence to Anatoly that I may pass back through Moscow, and as a result things started to develop and make way for a path back into theatre. It was around this time that all the lights were turned on, so to speak. Anatoly was jealous and talked often in his emails and letters of his dreams to travel and let slip that Alex and Evgeny had also been travelling a lot and had been away in Italy and Istanbul recently with Erik. Anatoly was upset that the family were taking regular vacations in Dubai with all the family but that he was unable to attend due to his heavy work commitments. He disclosed details of how he was now working for the navy on their nuclear propulsion systems and was excited to share how fascinating his work was, not giving away anything in his letters of course but it was obvious that it was all very intensive. Now that he was actually working in Sarov after he had graduated with honours, his career path seemed already well laid out before him, almost predetermined, which was of serious interest to the Steering Group as there were other communications that had been intercepted between Anatoly and Asad, who was back in Iran. It was such a ridiculous open line of communication into the heart of the lair in which hid the dealers and organisers of illegal arms trades and technical information from Moscow into the Middle East and Eastern Europe. This conduit was the catalyst upon which the Steering Group had pinned their hopes on getting right into the centre of Alex Markoff's world with Mohammed bin Shaban Al Zidjali.

Of course, I had missed Anatoly and Evgeny as friends immensely, and the correspondence was sometimes very deep and personal, probably a little too much in that it revealed my inner feelings which sometimes ran contrary to the mission directive. I often wondered what the Steering Group made of all the chit-chat but I remembered Spud's words of wisdom and how he had dealt with the whole Northern Ireland family he had lived with and loved so much. His surrogate family had been henchmen for the IRA and had so much blood on their hands, when you bring the truth into the conundrum it's easier to refocus. I had to remain focused. I don't think it would have been possible to have undertaken a second mission trip into the Moscow group if I hadn't developed some personal and lasting relationships. The official line to be toed was to just observe and record whilst not being noticed; this was fine on paper but once you're in as deep as I had become, the truths and the lies had to run equally as deep to avoid detection. There are a lot of contradictions in the policy, training and reality of the experiences and expectations in espionage work.

I think as long as you succeeded, were never compromised, a blind eye was turned on such domestic issues and personal attachments. This was always going to be a point of contention between an operator and his handlers.

I remember there had been a number of delays in the development and coordination of the mission, and I had drifted a little into a dull routine, keeping the communication conduits alive whilst keeping up with all the training and personal development with the guys from the squadron. It was intended that I complete a training package that the team had put together and tailored to my needs at the earliest opportunity and not be idle, so to speak, during this long pre-mission gestation. I was frustrated as always and wanted to bring things forward, but I had to be reminded by Cdr Brown and the Steering Group that there were other pieces on the chessboard that needed to move first. The planets had to align, and the collaboration with other governments and their intelligence organisations needed to be carefully choreographed to avoid a diplomatic disaster or a complete fuck-up in the coordination, execution and timing of the Steering Group's mission plan.

The team and the Steering Group met in Poole to discuss and outline the tactics that were in play to see Operation Segment concluded successfully. It was shaped into an interesting collection of strategies deployed in different regions with separate operations running simultaneously but autonomously. The overall idea was aimed at reducing the actual on-ground requirements in the build-up to any deployment by subduing the 'enemy' by making life really difficult without actually fighting. The word 'enemy' brings up some sort of defined group or nation in your mind with whom we as a nation had declared war. However, in this closed world of the Steering Group, enemy simply meant anyone or any group the politicians couldn't do business with. It can never be too defined, as today's enemy is more than likely tomorrow's ally, and vice versa. Our enemies are very rarely the kind of people who fly a flag and have a voting public.

Make no mistake, the biggest, perhaps most powerful weapon in any conflict is intelligence. Our operations would see minimum input by the smallest of teams for the biggest result. Our disruptions were intended to force a capitulation of the greater forces away from the bigger battle. That battle being for Israel, the race for nuclear technology in the Middle East, and Iran's play to become a nuclear superpower over Saudi Arabia, which equally supported and denied it, depending on who you wanted to believe. I guess the team and I had only to realise that we were but a small part of the bigger regime and were just instruments in a delicate operation who needed to tread ever so carefully in what we did, stopping the flows of weaponry and information in certain directions whilst avoiding initiating a global heart attack and creating a political meltdown or all-out war.

Don't ask too many questions and you don't need to worry as much, was Smudge's point of view. Hmmm, I suppose he was right, but we all needed to know that what we were doing was right, for our own sanity. Once we had that in our heads then the enemy could truly be our solemn enemy and good would prevail through our fervent desire to get the job done, or some bullshit like that. I think, looking back, it's a human need to just know what you're doing is right. So you can justify it. So you can cope with it later in life when you learn that maybe it might all have been a bit questionable. If you were to shine a spotlight on it or put it all under the public microscope years later, would you be able to blame someone else or truly defend your actions? That's where my mind wandered to when the team and I sat and planned for Operation Segment.

We stepped back from all the politics, we had to – it was driving me mad and was unproductive. We settled back into our relaxed state of readiness, our pre-op way of life, and were stood down in order to make the most of our free time. I took up their ad-hoc training programme wholeheartedly and did all I could to fit in and meet their expectations. To fail everything miserably, which may have been the intention all the while, would have spelled disaster in all camps. I can only speak from my experience as an intelligence operative, not a para or commando – I was never one of those boys. I can't even begin to imagine what they went through to be selected into the squadron. I fitted into their training programme as they saw fit. I wasn't selected and neither did I apply for any of this training, and I know that the SF teams rarely took on intelligence operatives or allowed them into their teams entirely. I guess their training package was a rite of passage in order to be assigned an SF support team – you had to earn that team's approval, or something like that. Fuck knows, I was N1 and the guys were tasked to take me all the way with my assignment. How they put us together remains a mystery, but I was pleased to know who I had watching my back as I played out the Steering Group's pantomimes.

This ad-hoc training programme was mostly conducted down south but with a few trips out of town, so to speak. If the all-arms course and the Green Beret thing was tough (and I now know I didn't do the whole thing), this shit was definitely the *agoge* of all military training. The training programme they had designed for me was an intense cultivation of loyalty, honour, discipline and mind control through intellectual adjustment, all delivered in nothing but the most unusual and most demanding of circumstances they thought I could withstand, to refine the subject into a *proxenos* for the nation, uncontrolled but at the same time controlled, a reactive component in a larger, much more complex disciplined machine.

The training included but was not limited to:

- Extensive diving techniques and maintenance
- Evasive driving
- Speed marching and endurance runs
- Jungle training
- Arctic training
- Language skills
- Middle Eastern culture and desert training
- Parachuting practice – HALO/wet jumping
- Demolition methods
- Infiltration of ships and oil platforms
- Canoeing skills
- Survival training in the wilds of Dartmoor, the Black Mountains and Wales
- Beach reconnaissance, including photography skills
- Maritime counter-terrorism activities
- Advanced weapons handling
- Submarine infiltration, escape and capture
- Concealment
- Interrogation training – both as the interrogator and the captive

I enjoyed the training and all the camaraderie of the group immensely; they were great guys and had my best interests and safety at heart. Looking back, I guess they needed me to see the whole thing through in order to play almost as an equal. I was a link the security forces needed and one the Steering Group wanted to use but was not yet fully integrated with the bag of hammers they wanted me to work with. Although I was very much a standalone asset, I felt a part of the team, and over time I think they took me in. I was well under their wings, I guess, after just a few months. Being very different to them somehow made me all the more interesting to them, and the fascination went both ways. I enjoyed being the centre of attention, to be honest, and having one-on-one training. It was mutually beneficial to have the team destroy me and rebuild me in so many different ways. From sitting in the mud of the Solent with a telegraph pole, up to my waist in mud, to jungle training, the team knew my weaknesses and strengths without any doubt. Yeah, I made for a good toy, but one they could trust and a toy they knew the strengths and weaknesses of. I think after spending so much time with them they actually wanted me to succeed in my assignment and, between them, secretly decided I was worth the effort.

It was my next assignment with the group that really tuned me in to developing a skill set that would be useful, and I was sent to complete the advanced evasive driving course, which involved almost unachievable timed transits using public roads and motorways whilst pursuing or being pursued by what could only be described as crazed drivers who were perhaps related to the Stig (from *Top Gear*). Such urban racing exploits usually ended in a dockyard, abandoned warehouse complex or deserted military base, with a counter-terrorism exercise to complete the training, and this was sometimes done with live ammo. I started out driving 3.0ltr Vauxhall Senator armoured cars at speed on main artery motorways with the Yorkshire and Humberside police driving units. They were great guys and I totally fucked it up a few times causing some serious damage to the cars. I eventually upgraded all the way to chipped Audi V8s, and I can now understand why those fucking idiot kids go out joyriding or do doughnuts on the street. There should be a skid pan in every town to let young lads get it out of their system, it's a great laugh.

After passing the evasive and advanced driving courses, I teamed up with a few of the close protection teams on occasion, to run VIPs about; it actually attracted extra pay and helped with a shit roster no one actually liked doing. I personally thought it was an okay job to do in my spare time, or more often than not in company time. Yeah, there were some stuck-up passengers but some were genuine enough to hold a decent conversation with me, which helped on the longer drives. I drove dignitaries, world leaders and some royalty all over the country. It was an interesting pastime, to be sure.

More than anything for some months we were killing time, but the guys were persistent in pushing me along; I was their little project. I ended up undertaking survival training after an extended field skills course which included a number of different training grounds including a trip to Belize for jungle training that lasted just over a month. I was transferred to the British Army Training Support Unit Belize (BATSUB), which is located at Price Barracks, approximately nine miles outside Belize City. We had nicknamed it 'bathtub' for obvious reasons. Insertion was into Belize by a HALO jump from 12,000ft and all the guys were up for it and came along to have a laugh at my expense I'm sure. HALO involves jumping from a very high altitude, only opening the chute at the last moment above the hard deck. The idea is to exit the plane, at night, above visual range of enemy on the ground and then open the chutes at low altitude, thus minimising the time spent suspended below a slowly descending canopy, which makes you a fucking target, and avoid any radar detection. The jumper sometimes has to wear oxygen breathing apparatus as the air is too thin at high altitudes. Keeping a stable freefall posture whilst laden down with a bergen (backpack), oxygen bottles, weapons and the parachute strapped to one's back is a nightmare. Yeah, it's the best adrenaline fix in the world.

In Belize City I would frequent a number of watering holes with Baz and Cheesy who had come along to assist with the training staff. The local sport was hot-coin throwing, which should be given a special mention at a child protection group or something. In downtown Belize a lot of the bars are on the first floor so patrons can sit on balconies away from the dust of the street. The local scumbags would heat up coins whilst holding them in a pair of pliers with a Zippo lighter before tossing them into the street below. Local kids, half-starved and homeless, would run out to collect the coins. The locals would count the number of times the child would toss the coin because of its heat before they were run over by a car. There was a lot of alcohol and gambling in this sport which would have most Westerners running to complain about human rights or something. What I found crazy was the drivers would make every effort to avoid hitting all the land crabs but almost no effort to avoid a child. Baz and Cheesy just looked on and enjoyed a cold beer and filled me in on some history of jungle warfare going back to the days of the Claret Operations in Malaysia and the Far East. Having a few wets with the boys was just perfect for me, I was starting to feel accepted. Feet up, cold beer after doing something high octane was like a drug. Just fuelling up for the next high. It was addictive to be with these guys.

Belize was an interesting episode and one I won't forget in a hurry. To plunge yourself into the mercy of a rainforest in which every living creature wants to eat you to some degree or another is nothing short of insanity. Just to stand still in the jungle is exhausting, and to do anything physically demanding is almost debilitating. The jungle is like a crawling humid sultry darkness that gets under your skin at every opportunity. The heat, humidity and sheer bloody mindedness of the jungle gets at you and can drive you literally insane. Rainforest it may be but you were always wetter on the inside from sweat than from any rain that might pour in to ruin your day. Belize jungle isn't all enclosed dark spaces, there are large open spaces, but you quickly welcome the shade of the rainforest canopy after a few hours out in the searing heat. The jungle is disorientating, full of wonderful disease opportunities and is actually a good place to prepare before going into the desert. If you can put up with Belize, the desert is a walk in the park by comparison in my opinion. Let me assure you, there's no real difference between light jungle and heavy jungle, it's all fucking jungle and you have to either survive it or become part of it.

It's such a difficult place to survive in and, like being on the ocean, can be a hard place to find something actually worth eating, plus water isn't as available as you may think. There were a lot of lessons to be learnt in that dark cupboard of nature, and some painful ones at that. Let's be honest, you have to wait until you're absolutely exhausted to get any sleep as there's no way any sane man is going to sleep voluntarily with the entire ugly bug ball crawling into every orifice you have whilst snakes are inventing their own way to attack you from above and below. Building a suspended hammock is tiresome and no defence against any jungle inhabitant.

Then there are the leeches to whom height doesn't seem to be an obstacle, as if they just teleport onto you from nowhere. I definitely could have done without those slimy things heading toward my private bits. Black widows, bull ants, brown recluse spiders, poison dart frogs and endless sea and land snakes make for an Indiana Jones adventure that you seriously might not actually survive. Then when you allow your mind to lapse just for a second in the dusky tranquillity of the forest, it's immediately broken by a flash of flying colour from a hummingbird that scares the shit out of you, or a howler monkey sounding like its being murdered. There's no real training by the staff; they don't need to do much, tell you how to deal with it all – the jungle does the training on its own and no one needs to tell you how fucking dangerous it is or what to look out for as the whole fucking place is dangerous and you need to be looking out for anything that's moving or has the potential to move, which means it's hungry. The staff do of course spend time teaching you how to survive in the jungle; there's a few tricks up their sleeves when it comes to finding clean water, food, how to build a shelter, when to travel and when to rest, a complete education in predators and how to use comms.

The government of Belize had graciously allowed and opened up 5,000 sq miles of jungle to the British Army for such training – bastards! The guys themselves did give up a lot of time to share some great skills, alongside the resident army staff: reconnaissance skills, working with the locals, foraging, water collecting, how to keep your fucking socks dry, the list is endless. I learnt how to paddle a canoe down mosquito-infested waterways whilst avoiding local traps, how to haul my ass out of the water up mud banks like a crocodile up a slippery earth travellator, and how to be thoroughly despondent, exhausted and on the brink of despair and share a laugh with an equally insane person standing next to you, whilst secretly ignoring your situation, simply storing the experience mentally as a living nightmare.

The end of jungle training really is a kick in your nuts. Starving, dehydrated and half mad from the lack of sleep and paranoia that something is eating you, they terminate your training by walking your ass over 50 miles of crazy terrain, which is like the Black Mountains on forest steroids, to a rendezvous point where you are greeted by the staff holding a beautiful white bunny rabbit for each trainee. Kill and eat it and you're through and it's home for tea and medals; if not, you do the whole walk again in reverse or it's game over and you're out the programme. The chances of successfully repeating the hike are almost zero, so that fucking rabbit tasted like fucking prime steak, cooked up with worm chips and some other fucking brown thing that was crunchy. Killing the bunny was enough to make grown men cry. However, it has to be said that the environment created by the people I was training with, coupled with the unpredictability of day-to-day operations in Belize, is part of what made it all so exciting and ultimately satisfying, and without that challenge I wouldn't have remembered it as I do today.

The team was happy to celebrate my completion of the training and we enjoyed a weekend in Cartagena, Columbia, drinking too much and kicking back, followed by a week in Aruba R&R before putting our serious heads back on for the trip home. It was good bonding that needed to happen, and I was completely enamoured by being a part of the team. The sense of belonging and loyalty that grows amongst such a close-knit team when pushing the boundaries is priceless, and it's a prelude to working together under fire in theatre. It's a drug – you just want more and more. You can't package it or build an individual course, it has to happen over time, a lot of time together, through various adversities, be it in military roles, private lives or just personal experiences shared to become more familiar with each other to the point of assimilation. You can't do it nine-to-five, you have to eat, sleep and shit together, do life together until you become brothers, sharing all your shit bits as well as all your skills and attributes. The bond that is created is tested of course, but you know it won't break because you would rather die than fail your brother. We were all becoming brothers.

It's always the good things you remember the most, and the exercises, training and fun times we had as a group before we finally deployed were awesome, to say the least. We spent endless days going over protocol, procedures, lost-contact drills, rendezvous methodology, navigation exercises and of course my briefings of the people we would ultimately be dealing with and the Steering Group's demands and mission statements. At weekends we would either head off home or be involved with other ops, but I remember one weekend the guys had arranged for an R&R weekend over to the Channel Islands and they had commandeered a Mk 5 LCU, or landing craft. The landing craft was well and truly loaded up with beer, beer, more beer, BBQ meat by the ton and some more beer. It was signed off as a diving and canoeing expedition but that definitely translated into a fun weekend. Once loaded up we departed from Poole on a Friday lunchtime and headed across the Channel. I was I/C of the engines, which to be honest I hadn't got a clue about, and Pierre took the helm as skipper. We had a reasonable crossing of around six hours, then spent Friday afternoon and evening anchored in a bay called Le Dos d'Ane. It was a beautiful bay with high-sided cliffs offering plenty of shelter from any weather but totally secluded to allow us to enjoy some privacy whilst we were let loose to enjoy ourselves.

Before the first beers were open we all opted to go diving together and catch lobster. Sark is famous for its lobster and the local fishermen sell it straight to the local restaurants. We had the whole sea garden at our disposal. We simply lowered the landing ramp down to water level and stepped off into an undersea supermarket. I was loving every minute of it. Cheesy was like a fucking sea lion and came up with a dozen good-sized lobsters within 15 mins and a full net bag of scallops. I think the rest of us just looked on in amazement at the seafood platter that Cheesy was singlehandedly putting together.

I loved the diving. I don't hold any qualification, the lads taught me in a swimming pool and then in Studland Bay, usually in the evenings to get used to swimming in the dark. It was nothing compared to the crystal-clear waters of the Channel Islands, which offered such an amazing experience and created such fond memories. We lit a fire on the beach and ate and drank the night away as friends away from the demands of the military. Time in Sark didn't count for anything that night, the clock had been turned off, the time was free. We were like family wrapped up in our comfort blanket of each other's good company and safety, the outside world banished from our private function.

We sailed the next morning and made the tide into Guernsey, which is a good thing as there is a tidal drop of about 33ft – that's about 10m! So, we berthed alongside and Pierre remained on board whilst the guys took me out on my first real piss-up with them. I don't remember fuck all after the first few hours, and I must have had an amazing evening because I woke up in the hospital the next morning to a very disgruntled nurse who threw the local newspaper at me after she had completed her checks. Apparently, I had been rescued by the fire brigade in the early hours of the morning from the mud down in the harbour.

Not really aware of the tidal drop, I had simply stumbled back to the boat expecting to find it as I had left it alongside the jetty in town. Of course, the tide had gone out and our little landing ship was sitting on the mud 10m below the jetty. Too pissed to realise, I had stepped off the jetty, fallen, bounced off the fibreglass canopy and then down into the mud. Pierre later described it to me like he had watched a sack of spuds fall off the jetty which bounced off the boat and into the mud. Unfortunately, the tide was on the turn and I was unconscious and about to drown where I lay. Fire brigade, big fuss, and now there I was the next morning in the hospital with a very sore shoulder that had been dislocated from the fall. What a headache!

I made it back on board that Sunday to get us back across the Channel to Poole. Fucking engine problems on the way over and I had a fire on the port engine caused by the shaft brake inadvertently locking onto the V drive, which was glowing red hot when a split injector pipe decided to spray diesel right onto the red-hot brake disk. There was an instant fire with a beautiful arc of flame back to the engine following the jet of high-pressure fuel from the holed injector pipe. I had to shut it all down in a hurry and then I fucked around with it for a few hours and was about to give up when Pierre commented that unless it was fixed soon and the port engine was back on line we would be back in Guernsey in four hours as we were doing four knots into a six-knot tide and going backwards. The weather was getting up to about a force 4 to 5 so we were going backwards, and fucking landing craft are shit in a swell – they roll around like a sick cow because they are flat-bottomed.

I looked like a chimney sweep having dealt with the fire, leaving the engine room completely sooted out from all the thick black smoke. I was totally exhausted and still a little high from the pain relief given to me for my shoulder and strangely wasn't too worried or even overly concerned at the mess the boat was in. I managed to fix the whole thing up and get it running again, which saved the day. We arrived in Poole in the early hours of Tuesday to a very upset engineer who ran the boats threatening to have my neck in a noose for all the damage caused, not that any of it had been my fault, plus I had spent my own money fixing issues that had arisen on the voyage over. We were a day late getting back after suffering all manner of setbacks, including the weather, and various people weren't too happy, but that's life. We did our best and got shit sorted.

To escape the whole military upset I had caused in the normal running of the hard and RM Poole, including that very upset boats chief and his disgruntled repair team, the guys had arranged for me to go out and complete the remainder of their training package, including the infamous 'fox and hounds' hunt. Cheesy wanted to do it with me all the way, which I thought was cool; I think he wanted to go deeper into my psyche, get into my brain perhaps – who was this guy and what's he like when everything has gone to shit? So, I was off again for a month away being crazy with the unit and it all sounded like a bit of a laugh. I think the lifeblood of the SBS is to be tasked, and if they're not tasked they will task themselves in order to remain at their peak, so I don't think there was ever a time when we didn't have something to do, and if there was spare time it was filled pretty quickly, and the guys wanted nothing more than to accompany me, push me and train me at every opportunity. I do suspect that at first it was all self-preservation – they had to support me in my missions for the Steering Group – but by training me to their standards I wouldn't be such a dead weight in the field; they didn't want an intelligence operative passenger, they wanted an integrated team member with multiple skills. Sure, they had their own agendas and self-interests. As did I.

Three memories come to mind during that last few months before we deployed: the dark room which I thought was just a piss-take at my expense but was actually an introduction to room entry & clearing; and then there was the fox and hounds hunt; and finally the submarine insertion and Arctic training.

The Dark Room

The dark room was/is an exercise for gaining access into a room containing hostiles and friendlies, engaging the right targets and covering all angles, all in a matter of seconds, and is a demanding challenge. The dark room is a building within a hangar. Think Iranian Embassy siege 1980 and you're along the right train of thought. The building is a two-storey house with walkways around each level and escape doors. Room entry is always done in teams, with each member given a spe-cific arc of fire and path through a room. When room clearing, each operator must not only shoot the terrorist but must avoid hitting hostages or other team members. This requires extreme levels of concentration and discipline, which is why the tech-niques are practised over and over until they become second nature.

Looking back, it was just a test of one's nerve, and of course it's always funny when I look back. Basically, the staff asked me to sit on a stool and not move. This guy asked me this about a dozen times, emphasising the need to remain on the stool. Stay still and whatever happens do not get off the stool, repeated and repeated again. Blindfolded, doors closed on the house, then you just sit and wait patiently on a stool in a dark room. How hard could it be? Then all fucking hell breaks loose, thunder flashes, endless release of ammunition, smoke grenades, tear gas, completely deaf at the end of it, but still holding on to that fucking stool. Eyes and nose streaming, snot everywhere from the gas, then the lights go on. Blindfold removed and the double safety doors are opened to a rugby line-up of the lads all in black with their respirators on, laughing their tits off at you. They were laughing because as soon as I stood up I felt the shit run down my leg. Everyone shits themselves apparently. I smiled and laughed my way to the shithouse to get changed, passing all the staff and simply whispering, "Didn't get off the fucking stool though, did I?" Then I swapped positions and became a siege team member with some other poor cunt sitting on the stool, and so it went on.

Fox and Hounds

There are many scenarios, and I've played a hound a few times, but for my first experience I was put out on Dartmoor late at night, dropped off by Land Rover, me and Cheesy with bags over our heads, then kneeled down in the mud at the side of a track, bags removed and then the tie wraps from our hands cut. I had nothing but a plastic mac, no shoes or any clothing, and Cheesy had a blanket and was bollock naked. I laughed at Cheesy, I remember him laughing and saying, "Let's see if you're laughing this time tomorrow." Now, we had about an eight-hour head start on the RM detachment that were the hounds. There were at least 20 of them out hunting us two idiots, not much of a contest really. Wasn't long before it rained and we were struggling not having any footwear. We stuck to following a stream for about four to six hours and did well to get to a farm that would otherwise have been hidden had we not followed the stream as it was in a depression in the landscape surrounded by tall mature pine trees.

Carefully we broke in and stole enough clothing to give us a fighting chance to make it to an extraction point that we had memorised prior to the exercise. Now, I'm sure the occupiers of this farm were well used to people breaking in and being part of the military exercises in the area and were hopefully well compensated. The farmer and his wife just sat on their settee and offered us a cup of tea and asked us to make sure we closed any gates. What the fuck?! None of this shit phased me in any way; my time at DECAF was training enough, especially having been a runner for the BUL's. So, I had a better chance than most of succeeding, plus there was no way Cheesy was gonna allow himself to be caught early days – he had a reputation to maintain. Usually it's all over within 8-12 hours. Cheesy and I managed 38 hours and 42 minutes of being out on the moors.

We were out on the run, in freezing cold shit weather, hunted by tireless marines, dogs and endless searchlights which appeared from every angle, cutting off every route and track we had chosen. Eventually we were surrounded and well and truly captured. Interrogation followed, with a three-day sleepless nightmare unfolding before me but one that the training teams in Wales had more than prepared me for. Before long we were back in the bar in Poole laughing about the whole deal. Cheesy had been one of my interrogators and was pretty cool in my mind after that. It was a double mindfuck well played out. My earlier training had definitely set it all up to be more of a recap than anything new. Cheesy became quite close to me after the interrogation. I've no idea what he had asked me but whatever had been revealed seemed to appease him in some way as to me being on the team.

Arctic Training

Now, contrary to what I ever thought I knew about the SBS, they fucking love submarines. I on the other hand hate the fucking things. We were all set to practise a range of launch and recovery methods from surfaced and submerged subs in the North Western Approaches and complete the training by boarding HMS *Triton* in Devonport, sail under the ice flows in the North Pole region and then conduct Arctic training.

We boxed up all our kit in the hangar at Poole and headed off to Portsmouth to undertake 'tank' training. I couldn't go to sea on a sub until I had completed the tank. The facility, which was located at Fort Blockhouse, Gosport, opposite HMNB Portsmouth, consisted of a water column with a single escape chamber (as fitted to some classes of RN submarines) mounted at the base, through which students can conduct a fully representative escape cycle from 100 feet (30m), closely replicating actions which would be required if forced to abandon a distressed submarine from depth. The 'tank' has been a rite of passage for all RN submariners and anyone wanting to go to sea on a sub, which included us crazy motherfuckers. Training includes ascents from increasing depths, but in addition is underpinned by lectures and practical training in how to survive within a disabled submarine, operation of emergency equipment and survival techniques on reaching the surface – a package of potentially lifesaving skills that had my attention right from the very start.

I remember that first time in the lower chamber waiting to be drowned. I was undertaking the training with four others who were potential 'sludge mariners', all looking equally terrified. You're hooked up to an air supply simulating the onboard life-support system whilst the chamber is slowly filled with water. It's just as the water level reaches your neck that the panic hits, but for the sake of appearance you give a thumbs-up out the window toward the instructor as the water goes over your head and then exit the chamber and ascend the tower. Once released from the lower chamber you need to be breathing out at a steady flow to avoid your lungs exploding. You do a test in a compression chamber equal to a depth of 200ft, then to the tank. Two ascents from 30ft and one from 60ft and finally one from the submarine simulation at 100ft. On reaching the surface you had to remain standing for four minutes to ensure you hadn't developed an air embolism, but it was comforting to know there was a decompression chamber on site.

Training for 'sludge mariners' as we called them was two days; my training was compressed into a day as I had to complete the BOSIET (Basic Offshore Safety Induction and Emergency Training) training as well, which was a civilian ticket allowing transit to offshore platforms. It's basically a good dunking in a swimming pool simulating a helicopter ditch scenario at sea, followed by more sea survival training. The SBS are responsible for the security of Britain's offshore interests so I guess I got the whole package. We enjoyed a night out in old Pompey in what became one of my favourite pubs, The Dolphin, before heading off to Guz to pick up our boat.

It was a cold wet morning in Plymouth and we arrived at the dockyard gates at Camels Head in two Ford Transit vans and were welcomed aboard by the XO who was waiting at the security checkpoint. Driving past various frigates moored in Weston Mill, I remembered my time at sea on the *Gainsborough*, the *Berwick* and the *Deptford*. This would be an entirely different experience. Boarding the boat was achieved by descending a long gangway onto the exposed outer casing through which watertight hatches took us through the outer casing and into the pressure hull. It was like descending into a motorised coffin. We were met by the captain and then allocated our bunks, which were all fibreglass cradles in the forward torpedo room. I was gonna be sleeping on top of a fucking live torpedo, which didn't make for a good night's sleep in any way, shape or form but it was my own bunk and one I didn't have to share, unlike so many of the crew. The *Triton* was a T-Class nuclear hunter killer sub, carrying Spearfish torpedoes and Tomahawk cruise missiles.

Although a nuclear submarine is significantly bigger than its diesel electric predecessors, make no mistake, it felt just as claustrophobic in that nuclear cigar tube as it probably did on the old diesel boats. The passageways were very narrow, hindered by electrical boxes, damage-control gear, BA lockers and fire reels, with any headroom significantly lowered by the endless cabling and systems pipework. Submarines are without doubt man's singular most destructive masterpiece of high-tech technology, delivered silently by stealth. The very fact that the boat itself is only limited by the endurance of the crew demonstrates the full intention of its designers. I was fascinated.

We sailed mid-afternoon to a pre-determined set of coordinates to submerge the boat. I can't begin to describe what it is like; it's best left to those who have earned their dolphins to describe how it feels to go under the water with a nuclear reactor burning away just metres from the open ocean. There are a lot of new sounds and motions that accompany the descent into the abyss; it's like flying an aircraft blindfolded, as the plainsmen react to the coxswain's orders to give a down bubble as the boat descends like an aircraft searching for the runway. Submarines glide and bank around corners, and once deep enough are relatively free from the effects of the ocean waves above, giving relief from any seasickness. I remember standing in the control room with the captain and asking how deep we would go, and he replied simply, "Very deep." To demonstrate the depth we were to descend to, he ordered a rope to be attached to each watertight door fore and aft of the control room and made taut by way of a Spanish windlass. That rope was as tight as a solid pole but by the time we reached the ordered depth was so slack the rope was actually touching the deck. Fuck, we were deep.

The captain put the boat through many drills on that voyage, some tedious and some very interesting, simulating any and every malfunction and failure that was possible. The drills became more and more complex and ran progressively, making life aboard unpredictable and very tiring. I spent almost all of my spare time with the engineers in the control room learning everything I possibly could from the chief of the watch and all the available manuals and operating procedures for the nuclear reactor. The chief of the boat was brilliant and spent many, many hours teaching me all the background theory and knowledge that I needed in order to pass the theory exams towards a Cat 1 licence and to hopefully be able to hold a valid conversation with either Alex or Anatoly when we next met. Once I had completed the Cat 1 theory I was put through my paces as COW (chief of the watch) to complete a series of multiple breakdown and emergency drills, operating the reactor, its control systems and all the auxiliary machinery. It was incredibly draining learning all the operating procedures and SOPs (standard operating procedures) which had to be executed exactly as in the operating BRs (books of reference). It included complete failure of the plant, testing my ability to restart the entire systems from a near dead critical state. Additionally, we as a standalone team had our own drills and exercises to run which were very carefully planned into the boat's otherwise hectic regime through the XO and approved by the captain. It made for a very busy and challenging transit to our exit point.

HMS *Triton* and USS *Portland* rendezvoused at the North Pole. It was quite an historic event by all accounts for both the US and the United Kingdom to have two subs rendezvous at the North Pole. The team and I went over to the USS *Portland* to meet with Paul who had decided to meet us in theatre, so to speak, and we enjoyed a smoke and a brandy on the conning tower of the *Portland*, almost free from the world beneath us. Looking over at the *Triton* we noticed how many acoustic tiles she had lost on the voyage, probably due to the cold or scraping on the ice. The submarines remained on the surface for 24 hours during which the crews played a cricket match which was simply a ridiculous thing to witness. There were some complaints from the Yanks about the failing light which was hindering their game, but it was soon pointed out that the sun hadn't actually set in months so the complaints were very politely overturned. The team and I left the subs and headed out onto the ice to our rendezvous point to complete my Arctic training, including an ice-hole plunge, before flying out on a US supply plane back to Brize Norton via Norway.

We were back in Poole exhausted but also exhilarated by our time on the sub and all aware and carefully watching the events unfolding in Kuwait, but it was after a regular day of fucking around down the hard with the RIBs that I was called into the adjutant's office and given the official deployment notice from London. I would deploy with the guys and an RM detachment to Diego Garcia (DG) for insertion into Dubai. The planets had aligned and it was all set. I was gonna have a two-week holiday in Dubai with Alex and Evgeny on my 'gap' year and hopefully set up the team for a successful elimination of the top two on the Steering Group list: Mohammed bin Shaban Al Zidjali and Ahmed Haddad. Alex's trips to Dubai were becoming so frequent that it was obvious to all in the doughnut that there were more than just holidays occurring. I needed to reinstate my presence within the family and then ensure Alex had no need of a return trip to the Middle East.

Before we departed Poole, the mess had arranged a regimental dinner. This was my first and only true mess dinner with all the guys, including a few guests from overseas and London. A mess dinner is a truly grand affair and is conducted with the utmost respect and detail to tradition. Best mess silver, battle honours, flags, finest linen tablecloths and napkins, bone china and fine crystal glasses. Each placement is perfectly measured as if all the regiment were royalty, and on each place a name plate with your medals and commendations copied for a souvenir of the dinner. There is always a master of ceremonies, two VIP guests, usually one member of the Royal Family (or the PM) and a guest from another service.

Mess dinners always came with beautiful menus, equally amazing food (usually five courses) and impeccable white-glove service, followed by slurred speeches and toasts to Her Majesty. There is no leaving the table, you are simply not allowed a bathroom break unless the adjutant or the VIP decides they need to go. It can get messy. Port is passed and the decanter NEVER leaves the table, and if you are caught breaking any protocol or tradition you are fined a bottle of port or a barrel of beer for the men. Once all the courses are served, you are finally allowed to 'ease springs' and get slaughtered. The rest I'll leave to your imagination.

These social occasions just highlight the brotherhood and comradery of it all. The drinking and the socialising are a glue that holds and binds a team together. It allows all the team to be as one. That's why if you're ever fortunate enough to attend a mess dinner you'll see some ridiculous sights. Grown men naked, dressed up as women, singing, dancing together or even fighting. It's not because they're gay or fucked up, it's because they are a family of impregnable brothers closed off to outsiders. Hidden in the silliness or weirdness of this bonding is a fight that lives inside each and every one of us. It can spill out because all of the guys have a battle inside them that is like a demon which they love and tend to. They keep it in a cage, prod and annoy it, like to hear it and fight it. The demon is a loud and annoying motherfucker. But we save the demon for the loudest of fights, the ones that attract gunfire, explosions and death. We all invite that demon to those fights because we want to know we can take our demon into the depths of hell, a place we cannot go alone, in order to know we can return; it's our own demons within that take us and bring us back from war.

Chapter 7

Operation Segment

So, there I was ready to go on the 'holiday' and a mission which would be entirely dependent upon my reintegration and successful acceptance back into the family after such a long period of absence. Adding to this were the complexities of a lengthy, very detailed and carefully choreographed training and correspondence period which I was glad was over and which had changed me, a change I needed to be personally aware of when I met Anatoly again. To write by hand and have mail, postcards and gifts sent from countries I had never even set foot in had been a mission in itself; the teams had worked long and hard with me, and I think the support teams in Wales and all those at GCHQ were more accepting of me now that the Russian sector was getting more serious. The stage had been set, rehearsals completed and the pantomime was ready for its audience. My passport looked pretty impressive and I hadn't even left Blighty yet. I just remember getting my No. 2 passport in the orders envelope and just smiling as I flicked through the well-travelled pages.

There was a massive emphasis from the Steering Group for me to get further under the skin of the Russian organisation and into the Middle Eastern connections, linking them to the developing Bosnian crisis, and to go deeper into their confidence. The possibilities of potential terrorist activity and involvement between the government transactions and the illegal piggy-backed transactions to support the Bosnian War were becoming more evident, especially due to the Russian support to the Serbs. The Steering Group was keen to link Russia with such illegal activities and transgressions against the UN and identify movements, travel details, new associates and what was being purchased or exchanged, particularly information exchanges, before termination of any targets. Details, details was what I was continuously hearing from London. We had some prep to do and we needed to plan the whole mission, from insertion to extraction, meticulously. Additionally, I had to re-rehearse my cover story for a two-year gap ensuring there were no holes in my story. The guys had their support systems all worked out, just a few minor adjustments. I was already very close to my team now and we were as one, sharp and focused for the mission ahead.

The whole team flew British Airways business class London to Singapore and had two nights enjoying the city before we needed to pick up our transport to Paya Lebar Air Base, from which we departed on a long flight in cargo nets aboard a C-141 Starlifter out to Diego Garcia. We arrived in the heat of the day and, as we circled the island, I caught a glimpse of the beautiful atolls that made up the archipelago. It's like the Maldives but much more pristine and completely unspoilt because there are no civilians allowed within the whole BIOT (British Indian Ocean Territory), and most of the islands, including over 50% of DG, are a marine reserve. What an amazing staging point for ops in the Middle East. The airbase aprons were littered with B52 bombers, P-3 Orion search aircraft, C-5 Galaxy transports and a complete US aircraft carrier detachment.

We were met and driven to the base accommodation, or downtown Diego, and allocated 'bungalows' which we expected to be home for the next 12 to 18 months. The whole base was like a military holiday resort. Swimming pools, bars, restaurants, the Brit Club (run by the Royal Marines), the seaman's mission for the guys off the merchant ship transports, and a beach club. Fucking paradise. It certainly didn't feel like work. For about a month we all just settled down into the routine of it all. We supported and helped out the local detachment and naval party, including undertaking security ops around the islands. Fishing trips, BBQs and long lazy days at the beach were the norm. It has to be the most beautiful beach resort on the planet – the film *The Beach* doesn't come close. We were getting totally off grid. No one knew we were here and there were no unwanted eyes to see us, and with no security issues to worry about we were utterly detached from the world and able to be ghosts when we made our insertion, without any fear of ever being tracked, identified or followed in any way. It totally allowed the team to bond, relax and prepare with no distractions.

Each team member integrated into the island community seamlessly with additional roles and functions in order to remain autonomous and to keep the boredom to a minimum before our insertion. I spent quite a lot of time working at the satellite station with the commercial guys from Cable & Wireless, as well as working customs at the airport, which was only really needed once when a civilian airliner needed to make an emergency landing. It was a bizarre experience to see unfold. As soon as the aircraft landed it was marshalled to a holding area while all the windows were covered over so the passengers couldn't see out. It was quite a security issue and I remember the passengers getting very upset when they learned they would not be allowed off the flight. They remained on that plane for five days whilst the mechanical issues were resolved, sometimes without air conditioning. It must have been terrifying, but on that airfield where everything from stealth fighters, B52 bombers, P-3 Orions, Galaxys, were unloading or loading every military appliance known to man, none of it was for public viewing.

However busy we were with either running island customs, police or simply running one of the bars, we usually ended up in some sort of trouble. My favourite pissed-up release was to go to the MT section with Cheesy and 'rent' (borrow without asking) an earth mover or small tank for the evening and go for a spin around the island. All the military hardware was left with the keys in, so to speak, as there was no risk of it actually going anywhere, except it's a bit obvious you were up to no good when you woke the next day to find a tank or Humvee parked outside your bungalow full of empty beer bottles. Apart from such shenanigans due to boredom, my claim to fame for island time would have to be my success at learning the guitar and singing 'Hotel California' in the island wide band. I was a hit – well, to the happy off-duty crowds for just a few gigs I was the base entertainer.

I guess you could say that most of my time 'on island' was in fact the real holiday – beautiful beaches and total isolation for the team. If we wanted to be alone together we would head down the plantation end of the island. We would enjoy a sail away on a yacht, enjoy scuba, snorkelling and chasing turtles in order to hitch a ride out into the abyss that we called the shelf. The shelf was where the lagoon's beautiful clear waters would give way to the black depths of the Indian Ocean, a sheer underwater rock face that descended from the island's coral reefs into the depths of the ocean. Sometimes we would float submerged at about 10m deep just on the edge of the shelf and look out into the black ocean beyond to be absolutely scared to death by inbound shark, tuna and wahoo that would literally zoom right past you into the lagoon, obviously escaping something much bigger that lay out in the darkness.

Then it was time. The team would find its own way into Dubai whilst I would travel back to Singapore, do a big shopping trip for the right clothes and everything else to give the best impression that I was on a gap year, then on into Dubai by civil airline. We had an extended briefing session in my bungalow. I explained my intentions and how I would identify known targets to the team, how I would communicate both in an emergency and once I was satisfied that I had the information the Steering Group was seeking. I needed to try and get transport details, shipping routes, storage facilities, as well as names and destinations. It was sort of a loose op, open-ended, and there was further opportunity on this trip but it came simply with the condition that at the end of the 'vacation' Ahmed Haddad and Mohammed Al Zidjali would be scored off the Steering Group's list.

I arrived in Dubai. Fuck, it was different this time – very serious, intense, more at stake and my neuro electrical synapses were being fried by an overload of information, excitement and expectation. It's the swan syndrome, looking smooth as fuck on the surface but paddling like mad underneath. I needed to settle into the role and get in control of where this was all at. *Relax, you're just meeting old friends*, I was telling myself but simultaneously trying to mentally reinforce the Steering Group's directive on overfamiliarity. To observe, record and investigate, not to become too involved, not to be overfamiliar, to be unnoticed like in the training modules. I calmly made my way off the aircraft and through the customs halls, picked up my luggage and was out in arrivals in under 20 minutes, back undercover doing what I was good at, doing the shit right at the sharp end, re-entering the underworld, adding deeper layers of paranoia to my already overactive mind for a future disen-tanglement nightmare. Fuck, I loved this job.

There was no need to have fired up all the engines; as soon as I cleared customs, I was in a bear hug with Anatoly and

Evgeny, the overfamiliarity clause busted in less than two minutes. It was emotional and I deliberately didn't hold back. I let the whole thing pour out, more genuine than anything else in a collision of emotions, so pleased to see my friend Anatoly. Fuck, I loved this guy, but it was a train smash of other emotions that were in betrayal of any friendship that I had. He was on the kill list, for fuck's sake. Anatoly was so excited as it had been years since we had said goodbye in Moscow and it was truly like we were brothers meeting up again. He was looking a little red from the sun and his now long pompadour-styled blond hair was bleached almost white from too much sunbathing and swimming. He was clean-shaven now, no moustache, and looked very smart indeed. He had grown up since we last met, matured a little and become quite the statesman. I don't know if it was harder or easier to play the part knowing there was a bullet with Anatoly Pavlovich's name written all over it, but I plunged myself deeper into the role and became more determined than before. This mission was different; the student scenario of my previous deployment was all spent and now I had a more serious and aggressive agenda and would need to employ all my skills to get what I wanted.

The fact that Anatoly and Evgeny had come to the airport to meet me actually meant so much to me; it was more than anyone had ever done for me before. None of my actual family members at that time had ever met me back from a trip abroad whether by sea or air. This was the family I loved and knew so well. It's fucking scary to look back and see how well I played this role, and outside all of the unwritten boundaries of the Steering Group. The point being, I had to go deep enough to extract the real diamonds of information everyone was craving and there wasn't going to be any fruit unless I was intensely engrained into their trust. We all stood admiring each other, how much we had grown, matured and all that bullshit. There was so much to catch up on and all the family were waiting for us back at the apartment. Evgeny carried my bags as Anatoly gripped on to me like he was never gonna let me go again. There was a nice Mercedes waiting for us out on the concourse, ice-cold air con hitting me and burning my nostrils as we climbed into the back, dark leather seats and tinted windows, all very bling but nice. It was an easy switch back into my old role and it all made for an easy day at the office.

We weren't staying in a hotel – this caught me by surprise – the family had purchased an apartment in downtown Dubai. Back in the early '90s it was very much still an embryonic building site to the vision it has now become. The main roads were like sleek straight black shoelaces through an otherwise barren brown desert, passing isolated building plots and bizarre green golf courses that were the initial parts of flesh being applied to the skeleton of the master plan of development. The Dubai skyline wasn't that impressive; there were a few exceptions but not the 'Everests' that pierce the stratosphere we see today. However, there were enough bright lights to satisfy any Westerner, and the culture was being slowly retrained to accept the US dollar and ignore, or should I say tolerate, Western habits in the tourist zone for the needs of the profit makers. The foresight of Erik and Alex to buy in Dubai at this time was nothing short of remarkable and I'm sure it was all part of a bigger insurance plan. Old Dubai and the markets or souks are still the same today and probably the best, or should I say the most authentic, areas in my opinion.

We arrived at the apartment block and in true Russian style everything and every detail had been thought of. Everyone was waiting. Things were obviously going much better for the family now, and everyone was dripping in Dubai gold and Western clothing. The days of being excited at a pair of Nike trainers or a few CDs had long passed. It was strange and intriguing to see what the family as Russians had adopted into their lives, all the Westernisms they had embraced which blended awkwardly with traditional Russian culture – heavy gold rings and chains for the guys, and too many of them, coupled with a substantial appetite for anything with a label, especially shirts and bags for the women. Evgeny had adopted the suit with Nike trainers, a look which I thought was ridiculous especially with his scraggy beard that didn't suit him, which both Anatoly and I insisted he shave off. I must admit I was fascinated by what I was seeing, how money was changing the family that I had seen cope so well in more humble times. Anatoly dressed a little plainer and more carefully. His immaculate appearance had only allowed himself to indulge in smart shirts and tie pins to accompany what must have been a nice selection of bespoke suits. His tie pin caught my attention, the Russian letters A P either side of a pearl embedded in white gold; it was very unique and he saw me admiring it a number of times. He had lost the moustache and was much more mature in his ways, very handsome and businesslike. Evgeny needed to catch up, and I guess Anatoly and I would work on that as our third wolf needed a little training.

I changed quickly into a T-shirt and shorts then joined the family on the terrace where there was a good-sized 15m swimming pool with views out to the Gulf. It was blistering hot, and as I came out onto the terrace I was greeted by Erik and Alex – shit, he was worse than me for emotions and welcomed back his little wolf, plainly excited and happy to see me again. Then I immediately sat down at a large table under umbrellas next to Natalia who held my hand like any good mother would do, with Erik endlessly welcoming me home to the family. Shit, I knew I had made an impression on my first mission but these feelings truly ran deep within the family. The mental battle for supremacy of loyalty between the family and the mission had begun, and compromises had to be made as to the levels of my engagement, or should I say entanglement. I couldn't be distant, it would raise a lot of suspicion, so

I allowed myself to slide into the safety net and open arms of the family. It felt great, and it released me from the stiffness I was feeling by being bound to the mission.

Erik told me how desperately sad Anatoly and Evgeny had been this last year or so. They missed their brother and I had to stay until at least the end of the month. I agreed, and Erik was just so happy that I would stay he kissed me on the forehead and thanked me, leaping around the room like I was the prodigal son or something crazy. I didn't know why he really wanted me to be back with Anatoly and Evgeny at the time; it seemed so important to him. Suspicious thoughts were always on my mind. Drinks were brought in by what must have been caterers, to accompany the biggest seafood salad ever seen. I was starving and overindulged in shellfish and ice-cold white wine, answering a barrage of questions about my travels, showing them proudly all the (false) stamps in my passport and telling stories of Singapore and all the beautiful sights and sounds I had experienced there. Alex and Erik continually tried to find a girl in my stories. Anatoly expressed his desires to travel with me as he came and pushed a chair closer to me. The afternoon soon became very relaxed and wound down away from any formalities, with the entire family changing into swimwear and enjoying the pool, all us guys ending up floating around in inflatable chairs with cupholders for our wine or vodka. It really was a bizarre but very happy afternoon. The family was complete and whole for this short and pleasant time.

As the sun started to set that evening, we all sat together in the lounge and huddled together as a family, and they argued who would sleep with me in the guest bedroom whilst playing cards and drinking. There were some surprise guests arriving tomorrow, and in the afternoon all the family were to go into the desert for a BBQ and dune racing. Everyone was so excited. I allowed myself to enquire of Alex and Erik how well the family was looking and how they must be up on their fortunes to be able to enjoy such surroundings. I laced the comments carefully with a subtle insistence that I should pay something toward the cost of the holiday. Alex was infuriated, in a nice way, and enforced the necessity for me to be here and spend time with Anatoly and Evgeny, which would be the price of my stay. Natalia squeezed my hand. I knew there was more to this than was being released, and she would no doubt fill me in.

It was two days later, while the entire family was out in the desert and I was getting some ice from the tent for my drink, when Natalia came and told me. The boys were racing each other on quad bikes over the dunes. Anatoly and Evgeny had become very depressed after I had left Moscow, and Anatoly had tried to commit suicide. His time at the military academy had been so hard and the pressures for him to do well had by all accounts been incredibly suffocating. He was a loner and didn't have any friends. I was his friend who couldn't be with him, and now it was just the government job that took up all his life, devoid and empty of personal friendships or relationships. Evgeny had visited Anatoly in hospital and had later disappeared for almost two months after he had been diagnosed with a heart condition prior to Anatoly's attempt to take his own life. The family was finding it so hard to comfort either of them. I remember standing there crying and saying, "Natalia, why didn't you tell me?" She never replied, just gave me a hug and beckoned me to go and enjoy being with my brothers.

Fuck, what had I walked back into? I was in a difficult position in which I had to contemplate every move very carefully, but at the same time the personal troubles of the family made for a window of opportunity to exploit. It's simpler to extract information from emotional people. I could use the situation to my advantage whilst being compassionate and showing empathy to each individual's needs. It was simply opportunity meeting requirement on an open playing field. I just had to capitalise on my position. I felt the betrayal demon creeping into my mind and into both sides of the game.

I remember that my talk with Natalia was the moment when the weight of suspicion was actually lifted; there appeared to be genuine reasons for the huge welcome back into the family. My support in Moscow for the boys following my time in DECAF had been a real tonic and a lifeline of hope for them I suppose, and I had been desperately missed. Neither of the boys had ever had such an amazing friendship like the bond we had together during my time with them in Moscow. I guessed it had been special but not of this magnitude. Thinking back, the family was probably guilty of keeping both the boys as isolated as possible from society because of who they were, who they were working for, and ultimately what they their parents were involved with. The family had to be tight, closed off, to keep things in check, no room for uncertainty in any camp. Who knows what had taken place but it allowed me to infiltrate beautifully in to the family and their business.

I promised Natalia I would stay as long as possible but just hinted that my financial situation wasn't as good as the family's. Erik overheard and said he would find me work if I was interested. I managed to park my suspicious and overactive mind to allow things to play out to try and extract all the information that I needed, giving myself time I didn't actually have. Unlike in Moscow I had a whole team out in the dunes watching and listening, a backstop of safety on this tour unlike in Moscow. I guess the build-up in London, the unveiling of the list and all the time spent with the guys at Poole made this trip so very different from my 'student' time in Moscow. I had real purpose now and I think that hit home. It was a passing moment of uncertainty in my mind that would resurface occasionally, irritatingly distracting me when

I needed to concentrate on releasing the sleuth from my toolbox and be the kind of emissary agent the Steering Group wanted, which was of course a complete paradox. In the end the Steering Group was only interested in solid intel and confirmed kills. The whole thing was now all being played out like in a bizarre TV soap opera or reality show with a loving Russian family in Dubai.

Our guests arrived at the encampment we had driven out to, and as soon as I saw the motorcade on the dune horizon I knew the day was gonna be of special importance. It was all starting to unfold. Six black Toyota and Jeep trucks threw sand and dust up in the air as they approached our little oasis, the dust lifting away from the rear of the caravan to the east as the wind caught it and then turned it into mini twisters that soon blew themselves out. The catering staff were going wild as the carpets were laid out from the main tents to greet our guests with cold towels and iced drinks. There was a lot of commotion and everyone gathered on the carpet. The cars pulled up and out flew Asad followed by his father Mohammed Al Zidjali, Ahmed Haddad and Nasser Tamei, with their wives and children. It was just a mind-fucking moment and I needed to take a minute to bring it all into focus. I managed to turn my twisted stomach cramps and nerves into excitement and greeted Asad, then allowed Alex to introduce me formally to Ahmed and Mohammed. Thank fuck for Asad, who insisted I race him on the quads. It later turned out that the whole event was being filmed and photographed by the team, and I am sure the guys were just as fucking amazed as I was at how things were playing out. I didn't see them and didn't want to; they knew what they had to do and I knew I was safe with them in the background. The Steering Group would have miles of tape to make fun of on my return.

I remember it was a few days later I had decided to take a walk while the adjacent apartment partitioning was being removed for the remainder of the holiday so as to allow our guests to be free to join us from one apartment to the other. Evgeny was always exhausted and hadn't recovered really from all the week's excitement, so Anatoly and I put him to bed for a daytime sleep after a light breakfast. I read him a story from *Kolobok*, one that he'd loved so dearly as a younger boy, and watched him drift off to sleep; he hadn't the energy he'd once had. Anatoly insisted he come with me and we headed off to the old harbour and took a dhow over to the souks. We talked all the way to the harbour, and on the dhow we sat together and looked into each other's souls and found ourselves at a loss as to how this separation sickness was ever going to be remedied. My mind was in absolute turmoil; none of this shit was supposed to be happening and it had thrown me way off course, so I was in a parallel of paradoxical worlds, in two lives each as attractive as the other. No amount of 'paper-clipping' was going to be of use in this scenario. I was sailing closer to the wind than I had hoped to; the realities of being so involved were suffocating my judgement, but somehow I remained mindful of what was purposeful and what was contradictory to the mission. It's like giving yourself a mental bollocking when your mind drifts into the no-go zones of an op.

Anatoly and I wandered for an hour or so between all the market stalls and shops. Like pinballs we bounced our way through the narrow alleys of overcrowded shops and stall traders, from carpet sellers to fig and date stalls as high as mountains; this, together with the spice sellers and the flower stalls, all equally contributed to the complexity of smells and aromas that filled the heavy humid air, giving you a full nose of pungent pleasant slow suffocation. Eventually we settled down at a café in the gold souk on some crap old wooden chairs that were synonymous with failing restaurant chairs in England, creaky, uneven and uncomfortable but exactly what we needed as we ordered coffee. I asked if they could bring some dates to share also. My favourite to this day is Arabian coffee and dates – it's a match made in heaven and the coffee is never reproduced as well in a packet back in the UK. We shared a hookah, or Hubbly-Bubbly , a water pipe with some fucked-up tobacco. It made us laugh and we shared a special afternoon together, just talking, wandering through a forest of issues and topics including poor Evgeny's health. We must have had a dozen cups of coffee and damn near smoked that pipe inside out before I plucked up the courage and asked him why he had tried to take his own life.

I think he was secretly pleased that I had found out from his mother Natalia, but pretended it was a shock. His time at the National Research Nuclear University MEPhI and Bauman University had been hard and he hadn't found any friends, deliberately distancing himself from Asad at the request of Alex and his father so as not to raise suspicions. He had basically been alone since I had left Moscow, and his move into a military research role at Sarov had isolated him further and further from human interaction on a personal scale which had slowly torn him apart inside. He had yearned for our friendship and, after all the hideous expectations that had been put upon him at the research facility in Sarov, and the endless isolation and secrecy, he explained that he had felt there was no way out. He was so lonely it was killing him, literally, and there was too much pressure from the family now with all the additional business and political entanglements his father and Alex had become involved with.

I had to let him tell me the whole thing over at least three times, and the words just ate me up and took me back to my friend Robert who had killed himself after sexual abuse by his foster parents all those years ago. The isolation, the loneliness and the pressures of life and work in order to succeed and be someone else's hero, devoid of true love, friendship and the fun of innocence, really is a dark path no young person should be made to walk. For Anatoly that path had only ever been lit up by my short presence in Moscow. When someone talks of suicide, as sick as it may sound, I can tell if they are genuine or not. It's that absolute loss of any hope and the unmistakable accompanying silence and utter despair that gives it away. Anatoly had found that despair and was only just surviving it. I remember telling him again all about Robert so he could feel my pain also and know I fully understood him and couldn't live through another suicide again. That encounter brought us to a new place as friends and brothers, closer still. Then he asked if he could come to England with me.

I was thrust into a mind-blowing mental dive by Anatoly asking to come to England. It had suddenly become time to get a proper drink so we headed off to a hotel bar, where I desperately tried to turn the whole conversation around to his work and why it was so depressing for him. The England thing needed to be processed later. I managed to get him talking about work and he described his employment at the Russian Scientific Research Institute for Experimental Physics (VNIIEF), Sarov (Nizhny Novgorod Oblast, Sarov). He explained how his life was like being in prison, especially following a number of security breaches and some of the offsite storage facilities being compromised on two separate occasions. There had been a lot of security checks and interrogation of the staff, which was wearing him down. Anatoly was without doubt a man of superior intellect, a genius set on a path that would be destined for fame within the Iron Curtain, but there were flies in the ointment, and those flies were the family which he could not squash.

The conversation was gold. I sat and learned everything Anatoly did and was involved in at VNIIEF. They conducted nuclear warhead design, within which Anatoly was a designer but was also engaged in teams and projects related to advanced conventional weapons, nuclear safety and intellectual property protection, and his latest assignments were working on Russia's most advanced supercomputers in the further development of an ISKRA laser-based inertial confinement fusion device. My mouth was literally agape. Anatoly laughed at me, and I just laughed back and said that it was all beyond me and joked that maybe he should come to England with me to escape it all because I didn't understand a word he was talking about. It was actually perfect cover for me; my true ignorance of what he was describing hid my true intentions, like a chameleon moving off the sand and onto a tree – my colours were all they needed to be.

I think he was sometimes in need of a mental escape outside of work, which I presented to him in the form of adventure and possibly misdirection. Anatoly wasn't really too adventurous or brave, even a little risk adverse, but loved it when I would thrust it all upon him. He pretended he wanted to do things like skydiving or scuba but needed a chaperone or someone who wouldn't make fun if he didn't see it through. On the quad bikes he wouldn't go fast; he would drive like a grandfather until I encouraged him to push the envelope. He knew that when I was around I would pick him up or protect him, I suppose; I was the brother he never had. He obviously never had the opportunity to talk about anything really close to him and felt it was okay to let me in on the outlines of what he did. He was stuck in Sarov all week and rarely got home at week-ends as it was about a nine-hour drive from Moscow and not always possible because of the weather. He worked mostly alone and only had a few work acquaintances. Speaking with Anatoly I didn't see why he was alone; I found him easy to communicate with and never found or thought that conversation with him was over complex or difficult to initiate. However, if you listened to him talking to Alex it would be almost a different language, and you would feel like a dustman discussing maths problems, like Cauchy's integral formula, with a mathematics professor, the conversation leaving you completely lost and with more questions than you set out with.

It was getting late and we decided to get back to the apartment as no doubt we would be missed and needed to get dressed for dinner. Anatoly was very specific that we should keep our conversation private as his father had such high expectations of him and now wouldn't be a good time to upset the family. Anatoly explained that there was a lot of business to be conducted whilst the family was here in Dubai and that he wasn't comfortable with it all and just wanted to have some family time and leave the world of work back in Russia. My mind was moving away from the mission and more to the possibility of a defection, a possibility that hadn't been considered as yet by the Steering Group.

Dinner was quite a grand affair with so much over-indulgence on offer. There was a huge buffet arranged in the dining room that opened out through bi-fold doors onto the pool area. There were tables of seafood layered with lobster, crab, prawns, oysters, langoustines and caviar, with forests of salads forming the foundations of the grand ice carvings. King crab and fresh caviar on lettuce boats were my choice of main course, an extravagant indulgence I wasn't going to refuse. I was sandwiched between Evgeny and Alex, who demanded my undivided attention. The humble dinners of Moscow had been surpassed by the unhidden abundance of money and the deepest desires to explore what could be gained from having so much of it. Food was a great expression of wealth and it was truly on display that day.

I think after talking with Evgeny I learned that he had become very dependent on the family, more so now that Alex had increasingly demanding deadlines to meet and impatient new customers. He was now feeling vulnerable with his heart condition which in turn attracted endless concern from all who knew. A deep breath or a slight grimace would have everyone standing. I sat with him and let him tell his story; it was quite sad because he expressed his desire to be free again – he would never hunt, run, swim or do any of the things he so wanted to like we did when I lived in Moscow. Alex and I worked hard to drive his thoughts to other possibilities like business and politics. The conversation was politely manoeuvred through the endless minefields of possible depression areas or negativities but eventually we ended up with drinks in the lounge with Mohammed, Ahmed and Nasser. Erik was pleased to isolate all the men from the women, who were now sitting outside conducting some sort of fashion show of shoes and bags, their laughter and overloud conversation gently silenced by the closing of the bi-fold doors. It was time for business.

Alex was blunt, and asked straight out if I wanted to take up some work for him with Evgeny. The family needed people they could trust and it would only be for a few weeks maybe in a few months' time. Nasser wanted only family and close friends involved in the logistics chain. Floundering, I remember simply nodding and smiling at Evgeny and not saying anything. Anatoly was upset and asked to come with me and Evgeny, the brothers should stay together he was beckoning, but Erik and Alex both jumped in, almost barking to Anatoly that the family needed him in Sarov. That was the first time I had ever heard Anatoly swear out loud; he was clearly not happy with being isolated from his brothers again and it was becoming clear why Anatoly wasn't the content young man I had once known.

Mohammed pulled out some folders and maps from a leather case he had politely disappeared to reclaim from his room while the domestic argument had taken place. There it was, the whole fucking secret revealed. Anatoly was supplying information from Sarov direct to Mohammed (Mohammed bin Shaban Al Zidjali – Syrian, now working in Iran with his son Asad, both nuclear scientists) who in return for this technical information was paying Ahmed to allow (and maintain approval for) the supply of illegal arms from Russia to Iraq and the Serbians (this included Scud missile parts and chemical weapon components). It was a complex system of payments and agreements, with some shipments having already been used against Ahmed, in that the Iraqi border with Saudi was becoming fortified with Scud missiles supplied directly by Alex, an embarrassment in some quarters of the Russian leadership who hadn't been aware of the trade-offs Alex had made on their behalf. In short, it was an insurance policy demanded by the end customers in Iraq to allow the arms build-up to continue and to ensure the funding and the bribery gravy train remained unhindered and fully operational.

It was imperative to the Russians and the Serbians that those groups controlling Saudi territories remained in approval of the movement of arms. The funding needed for the greedy underworld of Middle Eastern politics and terrorist groups would have been very significant to pacify and keep everyone onside in order for the bigger game to be played out. The Saudi regime would no doubt have been simultaneously and painfully unaware that some of the same shipments were being paid for by Iran to customers in Yemen and Lebanon in preparation to turn on their Middle Eastern brothers. (It's important to know that the relationship between Iran and Russia was good up until the late 1990s, so arms trading, legal or not, to Iran was okay from the Russian viewpoint.) Who knew what will never be fully established; besides, those with whom the Steering Group was involved were operating way below anything that governments of any nation could possibly be aware of. It was all the undertakings of lesser men who sought power but could never attain it.

The intricate, complex and sometimes hidden relationships and alliances across the Middle East were and probably still are a tangled mess that usually ends in a hatred trail for Israel, hence the involvement of the West and Saudi Arabia's face-value support to the US and Israel whilst allowing a neighbour to strengthen without apparent action. This, coupled with the entanglements of Sunni and Shia religions, made for an undecipherable code of alliances. The two questions that needed to be asked at the time were: why were the Saudis and their allies willing to forgo generations of refusing to recognise Israel as a country to now invite her to be an ally?; and why were the Israelis willing to accept this role? The answer is: because Israel has nuclear weapons (it's not a designated nuclear weapon state and does not openly acknowledge it); but until Iran takes her place (and that's what Mohammed and Asad's directive was from those seeking power in Iran) then these unlikely friendships must be maintained until the balance is moved. Mohammed was going to make that happen at all costs, buying it all from Russia through whatever means and at whatever cost, including the arming of unfriendly states and the creation of tensions and conflict to shift focus away from the main event, and the eventual development of Iran as a nuclear power. It's all enough to give an aspirin a serious migraine; and no matter how hard I tried to understand all the reasons why, it was just better and easier to simply obey the last order, fuck all the politics and pull the trigger when ordered to do so.

The best thing I ever learned from all my time with the Russians and all the tribes of the Middle East is that the enemy of my enemy is now my friend even if he was my enemy in the past. Welcome, friend, let me buy you coffee and give you the means to kill our enemies together. PS How much will that cost? Then kill your friend before any payment is due.

The family was supplying Nasser with the arms direct from Russia now, some under the guise of legitimate transactions; the source depot was not revealed and was kept a secret that only Alex knew, but the destinations were clear – deliveries would be made to Evgeny in Drobeta-Turnu Severin, a city in Mehedinti County, Oltenia, Romania (on the River Danube) before onward shipment to Nasser in Split, then the remaining cargo would be taken by ship to Iraq through Lebanon, Suez and the Gulf. Alex wanted me to be with Evgeny in Romania to ensure he was okay and see the first of the new shipments through. Alex would look after the initial loadings then it was up to Nasser. Ahmed stepped in and explained how the payment system would work from now on and listed the other beneficiaries. Dilip, our Indian transport contact, would cover all land transport, and Rolando Hernandez from Panama would arrange for the shipping of the cargos from Split to Iraq and Tehran. Mohammed then presented the details of the shipments and the target delivery dates, and fuck it was tight. Most of the arrangements had already been made. It was up to Alex to release the armaments from Russia but Anatoly had yet to pass the next package of documents to Mohammed, which was holding up the payment process. All eyes were on Anatoly, who had hooked a few looks at me during the conversation.

Anatoly in effect was the man in control, probably more in control than Erik or Alex. Erik was keeping the Russian politicians well fed and onside, spinning webs of half-truths and misdirection, whilst Alex was struggling to keep the lower bottom feeders in the military system happy. Anatoly entered into the negotiation of monies to the family and funds to support and appease the financial demands from the interior who all wanted their slice of the cake. So, as Anatoly had the ace card up his sleeve it was all up for negotiation and the biddings were high. I don't think it's possible for any agent involved in espionage or any undercover work to be able to fully process the information at such meetings where the intensity of information being passed is so far off the scale of rational comprehension. Here I was, sitting in an apartment in

Dubai witnessing probably one of the biggest illegal arms and information deals in history, with the top players all with their trousers around their ankles haggling out the details and finances. To say I had hit the jackpot would have been an understatement but this all sort of threw out the initial plans set by the Steering Group.

That night was a long one, a lot of argument from Mohammed, but Anatoly was firm and more professional than his father or Alex. It was clear that Alex didn't really have full control of the military, either in the supplying depots or in the higher echelons of Moscow KGB who were poised to leak information to the politicians, so he desperately needed the money from Ahmed to keep it all on track. However, it was Anatoly who wouldn't release the technical information Mohammed wanted so badly for the money initially on offer, which was annoying Alex immensely. It was a circular argument. The Arabs were watching, observing and applying pressure ever so gently. There were other agendas at play here; no doubt the information that Anatoly had was more than craved for by Iran, and the Russians were underestimating their determination to acquire it, and who knows what threats Mohammed had on his head to seal this deal with the Russians or what other promises he had made back in Iran or to splinter groups as side deals. Iran was desperate at the time to press on with its Bushehr Nuclear Power Plant, arms dealing was already good business, and the desire for the technology to build a nuclear weapon would be off the scale.

Nasser sat as intrigued and as neutral as me. Erik eventually sat with me as the floor was given up to individual conversations. Cigarette smoke and air conditioning blended together to form a cold atmosphere of foggy minds lost in frustration and anticipation that went on for some hours. Erik wanted to make clear to me that Alex was under more pressure than anyone. Erik could only keep the politicians happy and turn a blind eye for specific periods of time and couldn't risk unnecessary attention from the Lubyanka as his dealings were not always in harmony with Alex's arrangements further down the food chain, so the money needed to flow on time. This posed the question: would I talk to Anatoly? If so, I would be well rewarded.

This is the very moment any agent working this deep can almost get sucked in, and the possibility of going from agent to double agent is born. Espionage and counter-espionage, lies and bribes, mixed with targets that have become personal friends embedded within a trusting family on the brink of becoming extraordinarily wealthy all off the back of stolen military intelligence but endorsed by paid-off government officials and a known KGB agent is nothing short of astonishing.

We were all tired, and Evgeny wasn't looking too well. I beckoned Alex and Mohammed to end the evening well and for us all to go and re-join the ladies who had gone very quiet out by the pool, lit only now by the underwater lights. I remember looking at Anatoly and I knew right there and then he was ripe for defection if only I could find a way to offer it to him. I now truly knew why he had attempted to end his life. He had been well groomed by his father and Alex and prepared for this job he now found himself in; it was years of planning to get a family member into a position where knowledge is power but more importantly money. I think the Arabs were annoyed, becoming impatient; I had overheard them speaking in Arabic about their frustrations. I offered them whisky and we all took in the night air together. Tomorrow we would resolve our differences. They liked me as the mediator, family but not family, a middle man who could hear the lies, the frustrations and the needs of both parties but was able to see a negotiated way forward.

I remember getting up very early and ordering a cab. I had breakfast with Alex and Erik who had me firmly in their sights to get Anatoly to close the deal that day by agreeing to release the documents soon. I had to make contact with the team and get the information out to the Steering Group and get the grown-ups in London to agree to at least attempt to haul Anatoly in. I think, looking back, I was more intent on saving Anatoly's life than passing on all the other information regarding the planned arms movements and technical information transfers to the Iranians. I politely finished breakfast then asked Erik to send Anatoly to the souk café at midday once he had woken up, and said that I wanted to go and figure out how I could best talk with him about last night. Erik was pleased and asked me to bring him back some more cigarettes. He gave me a hug and wished me success for the family.

I was picked up by Hugh in a registered Dubai taxi – damn near scared the life out of me. I only had the time of the ride into town to pass him all the intel regarding the arms deals and technical information transfers that were being planned and a possible defection. It all needed to be transmitted to the Steering Group and I would fill in all the details once my 'holiday' was over. Hugh did nothing but take the piss and make light of it all. He looked like a proper scabby Arab driving that taxi but his presence was a very welcome relief for me. I would need a taxi again at about 1.30pm I told him and that's when he would get to meet Anatoly. No big deal to Hugh, and he said he would have the response from London to all my questions and any changes to the original mission directives by 1.30pm. I bailed out of the taxi and disappeared into the souks to get lost amongst the madding crowd and the heavy perfume of all the stalls.

I think that afternoon with Anatoly was remarkable. We ordered coffee and smoked as usual. He had relaxed into a shirt and jeans but with highly polished shoes. Looking fresh and more alive than the previous night he wanted to apologise for the family. I just sat and listened as he calmly explained the mess he was in, running his fingers through his blond hair and taking a drag of his cigarette. He was reticent at first but slowly let go and asked me to help him, brother to brother. There was a genuine look of fear in his dark and almost vacant eyes as that awkward moment lingered for longer than is usually comfortable as we tried to interpret each other's body language. The noise of the souk was drowned out by the internal silence we both secretly shared. I explained to Anatoly I was an Englishman, I couldn't get involved working like this for the family, it was illegal; he was trying to interrupt but I spoke over him to say I would do this one job for the family and the trip to Romania with Evgeny for him, but in return I wanted to know everything that I was getting involved with. I needed to know all the details.

Anatoly's retort was exactly what I needed to hear; he desperately wanted to get out of the whole thing. I couldn't offer the deal of defection, I hadn't got authorisation, shit, shit, shit. So I bungled the whole thing by saying something dumb like I would work out a way he could come to England once it was all over and we would work together. It was a sticking plaster on an amputated soul. It didn't work, and Anatoly was upset. I took him to one of the malls and we walked together round and round the shops aimlessly like a bored husband with a wife who won't buy the dress she saw in the first fucking shop. I needed him to buy us both some time. I coaxed him into engineering a stall for the information transfer that would allow us to pacify the Arabs for the rest of our holiday and to meet in secret outside of the family before he went back to Sarov and I went back to England. I encouraged Anatoly to conclude the deal, push for more money so it looked authentic, in fact to be almost rude with a proposed new price. Then we would simply meet again outside of the wider family and spend some time alone to figure it all out. Anatoly was desperate, and I was riding to his rescue in a way he could never have possibly imagined at the time. A bullet had his name on it and was all but locked in by my support team. Fuck, he had no idea how close he became to meeting his maker that very day.

It was probably about 3am one morning when we found ourselves awake in our bedroom in the apartment. We started talking about when it had all been fun, when we were in Moscow, how simple life was back then as boys. He turned to face me, allowing me to see how disturbed he had become. He was very restless about the betrayal of his country, the family pressure to deliver the documents to the Arabs and the sure knowledge it wasn't a one-time deal, there would always be another deal and another deal. He described himself as an information mule, but instead of drugs he was selling information which was more addictive than heroin and it would inevitably end badly sooner or later. He wanted to play the Arabs some more to get a deal that would help the family decide that it was enough money to quit and find a place somewhere warm to live out the rest of their lives. It was a ridiculous dream – the family was far too deeply involved in bribery and illegal activities involving the Kremlin, Lubyanka and our friends in the Middle East to be allowed to simply take the money and walk away to some exotic island. Either way, I was thinking the list would be signed off.

We talked about Moscow, travel, London and England, eventually returning again to the subject of the documents he had for the Arabs. I managed to steer the conversation round to him allowing me to see the documents he had prepared for the Arabs. He flicked on the bedside lamp and rummaged in his hand luggage before pulling out a neat brown file with only about 20 papers, each protected in a sealed plastic sleeve, perfectly numbered and labelled. Schematic drawings, formulae and shit I didn't actually understand other than there was no mistake regarding the references made to ICBM warhead assembly, which a child could have worked out from the detailed diagrams. I suggested that as there was so much pressure on Anatoly it would be easier for him and safer for the family to allow me to take custody of the documents before he handed them over to the Arabs, ensuring there was no sneak previews or discussion as to their worth before the deal was struck and the monies were transferred later that week. Alex had become infectious with the need to conclude business and was yet to understand the real value of stealing government technical secrets.

The days that followed our talk, however, were played out very calmly, each of us enjoying as best we could the family time and our holiday time with the Arabs, who had become more relaxed having attained the knowledge from Erik that my walk into Dubai with Anatoly had got a result that would bring his proposal to the table on the penultimate day of the holiday at the latest. The situation was diffused for the time being, but Alex was always seeking an early briefing that neither Anatoly nor I would give. Evgeny, Anatoly and I took a lot of time out away from the apartment to escape the politics that the Arabs, Alex and Erik so enjoyed discussing – who the business was benefitting and what causes deserved their efforts and how it all gave power to the right people in order to give control where they thought it should be. It was actually all very sick how they saw the world. I think Anatoly and Evgeny were more interested in the beach, a few good drinks and fantasising how we would spend millions of dollars should we ever be as rich as it then seemed possible.

I had managed to engineer some time away from the family on my own and rendezvoused with Hugh after ordering a taxi to go and collect ice creams from a special outlet in one of the malls after getting a list of requests from everyone. I took the documents. It was film night and Alex had arranged a big screen to watch a Russian war film. Hugh arrived to collect me. He was alert and serious for a change as I explained the developments in Arabic in the back of his cab. I needed the original documents replacing for an identical set that were imperceptibly flawed replicas for me to pass back to Anatoly. I needed them within two hours, I explained to Hugh as I handed them over, noting the time left on the film, the time an ice cream interlude usually took the family and calculating how much time was gonna look out of place and how to engineer the exchange of documents once they had been received. Hugh dropped me off for the ice cream at the mall. It was the longest hour and a half before Hugh returned, but amazingly with the new set of documents. The Steering Group was happy to end the show here on what I had obtained from Anatoly but would allow a defection. Hugh was exaggerating how pleased the Steering Group was and how I was their little pet, taking the piss all the time. The top two, however, must be eliminated and the supply chain funding destroyed. I was soon back with the family, overloaded with ice cream and other goodies, explaining that I had thought it would be good to share some traditional Arabian cakes as we had guests so I had stopped off at the bakery producing Luqaimat, baklava and an assortment of other sticky stuff I had thrown in a box, which all seemed to be well appreciated.

It was all very simple on paper. I now had a green light to affect the partial defection of Anatoly if possible. The transfer of false documents from Anatoly to the Arabs would be made in the apartment with everyone present. All monies needed to be confirmed as transferred by Alex and Ahmed before anyone left the apartment or Dubai; this would give legality to the Steering Group's plan to the politicians should anything leak. Once the deal was sealed, the Arab contingent would be eliminated before reaching their next destination. The Russian family and I needed to leave Dubai before the Arabs to give confidence no one was involved in the elimination of Mohammed and Ahmed. This in effect meant the team needed to execute the mission either in the apartment after I and the Russians had for all intents and purposes left the country, or eliminate them in the desert. The backstop was to eliminate all family members and the Arabs simultaneously if the deal was to fall through. The team would need to enter the apartment and prep for this possible eventuality.

It was all set for a Thursday morning. The family had their flights arranged for Thursday night so nothing needed to be manipulated, except that my spoof flight needed to be arranged a number of hours before the Russian departure. The Arabs would be exiting the UAE by road to Qatar and onward to Iran by plane the following day, so it would be an en-route motorised elimination that was anticipated. I was not really ready to approach Anatoly that day but it was the finals, graduation day for everyone. I was all set to have the big discussion with Anatoly at the souk café. It led to many dead ends. Our conversation was strained for the first time in the holiday so it was almost impossible to approach the subject of defection, and so I contained my inner desires and encouraged Anatoly to do this one transaction, go back to Moscow/Sarov and hide behind the system.

Eventually Anatoly gave me the look I was waiting for. His eyes were wide, deep oceans of tears encased behind a glass prison of fear in which servitude and misfortune reigned under the red flag of the hammer and sickle from which he so wanted to escape. This, coupled with the family, the guardians of his future, whispering in his ear not to betray them. I lit a cigarette and gave it to him with a newspaper. I asked him to pass it back after he had read the article about Norway. In the text were his instructions for defection. He looked at me calmly and took a deep drag on the cigarette before returning his concentration to the paper, which betrayed his nerves as it shimmered and shook in his hands as we sat together in silence. I had shown him a window into his future and lit a lamp so bright that it warmed his soul enough to give me a smile that simply meant *Thank you* and *Yes*. My friend and closest companion would be taken off the Steering Group's list.

Fuck, if he had declined I would have had to kill my friend, my brother, that very hour.

Alex and Erik were waiting at the Arabs' apartment for us to return, and Evgeny and Asad joined us in the Arabs' living room. The living room had three double settees and a matching pair of chairs all neatly arranged to accommodate our first official meeting trading technology for money and arms. The furniture was low but comfortable and encompassed high-quality Persian rugs which were deep red and made from only the choicest material, thick enough to dig your toes into. The bi-fold doors were closed and the blinds averted upwards. Drinks were available from a hostess trolley and it was as though we were all meeting for the first time. Mohammed sat unusually distant from the family with his son Asad and requested the documents from Anatoly. Asad had studied nuclear science with Anatoly in Moscow and was a Middle Eastern mirror of Anatoly but in Iran, a nuclear development specialist, scientist/engineer. Clumsy drinks were poured by Erik as Mohammed mulled over the documents with Asad. Asad, who had matured in some ways, was looking sharp on this important day. He had the authority of his father to accept or decline the documents supplied by Anatoly. He stroked his sharply trimmed beard so stereotypical of young Arabian men, trying to look important. I think Asad must have read all the papers through and was looking either perplexed by the level of detail in the documents or putting on a good show for the audience with perhaps no clue as to what was actually in his hands.

Mohammed lit a cigarette and asked Asad whether they should prepare to make the transactions, giving away his lack of patience. Asad was being a prick; he just nodded and said, "Maybe," leaving the room in silence. It was Alex who looked the most vulnerable. My understanding was that there were many party members wanting money from this arms trade and on top of this Alex was dancing the tightrope with the lower echelons of the army's officer corps to release the armaments on time to the transports. I'm still not sure to this day how high the level of corruption went with regards to the transferring of technical information, or whether this was the only leverage Alex and Erik could use to pull the deal off, and perhaps this sweetener was only really fully understood within the family.

The magnanimous Asad eventually returned and declared the papers agreeable, stood up and invited a toast. The room was elevated into the stratosphere of relief, and conversation broke out in a joyous manner as the whisky and vodka were poured and consumed. I was looking at Anatoly, and I held my glass up to him and congratulated him for his success for the family and the cementing of Russian–Arab relations, but was also inwardly relieved he hadn't double-crossed me by mentioning our plans for him to escape to the UK. Mohammed and Ahmed looked more relaxed now, easing back in their chairs secretly satisfied they had met their master's every wish.

The moment was short-lived as the computers were then immediately turned on, keyboards frantically tapped and then inevitable pauses as programs were loaded and internet access achieved. Anatoly went and sat with Ahmed and Mohammed, slipping them a piece of paper, obviously with the new price tag on it. Alex was watching carefully but there was no upscaling of temper or circumstance. Ahmed completely and professionally folded the paper away and looked toward Alex and said that, because of the level of cooperation, his clients were more than happy to pay double the amount Anatoly had passed. This was a gesture of goodwill by the end customers who would now be demanding on-time deliveries and a continued agreement for further technical information in the future. I think Iran wanted that information more than anything and at any price. And their true agenda was yet to be revealed. They were using the good relations between Russia and Iran to further their own nuclear abilities but lacked technology, which was soon to be limited again by the 1995 Gore-Chernomyrdin agreement which further fuelled the demand for illegal technology deals. There were some big smiles being restrained under the alcohol-fuelled relief from the family. Anatoly and Evgeny looked relaxed as the computers transmitted all the transactions to the banks and unknowingly to the Steering Group which had been waiting 48 hours to intercept all the transmissions from the entire street in Dubai back to London. If only computers could build trust or pull the trigger at the right moment, my team and I would have already reached mission complete.

That afternoon everyone dispersed from their business stances into a celebration as the women and children were invited back into the room and the doors opened up back onto the pool. There was no rushing off to the airport or apparent need to get on with the logistics. I think right at that moment the entire group needed to release the pressure that had been building up over the past week. I was the first to leave for my flight to London. I made my excuses and promised Alex I would look after Evgeny in Romania but begged him to make sure he didn't split us apart from Anatoly. It was obvious due to the success he would probably not allow Anatoly to be with his brothers in Romania as more information needed to be fed to the hungry wolves now at the door. There were some emotional goodbyes before I left, especially from Anatoly and Evgeny, who were in tears at my side as Natalia gave me a really affectionate hug. Saying goodbye to the Arabs was a longer, more intense affair: "Ma'salama" and "Allah Maak", to be safe in my travels and for God to be with me, then the touching of noses like in New Zealand Maori culture whilst shaking hands. I was then at that point accepted as a friend in the Arabian family. Mohammed and Ahmed were very grateful to me for bringing Anatoly to close the business deal on time and wanted me to accept a gift by way of invitation to a gathering in Damascus. Now I was family it was expected that the maximum time an Arab friend would be away from you would be three days at the most before they would like to make contact with you again, so I would have to be more available now, as they put it.

That was it. I was in the taxi with Hugh, ready to switch back and await the departure of Mohammed and Ahmed. Hugh drove the Mercedes taxi out of town, gently at first then frantically after reaching the city limits. The guys had been staying in a hotel near the port in Jebel Ali. It was great to be back with them, a relief in every way. I was mentally drained and emotionally exhausted from all the individual demands that had been put upon me, not just from Anatoly but from all the family. They had an ice-cold beer waiting for me and wanted me to debrief them quickly as they prepared to get underway ahead of the Arabs. Fuck, the paper-clipping and undoing takes a little adjusting when you switch roles so quickly, but I was soon back with the team with the original objective firmly in my sights. We packed, geared up and prepped for insertion into the desert and to shadow our targets to the border. The hotel room looked like a gangster's paradise, littered with small arms, ammunition, body armour and a plethora of other technical goodies, not to mention the shit Baz and Cheesy had been working on in the bathroom. The dustmen were next door waiting to sanitise the room from any explosive residues etc. on our departure.

We set out that night, just leaving Hugh to watch for the actual departure of the targets and be the tail. We would stay an hour ahead of them all the way, crossing the border into Saudi, breaking off the road into the desert, skimming around Al Silla'a and Al Batha, which was four hours out of Dubai to a point five miles west of any possible checkpoints, and picking up Highway 95 at a crossroads then driving on to a grid reference on Route 95 at an almost equidistant point between Qatar and the UAE borders where we would wait for Mohammed and Ahmed.

We had pulled off the road again into a ditch hidden by a rocky outcrop that shielded us from the road. The guys had a 360-degree view of the area. We were 10-15 miles outside of either border so not within sight of it but far enough away to avoid unnecessary attention from border patrols or other official traffic. It was then that Baz pointed out our exit strategy; we were positioned with Khor Duweihin 24° 21′ 32″ N 51° 21′ 43″ E military grid ref 39RWG3671194009 to our rear (and to the east), a sandy bay from which we would exit to RIBs, rendezvous with USS *Tarawa* and then sail with the ship en route to Australia, disembarking in BIOT waters. The team had done all the prep work and it was a perfect extraction plan avoiding spending any unnecessary additional time in the country after completion of the mission which had dovetailed beautifully into operation Red Reef III, the largest bilateral naval exercise in which the Saudi Navy had participated. The exercise involved almost two weeks of live surface-to-surface and air-to-surface missile firings and amphibious training in the North Arabian Sea and Arabian Gulf. The amphibious training was our extraction strategy – simply board a RIB amongst the chaos of an exercise and peel off to the safety of the US Navy.

We took up positions and hydrated ourselves whilst Cheesy our chaos man set up the mines and explosives to blow the cars off the road whilst hopefully keeping the road fairly intact. Baz had constructed the explosives in the bathroom at the hotel; he wanted the vehicles to be lifted up and thrown off the road towards us so the team could conduct a turkey shoot out of sight of the road. It took a little time for Baz and Cheesy to set up their little magic show. The binmen had been informed of the plan and would follow on our route after our departure by sea, making good the kill site, and then disperse themselves.

We waited. A light breeze kept us cool as the entire team watched the road leading back to Dubai. Every second a minute, every minute an hour. Out of the spotter sights we all simultaneously caught sight of a convoy coming down the highway towards our position. It turned off into the desert to a half-finished plot with a derelict building, partially hiding the possible targets. Smudge was on the squawk box to Hugh who informed us the targets were still mobile and over 40 minutes out – just two targets, as the women and children of the family had departed via Dubai, including Asad. It was a relief if I'm honest, as the possible elimination of the entire family may have been inevitable if we were unable to isolate the two on the list.

We had little time to reorganise and had to reposition between our initial road interception/ambush point and the new target zone. Rapid deployment tactics took us into the desert to a new vantage point, not great but good enough to be able to operate at each site if necessary, a small wall providing some cover from the road and the building. There were now six new targets at the building not active, just walking around waiting, smoking and generally stretching their legs. We split the team to give a better attacking position as the directive from the Steering Group was without ambiguity: to 'terminate with extreme prejudice Mohammed and Ahmed at any cost'.

With two more cars and a lone vehicle trailing close on the horizon, Hugh was at risk of being noticed. These cars turned off into the same compound area of the first convoy. Hugh continued and pulled into our initial staging point. Regrouping now, observing, Mohammed and Ahmed could be clearly identified talking with the six new targets. This propelled Smudge into some frantic radio activity to contact command in London via our US asset sailing in the Gulf for further instructions based upon the six new potential targets. It didn't concern me too much as the team's last order and fallback position was all targets to be eliminated if the mission priorities should become compromised in any way. Weapons and equipment were checked, but Cheesy was already available to deploy ahead with Baz and destroy the entire site. London wanted to keep the first group alive to give an alibi to the killing of Mohammed and Ahmed. Bollocks, re-think. Group huddle. Re-plan, last-minute reorganisation and strategy in place. Hugh, Smudge and I would head back south in the Land Cruiser in case the now possible information exchange led to the group dispersing in opposite directions. Smudge, Baz, Pierre and Cheesy would return to the original site and take out the six new targets if heading north, should Smudge and I fail. We were all to rendezvous at the beach on completion or the exchange site, depending on movements.

Bingo, drove right past the motherfuckers conducting the information exchange. The brown case with all the information re-written by London given by Anatoly to Mohammed was now being sold to this new group. Arabian but not businesslike, there was one guy in a suit and the rest in plain civilian clothing, well-armed and obviously well-funded. The team took extensive photographs of all participants whilst the exchange was undertaken. Then I made for a position of overwatch in a firing position south of the target with Hugh and Smudge. There was little cover for the team as Hugh with his 'broken-down' Land Cruiser was looking like the perfect stupid Arab without a clue what to do, looking under the hood of the Land Cruiser and smoking a cigarette, with myself and Smudge in the dirt. Mohammed and Ahmed departed the exchange site at speed and were heading in our direction, with the original six still at their meeting point. The tension inside was rising, but staying calm I was attuned to every tiny sound and was now sharply focused on any movement down sight. Sniper rifle loaded, noise suppressors in place, safety off, ready and poised. Baz had prepped a roadside bomb in the Cruiser which Hugh would now detonate if Smudge and I fucked up and failed to get a clean kill.

Time stood still. Looking down the highway, heat waves scorching the tarmac, a bead of sweat trickled down my back as I caught a glimpse of Smudge adjusting position. I adjusted my cap for shade over sight. There was a slight cloud of dust as more vehicles got back onto the road, which raised my heartrate and produced both a release of aggression and a sense of that welcome horrific expectation taking me back to the Asadi elimination. Black rubber tyres broke through the heat waves and I acquired a view of the Mercedes truck coming towards us down the highway at speed. My earpiece was crackling a little as the team were repositioning north of us as the first convoy departed from the exchange site in the opposite direction toward Qatar as predicted. Exchange completed. Communications silence, green for go from London. I could see the shapes enlarging behind the windshield, blurry and misshapen at first by the heat waves from the road but growing larger and larger. I paused and waited for absolute sight clarity. I could see Mohammed now, his eyes clear – *he's fucking mine, in the kill zone, in my sights, crosshairs aligned*. Gently squeeze, light recoil. Done. Smudge repeated for Ahmed almost simultaneously. The truck swerved just a little, decelerated as death took the pressure off the gas pedal, and then continued to roll down the road and bump into Hugh's truck – nothing dramatic, no Hollywood explosions or anything crazy, just two neat holes in the windshield and a mess inside.

It was a mad rush now, getting out of the dirt, gathering all my kit into the vehicle, double tap for each target, no mistakes, must be confirmed kills. We moved the bodies to one side, then got in, with Smudge driving and me in the back. Dust flying into the air, Smudge made a 180-degree turn back to the exchange site where we speedily parked up. Pierre repositioned the bodies and dressed the site to assimilate the kill was made where the information exchange had been conducted. Hugh then arrived and crashed his truck deliberately (he had stolen it that morning), then we were off, all kit, at full pace to the beach. Comms on, and we saw the RIB, our ride home, approaching the beach. I remember stumbling, like an asshole, into the water and then being lifted up by Smudge into the RIB before the twin V6 Suzuki outboards were at max chat and we were away headed for the horizon.

Forty-eight hours later I'm crashed out on my rack in the bungalow in Diego Garcia. There's nothing too glorious about the actual kill; it's the build-up, the anticipation and the fear of getting caught, the fear and excitement of a possible firefight.

I was totally exhausted but relieved it was all over for now. Mission was accomplished, making the Steering Group happy. Now for some downtime. We hit the beach and had a BBQ, cooking up fresh tuna some of the lads had caught that day on their fishing trip. I sat in the sea with my feet up eating fresh fish and drinking ice-cold American piss and it hardly felt like there was anything in the world to care about. We all simply got smashed out of our faces. We were left alone and kept out of sight by the island military police who had the beach secured off as we attempted to destroy every braincell in our heads to try and erase the whole mission from the archives of our minds.

A few months passed and the team and I slid back into island life, filling roles within the military community – customs, aircraft search patrols in the P-3 Orions, and of course Brit ops around the outer islands, which to be fair were just great little holidays, better than anything you'll find in the Maldives. We did a lot of diving and game fishing. I took two weeks' leave with Cheesy to Hong Kong and China to see all the tourist shit. We really got ourselves off the grid for a while – made it to the Great Wall, Beijing, Xian, the whole tourist package, staying at the Royal Fleet Club for free. Everything was sweet before we finally got the orders to see through the mission to Romania as promised to Evgeny and the family and disrupt the supply chain from Russia whilst detailing what arms were going where, with a particular interest in what was going to Iraq.

The mission and the methodology employed to cover our tracks appeared to have paid off, and the communications coming out of Moscow were fraught with fear, blame being fired in all directions, including Iraq, Iran and Saudi, as no one seemed to have the truth or a reasonable handle on it. Asad had apparently gone to Moscow to be with the family and there were tensions, not only because of his bereavement but also as to his real intentions or purpose away from Iran. Anatoly was complaining openly about Asad hassling his family whilst he was away from home and at work in Sarov. Everyone from the Steering Group down to the fucking cleaners at GCHQ knew that 'they' wanted to know who had killed for the technical information provided by Anatoly. Who were the Arabs at the exchange site? This would all add to the complexities of the Romania trip on which Asad now wanted to accompany Evgeny and Anatoly; it would be a huge risk, and to be in a country shutting down the arms transports into Serbia now that war had broken out, with Asad in the wings, would make everything incredibly complicated.

It was after the Socialist Republic of Bosnia and Herzegovina passed a referendum for independence on 29 February 1992 that the war got underway. In May the war for (the now former) Yugoslavia was firmly in play and it was clear that Erik and Alex needed the trade routes to remain open and continue working in that region. The routes from Romania through to Split had to be kept open at all costs. The onward shipments to Iraq were now erratic and uncontrolled at best now that Mohammed, Asadi and Ahmed were all out of the picture. There was obviously a missing link in the supply chain to oversee those shipments on to Iraq; now that war had broken out, it had all got messy.

With more and more shipments being lost in transit and more than likely diverted to the Bosnia war effort, communications and pressure were building from Moscow for Evgeny, Anatoly and me to become more involved, although it wasn't clear at this time who exactly the end customers were in Iraq, leading the Steering Group to question if we had been completely successful in the UAE or whether the whole thing had been taken over by a new third party who was at the exchange site. Maybe that had been Asad's directive, to ensure onward shipments weren't interrupted, supporting a secure future business platform for new technical papers from Anatoly, and be responsible for all future deals and shipments following his father's death.

It wasn't by chance that Alex had become more than a little spooked by the killing of Mohammed and Ahmed and put a halt to the trip to Romania, simply allowing a percentage of shipments to be written off despite the cost and reputational issues. He planned that we would all meet up in Bosnia at a date to be confirmed once he and Erik had revisited the politics, customers and funding. It was clear a new player was on the scene who had yet to be revealed, and it was definitely an Iran/Iraq player but only time would tell.

However, for me it was out of my hands for the time being. We had completed Operation Segment and it had been some 14 months since leaving the UK for the team and myself, travelling through Singapore and Diego Garcia and into the Middle East and back again. I returned to the UK for a full debrief at GCHQ with the Steering Group to then start preparations for what would be known as Operation RIAR. The team and I re-entered the UK, went our separate ways and got off grid whilst the politicians and the Steering Group engineered the politics, the legalities and the funding for Operation RIAR (Russia Iraq Arms Route) and the eventual insertion into Bosnia to uncover the missing links and possibly deal with the splinter groups or terrorist cells which were syphoning off arms from Russia to Iraq and into the Bosnia conflict and the genocide that was underway. I have no doubt that all countries involved at some point gave the green light to the Steering Group to remove those who were undermining the real peace talks and legitimate trading in arms. It was all going to be bad for business for the family in the end.

The Steering Group

Chapter 8

A Dangerous Distraction?

Returning to the UK for me was always a little depressing and this time was no exception, and in addition this was a major step down from the active role I so much enjoyed and thrived on. It was the next four years that were probably the most complex and demanding for me, both personally and professionally. Returning to the navy again gave me an entirely new direction as expected and a safety net to fall into whilst I decompressed and focused on the base job, which I actually enjoyed at that time to be honest.

I left GCHQ and all the issues behind, to disappear off grid for about a year or so into the world of NBCD, and let GCHQ develop the strategies and timings for all the communications to and from Moscow which were now mostly all lies; the innocent letters from one friend to another had all but been used up. The planning for a defection was simply out of my hands and would need to be woven into the fabric of normal operations, the correspondence and other military planning and intelligence. I had submitted a lot of intel and background information that needed to be taken to pieces by the teams at GCHQ with regards to the Russian arms and information deals taking place. The complexities of the Russian operation with regards to piggy-backing legitimate arms deals that allowed for the syphoning of arms to go relatively undetected to so many different locations was going to prove almost impenetrable as everything sat behind legitimate transactions, politicians and delicate relations on all sides.

I think what was of most interest was the technology that I had passed back to London from Sarov and how close it had come to falling into Iranian hands. The possibilities of getting further intel and the fact I may have opened the way for a possible defection opportunity from a major player in the nuclear arms programme in Sarov had made me very popular within the inner circles of the organisation. This allowed Cdr Brown to bask in all the glory.

I guess you could say the Steering Group was probably pleased to stand my team and me down for a while whilst they rebuilt the OPLAN (operational plan). The next few years of SIS involvement within the military followed the developments of Desert Shield & Desert Storm and of course the Bosnian crisis, with Moscow fuelling the workload exponentially. Bosnia was a NATO operation, and the successful planning of multinational military operations required a common doctrine which was aimed primarily at those engaged in operational-level planning, specifically commanders and staff employed in joint force command headquarters and component command headquarters. As Operation Segment had been purely a British operation, Ben Martin, United States Special Operations Command (USSOCOM) from the Steering Group, was now well and truly in the driving seat and at the centre of the politics and the planning for Operation RIAR. We would be working with the Americans now, under the wings of NATO.

I joined the Royal Navy NBCD (Nuclear, Biological and Chemical Defence) school in early 1993 following some well-earned leave. The Steering Group and Ben were now deeply entrenched in all the pre-emptive tactical planning that Middle Eastern politics and on-ground developments had led the teams to with regards to Iraq. Saddam Hussein would be toppled and a future all-out war for the liberation of Iraq looked inevitable (this was the period in the build-up to the Iraq War 2003). The team needed all operatives to be absolutely highly trained in all aspects of NBCD defence that had become apparent. Not only did British and coalition intel suggest chemical weapons were now on the move in Iraq, but following the Kuwaiti oil fires that were caused by Iraqi military forces setting fire to 732 oil wells as part of a scorched earth policy while retreating from Kuwait in 1991, the Steering Group wanted specialist operatives with engineering specialisations to be fully trained to NBCD 35 standards for chemical warfare and firefighting issues.

The focus had shifted within the intelligence services from the lessons learnt in the oil fields of Kuwait to the oil platforms and the tanker traffic in the Gulf which were all still operating in fear of future attack. Politically, there remained little app-reciation of the serious threat posed by the Iraqi military machine to the sea lanes of the Persian Gulf and to the Saudi and other Gulf Cooperation Council (GCC) ports on its south shore, a threat which remained relatively unaddressed and one my team seemed to be gearing up for. The whole assemblage of issues was entwined not only in politics in the Middle East but with global developments, especially within the former Yugoslavia, which was all interlinked into a bigger power struggle evolving out of the Middle East, i.e. Saudi Arabia, and Russia, which appeared to be planning a shift in power, opposite to the desires of the USA and the Western world. Russia was supporting Serbia whilst turning a political blind eye to the Iraq arms build-up, and secretly supplying technical papers (albeit intercepted by our good selves) to Iran in support of Saudi which wanted to see a power shift from Israel to an Arab alliance, with Iran being the major benefactor. This went against a main thread of intelligence and indeed Middle Eastern history in general that had Saudi deeply opposed to

Iran because of the whole religious divide between the Iranian Islamic Shia regime and the Saudi Sunni monarchy, and of course all the energy disputes.

I'm pleased to say I was able to stay away from the command and government politics which no one really understood, as our opinions and politics as a fighting unit were much simpler. We were just the pawns in the big games of deception and didn't really give a shit to be honest. Once that first bullet spirals at velocity out of the breach then they're all the enemy to me and the team.

It was whilst I was studying NBCD that the tensions in the former Yugoslavia rose significantly and the conflict became extremely complex. Muslims and Serbs formed an alliance against Croats in Herzegovina, rival Muslim forces fought each other in north-west Bosnia, Croats and Serbs were fighting against Muslims in central Bosnia, and all I could do was watch from a distance gaining a greater realisation that there was stronger and stronger support coming out of Russia for Serbia. The Russian foreign policy language on the former Yugoslavia at this time was neutral and simply called for Russia to cooperate with the UN in peacemaking efforts and to use its influence in the former Yugoslavia to encourage a peaceful settlement.

Russia was between a rock and a hard place as Serbia had always been a long-time ally. Later, in 1993, Russia, hoping to maintain its image with the West as a useful mediator in a thoroughly frustrating conflict, caused some tensions with the United States and its Western allies, who had hoped for straightforward Russian support of UN-sanctioned military actions against Serbian aggression instead of fence sitting throughout the whole ordeal. Russia was simply not helping, it was quietly supporting the Serbs whilst condemning them publicly, and this was where the arms were being syphoned off to and funded by Saudi Arabia which was diverting attention away from Iraq and the Iranian nuclear programme. The pressure on the family to keep the lanes open was now secretly sanctioned in the Lubyanka and the Kremlin. I had no idea what was actually going on in Russia at the higher levels but could see the turmoil in Anatoly's letters as illegitimate sidelines were being further explored by Alex for the kind of financial gain Moscow would never allow, and the words 'terrorist groups' were mentioned many times in briefing papers and indicated that a 'sweep and clear' policy would be sanctioned if substantial evidence could be gained by intelligence operatives to support such claims.

It was absolutely crazy to think that whilst the world was engaged in this silent turmoil and ready to implode once again, I was introduced by way of letter to Anna (who would later become my wife). Working at the NBCD school, and well away from any Bosnian nightmares or issues from Russia or the Middle East, a mate of mine Tom and I took Pete and Jackie out to a pub in Bursledon called The Jolly Sailor (Howards' Way on TV) for a meal and a few pints of real ale, Speckled Hen or Tanglefoot. Tom and I had often enjoyed going to Old Portsmouth for real ale evenings at The Dolphin pub and were always keen to explore further afield for the more genuine pub experience, including a medieval night out at the Fox & Hounds, not far from The Jolly Sailor. We had gone by train and were absolutely smashed out of our faces enjoying one of the most amazing evenings of my time in Portsmouth. The pub was by the side of the River Hamble next to the Elephant Boatyard. It was beautifully maintained and gave a warm welcome and old-fashioned feel, with the interior comparable to a hobbit's house, with old stone-flagged floors, oak beams and matching curved supporting structures. The whole interior was fitted out with traditional old wooden furniture and maritime memorabilia, with low ceilings and a warm hearth in winter. I remember the main drunken laughing point that evening being something to do with a gorilla shitting in your mouth whilst you were asleep after a night out – Jackie really thought we had been shit on by a gorilla and missed the joke completely, making her the target of fun for the rest of the evening.

Pete knew Anna through his wife – Jackie and Anna had attended a nursing course together previously – and went on to explain in great detail how amazing Anna was and how well suited they thought we would be. He had caught my attention and, after gaining Anna's address, I wrote a letter introducing myself. She drove down to Portsmouth a short time later and met me with Pete and Jackie in a pub called The Mermaid. I remember it well – I had been out in town and bought a completely new outfit from a clothes store in the city, seeking the shop assistant's opinion on everything from the shoes to the tie on suitability for a first date. Anna had a fucking Fiat Panda and drove that heap of shit all the way to Portsmouth to see me on a blind date. Now, I remember seeing her for the first time and nearly shitting myself. Pete was right, she was stunning, the kind of woman you just can't take your eyes off. Amazing. Anna went to the bathroom and, as soon as she had disappeared out of sight, Pete and Jackie demanded to know what I thought of her.

Now, I know it's a cliché but it really was love at first sight. I just didn't know how to handle a real woman, never really had to before this point. Life had just suddenly become massively complicated. We enjoyed our short time together and soon made plans for a second date to the cinema before she left to go back up north to Tadcaster. Having never been accountable in this way before and never having had a third party in my life, I must have fucked up a million protocols with the Steering Group whilst I sought approval to continue with this new adventure in my life. Anna and her entire family were undoubtedly screened for any possible connection to terrorists, foreign intelligence organisations, Russian and Middle Eastern contacts, through emails, internet activity, phones, etc., etc., whilst counter-espionage, counter-insurgency and MI5 (home security) made my life a nightmare. All Anna had to do was make me a sausage casserole and a birthday cake at her place and I was putty in her hands.

I actually had the minerals to introduce Anna to my parents and, more to the point, to my mother quite early on in our relationship. She was a hit at first, especially with my dad who gave his approval almost immediately. We had afternoon tea with my mother and it was a little strained to say the least but a pleasant enough afternoon with Anna looking all virgin-like in a white dress. I knew there would be a fight for this relationship, remembering the lengths my mum went to in order to try and dissuade my older brother from his previous girlfriend when their relationship appeared to be approaching marriage. It ended in tears. I would have a fight at both ends, and it got heated to say the least. It was worse than dealing with the Russians!

Anna and I enjoyed only the briefest of times together but I knew when we were together how much chemistry there was between us. I loved being in her company, and I remember our first dinner together at her home. She lived in a tiny terraced house in Tadcaster. She had made this little place home and on a tight budget. To be able to put everything together she must have had to work long hours. But as all young people are, she was desperate for her own space, her own freedom. She cooked me a sausage casserole and it won me over straight away. She often cooked for me and I always had to rush off, either to work or to my parents' house, as a curfew was always in place. Some fucked-up control my mother held over me whilst I stayed at home. If only she had known what I got up to in my spare time or in the service. Mothers! You can't control them. I often had to race my Jaguar down the motorway to meet the demands of my mother. There were many arguments. Love prevailed. Love conquers all and I was not gonna allow my mother to come between us.

It wasn't too long before I booked our first romantic weekend away to a hotel called The Montagu Arms in the New Forest. I remember driving Anna there from Portsmouth, with her continually saying that she really didn't want to stay in a hotel where we had to share a bathroom; she really preferred an en-suite room. The Montagu was a five-star hotel (it came in at around £350 a night – remember, this was the 1990s) and I had a four-poster room booked; it was the best money could buy and I had scouted it out a few weeks prior. The Montagu Arms Hotel was privately owned at the time and was the epitome of luxurious British country hotels. Set in a beautiful location with extensive grounds and gardens almost attached to the foliage that covered the old brick building's exterior, sympathetically hiding her age, it welcomed you through solid wooden doors to the smell of last night's extinguished coal fires and the sound of a ticking grandfather clock. A genuine welcoming smile greeted you as you stood on the homely rugs listening to the chinking of china plates from the dining room while you checked in, your mind leaving the big wide world at the door.

Immediately the hotel was a hit. We rushed up to the room eager to experience our first time together. Anna had forgotten something and I had to rush back out to the car to get it, and fell down the stairs – all of them! Landing at reception in a heap, I damn near broke my ankle. Fucking thing swelled up like a balloon. With a swollen painful ankle, bruised beyond belief, I managed to hobble back upstairs where Anna was waiting. She then put her nursing skills into action by putting a cold flannel on the offending ankle, swearing she hoped it wasn't broken as she didn't want to have to take me to A&E

and ruin the entire weekend. She elevated my leg on a pillow and laughed at me.

We made love and I was nervous as hell that first time. I lay with Anna in that big four-poster bed in a land so far from my troubles, in the quiet of the New Forest. We slowly undressed each other and kissed slowly and softly at first but then more deeply as we became lost in our passion, and I was allowed to forget who I was and become just a normal guy with a girl making love together. I had not had sex with her during the months leading up to this intimate time together, some sort of honour code or respect for a person I genuinely wanted to treat well. Trembling, my smile became a grin as our journey climaxed into a magical collaboration of need satisfying need. I felt more of a man that day than I ever had in my entire life. I guess a man needs to know he is at least capable of being able to satisfy a woman sexually. It was a completeness that allowed a transition away from my childhood, and a short moment in time when I was mentally free from the past and the world I was living in.

The romance was quickly destroyed by my father ringing the hotel and being put through to our room. It was classic – asking what on earth I was doing in a hotel (like he didn't know). This had all arisen because my parents had received a bloody booking confirmation letter for our stay, sent to my home address! I couldn't believe it. I asked my dad, "What the hell do you think I am doing?" It was like I was a teenager or something, totally bizarre. I could hear my mother in the background screaming her condemnation through the 300 miles of telephone wire. I think you could say that was the start of all the disapproval and negativity my mother showed towards Anna over the coming years before we got married. The turmoil included excommunication, fights and arguments, a curfew when I stayed at my parents' house and just about every disapproving gesture aimed to try and end our relationship prematurely. I'm pleased to say our love endured and we are still together to this very day despite these and many other obstacles.

Dinner that evening in the hotel was simply one of the most memorable occasions for us during our early relationship. It was sheer class and couldn't have been more perfect. It was indeed a grand affair. Just to get the accompanying bread was a display of amazing etiquette: you chose a type of bread from the bread trolley which was transferred to a carving board, then a slice was cut and placed on a serving plate prior to being finally transferred to your side plate. We giggled like schoolchildren and enjoyed the meal immensely, washing it down with a bottle of Dom Perignon champagne. I had tried to set the tone for the kind of future I wanted with this amazing woman, who I would eventually take to stay in some of the very best hotels in the world, including The Peninsula in Hong Kong and Raffles in Singapore. I wanted her to experience the finest life had to offer. I knew what the opposite was like being in a war zone. It was going to be the challenge of my life to keep my work and my private life both functioning alongside each other. But I felt and still do feel that the two had to be kept separate because of the very nature of what I was involved in.

It only took a few weeks for me to be dumped! I failed to fucking call Anna at specific times, which was damn near impossible being in the service. Failing to be at the end of a telephone every day eventually led to me being binned, and I remember the day because it was a difficult day conducting a disaster exercise at the fire school. I was fucking livid but there was no way of explaining it away; she needed to feel in control, and women, I learnt, want to be called every fucking day. I was shit at relationships really; in my mind when I was away at work I was away at work, and I needed for my state of mind to keep them separate and pigeon-holed. Of course, that was never going to work. I had to integrate my girlfriend more into the military way of thinking. Our relationship was never going to be normal like other regular navy guys who had their families with them all the time, our relationship was going to be much more complex.

The secrecy and difficulties of a double life in order to keep the innocent not only safe but ignorant to the risks at hand were slowly being realised in a world which was only going to become more challenging. I can remember spending some time with Brown on the matter, and the only solutions were to play harder at both ends of the system. He simply wished me luck but casually warned me that any slip in security would result in a very swift departure from the SIS and N1, in fact possibly the military altogether. I had, after all, signed my life away three times to be in the Steering Group's Russian operative programme. One thing that did stick in my mind was his comment that married men were 60% more likely to return from a war zone than a single man as the married man simply took less risks. It was an interesting thought that I believe I was able to substantiate later in my career.

I sort of introduced Anna to the navy when I joined HMS *Eagle* in 1994. She drove me to the ship after a weekend together in Cornwall. We had got our relationship back together and had survived a few bumps which were to be expected in any new relationship, but with a new set of guidelines from Anna, including the telephone requirements. I was forever trying to deal with her communication issues – I actually hated phones at this point in my life. Then there were the demands of the Steering Group and the build-up to Operation RIAR, its preparation and training, and of course my mother who was an entire war zone on her own. I think, looking back, the intelligence services were entirely right to have a younger generation driving the Steering Group's agenda. My relationships, both with Anna and my wider family, all looked incredibly average, normal, messy and unassuming to any outsider. But internally it was all tightly embedded in the absolute grip of secrecy and surveillance by the Steering Group, ensuring everything was kept on track and under perfect cover. It would be fair to say Anna was expendable at this time. She and her family were under surveillance the entire time I was on ops and they probably still are. I didn't find it difficult in any way to keep the interests of the Steering Group close to my heart. I had no reason to disclose anything as any scenario or situation could always be made accountable to the navy – cover within cover I suppose. It's easy to hide sand in a sandpit was the expression I learned.

We stayed in a hotel in Cornwall, at Cawsand (same hotel my parents stayed in for my passing out at Raleigh), and had a wonderful weekend together eating and drinking but also enjoying being by the sea. I remember the hotel wasn't up to much, had a busted shower and a split-level room with a crap bed. It didn't matter at all as we enjoyed a little restaurant on the seafront with perhaps only five tables. We stayed late into the night sharing candlelight and feelings of love for one another. She took me to join *Eagle* on the Sunday, and the only way to describe that feeling is if you were to watch *We Were Soldiers* as Mel Gibson leaves his wife in bed in the early morning to go off to Vietnam. The emptiness, the loss and the immediate detachment from the one you love is instant, like a knife to the heart. I don't know if Anna ever knew how much I loved her in those early days and it would be easy to just write about it years later as a love story, but those three deployments to the Adriatic made for a melting furnace of every emotion, commitment, loyalty and relationship in my life. It all came close to failing as I was never ever going to be able to keep up with the normal demands of a relationship whilst being deployed and continuing my role within the Steering Group.

There were exceptions. I remember being deployed the first time to the Adriatic and to the Bosnian conflict. HMS *Eagle* was to berth in Malta for Christmas, so I arranged for Anna to fly out from Gatwick to join me for Christmas and spend a week in a hotel. I had managed to call her from Trieste in Italy after an extended silence (a shitty container port) some months earlier after crossing back over the border from what is now Slovenia following a reconnaissance mission to the Romanian border with my team and prior to the eventual meetings with Evgeny and the new crowd the family were supporting. We were working with local services under the disguise of Wooltech International, a fake company dealing in woollen products from all over the world. It allowed for safe houses and easy transports, crossing borders with little or no interference.

The ship had been in Trieste a few days before our arrival and rendezvous. Trieste was an interesting place to meet up with the ship and allowed me time to readjust and unwind. The team and I had commandeered an office building near the port for the purposes of consolidating our intel and monitoring traffic movements behind us, so to speak, to ensure we had a clean exit. I remember phoning Anna from the office with my feet up on the desk, forgetting that I had no need to monitor the time or 'the cost' of the call. It was good to speak with Anna and we were very much looking forward to our time together at Christmas. I suppose it fits the horrible description of clocking in, where all the guys would clock in with their partners and then appear to forget all about them as we all concentrated on the job in hand – a magnificent way to deal with your loved ones and a way that can't be understood unless you have had to endure such situations where private lives cannot be allowed to enter and disrupt mission objectives. This is not to be callous or cold-hearted in any way but simply to preserve the integrity of the mission, the security of those involved and the very safety of the ones we actually love.

Time passed quickly and I remember transferring back to the *Eagle* and refocusing on the fact that Christmas was to be spent in Malta. Life seemed to be normal back on the *Eagle* and the prospect of some downtime felt very welcoming. The ship eventually berthed in Valletta against a backdrop of stone architecture and history, which I left behind in the rush to get to the airport. Waiting at the airport in Malta for her to arrive was one of the first times I truly got that feeling I would marry Anna. I can remember watching for her arrival through the glass partitions. Anna was and still is a beautiful woman. I think what attracted me to her the most, apart from the obvious sexual stuff, was the fact she was normal, grounded and my best friend. Someone with whom time could pass comfortably in silence as well as having fun, and she was a great travel companion. We were soon to gain a healthy taste for travel and the finer things in life.

Reunited once again after nearly five months apart. I picked up a hire car which we aptly named the foxy lady (VW Fox) and dropped off a friend and his girlfriend at another hotel before arriving at a shitty three-star hotel on the other side of the island away from the ship. Despite that hotel being probably the worst on the island, it had absolutely no impact on our time together. We were young and in love. With Anna I was able to briefly put the world to one side for those few days and have some fun and downtime.

The hotel really was awful. It had very average rooms with crap balconies overlooking all the other crap rooms around a central atrium. It didn't matter though. We were in love, and making up for lost time was definitely on the agenda from minute one. I had never been much of a ladies' man and had never gone looking for just sex for pleasure, but Anna had an insatiable appetite and it was like running a marathon to keep up. I don't think I was inexperienced or anything but it felt like a whole new experience with her, more intense, more exciting and definitely genuine. We gave each other pet names; I think we both ended up with many. Unlike our first time in The Montagu Arms this was totally undisturbed time together, despite the frequent fire alarms!

We spent a week or so touring the island, having fun and sightseeing. We loved the time together exploring in the car. I think this is a true test of whether you are going to last as a couple if you can spend all your time together as we did on that holiday. We passed the test and knew we would spend the rest of our lives together. I have some very fond memories of our time in Malta. We were young, in love and carefree. It didn't matter we had a shit hotel, a shit Christmas dinner in the hotel (which we walked away from) or a Chinese takeaway for New Year! Time together was the only thing that mattered.

Always wanting to get out and explore, we spent hours zooming around in the hire car taking in all the sights. It was a great holiday. We never really ate in the hotel and managed to stumble upon a restaurant called the Roman's Den after walking around hopelessly looking for somewhere to get a cold drink and get out of the sun and find a bathroom for Anna. I think it was in a town called Rabat. The restaurant door was not exactly inviting but the menu looked good. Pushed on ahead by Anna, who was and is very shy, we descended the stairs into an underground deserted restaurant filled with empty tables beneath brick arches and weird artwork. There was no one there and we sat patiently at the bar in the air conditioning for maybe 10 minutes. We were about to leave when a strange character by the name of Aiden appeared at the doorway from the kitchen, an explosion of curly black hair atop a beaming smile in chef's whites covered in stains – this was our host. Delighted we had waited, he prepared a tasting plate free of charge and we sat and enjoyed an afternoon of conversation with him as well as a few drinks, promising to come back for dinner.

We went back to Roman's Den for dinner and New Year's Eve. Back then there were no drink & drive laws so I was able to get plastered on champagne after eating the most amazing and, still to this day, best lobster thermidor ever. We each had a whole lobster tail taken out of its shell, cooked perfectly and re-inserted with a prawn thermidor sauce. I think it was maybe 2am when we emerged from the restaurant back onto the street and drove back to the hotel. Everyone was drunk and there was traffic chaos as people made their way home after the New Year celebrations.

I remember during our tours of Malta ending up at the film set of *Popeye* and spending a joyful day lost in fantasy land; I have a great photo of Anna behind one of those wooden characters with a hole to put your face in – it was Anna as Olive Oil. A few days later I watched Anna ascend the escalator up to departures. She turned and waved and was gone. I returned to the ship in Valletta harbour, which looked completely out of place, the modern cold grey steel of the ship against the backdrop of the stone fortress and Grand Harbour. I had a day and a night in Malta to explore prior to the ship sailing and managed to enjoy the fantastic Maltese hospitality to its fullest extent.

The ship sailed from Malta bound for Portsmouth, my first trip to Bosnia completed and a relationship still relatively intact. Heck, it was hard to adjust to having a person in my life who wanted to be with me all the time. It didn't compute, it was alien to me, and I guess I was suspicious in a number of ways. Suspicious that anyone would be interested in me for any genuine reason but also afraid I was being trapped into marriage followed by kids, a mortgage and boredom. Usually it means it's too good to be true. However, Anna was genuine to a fault which made the whole fucking situation harder to deal with. It would have been a damn sight easier to have ended it all at this early stage rather than go through the whole ordeal and the secrecy of the double life, not to mention the fact that I was actually in love which was a major curve ball, as it can be for anyone. Talk of buying a house in Portsmouth was simply crazy in my mind. I was always suspicious, and like all operatives I guess totally paranoid about anyone entering my life even if invited.

I had the voyage home and a heap of time to consider all the options open to me. I managed to get on leave back up north and would travel (not as often as Anna would have liked) to see Anna. She was a home owner at least so I wasn't a meal ticket! Fucking looking back, we should have just eloped and got married that leave, but it's never that simple when you're in the moment. Always in my left ear was my mother who found endless ways to make our relationship difficult: curfews and other ridiculous stipulations placed upon me whilst I stayed with my parents at the weekends. Then I had the demands of the Steering Group competing for my attention in the other ear. I know I should have just moved in with Anna, I know that now, but the fact is we do owe my mother a small debt of gratitude. She almost drove me to the point of literally squeezing the life out of her by gripping her throat after an argument over Anna. Believe me, I would have ended her life, but this moved our relationship to the point of no return, and I was certain that Anna was the woman for me. I would abandon my family for her if necessary, and that kind of certainty made other decisions regarding my relationship with Anna much easier. That was family dealt with, in my mind – well, one of them anyway – and now there was my second family to organise in my head. People, families and relationships, I find them all too difficult to understand sometimes.

What no one, including Anna, understood or was even aware of was the complexities of having a partner whilst being involved with the Steering Group. A partner is a bigger security risk than the operative because should she be compromised in any way then it's an open back door into the system, a breach that could open the doors right into the heart of the British Secret Service. The Steering Group had to put measures and resources in place whilst I was away to ensure everyone's peace of mind. Any pathway to the Steering Group, which operated behind the firewalls of MI6/MI5 and N1, would be an unacceptable risk. To expose a more fundamentally silent service whose mission is to undertake (by use of intelligence) the quiet option preferred by members of the House (known as the executive branch) to manipulate events abroad in favour of the Crown would be a catastrophic political and security disaster. Of course, officially we didn't exist. Funny, I still look for that resource outside my house today, however ridiculous that is now, as it's been some years since I was an active member of the group. I guess all those months that Anna felt alone, she was never actually alone.

Operation RIAR was set to remove any certainty I had of getting married, and all my domestic arrangements would have blowholes in them from every direction. My life's sureties would start to fall apart in the coming 12 months as I traversed the minefields of love with absolute commitment to the person I loved whilst battling with utter contempt for the military forcing me to possibly end the relationship because of the risk and danger I was putting Anna and myself in. If I had ever been discovered, captured or my true identity released, Anna would have been in as much danger as me for reprisals or possible recruitment under extreme circumstances through blackmail or threats from the other side of the espionage coin. This mind-spinning reality was the catalyst for all the uncertainties and the appalling treatment I unleashed upon my future wife in order to see and test her ability to deal with my attachment to the Steering Group, and withstand it. Yes, I admit I was a bastard as I tested Anna right to the edge and beyond that coming year. The Steering Group was aware and approved – fuck, they were only interested in the business at hand and wanted the results on the other side of RIAR, not a security risk in the UK, but they needed me so Anna was in for the ride for as long as she could hold on.

It was me who turned out to be the weak one as I saw my heart nearly break whilst continually trying harder and harder to push her away. But I sit here now believing that in the deepest corners of my heart I was, am and always will be Anna's soulmate, revealing only now why I did what I had to do in order to protect us both, uncovering who I was and what I had become under the veil of secrecy embedded in all the double lives, lies and confusion of who I myself wanted to be. The subterfuge that I had to employ to protect Anna and my military family was a nauseating obligation that was the very weapon one would employ to destroy the very fabric, purity and trust of the love I had been so privileged to be offered. Espionage isn't to be found in bed with love and trust, but yearns to be unmasked and set free when such purity enters its realm, yet it is too afraid to trust in return for fear of its masters.

I then left Anna behind and alone as I embarked on Operation RIAR.

Fuck, if only Anna had known what a fucking nightmare I was about to embark upon, could I forgive myself not only for my silence that I transmitted that coming year but for the whole fucking ordeal and aftermath that I'm still dealing with today? I still seethe with hatred for what happened in Bosnia. Motherfuckers, all of them. Bosnia was just another excuse for a racial hatred that saw Europe sit back and watch whilst genocide once again crawled out of the earth and into the darkest hearts of men beset on seizing power from those they knew could not resist or put up any kind of fight. Oppressing the weak and the vulnerable, then exploring and celebrating in the very filth and riches war brings to those whose desire is to immerse themselves in the quest for power beguiled by the very lies they have fabricated as the truth to obtain it.

Plato said, "Only the dead have seen the end of war." That guy knew what he was talking about.

The Steering Group

Chapter 9

Operation RIAR

It was back-to-back deployments for many of the British Armed Forces out to the Adriatic and the Bosnian crisis. I would hitch a ride aboard the various British naval platforms rotating watch out there, patrolling off the coast of Split. Although under the Steering Group's control, I was also working for NATO now, still with my original team attached to me and my assignments. This rotation was to last on and off for just under three years for me and the team, which made home life really difficult.

I can't remember how shit I was at maintaining correspondence with Anna back home but I know it was bad, and if I'm honest I probably ceased communications for the entire time I was in theatre. It was probably for the best as an average day at the office was looking like 20 hours and there wasn't much left in me after that which was any good. I'm quite certain it had been in my mind for some time to end the relationship, not only from a security point of view but as a kind of safety recoil in order to hide myself from Anna. My increasing activities overseas weren't helping in any way either, making it very difficult to make the books balance between home and the service. Having children had been talked about but there was never any way I would have brought a child into the world in which I was operating at that time. The possibilities of that child becoming fatherless were officially given the odds of 80%, not something you want to discuss with your future wife. I sent a letter to Anna implying it was best to end the relationship on my return to England. It's strange because some 20+ years later we have sort of admitted to each other that we regret not having children. We were better at good holidays, five-star hotels and fine wine.

I spent some transit time aboard HMS *Eagle* on my second deployment, getting re-familiarised with the team, attending group briefings from the Steering Group via sat link, discussing the high-value targets, priorities and secondary objectives they wished to explore and a plethora of background material that bored the team and me to death. I also managed to get plenty of time in the engineering department clocking up time in the 'chair' training to become an officer of the watch (engineering). It was my penultimate step to becoming an SNCO in the navy, which was tied to promotion within N1. This was a task the Steering Group was very keen to see completed, not only because of their plans for me to work with Anatoly in the future if a defection could be pulled off but also because it would make the transitioning of identities, posts, appointments, etc. easier to manage between various units. I do believe now that it's policy for any N1 operative to be of SNCO rank from any base unit. My time on the *Triton* had made this task easier as I had enjoyed endless study time. Gas turbines were easier to operate than a nuclear propulsion plant, so it was just a case of familiarisation and lots and lots of practice. It was a welcome distraction from the monotony of daily life aboard ship but one I really just wanted to tick off and move on from. There was no room for exceptions – to remain under the Steering Group umbrella, I needed to have two specialisations: language, which I already had; and engineering, which for me was an immense struggle.

There were obviously other Russian intelligence functions to be undertaken beyond Op RIAR, with all the source indicators pointing towards Anatoly and the information I had extracted from him in Dubai. Someone in the doughnut had developed a taste for Russian technology after our last success and was obviously keen to explore this avenue to a more beneficial conclusion, and submarine propulsion systems and subsurface-launched ICBMs were high on their agenda. Anatoly had become more popular than he could ever have imagined. I was destined to gain a more in-depth knowledge of ship design and construction whether I liked it or not before undertaking the assignments that were being lined up for me in the future involving Anatoly.

The *Eagle* arrived on station in the Adriatic as part of the Yugoslavian task force and joined up with USS *America* and the *Theodore Roosevelt*. I transferred over by helicopter to the *America* on the first flight off the deck one morning after the SAR helo had gone airborne. Day one week one on station. Lynx helicopters are just flying taxis, and I always enjoyed riding with the side door open until I learned of an accident where the side door had come off one particular helicopter and ripped off the tail rotor, then it ditched and all aboard were killed. I always had the door shut after hearing about that. I attended briefings with Paul and the team aboard the *America*. They all looked exhausted at those briefings. Paul was keen to point out he had been chewed up in the five-sided puzzle (the Pentagon) for the better part of a month and was pleased to be away from the politics, and he would seriously be up for coming out in the field if he could. Baz just laughed at him, retorting that the team didn't do combat tourism, not even for the Steering Group.

It had become painfully clear from all the continued and elongated correspondence between myself and the family in Moscow that Alex urgently wanted me to join Evgeny this one time on that transport out of Drobeta-Turnu Severin in Romania (as previously agreed with the family in Dubai).

Delivering this cargo, which Alex had now put all his personal guarantees on, to a place called Valjevo was of paramount importance to the family and Alex wanted me there to support Evgeny. I had to look it up in an atlas. Valjevo is a city in the Kolubara District in western Serbia, an area well known to be controlled by the Russians. Alex had made it clear that he controlled the entire route as it was in Russian-controlled Serbian territory, therefore Evgeny and I would be perfectly safe, but it had to be a personal delivery by the family as the customer was nervous following the disappearance of Mohammed and Ahmed after the last family gathering in Dubai. The letter and email exchanges danced around the issues in order to be non-specific, but it was pretty clear Alex was very much in the spotlight for this next exchange and no amount of bullshitting was going to allow him to sit this one out. The customer clearly didn't want to be exposed to any risk without the family being present, and he needed to be the living on-site insurance policy.

Tensions and suspicions were running high amongst the opposition groups, and the operation was given high priority as the Steering Group wanted to track the entire arms route and tie it in with operational surveillance, not only of the Russian supply chain but its intended onward route, possibly to Sarajevo (the syphoned route), and of course its final destination in the Middle East and the end customers there or any onward movements. The team's objectives were to neutralise all those identified on the primary list and destroy the cargo once I had separated myself from personal contact with Evgeny. Secondary to my role in accompanying Evgeny was to identify any Middle Eastern connections, gain their confidence if possible to expedite a meeting with them and the family under more controlled conditions, thereby facilitating solid intel confirmation that this new group was the same group at the information exchange near Khor Duweihin bay, and if so find out who the fuck they were!

On completion, the plan was to retract into Bosnia Herzegovina close to the town of Srebrenica on the Serb border, then currently held by the Dutch, and await extraction under the guise that we were UN troops. On-board pre-insertion briefing intelligence unveiled that there had been some reports from UN officials of a build-up of Serbian forces outside Srebrenica on which NATO had requested 'on one' intel as to the size of forces converging in the area. The town was supposed to be a city of refuge carved out by the UN and under the command of a Dutch blue beret force. It all sounded straightforward enough, just like picking up the takeaway on your way home from work.

Over the next two days we planned our insertion into Romania and how the team was going to cover the transport caravan on its final journey. The team was in agreement that it would be advantageous to follow the cargo for as long as possible, not only to gather information on the route etc. but the further it travelled into Serbia the less suspicion we would raise when we destroyed it, allowing for a cleaner exit on our side. This would all be dependent on my securing the final destination from Evgeny, the new customers, or it would all become a longer intel-gathering process. All the guys apart from Hugh would make their own way to the meeting point in Drobeta-Turnu Severin. Hugh would be 48 hours ahead of me and be my transport into the town to meet Evgeny. Hugh would then cover my insertion until the transport made Valjevo, and the team would oversee the entire operation out of sight. It was a 'suck it and see' type operation all the way to be honest; we didn't really know what or who I would encounter in Drobeta or Valjevo. Once I had made the necessary contacts and played the family pantomime, Hugh would assist in my extraction then we would destroy the transport and neutralise package four, that being Evgeny. It's still hard to say it, Evgeny being a target on the Steering Group's list, but he had become a ruthless bastard in the arms trading world and rumours from other operatives working for the Steering Group had made me subtly aware that he was into the people-smuggling business through Iran and Russia into Europe.

There was always a lot to learn from the team, and their planning and meticulous attention to detail for every possible scenario was nothing short of fascinating. Every building on the map was considered for use as an observation point, a refuge, extraction point, safe house, temp field hospital or just a landmark to be committed to memory – the detail was microscopic. Baz took me under his wing as he studied all the maps in detail, identifying all possible routes the transport could take – roads, forest routes, contours, towns, rivers, railways; every scenario was explored and dissected for operational possibilities. Baz ensured that all escape routes, evac and air support opportunities were listed for the command briefs. Transit times from one point to another, from one building to another, and shortcuts to cross-country and re-intercept points to avoid detection were all carefully considered and theoretically tested amongst the team, leading to discussions of how long it would take by road, on foot, yomping, high points for clear comms, and of course every 'action on plan' scenario the team could think of should situations change quickly or unexpectedly. Put simply, it gave me a lot of confidence going into this more than precarious scenario of unknowns than previously experienced. To be honest we had no firm plan when we would take out the cargo or Evgeny; there were a lot of 'play it by ear' type scenarios which didn't allow for a straight in and out op.

The next day revealed a beautiful dawn, the first light shimmering over the calm sleeping Adriatic Sea. I was on the sponson (like a balcony or viewing platform) having a coffee, taking in the air and listening to the gentle breaking sound of the sea against the hull of the ship. There were no signs of a conflict beyond those waves which seemed so gentle and relaxed in the morning sun. Time alone aboard ship is precious and to be savoured if you're lucky enough to find some solitude in a steel floating city such as the *America*. It lasted until I saw the very first glint of an object in the sky moving too quickly to be a bird, then a smoke trail as it throttled back, turning to make an approach, the night sortie returning to the nest, pilot tired and low on fuel; the plane aligning with the ship as she increased speed, to harvest her hawks, the decks becoming busy in anticipation, fire crews ready, all eyes on the pilot who's looking for the ball (the optical landing system – OLS), bright lights now from the landing gear, heavy smoke, then absolute thunder as it catches a wire at full throttle then whines down into an angry buzz saw screaming at a high pitch and looking for a resting place amongst the other tired fighters.

The entire team assembled in air ops for a safety briefing before our separate departures. An S-3 Viking carrier take-off is nothing short of fucking amazing. It's like a fighter aircraft but has four seats: the pilot and co-pilot in the front, with two seats in the rear for a tactical coordinator (TACCO) and sensor operator (SENSO), which we took as passenger seats. Taking off from a carrier for the first time must be equivalent to an astronaut's first launch into space – that sudden rush and G-force as you leave the safety of the ship behind and accelerate and climb at a rate that is nothing short of terrifying. Videogame stuff – hard banks and manoeuvres – before levelling off above the clouds, ready to vomit but swallowing it all to try and look cool and in control. The pilot must have loved taking passengers just to try and give us a scare. Hugh and I flew together to Eleusis military air base in Greece, coordinates 38°03′50″N 23°33′21″E, then I took a civilian flight from Athens to Bucharest. Arriving by civil airliner as a tourist into the country was the only way in without raising any suspicions. I was then back into the familiar role of being the N1 operative, undercover, a member of the Russian family once again. I think the team hit the silk (parachuted at night) into an area just far enough out of Drobeta to avoid too much of a hike into town to await our arrival.

My arrival into Bucharest's Henri Coanda International Airport was uneventful, despite arriving on a TAROM flight (Romanian airline). The airport was drab and very post-war, an arched terminal building clagged on to a box-like structure with low ceilings, giving that cramped overcrowded feeling no matter how busy or quiet the place was. To be fair, the airport was one year into an ongoing expansion and was a mess. It was only 16.5km from the city centre of the capital and lay just outside the main ring road to the north. Exiting the terminal building revealed an overcrowded car park and a chaotic interchange of passengers and vehicles frantically arriving and departing from triple-parked taxis and buses, typical of any Eastern European airport. Hugh should have been waiting for me in arrivals but was late which was initially a worry. He soon arrived and explained how fucking chaotic the whole place was and that he had been a little choosy in the vehicle he had acquired, an ARO 244 which sort of looks like a Land Rover but is completely inferior, ideal for what we needed. It would blend in and be useful to the team after Hugh had taken me to meet Evgeny; it was the best off-roader on offer but would not stand out in a crowd.

The drive from Bucharest to Drobeta is just under five hours and a distance of about 350km in a westerly direction and we set off by the most direct route via E81, DN65/E574 and DN6/E70 – what a fucking drag, but there was no direct train line. The alternative was to do 20 hours on a train via Sofia, and that wasn't fucking happening, so I had the use of a 'personal' driver hired in Bucharest, which was the best way forward; and besides, Hugh was itching to get closer to the action and I appreciated the close-cover protection on this trip. The truck was a sloppy drive but fun, and I think Hugh made every effort to try and roll the fucking thing on the winding roads. We got as far as Pitesti and picked up a tail. Now, we didn't know if it was serious or if the two of us were simply being totally overcautious. After a tense 30 minutes or so with us both checking our sidearms repeatedly, we ended up switching routes to the higher road and heading further north and then proceeding in an arc on Route E81, bypassing E574 altogether; we had lost the tail but were more alert now. We had to get in theatre mentally. It always starts out like a tourist trip, never feeling totally real for some reason when you set out. That fantasy can remain in your head until the shit hits and you have to get down to business; loss of focus shouldn't happen but it does.

The road wound through quiet villages and forests – quite a relaxing drive out into the country with only light traffic to annoy Hugh. The houses were quiet and quaint with red-tiled roofs and broken windows, some with rusted corrugated iron roofs holding up crooked chimneys that emitted the smell and warmth of wood fires being sucked into the cabin as we sped along. There's always a stray dog to watch out for and regular potholes to dodge, which no doubt kept Hugh awake. People would wave and smile as they stepped out over their little bridges across the drainage ditches that ran alongside the roads, which made us nervous, some selling their wares on the gravel shoulder on makeshift market stalls. They all looked tired and dirty; all the men would be wearing jumpers, denim jackets, with old trainers and checked shirts, many with bushy moustaches, accompanied by their wives who all wore headscarves and aprons or shabby dresses and broken shoes. Their faces were like leather, mapped with stories of hardship and cold winters, comforted by the smiles the scruffy children would bring to them as they played in the gardens and on the roadside. How innocent most of the world can be, living in absolute ignorance of the forces at play all around them. I had time to take in some of the countryside and then inspect the inside of my eyelids for an hour whilst Hugh concentrated on not driving us off a cliff!

Finally, we arrived in Drobeta, not quite the shithole we were expecting, and Hugh quickly managed to find the warehouse where I was supposed to be meeting Evgeny. We were on the banks of the Danube, the border between Romania and Serbia. Drobeta is home to a few historic sights and buildings, including the Iron Gate, Romanian Porțile de Fier and Serbo-Croatian Gvozdena Vrata, which is the last gorge of the Derdap gorge system on the Danube River, dividing the Carpathian and Balkan mountains and forming part of the boundary between Serbia and Romania, with towering rock cliffs that make it one of the most dramatic natural wonders of Europe. It was spectacular. The city hid behind a sort of beautiful façade, curious in its own way, busy but remarkably peaceful, encouraged by the central park surrounded by its history and other lesser tourist attractions. The River Danube itself and the Water Castle made for interesting sights to be enjoyed as a momentary but welcome distraction from the task ahead. Hard not to be a tourist despite the purpose of our visit.

Hugh navigated through the town and eventually pulled the truck up on a hardstanding outside an old warehouse complex just upriver from a boat repair yard. It was typical of any disused industrial site, and we got out and stretched our legs looking for Evgeny; as there was no sign of him we took it upon ourselves to walk around and familiarise ourselves with the area, do a bit of a recce. It was pretty bleak and looked tired; the successful industrial days had long passed and only the debris and abandonment remained for us to look upon. Lifeless machinery, old ship winches and disused cranes and cargo equipment nestled amongst the weeds and all the broken orphaned trucks. The warehouses were overlooked by five-storey concrete slab accommodations, dilapidated and derelict but occupied by desperate souls hiding behind their towels or bed sheets used as makeshift curtains. Rubbish and litter overflowed from four-wheeled industrial waste bins, some toppled over in the street amongst the rubble, others overflowing, spewing house waste for the stray dogs and cats to feast upon, the walls all cracked and damaged showing the iron meshing beneath the surface of the concrete as if there had been a recent earthquake. Strangely, however, all the walls were littered with endless satellite dishes for TV, some clinging to makeshift support structures, air conditioning units and other contraptions that had been hastily attached from nearby windows.

We were approached by four men, none of them recognisable, who were dressed in overalls with leather jackets, failing to hide the pistols beneath; I don't think there was any intention on their part to hide the fact that they were armed. Two of them were dirty looking guys, unshaven, matted hair, overweight, smoking cigarettes as they walked towards us laughing and cursing about something. As for the other two they were definitely Russian, thin with hard jawlines, crew cuts, Russian tattoos, jumpy and nervous, but there with purpose. Hugh and I gave each other a glance before I deliberately opened the conversation in Russian. They were quick to respond and looked relieved that I was speaking in their native tongue, and they simply retorted that Evgeny was waiting in the hotel across from the yard. We invited them to join us to take us over to the hotel as we preferred to drive over than leave the truck unattended.

A nervous but short silent drive followed as we headed over to the hotel, a four-storey yellow monstrosity surrounded by a crappy uneven bricked driveway which made for a parking lot, from which you were greeted by a poorly hand-painted faded hotel sign which hung from the second-floor balcony. The frontal aspect of the hotel was impregnated by uninviting dirty floor-to-ceiling sliding ranch doors giving access to each of the rooms they concealed. Wrought-iron railings were bolted to the balconies but were coming away from the rust-stained render, all of which attempted to safely enclose and protect the occupants from a fall. The occupants of these rooms were obviously not holidaymakers, smoking and drinking half-dressed, leaning over the railings, flicking their ash towards us as the net curtains behind them blew out of the balcony doors, some revealing the prostitutes who had obviously stayed the night. It was a dive, a complete dump, the kind of place you'd expect to conduct a dodgy business deal in, a place where should something happen it wouldn't raise too many eyebrows. A place where checkout didn't necessarily mean a nice smile and an invoice.

Now, Evgeny wasn't exactly himself, fucking jumpy as hell and pretty damn drunk in the lobby. We greeted each other briefly. He was so pissed. It was as though, on my arrival, I had suddenly relieved him of all responsibility for his purpose here in Romania. I was visibly angry and challenged him, aggravating the two guerillas he had sent to meet us. He was useless, and he hardly even noticed Hugh who I had introduced as my driver and transport back to Bucharest. Evgeny was straight into it, burbling in a semi-incoherent drunken state, trying to blurt it all out in one go. How it was all a fuck-up, how he was expected to perform a miracle on his own. He was completely panic-stricken about the cargo that needed to be loaded and on its way by the weekend, with no local labour and the customer coming on Saturday to ensure its departure. He complained endlessly about his father leaving him to do it all. He had apparently left several days ago to meet onward customers in Serbia.

Evgeny was in complete meltdown, pissed, only half making sense, it was a mess. I had just walked into a fucking nightmare, and Evgeny needed to be sobered up in order to get things rolling. In planning this mission no one could have come up with this scenario, so we had to play the part and get the shipment ready to roll. I would have appreciated Anatoly's presence at that time as none of this shit would have been allowed to develop. Anatoly was without doubt the brains of the two. The family was in trouble, it could all fall apart here in Romania, which we really didn't want to happen. I wasn't sure if it was all alcohol that was fucking Evgeny up or a combination of his heart meds, alcohol and all the stress.

I got the Russians to talk me through the consignment after putting Evgeny to bed. Fucking useless prick, I dragged his arse upstairs with Hugh to his shit hotel room with the welcoming committee in tow. The room was a cesspit, filled with really drab brown furniture, table, broken chairs, wardrobe and a bed, with an equally crap headboard adding to the sad-looking bed overthrown by a blotchy brown faded, almost orange, counterpane and grey sheets. There we were, Hugh and I, organising the two local guerillas to go out and get more reliable local labour as the two Russians showed us the shipment documents in detail, thankfully revealing some high-quality intel regarding the end users which included a cell in Yemen and a possible link to a further group working in Lebanon linked to cross-border attacks with Israel.

We all sat in Evgeny's room with a warm whisky and a cigarette each, smoke being swirled around by the ceiling fan which came on automatically whether you wanted it to or not when you turned the lights on. We worked through what can only be described as a somewhat questionable Russian military consignment order, complete with trans-border documentation from Russia to Romania and onwards into Serbia, together with shipping documents. The surplus illegal containers were piggy-backing a genuine shipment from Russia to Serbia, and there was an awful lot on that consignment order. The Russians were nervous. I talked to them about Evgeny and Alex, and as soon as I mentioned Alex they relaxed and the conversation became almost a test of who I was for a brief moment, but I spoke of my time in Dubai with the family and how we had done great business in the Middle East and how it was benefitting the Russian economy. I allowed the conversation to build and shared photos of me and the family, allowing them in turn to tell their story, and slowly they unwound. They had travelled with Alex from Moscow and showed a photo of him with me and Evgeny, but they were keen to learn who Hugh was. I explained about the awkwardness of the transport situation to get to Drobeta and how I had hired Hugh. Nothing to worry about as I was paying him good money and he didn't speak a word of Russian. It was a gamble, but safe in the fact that two of them were never going to be able to take Hugh out. I'm sure the team was probably real close and watching all the events unfold anyway.

Cautious but simultaneously under pressure from Alex and the customer, they were keen to have an extra pair of hands and burst into a barrage of questions on how we were to get the trucks loaded and away on time as there was a fucking entire warehouse to be moved. Anton was a nasty looking cunt really; he had a crew cut, very tight skin over a hard jawline and enough scars on his body to show he had seen some serious five-yard line action of some description. He caught me looking at his face and explained he had been imprisoned for crimes against the state but then later released and recruited by Alex as a personal runner. He and Gregori had joined Alex in the arms dealing business; they seemed almost pleased and even proud to be working with Alex and there was definitely a strong desire not to let him down. My guess was Alex had personally selected them for their talents from some hellhole prison in Siberia.

We put Evgeny into the recovery position and headed out to the warehouse. Pulling back the hangar-like doors, the

Russians were very quick and keen to inform us that some of the transports and containers harboured dangerous chemicals and we needed to wear respirators and protective clothing. It was nothing short of horrific. Amongst the stockpiles of ammunition, light arms and S-300 and Scud missile parts, we started to uncover the unthinkable: stockpiles, literally hundreds, of canisters in ammunition boxes labelled BZ, Substance 78 or EA-2277. Now my time at the NBCD school had just paid off. It was comparable to winning the lottery in military terms. US Army code EA-2277; NATO code BZ; Soviet code Substance 78 is all code for a chemical commonly known as BZ, an odourless military incapacitating agent, a stable white crystalline powder described as a "central nervous system depressant". It can "disrupt the high integrative functions of memory, problem solving, attention, and comprehension". A relatively high dose produces toxic delirium, destroying any human ability to perform a military task. This was chemical warfare in a tin, but this hadn't all come from Russia. Some of this shit was definitely untouched US stock, and there was no way Hugh or I were handling this shit.

Over the next two days and under the cover of darkness in the warehouse, with the help of a well-paid local workforce directed entirely by Alex's men and the two local guerillas, we coordinated from the safety of Evgeny's room a careful loading of all the munitions from the warehouse onto 10 articulated trucks. It was all done by hand utilising the Russian NBCD suits in the consignment to protect the workforce. This shipment would never make its destination. Hugh and I would see to that.

Exhausted and completely mentally drained by the whole ordeal, I sat alone with Evgeny who was now sober in his room, waiting for the customer to arrive. It had been nearly a week of organising his shit in order to move the mission along. Fuck, I wanted to kill him right there, but the links were too important. Evgeny was apologetic and pathetic, and even if he was a friend he deserved all that was coming to him by allowing this deal to go through. I asked about Anatoly but he was indignant. Anatoly had refused to be a part of this shipment and had relayed that he was confined to his work in Sarov. They had fallen out and the family was disintegrating under the pressures of international illegal arms deals coupled with their new more demanding customers.

We waited silently for the most part, Evgeny then trying to convince me how this would change our lives; the money was phenomenal this time. I ignored him. I wanted to know how many shipments there had been, where they were going and who the end customer was. Evgeny knew he was in too deep with his father, and I reminded him of how he had dragged me into all of this. I weaselled it out of him, arguing and demanding, playing on his conscience to let me know who the fuck I was dealing with. What had he allowed me and his family to become involved with? Fucking chemical weapons! He sat on the edge of the bed, a disgusting wretch of a man now seeking recourse from the situation because of his health, attempting to gain sympathy from me as a friend to see it from his perspective, the needs of the family, and his father, and the pressures from Moscow to support the Serbians. Then he told me there had been two previous shipments from other warehouses in Romania, heading to the Albanian coast now that Split had been compromised. All were mostly going to Iraq. The small arms and some of the chemicals were being syphoned off into Serbia to pay the way for the bulk of the cargo to make it through to the coast and onto ships destined for Iraq. Chemical and biological weapons, weapons of mass destruction, maybe with the delivery missile components already partly assembled, were what the customer wanted at any cost.

They were here – five Middle Eastern looking guys in the lobby, representatives of the Iraqi people apparently. Plainly dressed unshaven young men, trigger happy, uncompromising emerging leaders of a possible terrorist cell that had grand plans for the future of Iraq, Syria and the wider Muslim world. Fanatics that had greedy minds for recognition within their own circles, wanting to look important to the mighty hammer and sickle that was providing them with a future attempt to wage a war inside a war, with little regard for life. They weren't here for glory or for honour, just the means to cause death in the most catastrophic way and to receive the widest news coverage possible in the most shocking way conceivable. They wanted nothing more than to have accreditation for assisting a chemical warfare scenario in Europe, using the Bosnian crisis as a testing ground before releasing their new-found weapons on the West in Iraq.

Hugh brought them up to Evgeny's room, and we greeted them in pidgin English and shared cigarettes, crap coffee and whisky. Evgeny was being an arsehole, trying to make it look as though it was all his own work, attempting to appease and delight them with all the family's work. They conversed in Arabic, wanting to know who the heck Hugh and I were. There was some nervousness and unease as they hadn't met anyone except Alex and Evgeny. This was soon overcome by photos and polite conversation as I instructed Evgeny to introduce us and handed him some photographs to grease the way forward in order to complete business and get the trucks rolling. We were all family here and the Arabs were our friends, blah blah blah – underneath, we were seething with anger.

I attempted to make conversation and asked for a photo with our new friends, so that we could show Erik and Anatoly. They were un-obliging, squirming as Evgeny made it a big deal. His father would want us to be friends as this was a huge business transaction, a success and new partnership. Not a chance, they were not having any of it. I said I would speak to

Anatoly to invite them to the apartment in Dubai to celebrate once the cargo had reached its destination; they smiled and agreed to consider it. But then talking amongst themselves they entertained and discussed a possible future meeting in the desert in Saudi, to get their friend Owen to set up a camp in the desert so they would be in complete control, away from all eyes and any outside interference. It sounded like they wanted a meeting of some description, to enable a continuation of business arrangements and finances without the need for too much future interaction between the parties.

They smiled and looked at me and Hugh as they conversed, unaware of our ability to understand Arabic. They wanted us gone now. They wanted to take it from here with just Evgeny riding with them to Valjevo. They would pay Alex in Srebrenica once the cargo had been tested. Evgeny relayed their requirements. We smiled and shook hands and I wished Evgeny a safe trip. Hugh had my back as we exited the hotel with that heightened realisation of being watched and possibly seconds away from being shot in the back, not sure if we had won their confidence in any way at all or raised their suspicions in some way. My heart beating out of control I was fucking angry beyond all belief. Hugh slammed the truck into reverse and we were off to rendezvous with the team. There was uncontrolled laughter for a moment and then we fucking looked at each other and realised what we had to do.

Meeting the team in the hills was a fucking relief. We were still laughing but a bit shaken by the last few hours. I had thought we had reached the end of the line because the Arabs weren't keen on our participation at any level with the transport, and the whole situation had changed. The disconnect from the Arabs was a possible significant loss of intel and it had really felt like they were prepared to eliminate us at the hotel. However, time to move forward – the guys were well set up and Hugh explained how he had rigged all the trucks up with explosives. The chemicals were all on two trucks, and only the cabs on those rigged with shaped charges. We didn't want to release any of the BZ into the atmosphere, so would need to separate those trucks from the convoy somehow. We got underway to intercept the convoy, with Hugh diverting to call in all the intel to the NATO commanders and Paul waiting in the Adriatic.

The team and I were off, max chat/full speed, to an interception point on the route Hugh had managed to copy from the Russians at the hotel. Valjevo is about a five-hour drive on a good day with good transportation. We had a great advantage now: the trucks rigged with explosives, the route confirmed and a green light to eliminate the fucking lot. It was silence in the jeep, just concentration and the smell of gun oil on my fingers from cleaning my sidearm and assault rifle. I was rigged, full kit, webbing, weapons, grenades, rifle, anticipation, excitement, nerves, hatred and determination bottled inside, carbonised ready to be released at the right moment.

Evgeny had royally pissed me off, drunk, useless bastard, betraying his family, claiming glory and respect from the Arabs, dealing in chemical weapons, lying to me and now riding to victory with his pockets stuffed with money from a death deal. My anger was at 110%. Breathing deeply now, I was trying to control the software of my brain in order to control my body's hardware, sweating and swearing under my breath. Cheesy punched me in the arm and said I was with him on this one and to be ready to undertake a final reconnoitre of the intersection before the convoy arrived.

We arrived in a long narrow valley with steep hills, perfect for cover and escape. The eastern end of the valley ran into another valley which saw the river part in two directions to their individual sources upstream. Near the eastern end, mainly on the steep slopes of the hill, was a long, bent, narrow ribbon of woodland, planted to connect one end of the valley to the other. This is where the road passed over a bridge and was perfect for the detonation of the explosives on the transports. Baz would give sniper support from the woodland position. Hugh would conduct all the detonations in a sequence to facilitate elimination of all the transports but safeguarding the chemical trucks. This strip of woodland was not remarkable in any way, but simply a copse hanging on a steep bank from where I would position myself with Cheesy to erase Evgeny from the Steering Group list.

Waiting is a discipline; it's so easy to get distracted, lose focus or concentration. The whole enigma of being an intelligence operative is the ability to decode the target in every way, befriend the target, understand it and its needs, desires, goals and most importantly its fears. You need to be patient with the target, it needs to feel confident, relaxed and eventually dependent upon you. Once the DNA has been unravelled you simply have to wait until the target makes the mistake or the move you knew was coming because you planted that seed, idea or task in their mind. It is in the setting of these codes within your adversary and in your building of their trust that allows you to break them when they least expect it. Because they don't fear what they have planned or organised, the unexpected strength and surprise summoned to destroy them is completely overwhelming, terrifyingly quick and remarkably accurate.

The trucks were approaching. There is nothing quite like the build-up to a firefight. Months of dull preparation, training, planning, talking, endless talking and more preparation leads to about 10 minutes' worth of high-octane, intense, adrenaline-fuelled, calmly administered chaos and death. Some of what the team and I did that day was nothing short of nasty, enough to put fear into the devil himself. You simply don't think about it, targets are just targets, nothing personal, it's just business. The fact that biological weapons were now in play was to me and the team a game changer; there was no longer any doubt in our minds that the task ahead was justified and totally legal, in so much as these people were absolutely intent on killing millions of innocent civilians.

I could see the black smoke coming out of the lead truck's vertical exhaust pipe as the revs changed and the driver dropped down a gear as it approached the bridge. The convoy was conveniently close together. I wanted to take my time, feel the moment, take in the satisfaction of stopping this trade of munitions, but also deep down wanting to ensure I remembered this kill. It was like I wanted to record the event in some way mentally, so I could use it as proof that I did some good, at some time in the distant future. Or was it to justify my killing a friend? Not sure. I don't think anyone could consciously allow this shipment to get through.

Killing on licence is weird. It comes with self-satisfaction, denial, truth, lies, doubt, belief and apprehension all at once. However, all these emotions are held beneath the surface in your subconscious, whilst your conscious mind enjoys releasing the caged animal from within. It can only be released for just a few controlled moments when the adrenaline is running at full flow and you are authorised to actually enjoy it, because for some fucked-up reason killing is legal when you're holding a piece of paper from a government. Now, that is fucked up if you sit and think about it. It's this that sets the conditions for the mental cloud to form, a swelling of thoughts and emotions that won't be realised until much later on in your life. But the first cloud was forming and it would rain, of that there is no doubt. For now, I had to concentrate, let the mental cloud form, ignore it, just do my job and deal with my cloud of conscience later.

The first truck reached the near side of the bridge. It was going to be a moving target, so patience was needed before I could place the crosshairs on Evgeny. It had to be a head shot. I was about to eliminate my third wolf and Russian brother; the thought was there but not enough to interrupt my determination to complete the task. I always felt my heart pumping before the first round was released out of my weapon. It was the release of my anger, frustration, childhood and training, a climax of months of preparational foreplay. It is an utter release when the trigger is squeezed that gives notice to the noise that starts a firefight. Like the starting gun, or the ringside bell, my first shot signalled the beginning of the fight and I was able to take out Evgeny with one high-calibre sniper shot from my L96 7.62, like a single punch to succeed a knockout shot, that passed cleanly through Evgeny and into the driver.

My gunsight blacked out immediately from the explosions that followed. The quick succession of minor shockwaves increased my heart rate but not before Cheesy was tapping me on the right shoulder indicating targets right. Selecting targets, breathe and squeeze. I could hear rapid fire from the team below and from the vicinity of the twisted wreckage but I remained focused. In a firefight now, rounds thumping into nearby ground and cracking through foliage as the targets below fired randomly into the trees around me. Not afraid, I was satisfied they couldn't see their target and was happy to have a clear line of sight into their tiny soon-to-end confused world. I remained in position within the trees, their falling branches adding to my cover, and took the fight to its conclusion. Silence falls after any exchange, and as I breathed the scent of my spent ammunition my appetite was satisfied.

Baz came over comms with an all clear. Taking my eye away from the scope I could see the chemical truck cargos were intact, cabs obliterated, making for a nice mess for the dustmen to clear and some pretty interesting evidence that needed to be relocated. Never knew where that shit went; the dustmen would come with their support team, bulldozer the mess into the reservoir and tow the chemical trailers away. We never made contact with them; they did their job as we did ours.

We were on the clock now to make the rendezvous point whilst accommodating the request to assess the situation the blue forces in Srebrenica were in. Rapid clean-up, reposition and back on the road. We were soon in the hills near Obadi on the outskirts of Srebrenica and were back under the air cover of 800 NAS from HMS *Eagle*, which seemed bizzare, a bit of home above us. We approached from the east, the team exhausted from the past few weeks. For me the long build-up entwined with my own thoughts about Evgeny, his end at my hands and how this would impact the family was fully occupying my mind, which in itself was a tortuous mental-fatigue process. We had almost another two weeks to go before the rendezvous for extraction, and would conduct our reconnaissance and surveillance from higher ground overlooking Srebrenica and the other surrounding villages. Extract would be by black helicopter to a naval platform stationed in the Adriatic, and that day couldn't come soon enough.

We could not make contact with the NATO UN blue beret forces in Srebrenica and so the team entered the town masquerading as Serbian fighters. The team limited their time to undertake a recce of major buildings in the town and warehouses, trying to identify if there were any weapon dumps or other chemical weapon hoards from previous shipments. There was a heightened sense of tension as Serbian forces continued to build up their presence in the town under the lead of Ratko Mladić, the army general who became known as the 'Butcher of Bosnia'. The Dutch battalion under the command of NATO was there to implement United Nations Security Council Resolution 819 in the Bosnian

Muslim territories. But as I later learned, the Bosnian Serb forces, under the control of General Ratko Mladić, were set to take over the town, and the Dutch forces were vastly outnumbered and outgunned. The Serbian forces, under Mladić's control, then undertook a process of ethnic cleansing leading to the deaths of more than 7,000 men and boys. This was later declared in 2017 as being genocide at the International Criminal Tribunal for the former Yugoslavia, which also convicted General Mladić of war crimes and crimes against humanity.

We had very little time to react to this sudden influx of Serbian forces and were powerless to actually achieve anything other than to observe and report. It was on one unexpected day in early July on a routine patrol around the town and surrounding villages that I saw Alex. This was just after Mladić made a speech to TV cameras in which he announced that he had given Srebrenica to the Serbian people and it was time for revenge to be taken against the Muslims in that region. I remember talking quietly to Cheesy as we lay under-cover and casually pointed out Alex in the scopes and that we had found a way to finally complete Operation RIAR. The Dutch were soon rendered useless by the Serb forces who had rapidly taken over the enclave.

We were not able to stop the unfolding events, and being just a lone unit with a different target package we were totally unprepared for this level of aggression so we regrouped up in the hills. We were living out of an old shipping container that had once been used as a logger's hut but was now abandoned deep in the forests above the town. There were many refugee families living in the woods, as well as what we thought were small guerilla units, which made it difficult to stay completely unnoticed. I think that mostly those who came across us were displaced families and just thought we were in the same situation as they were. Usually, any encounters with the local populous in the hills resulted in them fleeing in the opposite direction. However scared they were of us we were equally keen not to engage to any extent with them. The Kamenica Hill area was becoming full of civilians whose growing numbers we had been monitoring and reporting to NATO commanders on the naval platforms to assist with any air surveillance. Most of them were just starving and desperate to find food and water; they weren't up for a fight. We helped where we could. Thousands of refugees seeking an exit route were being hunted down by Serbian forces; you could hear calls from passing vehicles from the roads below for them to surrender, despite random shooting and shelling coming in from all directions.

The team sat down on the ammo crates and other makeshift seating as they looked at me and asked, "Who the fuck is this Alex?" I explained to them how much it made my stomach churn to see him here. I didn't know if he was here selling arms and the chemical weapons or ensuring a safe passage through to the Middle East. I needed the team to consider the wider picture. They knew I was involved in the intel side of it all and the full game board was never going to be revealed to me but they should understand we were close to closing down operations that were not only possibly fuelling this conflict but other planned conflicts in the future. It all had to be called in and the risk to make the transmission wasn't even considered as a risk by this latest development. We sat smoking, with the brew on, discussing what we had witnessed.

Hugh, as the main comms man, dialled it in as we all sat and waited for the brew to boil. We had to get that transmission out and let the world know what we had uncovered. It wasn't long before the TX was received and the reply was nothing short of astounding.

```
STGP
SG RIR SG 117
NS XXXXXX JUL 95
FM RIAR 1
TO SG / SHAPE /
WBTS
BT
NS /

Tx

RIAR 1    Package 3 available for immediate
          delivery
RIAR 1    Request delivery method
RIAR 1    Delivery area now compromised.

Rx

SG        Acknowledge transmission
SG        Follow White Card Delivery Policy
SG        Package 3 was expected at your
          locality
SG        Urgent delivery of target package
          required
SG        Delivery town to be abandoned
SG        Extraction <12 hrs local - Priority A
BT
NNNN
END
```

Translated, we had Alex in our sights, permission to engage was sought from the Steering Group, our request to engage was approved by way of an executive order and the white card meant we could do what we had to in order to secure the kill at any cost. The fact that they knew he was in our area was a surprise to me as I had expected him to be with Evgeny in

Romania, not here in Serbia. Thinking it all through, both ends of the deal were being overseen by direct family members, making the Romania/Serbian transit less difficult. The value of the shipments must have been high for Alex himself to be here. We needed to deliver the package and secure our own extraction as the entire region had become untenable.

We hadn't time to process it. I passed a cup of coffee over to Hugh who was sitting out the front of the container. He was waving his arm around in the air with the aerial (he had his earphones on trying to reconnect) as if to swipe a bee or a wasp – but it wasn't either, it was a fucking sniper shot. A delayed sound, fired from a distance, snipersonic (supersonic) round, crack – thump, no time to compute, and the whole team was on the floor in the container now. Large-calibre sniper fire is so loud it's the loudest whiplash you'll ever hear, like a massive crack of a whip in a circus right next to your lughole. No silencers now, contact from the west through the clearings directly at us, with the container being slowly converted into a metal box sieve. A firefight. Multiple cracking of semi and automatic fire was echoing in the valley and confusing me as to the source. There is nothing to compare to the sound of a round going through steel. It's that horrific bang with a grating, ripping noise that follows; the very sound chills you to the bone. It was chaos now. We grabbed the gear and dispersed to regroup at RV 1. It was a scramble but that fucking adrenalin kicked in and Baz had a death grip on me to ensure I made it out of that shipping container. We had found ourselves in among a swarm of battle-drunk Serbian fighters.

Mortars, indiscriminate shelling in all directions, then it began to rain, the light faded and I lost my sense of humour, although I have to say there was a crazy giggle inside me when it all hit the fan. It's not funny, it's just nerves gone crazy. Cheesy was returning fire now, strategic positioning within a coordinated dispersed retreat. Small arms getting closer and fucking bark was flying off the trees ahead of us and the dirt was leaping up from the ground into our faces as automatic fire strafed the forest floor amongst us. Veer right, and RV 1 was compromised by mortar fire splintering the tree trunks and leaving giant matchsticks everywhere. We had to make RV 2 now on the edge of town, and we were leaping over impact craters to make for cover. The guys are in auto now, but yeah, I'm shitting my pants as the devil of uncertainty crawls inside my head for a dig around as I randomly return fire, changing mags twice, ears ringing and eyes all messed up from splashed dirt.

I was my own for a short while as I caught a glimpse of Baz as he let off some grenades from his M16 A2 with its grenade launcher and disappeared in support of the group to outflank the incoming troops. I could hear them but I was detached. I made it to the farmhouse about 15 minutes later and laid low. I could hear contacts moving around me to the east. Baz, Hugh, Cheesy and Smudge cut across the front of the farm-house out from the cover of a community hall and piled in on top of me. I remember Pierre just casually strolling into RV 2 like nothing had happened and laughing at me hiding under the five guys piled on top. He just stood there looking down at us, laughing. We did an equipment check and body check. All good to go. Then we set ourselves up in the farmhouse to make preparation for a run to the extraction point. Hugh was on the blower as the rest of us set up to cover the farmhouse. A drag on a cigarette after that kind of encounter is nothing short of heaven. One all round, and Cheesy was looking to make a brew, fucking calm as fuck. That's the thing, that's the moment, that's the second it all becomes okay, it becomes normal to be shot at. No comments about the attack, just a fag and a cup of Rosie Lee as the guys very calmly got their shit all in one sock ready for a second sitting. It's not meant to be like that, no training teaches you how you're really gonna react, and training never talks about having a brew or a smoke in the middle of it all. The guys just set up for a breather and gathered it all together. It's focused, you must understand, not messy; it's personalised discipline being displayed in very unusual individualistic ways whilst under immense pressure to be ready for the next fight.

Heads up. Activity was now growing across from the farm as the hall and surrounding buildings were brought under siege. Now it turned out that the forces at play were not in direct contact with us because they didn't actually know we were there, but this was a series of clearance operations their forces were undertaking to round up civilians they knew were transiting or hiding in the hills. We had simply been caught up in the crossfire. The events that followed in those hills were insanely barbaric and many innocent civilians lost their lives.

The extraction point had been set for about eight hours' time and our last order was the white card approval for Alex. Team huddle was convened after agreeing to defend the Muslim civilians, or create enough diversion to allow maximum preservation of life long enough for them to escape out of the hills and for Hugh and I to find and eliminate Alex. It was a huge risk but package 3 had to be delivered – after all, it was our last order – but with the unfolding atrocities now being undertaken in plain sight of us it would be a hard choice to do nothing for the civilians around us. The soldiers were now dragging women and boys out of buildings, stripping then raping them in front of their comrades, whilst others were being beaten and tortured. Babies killed in front of their mothers, who were wandering aimlessly in search of help, screaming – sights no person should ever see.

The screams were the piercing sounds of hell in surround sound, a man-made recreation of the urban legend of the Siberian 'well to hell' sounds from 1989. Hell unfolded through the hands of men. Houses were emptied, looted and set on fire, men dragged out to be shot. Boys' heads cut off and throats slit as soldiers laughed and encouraged each other in their chaos. People were committing suicide to avoid the torment and the wrath of the Serbians who were seeking them out. We fell into a place covered by dark clouds.

A cloud forms in your mind from such sights as these.
A cloud of tiny droplets, each reflecting the sights you've seen.
A cloud, a personal i-cloud, collecting, storing, preparing for the storm to come.
A cloud in which to POST all your images, and all you've done.
A cloud that knows you, lies about you, twists everything you have seen.
A cloud that fills the dark voids with every place you have been.
A cloud swelling with the sounds and screams from those you've seen.

A cloud full of those who have seen such sights as these.
A cloud filled with all those TRAUMATIC sights you've seen.
A cloud that will wait, is not proud or gentle, but silent and cunning in its deed.
A cloud that wants to become a storm in your life indeed.

A cloud full of time and pain from all the sights such as these.
A cloud under STRESS to deliver the torment of where it's been.
A cloud that just wants to linger, waiting, seeking to hide your very needs.
A cloud that always returns to you. You, the one in need.

A cloud full of those who have seen sights such as these.
A cloud in DISORDER where nothing is clearly seen.

*A cloud which will release its rain with added thunder in
    the night.
A cloud that gives you strength and anger from all its
    might.
A cloud that drives you out of sight.*

I remember getting my shit together to go off with Hugh,
shaking with fear, excitement and anger, swearing under my
breath as Cheesy took my arm and gripped me hard as his ice-
cold eyes locked into mine, revealing a real hatred behind his
calm exterior as he gently whispered:

"Kill Alex."

Hugh was at the door and the Serbs were now approaching
the farmhouse from the front. We bolted out the back as the
guys unleashed all they had to cover our escape. The Serbs
were firing through the civilians now to get to the team. We
had been surrounded, so a rapid escape right through their
lines was the only option open to us, and there was no looking
back and no time to process the carnage that had just been
revealed. No time to dwell on the cloud we had seen.

Rogue Serbian soldiers came into our path. Hugh laid down
automatic fire and cleared the path ahead, whilst I reacted
with my weapon to the right flank on a number of occasions. I
see their faces briefly but not long enough to feel anything for
them; they were the painters of genocide in Europe and I don't
believe my mind should be occupied with their images. But
here they stay with me to be remembered forever.

We had made it out of the killing zone and into a clear space
before descending SW towards the town, picking out a vantage
point over the main square and with line of sight through to
the Town Hall in which we hoped Alex would be. I had my
sniper rifle and took up position, loaded and expectant. Hugh

was beside me with the spotter sight, searching for the solution to our limited time. We were at a good range, 1,000m, and still in good cover of the trees, but we needed something to empty the building to get a shot if he was indeed still in there. It would have to be a good shot to hit the target cleanly but I kept reminding myself what my instructor had told me in Poole: a Billy Dixon in June 1874 killed a buffalo at 1,406m (1,538yd) with a Sharps .50-90 rifle, so this should be easy. Hugh was getting impatient. We could still hear gunfire from the farmhouse and it wasn't easing up. Time was against us. Hugh looked at me and simply said:

"Don't miss. I'm off to empty that fucking building. You kill him when he emerges and meet me at the extraction point."

Then I was suddenly on my own amongst all the confusion in a forest with my support team split between a firefight against a battalion of Serbian fighters attacking the civilians and Hugh, who was clearly fucking nuts and about to go and poke the hornets' nest with a big stick. Time passes quickly as all the thoughts and actions you've just experienced jet through your mind in a brief moment of silence. But it's all about preservation, attack and attack, never defeat.

I'm well camouflaged now, got myself almost buried in branches and I'm looking through that perfectly clear sight waiting to see Alex, waiting to see the old wolf come out into the open. Then I see it, Hugh at the fucking front door, and in he goes bold as brass, lets off a few stun grenades and a smoke, and they all come pouring out. Could have left the smoke out, Hugh, I was thinking. Artillery fire now inbound, it was all falling apart. Chaos was master here today but it made for an easy shot. No need to silence the shot, it would all just blend into the chaos. Alex wasn't in the building but had come out into the street to help some people from another building hidden from Hugh's view. He turned and came directly towards me in a NE direction. Safety off, ID confirmed. Clean shot and he was on the ground. Reload and make the confirmation shot, watching the body jump off the ground.

I was up and moving, and damn near knocked myself over running straight into Baz, who was with Cheesy, both in full-scale retreat, about turn down toward the town, pick up Hugh and then skirt our way north and then east to pick up the transport home. The entire enclave was pretty well secured by the Serbs and I can remember being fucking knackered running out of that place, but was soon reunited with the entire team all yomping our way to the RV. Running towards a forest road, getting dark now, the road littered with an endless trail of personal belongings, rows of bodies, hands tied behind their backs, faces down in the verges, bullet casings, small fires, the occasional blue UN helmet lying abandoned.

With the checkpoint ahead, we casually tore down the unprepared occupants where they stood and were then quickly mobile in a Serbian LUV (light utility vehicle). Damn near drove that fucking thing to destruction to meet the black helicopter at the RV point. We passed the unthinkable, mass graves with piles of bodies stacked up next to burnt-out buses pulled off the road and in plain sight. The carnage went on for miles and nothing was said; we kept going, ditched the vehicle and made the helo for our extraction to USS *America*.

There are no words to describe the previous 48 hours we had experienced together. We were debriefed and then signals were sent confirming the delivery of package 3. The NATO commanders were totally focused in on the developments in Srebrenica and had no doubt bigger issues to be working on. Baz handed over his camera, no doubt full of the worst images imaginable. Srebrenica had just seen the worst mass killing since WW2. Fuck. Just fuck. I mean, how the hell are you supposed to process that shit?!

The team and I were allocated an entire command briefing compartment on board where we slowly got our shit together, had food brought in and then sat on camp beds assessing the situation we had just escaped from and then each other's condition, supporting each other in the best ways we could and the work we were doing by focusing on the bigger mission, but also taking in that we had actually made a difference in the war today and the wars being planned in the Middle East. The guys had at least put up as much resistance for as long as possible in the field whilst our prime objective was still achieved. Our thoughts turned to the civilians, then to the firefight, our mistakes, and finally to the trip into Romania. I wasn't comfortable returning to Bosnia from Romania, and now Alex was gone how the fuck was any information reliable and how was the route from Romania being protected/overseen? Was anyone aware in Srebrenica of Alex's death? How was the team going to cover the insertion into Romania and the transport destruction? The customers that Alex had been doing business with needed to be identified and the source of arms halted.

I think we all lay awake that night listening to the sound of the air conditioning howling through the punkah louvres and the roar and gentle vibration through the ship as jets took off on their undisclosed sorties before trying to catch just a few zzzzs. A naval mattress and a cooked breakfast were most welcome. It was now, after spending many months being cut off from the world and deliberately focusing on the mission, that my mind turned back to thoughts of Anna. I had excommunicated myself from her but the truth could not be hidden from my heart.

Lying on my bunk, the utter realisation was that nothing else mattered because when you know your soulmate has come into your life everything else is just an addition to the main event. This of course was a paradox, an absurd ideology, because during this trip to Bosnia I had tried my hardest to push Anna out of my life. Now, you have to understand that although I loved her so very much I needed to know where her breaking point was. What a prick. I know, I know. I had to test the water to see how much this girl could tolerate. I even wrote to her whilst I was away on deployment, trying, in a not too delicate way, to end the relationship. I guess what you need to understand is that in an awful way I was trying to protect her from who I was and what I did for a living, all the necessary lies and deception and the inevitable fallout that would follow later in life. I couldn't see it ending well after the latest assignments by the Steering Group.

Eagle's next assignment took her back to the Balkans during the Yugoslav Wars for the rest of the mid-1990s and then she later made up the coalition contingent monitoring no-fly zones over southern Iraq. She returned to the Balkans under the NATO flag to battle Yugoslavian elements and conduct humanitarian missions. My time on board her was to take a different turn and encompass a different role the Steering Group wanted me to undertake, and one I was wholeheartedly grateful for – to engineer and perfect the transition and defection of Anatoly into the UK.

The Steering Group

Chapter 10

Interregnum

On my return from Bosnia, Anna very graciously came round to my parents' house to meet me. At the time my parents were living in a bungalow on the posh side of town; they had moved when things had been going well for Dad at work. The underlying reason, though, was to get away from Curly and all his hellish noise and the DIY ventures he'd embarked upon whilst I had been working overseas for the Steering Group. Fucking Curly! All those memories! I think if they had stayed in that old house too much longer, Mother would have ended up in a mental asylum. The bungalow wasn't anything too fancy, a 3/4 bed with a conservatory and reasonable garden in which stood my dad's shed. My dad spent most, if not all, of his spare time in that shed. He would sit in the freezing cold smoking stubbies (butt ends out of the ashtray) whilst he built the most amazing model ships, two of which I still have in my office to this day. They are actually worthy of a maritime museum such is the detail and quality of the craftsmanship. I used to like sitting in that shed, smoking enough Benny Hedgehogs to infuriate my mother badly because we both stank of cigarette smoke. Sometimes Dad wouldn't even be allowed into bed at night because he stank so much. He would be ordered to have a bath and this could be as late as midnight!

Times had been hard and Dad had been out of work for some time. I guess my parents were not only pleased to see me and my older brother when we came home (my older brother Phil was serving in the army), for the company, but also because Phil and I would always fill up the larder from Asda to last them the month. My younger brother and sister were still at school and it was hard to see our parents struggle as it caused so many upsets. Money, the root of all evil and all that. It's so easy to say money isn't important if you've got plenty of it. For me and my brother, spending £150 at the supermarket was just a night out on the beer when we were away, but to our parents it was a lifesaver. They had but £10 a week to spend on grocery shopping whilst begging on the dole.

My dad would have to prove to some young girl down the DHSS office every week that he'd been job hunting. Fucking bitch – I could quite happily have shot her after the way she spoke to my father one time I accompanied him into town, just no respect. I think the real low point was one weekend when I had come up on the train because I had left my car at another base. We had to walk into town with my dad to get the fucking shopping. We walked all the way into town in the pouring rain (a good couple of miles) and lugged that fucking shopping all the way home. It was just a really miserable point in time to say the least, for all of us. Not being in work is so demoralising and it takes away a man's self-worth. It had crippled my dad mentally and stolen his self-respect. Although, he always wore a shirt and tie even when he cut the grass! Old school, I guess.

So, here was Anna standing on the family driveway. I knew I had been a terrible communicator and was fully aware that she was possibly there to end the entire relationship. It was without doubt the weirdest thing ever for Anna to come over to my parents' house that day. I'm not sure if I was simply surprised or secretly happy to actually see her in the flesh as I had been sure I had pushed her away so hard by this point and it was all unrecoverable. I was ready for the argument and the deserved anger that might ensue. However, anger was and never has been in Anna's character. Instead, whilst waiting for me at my parents' house she disclosed a letter I had wrote, to my mother, who naturally said to Anna that she should stay with me, that there was a good boy underneath all the silence and I wasn't serious about ending our relationship. Give love a chance, give her son another chance. Anna and I were boxing clever, each with our own hidden knowledge of the other. I deflected the conversations and invited Anna to escape my parents' place after an hour and several polite cups of tea and go with me to an inn called Ye Olde Bell in a really peaceful country village, just to talk.

Ye Olde Bell is an old country coaching inn and is still there today. We sat in the snug part of the bar surrounded by the dark oak wood furniture and panelling strewn with pictures and ornaments from times gone by, stereotypical of a true old English pub. Great pictures and memorabilia of the harvest and of the hunt. Elegant English gentlemen in red tunics aloft their majestic horses sipping a whisky before the chase, hounds at their heels waiting patiently for the bugle to be blown. We sat and ordered a drink. The room smelt of old extinguished coal fires and tobacco smoke, not in a dirty or unpleasant way but more rather in a relaxing homely manner that must have greeted weary travellers and coachmen of a bygone era in only the most welcoming of ways. How they must have enjoyed the welcome of hot food and a warm hearth to sit in front of to warm themselves after being out on the Great North Road in all weathers (Ye Olde Bell is actually on the old Roman Great North Road).

I'm sure that during that ride in the car Anna was thinking, *I need to tell him it's over unless he changes*. She had been out with friends the night before and had met a man called George who was waiting in the wings should things not work out with me. Anna had surely reached the end of her patience with me. A woman needs to be able to communicate with her boyfriend, especially in a long-distance relationship. She needs to know you're always thinking of her and that she comes first. Shit, I got all that wrong, and got a full lecture and a heap more in that pub. There was no holding back, and she calmly let me know what a shit I had been, and she was right. I pulled out a cigarette and took in the heavy smoke as Anna gently released her frustration. I tried to drown myself in the nicotine. This was a new emotion for me, a new sensation. I wasn't able to cast aside my real feelings, I couldn't paperclip this. I was not able to simply walk away or 'remove the problem' as I had with anything and everything else that I didn't agree with. My greed for success and my selfishness to be No. 1 in everything at work just felt miles away; and besides that, attitude doesn't work in a relationship. Funny old game. I can't deny I wanted to be back at Poole most of the time I was at home, as being with the lads was less complicated and infinitely easier to navigate.

The only thing that really happens when a relationship breaks down is you become a shipwreck whose heart is open to anything to fill the void of real love; this is usually coupled with a dramatic increase in alcohol consumption once the shit news has been shared with the guys at work. I wasn't really ready to go back on the market, not that I'd ever really been on it in the first place, or ever for that matter, in my life. To be honest, all this was new feelings for me. We sat in a short but not uncomfortable silence with me twisting off the spent tobacco ash from the cigarette into a clean ashtray, exposing the red embers. Even when things weren't right between us, I couldn't help but lose myself in the loving pools of her eyes and be consumed by the safe knowledge that she was my soulmate. I was incomplete without her. In that moment of doubt, I was hit by the tsunami of emotion that is love, whatever that is. I think it's beyond poetry and all that shit. I think true love is a vacuum of wasted time, a void of time that you never knew existed until it's brutally pointed out by a random person who transpires to be your true love. You then suddenly allow her into your life to fill all that is empty in your life. Then you desperately yearn to fill your life with that person with every waking moment, to stop a vacuum ever forming in your heart again.

Just before she had chance to say 'It's over', I interrupted and said:

"Anna... what would you say to us getting married and buying a house together?"

Anna was completely taken aback, shocked. She had been sitting waiting for the 'let's end it' conversation that simply didn't happen. That conversation wasn't actually on the menu for me, instead I opened a door for Anna to marry me and become a military wife. A different world, an unexpected one and probably a little scary, but one I think she was actually very keen to explore. It was easier now that we were able to sit face to face and look into each other's eyes and see into each other's hearts. The deal was negotiated very quickly by my agreeing to buy a house in Nottinghamshire! To be fair, living in Nottinghamshire was cheap and away from all the noise I so dislike about big towns and cities. It came with only one caveat, that we would move to Plymouth (or wherever I was stationed) within two years. Now, believe it or not, we went down the estate agents that weekend and bought a house. We saw one property we liked the look of in the display window, arranged to view and bought it that very day. Anna had her own place in Doncaster but, me being me, I wanted us to buy a house together. I didn't want to live in her place, I wanted us to have the right start where there was no 'mine' 'his' or 'hers', just ours.

It should be Anna writing these paragraphs about how fucking dreadful I was at keeping in touch all the time I was in Bosnia. I hadn't really kept in touch apart from our time in Malta and then later sending that letter feebly trying to end our relationship. I had spent three years in total dedicated to the Bosnia Campaign in one form or another, three fucking long years. There were many strings attaching the Russians to that conflict and I can't even begin to describe what that actually means, I can only show you my certificates from NATO and my medal, neither of which will ever replace the time I spent in that hellhole.

There were two agendas behind my poor behaviour, neither of which were gonna make any sense to Anna, and she clearly would have never understood or believed what I had been doing or what I was involved in. It would all sound like lies to her ears. Besides, I had been executing a need to prove to myself (before any firm commitment – and I wanted it to fail) that Anna would be able to deal with the lifestyle, the absences, the not knowing and the poor communications that came with me and the Steering Group, my surrogate family. Seriously, you couldn't just call home from the battlefield on a satphone, and if you could we wouldn't have anyway. There was no just flicking off an email on a smartphone or anything like that back then. Besides, N1 and SF operators maintained absolute silence when deployed on ops. Additionally, the Steering Group wanted to see who this girl was and what impact she would have on their asset. Being a lone operator was more beneficial. Independents will do shit that married men wont. It's a simple statistic. Anna was like a glitch in the machine, a bug in the espionage app.

However, the other side of the coin is that more married men come back from war than single men, and that's because married men think before they act, have more to lose and take less risk. Single operatives will by nature go further, take more risk because they have more to prove and less to lose. It is this very nature within a person that the Steering Group wanted, because they can train a single man to harness the adrenaline and manage the risks. How marriage would change me was a question probably at the front of their minds whilst on the brink of securing the most valuable defection since the beginning of the Cold War.

All of this would have meant absolutely fucking nothing to Anna, especially as she was and still is a woman who is good, kind, gentle and faithful, and completely in the dark as to what I was, who I was and what I really did for the navy. *Fucking N1 Naval Intelligence operator, my arse*, I could hear her say! It means absolutely nothing to a woman that you're doing some serious shit in an unpronounceable place, all hidden behind a silhouette of deception and lies. The idea of being completely honest was always there but completely inappropriate and fucking dangerous, not just for Anna but for her family, me, the team and the Steering Group – none of whom officially existed, but we did, and we all remain targets in our own rights to this very day. All that aside, who'd fucking believe it anyway?! It would be on a scale of saying to your future wife: "*I need to tell you I'm actually a rock star*" or something equally as ridiculous. I don't think so.

I admit I had been a complete bastard. But for all the bad shit, underneath I wanted to know if she really loved me and at the same time wanted her to walk away because I knew how fucked up it was all going to be in the end marrying me. The fucked-up abused kid, who had got himself a bigger life immersed in all the utter reality of war, political warfare and all the deception of the service, the doughnut, the circus and all the potential this dark world of being an intelligence operator could offer to a young man willing to risk it all, was now trying to be Mr Joe Average. There was going to be some collateral damage, some serious fallout eventually should

I survive the endgame and complete the list and make it to retirement.

No matter how many missions I completed or how many successes were applauded by the Steering Group, it all amounted to nothing. What I had become was as dry as a desert by comparison to the true belonging to Anna who was my eternal love. The reality I actually faced was that the Steering Group would eventually use me up and discard me should I become less useful or, God forbid, become a casualty either in the field or mentally. All this was unlike the eternal love of Anna which was now within my grasp and offered freely to me with no small print or any requirement to complete a set of trials or training courses or a hideous list. To have a real family, a wife and a lover, is something the Steering Group could never offer. Their family was just another foster family for me, a stepping stone to belonging. Subconsciously I knew all this and had suddenly begun to resent this reality that had surfaced after meeting Anna.

Looking back, for all I was and for all that I am today, I fucking love this woman. The thing that still fucks me up above all things is the fact that no matter how messed up my spaghetti-wired brain is, the one strand holding it all together is the bit that knows without doubt I love her. She was and is my soulmate. We argue and fall out, but fuck I could never live without this woman. She is stronger, wiser and more caring and loving than I will ever deserve. She is the only living person who I can trust with my life. The Steering Group only had its own desires and agendas at heart.

She was my link to the here and now, to normality and a conduit back to life outside the Steering Group. She was already at this early stage in our relationship keeping the Russian family deaths from the door of my mind, allowing me to focus on my dear friend Anatoly's defection and his last chance for life; a chance for me to do something good in payment for the list I'd had to fully execute. She kept my mind open to the tasks in hand and gave me reason to keep going, but more importantly a reason to return home. Anna's most important role was to allow me to believe I could return to my own true life and not be afraid or ashamed of all the bad paint, the damage or the graffiti made on the canvas of my life. Underneath all the damage and unwanted smearing of the portrait of my true self was still just a boy who was deeply in love with a girl and wanted to be free – free not only from war, terrorism and the Steering Group but to have the security of a lifelong companion which I now had fixed in my mind as a minimum reward for my work. I wanted that reward before I quit. Freedom for my mind would not be easily acquired no matter how hard and deep I tried to hide everything. But let me tell you, there is no cure, not even time, that will take away the memories and the fear of the future.

We moved into our new home together after three months. I had to sell my Jaguar and trade down to a Vauxhall to help pay for shit. There went my dream car. Anna hated the Jag anyway, it never impressed her. I remember when I first got it, I raced over to pick her up to take her out for a meal at an upmarket Chinese restaurant and released all my excitement about the car in a short telephone conversation, saying I had a surprise for her. Anna was expecting a ring for her finger, not me getting a new car. It wasn't the evening she had expected, but we had a great meal. I still loved the car!

The time finally came when I had to pluck up the courage to ask Anna's father for permission to marry her. I've always been a bit old-fashioned in that respect and thought it would be one of the few things in life that was worth getting right. I drove over to his house in Doncaster and damn near bit my lip off building up the courage to go and knock on his door.

John was an ex-Coldstream Guardsman and a retired police officer, so plenty of self-induced pressure not to fuck up! John's reaction was nothing short of remarkable. He simply leapt to his feet in approval once I had asked the question. I've always liked John because he did his bit, wore the uniform and served in Kenya, the same as my father, so he became my surrogate dad in more ways than one.

I actually proposed to Anna on a trip up to Northumberland. It wasn't like in the movies, although I had planned it to be so at a posh hotel. Instead, after nearly running out of time and nerve, I proposed in Seahouses in a local pub in which we were staying. I wish I had done something more for her. But it never really works out the way you plan it. Besides, I don't think any of those melodramatic proposals enhance a true proposal from the heart. This was my first true commitment to anything, made entirely free from any work agenda or desire other than pure love.

Typically, I left Anna to deal with all the arrangements, including the sale of her home and the entire move, whilst I was deployed to the Middle East. Anna moved in and redecorated the house with the help of her sister, whilst I was oblivious to the whole episode, buried in the bullshit of the Middle East and focused on new and outstanding tasks for both the Steering Group and my promotion. I wasn't 'hot' on this trip. I was getting acclimatised, I suppose, to this new enemy – the stench, the heat and the unforgiving rawness of being a Westerner in the Muslim world, trying desperately to respect their rules and customs but feeling utterly despised at the same time. The time would come when I would respect the Middle East unreservedly, but now was a different time. I resented this time when I was apart from my Anna. It was as though the sand people had laid claim to my private life as well as completely ruling almost everything in the minds of the Steering Group.

Anna was commuting to work and had taken on the full mantle of being a military wife – well, my partner at this time – left to organise everything, sort everything out alone and all totally unsupported. She was a very independent woman and that was a great comfort to me; she wasn't needy or anything. She was completely able to deal with situations that arose on her own. Our first home was a modest three-bed semi-detached house. I remember the fantastic power shower, that leaked through the ceiling onto the cooker below, the bubbly wallpaper Anna's cat loved to rip off the wall in the living room and the moss-ridden grass in the back garden that would drive me mad. All these little idiosyncrasies made the best memories and became a path allowing me back to a normal kind of life at weekends when I was back in the UK. Work was playing on my mind heavily and I couldn't overthrow those thoughts all the time by being with Anna. It distracted me from our relationship at times and I'm sure she noticed but these were good days free from the burdens we carry in life after the passage of time.

Going home for the weekend was a great escape from reality and all the military shit. I know most guys in the military would have you believe they are having sex with women every minute they're not at work, be it with their wives or one-night stands; in truth, it's all mostly bravado. For me, time with Anna was much more special; when I was with her, I truly felt like a complete man, complete in every way. When I was with Anna there were no absences in my life, I felt utterly normal and complete, almost an illusion to fool me each and every weekend. From the outside we were just a great young couple starting out together, and that was true, but like the cans that jangled along behind the wedding car I was pulling a few heavy loads that were yet to be unhooked.

The garden was the size of a postage stamp and consisted of mostly moss with a crap wooden fence. George and Mildred, the couple next door, reminded us of that same-named TV show, although I think George was more of a Victor Meldrew. On the other side was a fucking lazy bitch whose shit was spread all over the front garden, bringing down the entire neighbourhood. None of this mattered as we were probably the noisy ones in the street. We loved to turn up the music at the weekends, get drunk and then dance like Mia Wallace and Vincent Vega from *Pulp Fiction*, trying our best to win the twist contest at Jack Rabbit Slims on top of the sofa. Fun times. It really was a carefree time, lots of relaxing and weekends at home together. No real shit to be worried about as training was just training, no one's life was on the line; it was like being back in Russia.

We had BBQs with Anna's friends at home regularly and I started to put my feet outside the door of military life, if just for the briefest of moments. It was great, every weekend a party. The thing is, though, civvies don't understand military guys. Civvies are usually tight and can never afford a round at the bar, probably because they've got a family and a mortgage, which as a young member of the armed forces with no commitments made most civvies generally boring. They're not of course, but how do you have a polite conversation about blowing some fucker's head off during a firefight or how you saw women being raped and men burnt alive in front of your very eyes? You can't, so you talk about all the other mundane shit they want to talk about – work, football and fucking soap operas. It all directs you back to the solitude and the more accepting bubble of military life, being with the guys. It remains easier to avoid letting non-military people get too close to me.

It's not that you even want to talk about anything to do with your job or what you've seen or experienced, which is what makes it so much easier to hang out with other military guys. You just know, you don't have to ask, you don't need to discuss any of it because it's all understood and easily recognised by the way you act, talk, are silent, get angry, get pissed or whatever. It's all perfectly acceptable and normal because you've walked the same patch of earth and just understand and respect each other without saying anything. You know when you're with someone who has seen the other side of war because there is nothing to explain; you can both mutually accept each other as equals, accepting without reservation the other's mannerisms, imperfections, or the inability to communicate effectively or communicate at all, and still be at ease. Trying to have a complex emotional conversation with someone who has PTSD is just gonna go in the 'too hard' basket for most civilians. That's why no matter how fucked up veterans or serving members of the armed forces get down the local pub, it's all okay to the military eye. Let them get on with it. Civvies will never comprehend that level of brotherhood and will never understand why sometimes servicemen just need to get smashed, be left alone, get upset about nothing, be withdrawn, difficult and sometimes just fucking annoying and appear to dislike people in general. It can and does sometimes lead to a pretty miserable lonely existence because you want to keep it all in without upsetting the public, but the more you keep it in the harder and more aggressive it all becomes in your mind to try and break out. It's always the family that has to pick up all the pieces. Trust me when I say that all servicemen respect you, the public – that's why we want to protect you. Just sometimes, some of us might lose our way home in more ways than one. Sometimes we need help but don't want to ask and definitely don't want to be a burden. I think above all, speaking as a veteran now, I don't want to show any weakness, as it would translate into failure in my own mind.

The minute we moved into the house, my mother made things doubly difficult for the pair of us. Anna had made a card and gift-wrapped up the front door key which compensated for all the negativity I was getting from my side of the family. I remember my first time at home, my new home... My mother rang and asked when was I coming home. I simply replied that I was already at home, I'd bought a house and that was my home now. It went down like a lead balloon and within the hour my father had delivered the rest of my belongings to my new front lawn! I guess however stupid it sounds at that time in my life my apron strings were finally cut. I had defected away from one life to be with the woman I loved. I was happy to end that part of my life and get on with making a new life for myself. I think there was a lot to move on from. I had to stop the truth from my childhood hurting the new me and my future wife – find a shovel and bury it. The love-hate relationship between me and my mother ran deep. God rest her soul. I fucking loved her but equally felt like killing her at times.

To say that the build-up to our wedding was difficult would be a complete understatement. My mother made every effort to make the process as emotionally and practically impossible as she could. She tried to sink our ship at every opportunity, right to the point where threatening ultimatums were made on both sides. We had arranged for all the family to come to the suit-fitting party for the wedding. We laid on some food for everyone so both sides of the families could be formally introduced. Now, my mother nearly destroyed that afternoon, I guess probably for three reasons: firstly, the realisation that I was actually getting married; secondly, she wasn't the centre of attention; and thirdly, she was not in any way able to influence any of the outcomes for her son and future daughter-in-law. One of the chicks had decided to fly the nest, and I guess it must have felt too final for her. It was to be a Christmas wedding, so all the colours Anna chose were reds and greens, completely unappreciated by my mother who swore she would not be wearing green to the wedding. The response from me that nearly destroyed the entire event was simply: "Well, don't fucking come, then!" My father must have smoked 50 Benny Hedgehogs that afternoon as he navigated an impossible course through the whole damn event.

Life went on like this until her untimely death. I think it's the same in most families to some degree or other. Families, you're born into them, you can't choose them, change them or even communicate rationally with them sometimes, especially when emotions are involved. I don't, however, believe they stick together. In my experience they self-implode and retain bitterness and memories. My childhood was to remain hidden, undisclosed yet inconveniently raw in my mind, but like impurities in molten steel the slag would float to the top and come out on the surface every now and again; this and my recent military experiences were starting to manifest themselves through anger. The Steering Group had given me the tools and mental capacity to harness, focus and utilise this anger to their advantage. Their methodology allowed me to almost tame the dragon inside, but all those tools and mental games do fuck all within the family environment. The on-off switch can never be turned off where family is concerned. This is probably because I refuse to employ military methodologies in such a personal part of my life, because family sit in another dimension. This is why interrogators and terrorists love to threaten your family, because it prods you in a different way and can break you quicker and harder than a sledgehammer. Family is not an escape for me, it's problematic. As an operative it's just so much easier to turn family off before and during ops because it clouds everything.

My family was and always will be the boys in my unit and Cdr Brown – the godfather of the Steering Group. He knew where I had really come from, he knew what lurked behind the collection of masks he had equipped me with. He knew what he had created and had made a home for me with the boys from Poole. These boys were fucking nuts but in a great way. I wasn't one of them but I belonged to them, if that makes any sense. But now there was Anna, who could see my potential and my desire to be good and succeed but was unable to understand or be a part of the man I was becoming, a man who so wanted to be free but remained chained to a life built on the desires of evil men, hell-bent on a list of names which must be expunged from the human 'razza'. The Steering Group's grip was tight, from which there was no escape, except by completing the climb of their Purgatory, each step of which was carved with the names of those from the list who must be killed. It was the only way to true freedom for me now, the stage had been set. Although, such a freedom would come with a price which will always have the memories that the drink won't ever drown or a night ever fully extinguish. Insomnia was in the post already and hard to disguise. But insomnia is a friend to the intelligence service. You can work longer, achieve more and deliver the impossible despite the fatigue and the anxiety as you over-process everything you get involved in.

I guess, looking back, the Steering Group was like belonging to a cult, a very, very religious one. Once you were in as deep as I was, to leave the cult would be devastating and the excommunication would be catastrophic. The utter loss of all the family, all the team. No contact. A vacuum in space awaited the defector, in utter darkness, and there was never any return to the light permitted. What was once simple and easy in life would become incredibly difficult. Life was made smoother providing you remained faithful. Your life's struggles were sometimes made easy all of a sudden, things fell into place naturally for their members. It was wise to stay within the group and leave when the job was done and become a veteran with honour. To leave would be dangerous; people outside the group wanted me dead. The protection offered by remaining was overwhelmingly and magnetically attractive. The Venus flytrap of the group caged you safely away from the outside with only the strongest of defence mechanisms in place, allowing the occasional peak in from the outside world before the curtains were drawn in utter secrecy. To belong was everything. To leave was suicidal.

But even in that first home with Anna, I was always looking out the windows, looking to see who was there, what cars were parked, all movements monitored, all number plates recorded, each person a possible mirror and every child a delivery boy who wasn't delivering anything from Amazon. This surveillance remains with me and haunts me to this very day. Who might walk down the drive looking to remove a name from their list? I'm often at the window at night and often go out to check the cars, the garage door, have a walk around and then at 2, 3 and 4am checking again through the windows, monitoring and recording. It drives me fucking mad, the paranoia and the endless fear of it all. Surely I made it onto a list of some other overseas fucked-up organisation.

My final deployment to the Middle East on *Eagle* was coming to an end and had seen me spend a considerable time away from the team which had been deployed elsewhere on land in Iraq in preparation for Operation Desert Strike and whatever else they had in their assignment package. I had little involvement, except some minor intelligence gathering, and played my part in a more observer type role. I would soon be seconded back into the full throes of the Steering Group. I had actually enjoyed the reduced responsibility, less tense yet remaining involved whilst I prepared for my wedding!

It had been a long six months away from Anna this time going through the Suez past the Adriatic and Bosnia and out into the Red Sea and then the big left turn into the Gulf through the Strait of Hormuz and the ever-present silkworm envelope. This deployment was a step down, a time to gather my shit together and prepare for the next assignment from the

Steering Group. I had spent endless nights putting together suitable correspondence to Anatoly. It had to be carefully compiled with information subtly included in the innocent text that would be just enough to get a message through prompting him for a date, a place, a trip, anything innocent. Our last conversations together in person had opened a way of communication that allowed us to trade ideas in ways that would be extremely difficult to gain any intel from. Besides, most of what we talked about was rubbish anyway.

I was on the brink of my wedding and my promotion, which would all come together should I make the flight out of Dubai! I enjoyed a few parties in the SNCOs' bar aboard, getting fucking bladdered (drunk) and spent long nights bonding with the guys and the crew, often ringing the bell to buy everyone a beer. It wasn't unusual for me to see sandy bottoms in a bottle of whisky after a couple of bottles of wine or several beers. It would all start off very sensibly but always end in a mess, often being put to bed by one of the crew as they got up for breakfast. The best nights were in the Aruga room, an all-ranks bar deep in the bowels of the ship. It was a regular nightclub. Entry was only permitted after shooting a can of beer and then screaming at the top of your voice: "Arrrrrruuuuuuggggggaaaaa!" It passed the time. As was so often the case in my line of work everything was fucking boring for such long periods of time, months, even years before a brief interlude of crazy action-packed adrenaline-fuelled nonsense hit the stage. So, to pass the boring times we got smashed, spun dits (told stories of war, etc.) and generally made a nuisance of ourselves.

Anna had threatened to cancel the wedding should I fail to make the flight home. There were many things lining up to fuck up my return home. The ship was deployed with heightened tensions in the NAG and it was looking increasingly likely that the ship might not dock in Dubai. I was frantically trying to arrange alternatives. Operation Desert Strike kicked off and saw cruise missiles released from USS *Laboon*, USS *Russell*, USS *Hewitt* and USS *Jefferson City* (attack sub) against Iraqi air defence targets. I gotta say, the targeting was pretty accurate for some bizarre unexplained reason. But tension in the Middle East was rising fast. I was pleased to make an exit. I felt relieved to get out of there.

The ship eventually docked, and I got a transport to Dubai airport and picked up an RAF flight to Brize Norton. The RAF wouldn't ever get any awards for airline of the year or anything. I flew fucking backwards in a VC10. I think the flight was like seven hours of uncomfortable torture coupled with a shit RAF packed lunch consisting of a mushy apple, a wet cheese sandwich, a carton of warm Kia-Ora orange juice and a biscuit, all in a flimsy white cardboard box. Anyone who has flown RAF will have a similar story to tell. However crap the flight was it didn't matter as I landed to meet Anna, the only person who has ever come to meet me back from deployment, either at Brize Norton or any other airport or port. No one else had or would ever do that for me; Anna did several times. That meant so much to me. Coming home after time away to be greeted by an empty arrivals lounge is dreadful, but worse is to see all your comrades' families waiting expectantly and no one there for you. It makes you feel more alone than if you'd landed on Mars. It was late at night and England greeted me in darkness, wet and typically miserable. The only warmth or sunshine I received was from Anna as we made it home to our little secret place away from the world and all the shit floating around in its oceans of demands, misperceptions, conflict and utter chaos. I allowed my mind to turn off, if only for a short time, as I dissolved into her comfort.

Last-minute preparations for the wedding needed to be finalised and I was thrown into all the frenzy and chaos of it all. But John (Anna's dad) came to the rescue on many occasions to support and help pay for a huge chunk of the entire day. Anna had done really well; she had saved up heaps. She had booked us to go to Bali for our honeymoon, only because it was one of the few places left on the planet I hadn't actually visited. Between all the preparations, I needed to get fit, so I did a lot of running out to the second village from our home, about 15 miles, and practised the BFTs and all that meathead stuff. I never really liked the fitness side of the job and usually only managed to stay just within the requirements, no wasted effort. I had to pass the BFTs (Battle Fitness Tests) and the leadership courses, which were all lined up for my return after my honeymoon, which wasn't great planning if all you intend to do is eat, drink and have sex. Poor timing but necessary. Promotion was waiting in both camps. I would soon hold SNCO rank in the navy and in return gain combat commander status in N1. You never hold the same rank in the regular service as you do in Intelligence; you go to the bottom and start again; it doesn't matter if you're an officer in the regulars, you're nothing when you step over. It's a different world, which can really piss people off. You can literally have your commanding officer beneath you when you switch over into the underworld of N1, or indeed the UKSF Intelligence division. I had eight months of courses to complete ahead of me – leadership, command training, engineering and personal development within the Steering Group. I put it all to one side as we headed off to be married and then take off into the sunshine, newlyweds away on our honeymoon.

The wedding was fantastic, the happiest day of my life. We, or should I say Anna, had organised everything beautifully. Both our families came, with the exception of my younger brother. I hadn't expected his attendance. Families are unreliable. Perhaps all the medals scared him off. The wedding was in my old church in defiance of my childhood. A proclamation to the world that I would move on from my childhood was to be sealed in joy through my marriage with Anna. The old phoenix was rising from the ashes to be remade, a deliberate movement, a shamanic journey further strengthening my love for Anna, affirming my resolve for life, and like a penicillin for a diseased soul I received the belonging I had always searched for in the sharing of two rings and two hearts. This union was beyond the control of the Steering Group. I was in control now.

Like a renegade I was accessing new resilience in order to be a better man, a reason to pick up my courage from where I had left it, freeing my mind from the strands of life's complex webs holding me back from mental freedom. I had found love, but more importantly a real tangible reason to do well in life. I had found a person so precious that the responsibility to protect her was crushingly beautiful. Such love diminishes all other past thoughts and failures, but above all the weight of loneliness and rejection that once was and had always been buried in my heart was now overthrown. I didn't need the military to feel I belonged anymore. I now needed the military to provide for the one who had chosen me above the military. This was a fundamental shift in my mind, a change not only in the way I thought and processed decisions but my entire outlook on life. I think I had finally acquired something I never wanted to lose. It was worth fighting for. Anna gave me new reasons to succeed and be fucking determined at work to see it all through.

The wedding day was perfect: good food, good wine, Anna and I had champagne on our top table, it was perfect. Some of the lads from the *Eagle* came up to participate in the drinking, as well as a watchful eye up from the circus. It went unnoticed as it should. We floated through the day then consummated our marriage in the afternoon in the Dukeries Suite of the hotel. I know the suite was amazing but I don't remember anything other than being with Anna that afternoon. It was the most important moment of my life and I wanted it to be perfect. And it was. I truly felt like a new man. Then I donned my James Bond outfit for the evening reception, a white tuxedo jacket and bow tie – the real 007, stand up! Haaa, it's not anything like that, it's dark and lonely and there's no glory or reward in any of it. I hate discos and all that shit, but I danced my heart out that evening with my new wife and still look at the photo each night as I go to bed and inwardly allow myself a little smile. I was truly happy that day, beyond question. Everything was in balance, if only for a short while.

The honeymoon followed immediately and was equally as awesome with all the right mixture of romance, excitement, exploring and adventure. We stayed in a beautiful hotel outside Gatwick, Langshott Manor, which set us up for the start of our trip. A five-star luxury hotel, very English and very proper. Garuda, Indonesia made for a long ride out via Bangkok and Jakarta from Gatwick to Bali. You were still allowed to smoke in the back six rows of the aircraft, which seems so bizarre now writing about it. Bali is life, full of colour, noise and new smells. Anna was initially shocked by all the street and beach hawkers, which were overwhelming for her, but she has since become a veteran of British tourism. The hawking and bartering dialogue soon transformed from a simple 'No thank you' all the way down to a firm 'Fuck off' which did the trick. I found it amusing as we walked the beaches and the town, but I had experienced it all before in Africa. We spent long days by the pool as well as long days out exploring, driving around the countryside trying to cram in every tourist site listed in our little guidebook. We explored everything from temples to monkey forests and were exhausted at the end of each day. It was great that we loved spending all our time together and we were both drawn closer still by all the adventure and exploration. I think for Anna it opened a new portal to the world of travel; it wasn't just about sitting on a beach and sleeping in till late afternoon after a heavy night. Indeed, we would go off and explore many other countries in the years to come, from America to the Gambia, Kenya, Seychelles, Singapore and Hong Kong, Dubai, Australia and New Zealand, the list is almost endless.

I remember we would often sit at the swim-up bar and character assassinate the other guests as an amusing pastime. One hot afternoon we sat at the swim-up bar in the pool together taking the piss out of a woman who was the spitting image of Margarita Pracatan, an older woman who sat at the bar on the terrace with every inch of her skin covered in makeup and overloaded with fake jewellery. She was funny, drank neat brandy and went to bed at about three in the afternoon each day. This was after demolishing an entire bottle of Hennessy and embarrassing herself endlessly, especially the lower the brandy got in the bottle. Our time in Bali came to an end atop the Satay terrace where we watched a perfect sunset and ate far too many chicken satay skewers, drinking fine wine to the sound of the ocean breeze through the palm trees. Gosh, it was a wonderful trip.

As with all good things it came to an end too soon. The flight back was a disaster, cancelled and then reassigned to another flight, like escaping Vietnam at the start of the war! Some 40 odd hours later we found ourselves back home in the snow and had a dreadful drive north from our hotel near Gatwick all the way to Nottinghamshire. I had a few short days to prep for my courses. This wasn't a particularly exciting time for me or Anna. We started the military married life together being mostly apart from each other as all military families experience. I travelled at weekends, every weekend I could, and officially joined the weekend warrior exodus on Fridays. I travelled as often as I could whilst undergoing all the compulsory promotional courses, each course presenting its own challenges but nothing to match the challenges and courses I had already passed with the guys from Poole, or indeed the Steering Group courses and training in Wales. By comparison it was all rather dull, with the exception of the engineering courses that seriously challenged my intellect and my ability to maintain focus. I'm not really a very good engineer, I sort of just got dragged along in it all over the years, especially the more the group learned of Anatoly's talents and made their plans to use them.

Engineering training was shit at first because, as always, I just couldn't find the reasons behind what I was supposed to be learning and it was all starting to feel pointless. Why and how all this was of any relevance to the next mission was escaping me. But I remembered how Captain Pies had changed how I had thought that day when I was a boy on board the *Atlantic Star*, how he'd shown me how to navigate and how that useless maths lesson years before at school could be used for something purposeful. Those memories reminded me that all things fit into the jigsaw puzzle if you allow the pieces to be placed on the table. Trouble was, I never had enough patience to wait and see what was unfolding.

On my engineering courses I covered everything from thermodynamics, electrotechnology, gas turbine theory, hull and construction, naval architecture, power and distribution, ship's systems, reverse osmosis and evaporators, refrigeration and air conditioning, nuclear theory, welding (to nuclear standards), TIG MIG and gas to fabrication, design drawing, including CAD, and everything else I've not used for years! The engineering training was eventually unveiled as being of significant importance, with the need to be able to understand and converse with Anatoly more in his conversations regarding the projects being lined up for him. I needed to be able to support and encourage him. Also, there was the underlying fact that my promotions depended on me having the trade and a core rank. I knew Anatoly was going to be working with me on a project in the future, it was all lining up, I could feel it; my grooming hadn't been completed yet and I was aware of this and the fact that Anatoly was going to be utilised in ways I had yet to fully understand. As usual, don't ask too many questions and you won't get told any lies.

I do recall being overconfident for the leadership and command course held at HMS Royal Arthur. A young lieutenant as green as grass opened the course with self intros, etc., etc. and we all had to follow his lead by way of answering a set of pre-determined questions on a board. Apart from all the usual shit like name, family and all the usual bullshit, in response to the question:

"What do you expect to get from this course?" I simply responded: "Nothing."

Enraged by my negativity I was hauled in to see the commanding officer of the Leadership and Command School and invited to explain myself. Quite simply, I responded with the truth.

"If you can get a group of men to do a job they don't want to do, and get them to do it well, that's leadership, and I can already do that, so what the fuck are you going to teach me about leadership?"

There was a look of disgust and my comments were met with distaste but also some interest. What followed was basically an attempt to make things very difficult for me over the four-week course. For me I found the whole thing amusing and relayed my thoughts back to Cdr Brown on how best this course should be changed to meet the leadership needs of the future and how we could use this course to spot potential candidates for the group. It wasn't anything close to the all-arms course or the field training I had done with the boys. I just found it amusing how hard a lot of the trainees worked at getting off the course rather than focusing on completing it. Complaining of injuries like twists and sprains instead of just fucking getting the course done. They were not like the team at Poole whose attitude was very, very different – it was do it or fuck off, no giving up.

Nothing ever came of my suggestions, I just had to get on with it and tick the damn box. To be fair, most of the guys on the course were great and I was lucky enough to have a relatively solid core group of high-performing and high-morale guys. We ploughed through the eight weeks and completed our training, ending with the 54-mile yomp over the Black Mountains in the pissing rain. It was easy. As a final insult I got to play the lead role in the course play as King Arthur – what a load of shit. Anna even got me a McDonald's crown for the big show! At the end of it all I think Anna liked my new uniform better so there was at least one plus. She found the new uniform much sexier!

Now, some eight months later I eventually found myself back under the command of the Steering Group. Seconded back to the group I was drafted into submarine projects. This was the journeyman's time in which I needed to get under the skin and become familiar with all things nuclear and all things submarine. A more than deliberate move to prepare me for the defection of Anatoly, I needed to be submarine savvy and get ready to be deployed again with the boys. I was drafted to HMS *Drake* and immediately put to work within the nuclear site at Devonport docks. My education was to begin in more ways than one, and it started with a meeting with Ben Martin (US Ops) and my old friend Paul Seely from those early Moscow days. He was back in play for the next step after the defection, which was to get Anatoly involved in the new sub project being undertaken by the navy for the RN/USA joint projects utilising possible stolen Soviet technology and inside information yet to be extracted from Anatoly.

He would be working with me on a submarine build project upon his defection. There were some high-value assets who would be ready for any design changes or reworks in order to be one step ahead in the arms race. I wasn't exactly fully in the picture as to what the team wanted Anatoly to assist with, but from all the hype I was guessing they knew more than me as to how Anatoly would be employed upon defection and I was key to ensuring my friend cooperated in every way, to make sure the investment of the Crown paid off. Nothing to do with me, you must understand, I was only important in so much as I needed to be there to keep my old friend Anatoly engaged and useful, keep him happy. I suppose you could say he needed to pay for his defection in this manner. I didn't give a shit, I just wanted him alive and happy in England if that was at all possible.

Of course, I feared that all the secrets of how he was targeted by me and the Steering Group would eventually enter his mind for a showdown, and I needed to stop any repercussions that might arise. He had been granted a chance for a new life, and I needed to remind him that there were a great many people and organisations that had the polar opposite in their minds, especially as the list hadn't been completed yet. Word would get out very quickly of his disappearance from Russia. I was going to be his only link to any sort of a life and a future with his new identity, but also I needed to ensure he gave me *every* link his family had with the Middle East, once he was safe in England, as every link needed to be severed.

I was eventually summoned to a meeting with the Steering Group in London. All the players were there ready to unveil the defection plan. Whenever I went to London it always felt like a family reunion. Walking down those echoing halls again reminded me of the first meeting I'd had all those years ago at the beginning of it all. The meeting room still looked like a fine dining room, the oval walnut table looking more worn from endless meetings of heavy files being pushed over its once smooth highly polished surface, it too now showing the scars of the last few years. The carpet had started looking tired and darkened by the heavy steps of those carrying the weight of their responsibilities, creating distinct carriageways trodden in the once vibrant pile. The same simple water jugs and glasses placed at convenient points between the 16 chairs, some now creaky and unstable. A few pictures were now on the walls, and some very poignant to me. There was one picture that I stood and stared at for some time – it was of me on the ice at the Pole. HMS *Triton* and USS *Portland* had rendezvoused at the North Pole back in 1991. Shit, it was a good picture. I thought briefly about stealing it...

The entire team was assembled, Cdr Brown, Anderson Chaplow, Marcus Branford, Paul Seely, David Crowle, Ben Martin and all the boys, Cheesy, Pierre, Smudge, Phil, Hugh and Baz. We were joined by the captain of the *Cavalier*, and the captain of HMS sub *Triton* who walked over and joined me for a cigarette, staring into the picture with me. The reflection in the glass betrayed his true feelings. He was uncomfortable in this room, unprepared for this kind of meeting, or perhaps unnerved by the sheer informality of the gathering. Perhaps he felt a lack of respect. Our meetings were, by comparison to naval high brass meetings, a bit of a disorganised argument and debate with no real solid agenda. I looked into the glass of the picture and caught his attention and his displeasure. I think he was just pissed about being roped into a role he felt really uncomfortable with.

I suppose he had a right to be pissed as everything was getting complicated, but there's really no point having such a negative agenda at these kind of meetings as everyone brings issues to be table-topped that outweigh personal agendas. Besides, with so many possible scenario outcomes at the start of such meetings we could all fret and worry about it and achieve absolutely nothing. Everything is a moving feast, it's all fluid and it's all a game. I don't think anyone really has a plan in these situations, we all just get together in the hope that someone will dream some shit up over coffee that sounds half doable, then we make it happen. It's funny because all the things that would trouble my mind would be calmed by being in that same old room with the team. Everything was made to sound simple and less complicated than when you're left to try and pull things together in your own mind. The meeting rambled around all the usual logistical issues, the insertion and extraction options, support teams, etc., etc. Then heavy discussions on how best to meet with Anatoly, where, day or night, time to transport the package to the extraction point, plan B, plan C; every possible option was to be explored in-depth and either considered further or quickly dismissed.

The really big shit sandwich that needed to be devoured undoubtedly fell to my old friend David Crowle, MI5, political division. This would be where the hammer would hit hardest should the whole thing fall apart – the political and public fallout would be of biblical proportions. How the fuck to play down any known UK involvement? The minister wanted assurances that no one political would ever be found to have had anything to do with Anatoly, his defection or indeed anything else that might be of public interest or embarrassment. Of course, a pre-rehearsed script of political bullshit needed to be broadcast should we be caught, and what backdoor settlement, if any, could be negotiated quietly in the House to appease any Russian backlash. There needed to be a peace offering in place should it all go politically sour, and the excuse book needed to be fully loaded for rapid deployment to the press.

The Steering Group didn't see the need to worry the politicians – do it and get the praise if it all went well or seek forgiveness and plead ignorance if it all went south. Myself and the team played down Anatoly's defection as a light operation but with a few risks. We simply needed to be covert, go in, pick up Anatoly and get out, avoiding any detection. No planned engagements. But we all knew that as simple as it all sounded, we needed to, as they say, plan for very different scenarios – if you want peace, plan for war. Adaptation to unfolding unknowns was the team's bread and butter and so Baz and Pierre calmed the whole meeting down from a brass band to a gentle harp. Besides, no matter how well we planned shit it always looks different on the ground, and therefore it's all just a game of improvisation after the plan starts to fall away to real-time events. This was what we were all good at so it all felt a bit ridiculous to be planning things too tightly. Someone's arse was puckered up too tight higher up the food chain was our final assessment of the situation.

Eventually the elephant in the room was finally mentioned – my attachment to Anatoly. It wasn't an unknown, there was no secret about my relationship with Anatoly, that it was a very close one. There were feelings of serious risks here to some of the team, especially Paul Seely. My loyalties were brought into question – hard questions to face but I guess necessary. I didn't deny my closeness, what was the point? I knew all my mail had been read, private mail and email monitored and intercepted, dissected and analysed and even changed by the group before anything went outside the circle into Russia. For some reason and from out of nowhere there became a distinct atmosphere and pressure to count me out of this operation. Without doubt this became a serious conversation and consideration for the group but conversely there was no way Anatoly would ever leave Sarov and come to the UK without me. I stressed this point. I had his trust and it was my fucking operation and had been for years. It was I who had introduced the family to the world of UK intelligence and I who had betrayed the family that had looked after me. It was I who had eliminated Evengy, my third wolf, my Russian brother I had betrayed callously and deliberately – a cold killer deep within the enemy's council without which the 'list' and all the intel would never have been delivered to the Steering Group.

I resented the accusations and it showed, raising a smile from Cdr Brown. When I promised I always delivered. There was no lie in my eye when I stood at the head of that oval table and delivered my speech regarding my involvement with the family, and Anatoly. But above all I was bold enough to be honest and admit I wanted my friend to come to the UK and remain alive. I had no issue pulling the trigger on any member of the family but Anatoly could offer more if we brought him over. Perhaps there were some underlying suspicions about my loyalty or commitment that needed to be laid to rest. My commitment to see Anatoly move over and then for me to be free for the completion of the list was my goal. My support team was watching intensely. The guys hadn't been involved in the Moscow years, that was all my own work. But the question that was sewn into their minds was: would I give up Anatoly for one of them should the situation demand it, and when shit goes south who will I protect first and more importantly last? The guys from Poole don't operate like that. They're tight and you don't get to work with them if you don't follow suit.

It was a test, an internal and deliberate test of my loyalty and integrity. I guessed that maybe silent whispers had taken place behind closed doors, a whisper of a doubt uttered quietly in the halls outside this very room or in the labyrinth of the doughnut at GCHQ. An administrator, an overthoughtful fucking analyst or non-operational member of the support team perhaps, making a comment to a member of the Steering Group, who allowed the whisper to grow into a tiny suspicion after half reading some papers in a file. Or perhaps a single misplaced comment in one of my letters taken out of context or misinterpreted by some poorly informed nerd of an interpreter who couldn't understand written Russian slang or humour. This tragedy of suspicion was now arising out of the dark against all my best efforts to hide my desire to keep Anatoly safe but ultimately for him to defect. Was the Steering Group looking for a mole or a double agent? To be frank, at this point in my time with the Steering Group I hadn't the energy to play both sides. It would be too much. The mission, the family and the list were suffocating enough. It didn't matter in the mists of being an N1 operative; it is utterly allowed to have suspicion enter every part of your life and I should have expected this sooner after RIAR and Segment, but my loyalty was intact and my nerve had been tested beyond question in the company of the team and the group in the worst situations. Besides, I was the one who always pulled the trigger on the main target and the team knew this. I think it had been engineered in such a way.

I think everyone needed to see my reactions, to see if they were rehearsed or paperclipped, or genuine. I knew the core members of the Steering Group were decoding me in every way. I looked into the eyes of the team, into Cheesy's eyes, Baz and Pierre, Hugh and Smudge, telepathically transmitting my commitment to them. Besides, if shit went south and loyalties were not solid then the team could easily eliminate the bridge, hang me out to dry to the other side. It wasn't hard for the group to know they had the upper hand and I was on their leash should there be any unplanned actions on my part in the execution of this most sensitive transfer of Anatoly to the UK. Cheesy let out a loud laugh and threw a napkin at me, breaking the tension. Cigarettes were lit and coffee poured. Everyone knew this operation was fucking massive, no matter how much we tried to compartmentalise it all into a simple op. We knew its true significance and it wasn't just us and Anatoly who would reap the repercussions from behind the curtain in the Lubyanka if we were caught. The other side would hunt us like dogs, and we would all carry a high reward if captured or if we found ourselves in an unplanned firefight on their turf.

Cheesy took the floor, calmly approved my involvement and recollected my actions to eliminate Evgeny, how calculated, focused and fucking ruthless I had been, not to mention the absolute deception I had employed with the family to see the job done. The room was in silence as Cheesy gave his testimony of my ability to complete a mission; he spared no detail and gained table-banging approvals from the team, mustering to a well-supported accord. Cigarette smoke lay heavily across the room at head height waiting to be dispersed by a change in direction. It was clear my bond with the team had been forged in the fires of war in Bosnia and could not be undone by such a misplaced whisper by any desk-driving paper shuffler. The doors opened and Spud stood in the doorway. He casually walked in, took a place at the table and simply nodded at Cdr Brown. The elephant had been slain by a silent witness, but fear was now sown in my mind for this next mission.

My support team was invited to leave as the Steering Group moved the meeting on to known KGB activity. All the guys got up and wished us well, and offered some banter and words to the effect of offering the Steering Group the advice not to fuck this one up. Cheesy came over and patted me on the head like a pet dog and play punched me as he left the room. Smudge just said it was all getting boring anyway, to which there was a communal laugh as the guys left in high spirits, shouting back that they would meet me in The Red Lion on Parliament Street for a few wets once I'd done talking shit with the grown-ups. The doors closed behind them and there was an uncomfortable silence that swallowed up the diminishing joy of laughter and banter that disappeared down the corridor with the team headed for a beer in less uncomfortable surroundings.

Intel showed that the KGB had mirrors who had been following all the family, and I was in their portfolio of interested parties. It was a sure by-product of spending so much time with the family, plus no doubt a reaction to RIAR and Segment. There were photographs of me with Anatoly in Moscow, at cafés and at university. Innocent or not, the intel suggested it was Natalia who had leaked my name to the Lubyanka after that first chance encounter with Rashid Mohamed Asadi on the Metro. These were older photographs. I had known it must have looked too good to be true to the family, but I thought it had all gone unnoticed. There was no intel to suggest anything other than a friendship with Anatoly but the suspicion and fear had been planted in everyone's minds. There had been Russian operatives following Rashid, and me. Yes, we had mirror operatives to consider now, but they had been there for years – this was old intel to my mind. I was unflustered by it. Time was getting short and the walls were closing in, and the Steering Group wanted a conclusion to the Russian chapter a little more urgently than we had first understood. The list needed completing and Anatoly needed to be extracted. I found it of little importance or any significance that we had mirrors back in the Moscow days; I was fucking living with a KGB family. for fuck's sake! I would have been more concerned if there had been photos in Dubai from other lesser-known sources, or more recent photos of me with Evgeny in Romania or other shitholes.

Spud calmly released that things in the US hadn't been too watertight either. Joint teams had uncovered a possible leak through FBI Special Agent Guy Mitchell. Because of his position in the FBI Foreign Counterintelligence Unit and his use of computer technologies, Guy Mitchell was able to pass extensive and highly damaging information to the Soviet authorities on all things linked to operations behind the curtain. An intercept had managed to stop information regarding Anatoly. Ben Martin interrupted and stated that our friend Guy had been left in play deliberately until such time as the Steering group had used him to relay the right amount of false information to create a sufficient diversion to allow a confrontation between the Arabs and the KGB whilst we executed a left-field approach to the removal of Anatoly.

It was Spud and Ben who now suggested that rather than extract Anatoly as a defection, the team should fake his death to avoid all the other issues aggravating the politicians. A pregnant pause, a silence for just a few deafening moments, then huge conversation, ideas flying back and forth, opinions and strategies, an all-new electric atmosphere was unleashed into the room. Then silence before a new barrage of conversational engagements. A new direction, directives would follow, and the team was simply to be put on immediate standby in readiness to execute any new approved order. It was a no-brainer: avoiding a full defection scenario would remove the shadow issues, and a terrible accident for Anatoly would remove all the inevitable defection fallout on both sides of the fence. No engagements and no witnesses.

It was Spud who stood up and let the bad news drop like a sledgehammer into a glass bath, and all the plans and aspirations simply spilled out like lifeblood from a patient on the table in an operating theatre.

"There is a double mirror in our group," he calmly stated.

The room flatlined. We had a sleeper agent, a spy, a fucking two-headed coin! Spud had been assigned as cover agent to the group and team for some time. He had my back. He had been working very closely with Ben and found communications between their man in the US and a contact in the UK, completing an intelligence circle. Spud and Ben were our anti-virus, deployed to keep the back doors sealed and await any trojans or worms looking to get in amongst British operations. They had uncovered a sleeper cell in the UK linked to the Arabs assisting the family business in Drobeta during Operation RIAR. There were photographs of Hugh and me in the hotel room and with the trucks we had loaded with the local hired hands. The entire operational plans of the Steering Group seemed to be looping back to this cell in the UK from the US mole in an attempt to obtain a backdoor entry to Russian operations linked to the Middle East and Anatoly. We were clearly a target now for these terrorists right here in the UK.

To betray us and pass the list to the terrorists, take payoffs and accept a false offer of an exit was what we concluded for the US mole. Our job to complete the list would be near impossible now with the Middle Eastern terrorism groups possibly knowing not only the identities of UKSF and intelligence operators but the entire portfolio of Russian ops led from the UK. Of immediate concern was the fact the Arabs would seek to steal Anatoly during our defection attempt for the benefit of the Iranian nuclear programme *and* more than likely use his knowledge to build a fully operational ICBM. Fuck! It wasn't about the chemical weapons or the passage of arms to the Middle East, or any of the sordid underhand deals between governments and terrorists, all this was small fry by comparison. This was about getting to the source of the intelligence the family was selling on the side from Anatoly in Sarov. The family had never intended for Anatoly to become the sole goods for sale. No longer did anyone want the crumbs from the tables at Sarov, we all wanted the main course. My friend had become the main target and his safety would be very hard to ensure.

There would be no further negotiations between the family and the Arabs in nice cosy apartments in Dubai, they were going to kidnap Anatoly and make the whole thing hang on the UK by exposing the team and the Steering Group on Russian soil. The Arabs were planning on using our plan to cover up their plans and bypass all the issues we had been discussing. Guy Mitchell was going to allow the Arabs to know where the defection (and accident, if we now leaked it) was going to take place and have Anatoly probably held up in captivity in some hellhole in the Middle East, and at the same time open up an international crisis between the CCCP, the UK and USA. Bastards.

Spud laid it all out on the table: photographs of Hugh and me in Dubai with the same Arabs photographed in London with the sleeper cell; photographs in the shopping mall, and our meeting with the Arabs in the desert before our extraction after the deal had been sealed in Dubai before we executed Segment; more photographs of Hugh with the Arabs in Drobeta. It was all fitting together now; no wonder there were no issues with the Arabs in Drobeta, Mitchell had worked it all out ahead of us and arranged for the Arabs to drug Evgeny in that hotel room, set up the meeting with the Arabs, taken his payment and sealed his fate to chance, falling deep within the embryonic machine of a terrorist organisation and setting up a backdoor with the FBI into MI5 and the Steering Group. Ben assured the Steering Group that the US had Guy Mitchell on a very short string and that operational control was with the group and supported by the head of the CIA in Langley.

What was eating away and tearing my mind apart was what did the Arabs actually know of me, the family and our connections, and my connection to UK intelligence? Or was their undivided attention simply on Anatoly? Perhaps they believed I was KGB as I had spent so much time with the family in Moscow. Unanswerable questions. But without doubt was the fact that they had me as a close associate of Anatoly. Perhaps that was it, but equally they could be seeing my relationship with him as a threat to their plans, especially after seeing me at work for the family both in Dubai and in Eastern Europe.

I remember sitting and reflecting that Evgeny had actually been against the entire plan to betray his brother and me but had been defenceless, a lamb to the slaughter. No wonder he had been in such a mess, drunk, lazy and incomprehensible, it had all been the work of an FBI mole in league with the Arabs, whoever they really were. Evgeny had been used and compromised by all sides whilst remaining loyal to his brothers. How many more WOMD (weapons of mass destruction) and chemical weapons had left in earlier shipments to destinations he had no control over? Where did they go? The removal of Evgeny may have been unnecessary or at least somewhat premature reflecting on the fact that the whereabouts of those shipments would later become a prelude to war. We had reached the point of utter compromise, a state of complexity that had everything we had planned completely undone from the inside. A re-think had to be undertaken to analyse the mess, plan on a double hit when we got to Anatoly and make a new pathway for his entry into the UK. But before that we would need to fully identify and eliminate the Arab/Middle Eastern components then turn the whole thing upside down and engineer their demise in Russia.

I understood it completely, why it was so easy to become a player on both sides. Guy Mitchell had seen an out that would furnish his future beyond anything the FBI or the Steering Group could ever put on the table. To escape and hide in some sunny hideaway in the Caribbean perhaps, or disappear into South America. But now with a price on his head so high from three organisations, let alone any mercenaries who may now have his number, this would ensure his ultimate demise. I think it's the secrecy and the wanting to be caught feeling that all spies openly deny, but secretly, like serial killers, we want to be caught, to be captured in order to show the world our masterpiece of undercover work, how far we could go and remain unnoticed. It's against everything we are trained to do but when you become good in the espionage world it's never possible to tell your opposition, or anyone else for that matter, how fucking good you really are without revealing your identity. A paradox.

Guy Mitchell would be wanted by the entire circle: us, the Arabs, the Americans and very soon the Russians. The Steering Group had to leak this information. We needed to leak the right amount of information at the appropriate time in order to facilitate a clean departure for Anatoly. Thank fuck for Guy Mitchell; he was now the key to the entire puzzle, a way for us to clean up. We spent 12 long hours in that room with the Steering Group coming up with a way forward. By early morning I left Whitehall with a thick fog in my brain and walked the streets of London for a further four hours, drinking a few lonely beers amongst the crowds, before getting on a train to Plymouth with new orders in my hand. I was beginning to think it was all a fuck-up.

The Steering Group

Chapter 11

Defection

The entire team assembled in MHQ Mount Wise Plymouth some months later, I think around June 1998. MHQ (Maritime Headquarters) was a mainly disused building at the time. However, despite its state of semi dereliction here we were for our planning meetings. MHQ consisted of a complicated nine-sided two-level bunker, built half submerged into the ground to afford some sort of protection from air raids I imagine. Behind MHQ and beneath the lawn of Admiralty House is a network of underground tunnels called the Plymouth Underground Extension which connects MHQ to Admiralty House. The rooms we occupied had been stripped bare apart from a number of whiteboards, wiped clean of previous ops long since completed or abandoned. On the entrance door a simple sign saying 'DCSA Communications Centre Plymouth' hid our gathering (DCSA – Defence Communication Services Agency).

We assembled in the heart of the bunker at the joint operations room which was two storeys high with a number of different rooms on each level. We had been split into three teams, and some cross-pollinating between teams and rooms was expected during all the briefings and discussions to find a way forward. I was with the Steering Group in the main planning and coordination room; the SF team was in another room and would oversee all the dramatics where the metal meets the meat, the false death and the defection; and the third team consisted of the dustmen and their various support teams.

David Crowl, Ben Martin and Anderson Chaplow were overseeing every move, decision and idea, sometimes abandoning us in the main meeting room to throw ideas into the other meetings. It all seemed a bit of a non-event in our separate briefing rooms when I compared it to seeing Marcus Branford with his own personal team assembled in a locked room. Marcus looked older than before, holding up his heavy head in his hands, no doubt troubled with the demands of Government and the doughnut to remove the mole, eliminate this new sleeper cell and pull the whole thing off. Marcus was the upper tier of the political/non-political commanders and sat both with and above the Steering Group. He was a true polycephalic (a creature with two heads), smiling with the politicians in polite and comfortable surroundings, but then devouring any enemy discovered amongst the many briefing notes and files fed to him by the Steering Group teams. His teams were only ever assembled in order to execute the Crown's will, whatever the cost, no matter what. He had been given quite some mandate. He needed a plan to take forward to be quietly approved higher up the food chain.

The planning and briefings that go into some ops are nothing short of remarkable, the attention to detail has to be perfect, there are no second chances. We would always remind ourselves of the six Ps: 'Prior Planning Prevents Piss Poor Performance'. It's this attention to detail that was the very real difference between success and failure in the intelligence world and probably more so for the boys from the boats squadron, who were and remain the true epitome of military perfection. Not actually knowing exactly how we would execute the extraction opened up a lot of discussion. To plan for the unplannable, that's what we did. We had an objective and had to find as many ways as possible to achieve it, maintaining the ability to adapt as nothing can be too rigid – shit on the ground changes by the minute. We needed cover stories, for both myself entering the Soviet Union as well as the team, that were plausible yet unremarkable. Transport methods, equipment for the team and the dustmen, insertion and extraction points. Safe houses, alternative routes, the list goes on.

I'm very proud to have been able to know all the support team members for those short times we actually worked together in the field. It's true that in my many years of service the actual time spent on ops was actually very short indeed. So much of my time was spent patiently waiting, planning and training, which can be tedious and sometimes very dull, just like life sometimes is. This patience is required in order for the other side to lose their patience or to start their game prematurely, believing you're not waiting or watching. Your adversary's conscience will eventually take its leave and seek an audience with those faithful to the inevitability of conflict brought on by the needs of powerful men and their desire to dominate. We wait because we are not in possession of an order, and are patient because we are trained to be prepared for the right time to strike, when the enemy least expects it.

Time on ops is like a flash of lightning in a very long, wet and miserable storm as you seek passage to the silence and peace of the shores beyond, a flash of light and excitement that although very powerful only lasts for the briefest of moments in time before it's gone and committed to your eternal memory. There it stays, patiently waiting for the thunderous outcomes of your actions to be fully realised and then played back to you at the most inopportune times. I grew a taste for those brief moments of excitement because they truly reminded me of my time in Moscow when every day was 'active'. Each day had made me feel alive in Moscow and I missed it very much. Although bizarrely back then, the family and the life I lived so easily felt like a pleasant reality at the time, not a mission in any way shape or form – a delusion of peace. It was a false security in which I was a stranger in my own life; that is until much later when a trigger had to be pulled and when fate would catch up with the temper and strength of those against me and the organisation. Time always rushes to reveal the real world, for just the briefest of moments, when decisions become very real actions.

It was cold, damp and musty down those old echoing corridors. The smell of old stale air mixed with the corrosion of obsolete equipment left to the decay of time and wary memories. Each corridor and room was tired and overpainted, the walls flaky and chalk-like to the touch. The air was perfumed with the scent of gun oil soaked into those little red-lined cloths littering the old armoury floor, entwined with the echoes of old secrets that cannot be discussed by anyone. It's a smell that can only be remembered by men who have spent time in such dark places, cleaning and preparing their weapons, arming themselves ready to perform the quietly whispered orders from the people occupying those dark rooms, sending them to unnamed locations.

The tension and intensity of the planning were enough to bring the old rooms back to life. Like a re-powering of an old factory, life was temporarily breathed back into the old lungs of the bunker that day. This increasing hum of activity joined with the uneasy movements of commandos drawn in from the local citadel, unsure of what exactly they were hiding or protecting. It all added to the heightened sense of expectation as they nervously asked for identification at the many checkpoints along the corridors and rooms. No doubt the wall maps, one of the entire Soviet Union, the Middle East and a more detailed map and satellite imagery of Sarov, made for rumour amongst the security teams. For me it was more than exciting, it was up a level from anything I had done previously, like coming out of hibernation as it all came alive around me.

It was all much bigger now, the fear and the excitement very real. I was more aware now than ever before of what we were setting out to achieve, what the Steering Group had been engineering and dovetailing over years and years of planning. Who knows how many other operatives had been involved or been simply transient to the needs of the Steering Group? The curtains were set to go up.

Things had grown out of my control, nothing like back in the Moscow days; I no longer had control of what information flowed into the machine. It was self-sustaining now, feeding itself, growing significantly bigger and bigger. I was truly becoming nervous, afraid, and for the first time, in a way I hadn't felt before, unsure of my own abilities, or perhaps I had become afraid of what I had created, unable to stop its progression. I was truly a castaway in my own creation.

It's like when you tell a lie, you have to remember the lie and then tell lies to hide the lie and on it goes, you can't control it. It sort of took my breath away as it eroded my inner independence as an N1 operative. The thought of losing total oversight and control of it all freaked me out. It fed paranoia and gave rise to a quiet mental rumour. I had begun to feel vulnerable and alone in it all as though the teams were working to find a mistake in my work. I was secretly pleased to have the team with me; like a safety net of reassurance they made light of all the heavy briefings and reminded me that no matter what the top brass decided, once the first bullet left its chamber out there in the real world it would all be back down to me and the oppos next to me, just me and my brothers. Forget the politics, concentrate on my job and the safety of the man next to me.

It was knowing this that allowed me to focus and put doubt and fear in a box for a much later discussion with myself. I think it was about this time that I realised I wasn't really a big team member or player, I worked better alone, more of a lone operator when it really came to it. I could feel the unease growing in me as the realisation that working as a solo operator might be at an end. I didn't like it. I would have preferred to have kept it more personal. The family was mine. I would see their end and save my friend Anatoly. That was the glitch, the chink in my armour – I had become friends with the very people I was sent to bring down. Maybe they had all been right to question my loyalty, or was I just being fucking human? Round and round the thoughts would go, betrayal, loyalty, duty, honour, guilt and confusion, all equally malleable on the anvil of destiny before me. What was I to forge from my assignments now?

I don't think I really knew anything other than I wanted to save a friend and go back home to Anna. Everything else seemed like white noise now. I couldn't fully engage with it all. In my mind I had my own mission, and it wasn't too far away from what was happening around me. I just wanted to feel valued, to be in the middle of it all. It took me back to my childhood, the detention centre, the thought of wanting to be recognised and be a key player, the incessant need to feel valued and to belong, not discarded. Old demons were playing with my mind, when in fact I was the centre of the entire gathering. To be surrounded by people who are all working because of you and for you but feeling alone and isolated is like being an animal in a zoo – very interesting and valuable but still caged. Looking back, maybe it was because I did feel a deep belonging and loyalty to my friend Anatoly. The whole deal was a complete mindfuck.

In a separate room, I joined the support team briefings, much more relaxed yet at the same time focused. Being with the team always reminded me of my place in the world. I belonged to these guys and felt very attached to them, always the best place to be when I had doubts or messed-up thoughts.

The plan was to extract Anatoly as he made his way on a pre-planned holiday from his workplace (the Russian Scientific Research Institute for Experimental Physics (VNIIEF)) in Sarov to Yaroslavl, the holiday home where we stayed all those years ago with all the family. This holiday had been in Anatoly's calendar for a long time, and I think only Cdr Brown, Marcus and I knew the actual dates. All correspondence I had seen from Russia had the dates removed in all briefing papers, orders and the like. Where does all that correspondence end up? I remember thinking. In the hands of a fuckwit FBI agent or discarded in the CIA's in-tray. Being old-fashioned in some things, like sending teams away on ships to see what follows them or stops following them and destroying shit immediately after a briefing, was the norm for the Steering Group.

Computers, they're our weakest asset. There's a lot to be said for disappearing off grid into a bunker and writing shit down on paper then burning it all on completion after it's all committed to memory. You can't hack ash! Seriously, every fuck-up I ever heard of in the intelligence world involved a human, a computer or a telephone. They are all dangerous. Yes, Big Brother is watching us all, every day and every night, through our new smartphones, smart TVs and the incredible global CCTV network and internet. The system knows everything about you – who you spend time with, talk to, what shit you watch on TV, your favourite takeaway, how long it takes you to get to work and how you got there, even what you bought at the supermarket and how you paid for it.

If you're one of the millions who have Facebook, they now know almost every detail about you, your friends' details and their friends, and their friends' friends, and the terrorist group sitting in London watching you and your friends through your new iPhone camera. Before you know it their friends have befriended you, or someone you know, and are now piggy-backing your accounts from Kazakhstan, then they're hacking your work computer or emptying your bank account because you have told them everything – indirectly and innocently of course. Happy birthday! Now I know your date of birth, your name and I'm almost ready to get a mortgage in your name.

The intelligence service and the terrorist especially like all the photos the public like to post online, it's a great help to both sides. We know who to target and what you look like, and best of all where you're gonna be. They know everything about you, exactly where you are and how to get hold of you and, if they do, so do all the other intelligence services around the world and the bad people we don't talk about. It's called the internet and it's the most used item in the intelligence services toolkit. We use it way, way before we redeploy a fucking satellite or something that might cost hard cash. That's why it's so fucking great, because it's free.

It was a 572km drive to reach Yaroslavl from Sarov, a journey during which the team would engineer a disaster for Anatoly, avoiding the whole unpleasant defection issue. There was plenty of open country to find a suitable stage upon which to create a masterpiece of illusion. A performance worthy of an Oscar is what was needed. It was widely agreed the accident needed to take place somewhere remote but not inaccessible. Route 72 was the preferred road from Sarov to Yaroslavl and the ideal point would be a river crossing on the Murom Bridge over the Oka River north of Murom. We all pulled our seats in close around the table as maps were pulled out of the files. We needed an exit route, a sea exit north of Yaroslavl/Lyubim.

We looked at the possible routes for Anatoly to take. Our main issues were the distances involved and the precarious proximity of Moscow just to the west of all our plans. We needed to conduct the accident and head in a direction that would be unexpected, a harder route than anyone would think of if planning this operation from the other side. There were only a few options: go south to Kazakhstan, an immense distance of 1,422km to Atyrau; or go west into the Ukraine and on to Mariupol, some 1,311km, where we could pick up a sub or small coaster in the Black Sea and exit out through to the Mediterranean via the Sea of Marmara, a tricky manoeuvre to go unnoticed in such a busy sea lane.

The captain of the *Triton* exhaled a sigh and muttered, "What an impossible task." He wasn't fully submerged in the briefing. He was disengaged from the meeting, probably feeling as though he would only be used as a stealth taxi should the need arise. His mutterings were silenced by Cdr Brown.

"Nonsense! Let me remind you of Gallipoli. The success of the Turks in frustrating the Allies in Gallipoli overshadowed a very little unknown fact and an aspect of that campaign that was a complete success for the Allies."

Brown had everyone's attention.

"Sir Winston Churchill saw the penetration of British submarines into the Sea of Marmara by daring and brave submariners navigating the narrow strait that connects the Aegean Sea with the Sea of Marmara, with depths as shallow as 200ft, and managed to safely navigate and cope with complex and unpredictable currents."

Everyone was scouring the charts and maps, smoke rising, blowing ash off the charts and intently listening to Cdr Brown at the same time. It was like a bedtime success story or a rousing speech, and to be fair we were all totally immersed in listening to a success story. I had been daydreaming of a more simplistic approach.

"Also! Let me remind you of Lt Cdr Holbrook who took the first British submarine B-11 some 12 miles up those straits and through the minefields to sink the Turkish battleship *Mesudiye*. He was awarded the Victoria Cross, gentlemen. It is totally possible to extract our man out through Turkey."

There was a lot of laughing, desk banging and cheering as though we were celebrating being fucking British, a boyish bravado to compensate for the difficulties that needed to be overcome by the team once a course of action had actually been decided upon. Brown was just wanting to open everyone's minds, clear the air, get the guys pumped up or something. There had been without doubt a room full of blank minds hiding behind eager faces, but this was how ideas were brought into play for the team, put them out there to see if there was any merit in your thoughts; if there wasn't, they just got laughed off. Insertion through Europe and extraction with Anatoly through Turkey was possible... I think, however, the guys preferred the Kazakhstan route. The final decisions would be made by Marcus, and however fucked up it all looked or however difficult it was being perceived a way had to be found. I guess Brown wanted the mood lifting or was getting tired by it all so late in the day.

The briefings and discussions were wound up and brought to a close late in the evening. Each segment of the orange remained separated, only Marcus knowing which to use in order to create the final plan. Marcus would decide what orders were issued and when. The guys at the doughnut would be charged with placing only the most relevant of articles on record for a trickle effect to our man in the US, Guy Mitchell, and then hopefully on to the Middle Eastern/Arab contingency and with a bit of luck the sleeper cell here in the UK. I guess the Steering Group wanted to sit back and watch where all the information went, and what came of it. Of greatest concern was how it looped back through the FBI into Russia and the

Middle East. It would be a perfect opportunity to see what colour the chameleon would turn back into in the US and how big the mess really was. Allow him the opportunity to get the Arabs right next to Anatoly and take the package in either direction, to the Russians, to the Arabs, or would he come running home to Mama?

We parted ways, each with separate orders. I suppose they were sort of holding orders, nothing more. Marcus met me at the exit door of the bunker. We stood with the double-sided steel door wedged ajar and he shook my hand and asked if I was okay. I wasn't. Brown came up out of the dark to join us. I lit a cigarette and gently allowed myself to explain that I could take Anatoly alone. No need for dramatics, they could rely on me. Marcus was calm and gave me a smile and then turned to Brown said, "Look after this one." Brown laughed as we briefly enjoyed the night air together, each of us probably overwhelmed by the day's events and where everything had ended up in our lives. Both Brown and Marcus were keen to warn me about the American issue as no one was really sure how deep this went. FBI agents working alone didn't seem plausible, and Langley and the CIA involvement remained a mystery – either they were on the other side or they were internally trying to flush out a 'Boris'. Who fucking knew? We shook hands, Marcus holding on that second too long before we parted ways.

Of course, as things turned out the op that unfolded on the ground was going to be somewhat different than what the team was expecting from those briefings, which to be fair had probably been more of a pooling of ideas, or even a complete diversion. Most of what had been agreed wasn't actually going to happen at all anyway. The key to pulling it all off was to set a trap door for the terrorists, the Arabs and the Iranians, whoever the fuck they all were, to fall into, allowing the team to dissolve all players and hang it all on the Arabs at the accident point. The mastermind of what follows was the work of my very close friend Marcus who no doubt had a few sleepless nights as we all went off to play our individual but highly connected games. Ben and David were no doubt simply left to watch in awe as Marcus orchestrated his plan. They must have been totally enthralled as they learned from the master how to do the undoable.

I would join HMS *Cavalier* in Plymouth, integrate with the crew, do work-ups in order to prepare for a quiet insertion, possibly from Norway, and make my way overland to Sarov. I would train for any possible hot exits with an elite group from 42 Cdo and the team over the next six months, building in all the training packages with the ship's work-ups and exercises. I would eventually meet a new operative on board who would be working with me and receive further instruction once deployed. My orders were very simple and kept completely sealed and undisclosed to the other groups. There was nothing in those orders that I was aware of that differed in any way from what the team was being briefed, and I was never fully aware of the entire plan forward from this point. However, I suspected that a very different and complex operation was being orchestrated beyond what the teams and I had been working through at MHQ that day. That was why Marcus was there; he was the big cheese, the top brass, the man with the egg on his cap. Marcus was labelled 'only consult in the event of a fucking disaster', and there he was, open for business. All briefing notes and agreed orders disappeared into his room and into the master plan, concealed from any outside opinion or influence, to be considered but not necessarily used, leaked and transmitted where deemed appropriate, to set the traps, set the scene.

I was soon aboard HMS *Cavalier* and enjoying my new life based in Plymouth. It didn't take long for Anna and I to move from Nottinghamshire to a village in Cornwall only a few miles across from the Tamar Bridge. It was nicely isolated from the main city but pleasant enough, with a local pub and shop both as welcoming as a dose of the flu. However, we could forgive them for that so long as the Cornish pasty shops remained open! It was exciting for Anna I think, returning to Plymouth where she had done a nursing course. Old haunts, pubs and bars bringing back good memories. She got a job in Plymouth Hospital in the neurology department and we had a few months living a relatively normal life together. House-hunting had been swift although a little painful as prices were much higher than in the north. The move had been a bit messy, but with an interest-free loan from the navy things were made a bit easier financially.

Moving into our new link-detached house we were amazed by those wonderful storage heaters that used up all your electricity at night and released all the heat the next day while you were out, leaving you fucking freezing when you got home from work! This, coupled with wooden single glazing, gave rise to an expensive priority list of home improvements. We soon made it feel like home though and in no time became very fond of Cornwall. We enjoyed our weekends out and about enjoying the many attractions, beaches, village pubs and of course Dartmoor, one of my old training grounds. We became very fond of coastal walks from Cawsand round to Rame Head and back, and the 24-mile run I used to do over Dartmoor. Anna and I did well on these walks together, even in the snow.

Anna's sister and family visited often with their young children. They would take the 300-mile drive down from Sheffield to spend the weekend with us. We would always try to get to a beach or something, trying to keep the kids amused, which made our exploration of the South West very comprehensive. We always found a pasty shop or a good local pub for lunch before heading back home and all getting very drunk. These were good times and it was great to have her family so close and able to come and visit often. It felt like we were a normal couple with a normal family life. I was now commuting by moped to my job in the dockyard as I had to sell my car to help pay for the removals, etc. It's funny to realise that the best times in your life are perhaps the quietest or seem to be the dullest of times. You don't realise how happy you are until something much worse comes along to fuck you up. Then you wish you had been content as you were, where it was perhaps a little quiet but safe, happy and settled with a routine. But such times are never allowed to endure, they are time capsules in a world that won't stand still and you never appreciate what you have until you, time or someone else fucks it up. Cornwall really is a great place and we still visit to this day. It never compared to Moscow; this was different, Anna was different, she wasn't controlled or engineered by the intelligence services. Anna was pure and unspoiled, a virgin in a world of deception, such a gentle and beautiful creature, a floating butterfly in a sky of ash.

Often, Anna would drive me into the dockyard very early on a Monday morning and pick me up on a Friday as the ship underwent all the many trials and exercises that had to be undertaken for the ship, her deployment and our ops. The support teams and I worked through every possible op scenario gained from the briefings. It all got to be a bit routine for the crew in the end as this went on for about six months or so. But for me, the guys always had something new to teach me so I was always kept very busy and engaged. Sometimes the ship would go to sea for just a few days, a week or up to a month but nothing too heavy, which allowed for Anna and me to have some normal life together at the weekends when I was home.

Life was better for me now on board, I had my cabin which was very comfortable compared with previous ships I had worked on. I was very much left alone to my own devices now. I had plenty of engineering study to keep me occupied, which the Steering Group had passed on to me. They wanted me up to speed on a number of topics in order to be ready for Anatoly's arrival, as I would be babysitting him on his new job. With this to think about and all the diving equipment to maintain for the team in my spare time, it made for a welcome boredom breaker. The diving store/workshop soon became a tea shop for the boys and all those interested crew members who liked to sneak a fag when they should have been turned to elsewhere. ('turned to' means to be at work)

All of the team, especially Cheesy, were very particular as to the standards of maintenance I deployed on those diving sets and to all the other equipment we held on board. The new UWCS (underwater communication systems) were a new toy for the boys to play with and, as we all believed we would be leaving the ship by water to join a Norwegian sub in the fjords, we were keen to get to grips with the new kit. I was deeply entrenched in the planning for that day when we would finally depart the ship. We spent many hours in the workshop, in the pool at Drake and down at Pier Cellars, checking and testing the kit as well as trying to break it!

The ship was soon to sail away from British waters and the programme released to the ship's company. Joining STANAVFORLANT (Standing Naval Force Atlantic) was a great opportunity for everyone to get lost in and amongst other naval groups. The full teams were soon aboard and we had taken over our little section of the ship. Everything was setting itself up for a nice trip, the ship was comfortable and a good sea boat. Sailing out on a pussers' grey is the Steering Group's standard disconnection policy for all Naval Intelligence personnel to get away from all unwanted eyes and ears by being at sea like a satellite before ordering the execution of any mission package. Being away at sea was like disappearing into a communications abyss from which we could emerge confident that there was no tail and we were truly free from any shore-side connections. This gave huge confidence to the Steering Group knowing we had all been 'sheep-dipped' clean of any contacts, both in person and electronically, before they pressed the final green light. When I look back it's a very clean way to ensure your operatives and SF teams really are detached from the world and can be readily reinserted anywhere and at any time in the world totally confident of anonymity. It's easy to control what goes in and out of a warship at sea.

Leave had been granted before our deployment, offering the teams and me some downtime whilst the ship undertook the transatlantic crossing ahead of us in the New Year. I worked on board over the Christmas period. There was a lot of preparation to be made out of sight of the main crew who were away on their Christmas leave. Baz, Cheesy and Smudge stayed on over Christmas with me, which turned into some major drinking sessions. During the working day we jointly went through all the kit that was being delivered to the ship over the holiday period. It all had to be prepped, checked and made ready for use, and we worked methodically to ensure nothing was less than 100% perfect. Each team member's weapons, Sigs and Glocks, SMGs, assault and sniper rifles, L119A1s, an L82A1 50cal anti-material rifle, sniper scopes, sound suppressors, grenades, rocket launchers, bergens, secure comms, tactical webbing, NVGs, diving kit, clothing, CamelBaks, goggles, rations, etc., etc., all had to be prepped and ready without too many prying eyes seeing it all laid out in the ship's hangar. A lot of the kit was dispatched directly out of RM Poole from our cages there, but there were a lot of new toys the boys were playing with and it really felt like fucking Christmas the number of parcels we had to open from the many stores' deliveries that seemed to come endlessly to the QM who was always piping (broadcasting) for me over the ship's tannoy.

On Christmas Day Anna came on board. It was kind of weird having her aboard the ship but at the same time made everything feel normal. She stayed for Christmas dinner and the chefs actually did a great job. We ate with all the crew and were both genuinely impressed with the spread laid on: three meats to choose from, turkey, ham and beef, with all the trimmings, and a great selection of duff (puddings). Later we retired to the mess and got fucking smashed, with our friends who lived in Plymouth joining us later in the evening. It worked out at about 50p a pint and 20p a short. There's no cash in an SNCOs' bar, you just fill in a chit with what you've taken and then pay your mess bill at the end of the month. I think 20 quid covered the night which turned out to be quite noisy, and the OOD (officer of the day) sheepishly came and asked my guests to leave at 1am. I went on leave two days later as the crew returned from their leave plainly jealous of those who had stayed. They would now take their turn whilst the ship endured a three-week Atlantic crossing. Naval ships never go in a straight line!

Leave passed and I was picked up by a few members of the ship's crew in a hire car in the New Year. I remember getting into the back of that car early in the morning outside the house and looking back at Anna. She was still in her dressing gown peering out the half-opened front door as I departed in the snow with airline tickets to New York and onward to the Caribbean. Our eyes met as the car drove off. How I wanted to stay at home with that girl, her sad eyes filled with the knowledge she'd be alone again now for months whilst I disappeared. So very sad. There's nothing quite like being amputated from your soulmate as you disembark on a deployment or mission. It's quite debilitating to your mind, soul, morale and purpose in life. There is no antidote for this feeling, it has to be supressed and covered over by a false engagement and enthusiasm with your teammates in the form of morale-boosting piss-taking and eventually getting drunk at the first opportunity. I often wondered what it must be like to be left behind. Fucking boring, I think. I would later learn from Anna that being left behind was so fucking lonely too.

The transit out to the ship was uneventful and I was greeted by the unpleasant fact that my entire support team had been diverted to another location. This was not some last-minute decision made in haste, it transpired that the decision had been well planned by Marcus back in MHQ that they would not accompany me for my part of the extraction of Anatoly. My operation was to take a new twist from previous instructions and new orders now awaited me, sealed in the captain's safe aboard the *Cavalier*. These new orders would unveil my part in this new unfolding saga. I re-joined the ship in Puerto Rico and soon discovered that all the team's kit had disappeared, their cabins abandoned, all the equipment and any sign of their presence removed. They had already deployed, or had other business to attend to before Anatoly. I didn't know anything more at that point in time.

Only my kit remained, one kit bag, a holdall and a suitcase. Keith, the short cockney I had met years before with Pierre in a pub in Weymouth, had joined me and was sitting patiently in my cabin reading a book. After a brief introduction I asked who the fuck he was, to which he simply retorted that he was my No. 2. He was from the same ilk as me, only about five or more years behind me, had finished his training with the Steering Group and completed his first solo mission unsupported overseas. I think going solo is the rite of passage of an N1 operative into the group. If you can work solo then you've got the fucking balls to do anything, because when you're solo if it all goes pear-shaped the group can just dump you and deny your very existence. So you've got to be fucking good and completely committed to what you signed up for, prepared to get out of any mess you make for yourself alone and unsupported. I think that was the difference between myself and the SF boys. I think it fascinated them how long a guy can work incognito and alone, waiting patiently, working with the very people who'll end up on a kill list. Don't get me wrong, having the backup was great but the trigger was always mine to pull and that's what joined us together. At the end of the day I guess we were all just tools in a box.

I have to say that at this point in my career I wasn't too keen on the idea of being without my full support team. Maybe I had come to rely on their support too much, or was getting soft. Or maybe Marcus was thinking this part was better off back in the hands of an N1 operative – expendable? But now I was given an unknown to assist me in this next phase which to me was nothing short of crazy. I hadn't got a fucking clue as to his abilities, let alone had any level of trust with this guy.

Keith reported that our gear was safe in the 4.5 magazine up forward. Oh and by the way, the captain was waiting for us both in his cabin to read our orders. All I could think was *Fuck off, you little prick*. I was angry about the change in plan, and my thoughts were on what Marcus had in mind – was I losing my nerve, was I really too reliant on the team? Was this a test of my loyalty? Paranoia? Fuck yeah, in a massive way. Or was it just that last conversation I'd had with Marcus outside the bunker: "I've got this, Marcus, you can rely on me." Hmmm, be careful what you wish for.

We attended the captain's day cabin. I let out a laugh as all the seats were fitted with those annoying hideous cream seat covers with the green floral arrangement which reminded me of my first interview with Cdr Brown all those years ago in Raleigh. Some shit never changes. We stood up as the captain entered the day cabin. It was a calm relaxed atmosphere and the captain introduced himself as Cdr Bolton, who had just taken over command after the ship arrived in the States. Cdr

Bolton was a 'see and forget' kind of guy, neither pleasing nor annoying in any way, typical naval officer, well presented, too much aftershave lotion and terribly polite, perhaps even a bit delicate.

The Caribbean sun beamed through the scuttle, beckoning us ashore for a few wets just as soon as business was concluded here. We had a nice friendly sort of chat, low-key, as he welcomed us aboard, explaining that before we opened our orders we should read and study the ship's programme which had been published. This meant it had been passed to the NOK (next of kin) of the crew and was public knowledge. He was very subtle in his approach which for me clearly laid out the fact that we should try and fit all our plans into what would appear to be a normal deployment for a frigate attached to a NATO group. He didn't want to break away from the main flotilla. I respected the fact he wanted to keep everything looking routine whilst allowing us to make our own arrangements hopefully without troubling him to change the programme. It was obvious that he was very pleased to have us aboard in our capacity, which was a little strange but I took it as a compliment because sometimes cruising teams get jittery when they have guests from Poole or London on board.

Keith sat back and watched me as I opened the envelope from the safe. Typically, the document was encrypted and left to us to de-crypt in the EW (electronic warfare) office. We both thanked the captain for his time and reassured him that our presence would be unnoticeable right up to our eventual departure and we would keep him informed of anything we thought of relevance to the ship, its programme or the crew. Being on the *Cavalier* felt homely and it was an absolute oasis away from the world in which Keith and I really operated. I loved walking down the main drag of the ship which stretched almost all the way from Charlie section, the buffer's store, to Zulu section on the quarterdeck. Always plenty of people wanting a chat or to pass comment on something they didn't approve of, like the time of liberty, duty lists or fucking rounds (inspections) coming up. The Royal Navy really knows how to moan – it's called having a good drip sesh (moaning session).

The journey from fwd to aft made for a stroll along a long passageway broken up by watertight doors, passing tiny offices, switchboards that hummed away all day and night, A/C compartments, the stench of the garbage compactor room, stores office and of course the Colonel Gaddafi (NAAFI) and the main galley. The *Cavalier* gave me the welcome of the orchestra that I remember so well from the *Atlantic Star*, all so familiar but strangely different now. I think this ship was probably the best ship I ever served on for the morale and the welcome from the crew, who assisted but didn't pry, were inquisitive but didn't ask. Then of course this was probably due to the cruise that it had been allocated; it was a cruise ship itinerary. Plus there was the issue of the fucking scran (food) on board which was unrecognisably awesome. In the main it was pretty damn good. To answer the question, who is the most important person on a ship, the answer is without doubt not the captain or the chief engineer but the chef. However, there was one chef who should have a special mention as he could single-handedly destroy a potato. How the fuck you can turn a potato into a completely hollow piece of coal using a steamer is fucking amazing, but if that fuckwit was ever on duty on a Sunday to do Sunday roast it wasn't worth the time to get changed to go eat.

Keith and I went off to the EW office to read our orders and study the ship's programme. It felt like it had been almost arranged by a tour operator. We had the most amazing itinerary of Caribbean islands coupled with mainland ports in North and South America to visit before heading off back over the Atlantic, all of which presented itself as a great opportunity for Keith and I to gel as friends. Keith and I became the closest of friends in literally a matter of minutes. We sat together for many, many hours in that EW office, and we saw the sun set and rise again as I brought him up to speed with Moscow, the family and how it had all come together for this mission and the defection of Anatoly. The thing is, Keith didn't interrupt, he was engaged, respectful and very knowledgeable of how to run a mission from his own previous experience; he was my link to the Middle East where he had been working solo. He helped complete my jigsaw puzzle when I gave him an opportunity to input, and his input was nothing short of remarkable.

Things started to click into place – why Marcus had put us together. Keith had met Owen, picked up and followed the stink trail we had used in the Middle East to find Rashid Asadi and Ahmed Haddad, and brought intelligence of the Arab/Iranian links of the sleeper cells in the UK and the Russian sector back to the Steering Group. Clever bastard. They were all linked to a new terrorist cell in some way. I have never fully understood any of the terrorist groups that may or may not link to Iran or how the whole terrorist circuit worked because it was a complete mess and above my pay grade! But the people who wanted Anatoly as much as us were serious bastards, their origin was mixed, their history complicated and their intentions unpredictable. However, the people we sought were most likely Iranians looking to acquire the ultimate weapon, or a person who could build it, and that's where Keith's path crossed mine.

We talked generally about our solo assignments. His assignment had been in the Middle East. This guy Keith had spent three years in and around Tehran, for fuck's sake. It would have been very different to my time in Moscow and definitely more complex and much higher risk. He knew where the final games would be played out, but more importantly all the names on the list, OUR LIST!, their groups and the people and places that tied it all together with his solo mission. Our solo missions were now inextricably linked, which made us strangely partners. Keith was very knowledgeable about our final goals and the needs of the Steering Group to get this and his mission in the Middle East brought to a conclusion cleanly. I had underestimated him and this wouldn't be the last time. He had his finger on the pulse. I can't explain it, we had a connection, and not just because our work had been linked; he had my back from that very first day, way before we came together for the endgame.

He was definitely a weird cunt, but despite his outward appearance of a short stocky bulldog this man was as ruthless as they came. He was a true assassin and a man of the utmost integrity and loyalty. A talented linguist, engineer and fucking great under pressure in environments you'd want to avoid. Fuck, I was actually pleased to have him alongside me. We fed positivity off each other, our friendship grew quickly and soon our brotherhood would know no boundaries. I think it was the amount of piss-taking that brought us so close together and the fact that operatives so very rarely work together, it's almost unheard of. So, there was a mutual respect, that we had both already overcome some impossible operational requirements involving personal sacrifice and difficult and challenging times in the field. I loved to wind him up about being a cockney, and how the fuck an East Ender got away with working in the Middle East. I tried to do a London accent whilst speaking Farsi and managed to flash him up so violently he got to throw a few punches at me in jest.

We set about it, spending a lot of time together. We ate, drank, slept, partied, went ashore together, worked and planned for months, always hidden away, focused on the mission. We took over one of the engineering watches for a while, allowing us to spend more time thinking and working together. Not only did we bounce ideas off each other and assist each other in our studies, it opened up new avenues for us getting rat-arsed in the middle of the night. We would come off watch and dive into the mess so no one could interfere or overhear. We talked about past experiences, all the people we had engaged with and the skills we had developed, and of course endless conversations about our support teams and our time with them in training, theatre and at home.

He explored my weaknesses as I did his, and we got to know what each man was about. Keith was a sensitive guy, couldn't take any shit about being a fat cunt (even though he wasn't really), and his mother was off limits. He drank too much as did I and we both never knew when to stop. I learned his trigger points, his character and I enjoyed his humour, his goodwill and generosity. He always bought the first round, always saw us back to the ship no matter what fucking state we got ourselves into or if we had gotten lost in some shithole bar in the middle of nowhere. He found my temper, my anger, and quickly found ways to use it to get me in to as much trouble as I found for him. I had to bail him out of the shit a few times; he liked to go shagging whores in the seediest of places and didn't like paying. But generally we were bulletproof on that trip. We laid the foundations for our friendship and loyalty to one another. Yes, we made promises, both during drink and soberly, that only men in our position could even dream of making, promises he and I would later uphold.

Our daily activities were planned to be mutually beneficial to the crew as we had no intention of upsetting the daily running of things for everyone but rather to get involved and get stuck in. It gave relief to the crew as both Keith and I were qualified engineers. It gave them a rest from the tedium and it passed time very quickly. Our watch loved working with us because we were so relaxed and we always had access to food, often inviting the lads for a free beer in the mess on occasion. If, however, we ended up down the stoker's mess or as often happened the chef's mess after the middle watch, we usually got so fucked up we ended up having breakfast brought down to us at 6.30am before we slid off to our racks and slept through the ship's daily routine.

I think it was about a week before we were about to leave the ship, I remember sitting down with him in the cabin going over our plans. Keith didn't know when we would go, I never told him and he never asked. He was just ready, ready mentally and eager to get going. We sat just having a laugh looking at some photos of a banyan we had gone along to with the ship's company. Fuck, when we let loose, we fucking let loose. Unlike me though, after a day on the pop Keith was either rough as fuck or back on it. He was a bag of shit after a heavy session. I didn't start suffering from hangovers until my mid-40s so I was the wanker up at 6am for a full English every time, and always first in the dining hall banging the shutters to get the chefs all riled up! As we talked, I let him in on our departure date. We needed to do an equipment check. I had made arrangements for the SR's mess to be out of bounds whilst we went through all our gear and over our plans. His mood and stance changed in a second like I had flicked his switch over to sensible or operational mode. This was it, I would now see Keith as a team member, not a run-ashore buddy. His demeanour fascinated me as he set about his personal prep.

We departed the ship in Jacksonville. Keith and I were picked up by a US Marine security team at the ship at about 3am. A few crew members were coming back to the ship properly pissed up and were wanting to get in and have a go in the Humvee. They unfortunately were very strongly denied and a scuffle broke out. The security team was not diplomatic in any way and one of the lads was brought to the deck really quickly with a busted nose. Keith and I carried on, ignoring the incident, jumped in and hid in the back before being taken the short distance to the Admiral David L McDonald Air Field with all our kit. It wasn't a fucking arsenal, we had limited our kit and had stripped things back to mostly essentials only. We jumped out the transports on the airfield adjacent to a burning and turning Sikorsky UH-60 Black Hawk, DAP (Direct Action Penetrator). Fucking cool as fuck, operated by the 160th SOAR (Special Operations Aviation Regiment). They call themselves the 'Night Stalkers'! Yanks! Fucking typical. It was a sweet ride, thanks to Ben Martin I'm sure. The flight crew welcomed us aboard. I guess they must have guessed by their orders to undertake this early morning flight that it was all a bit, let's say, unusual and we weren't the usual characters they gave rides to.

We were assisted in stowing our kit and given a short safety brief. Standing on that airfield in the middle of the night not knowing where this fucking helicopter was going to was a strange feeling. Not even I knew how we were getting to our insertion point. There's something about helicopters that just aren't natural. I don't think according to the laws of physics they're even meant to fly. I just paused for the briefest of moments after checking the Humvee for left belongings and looked at Keith in the helo. He was so fucking chilled out, already trying to catch a few zzzs. I took in a deep breath and savoured the smell, a deep pungent perfume of spent aviation fuel exhaust forced into the air by the turning rotor blades. This, accompanied by the noise of the jet engines and the flashing of the strobe lights against the tarmac, gave a formidable silhouette against the backdrop of a moonlit night. This was minute zero. On board I gave the pilot the thumbs up and a post-it note with the coordinates and time we had to be there. The noise increased as the pilot increased thrust, pulling up on the collective, the helicopter gave that little unusual wobble in the fuselage just as the wheels left the ground, the vibration increased and we climbed away into the darkness, soon leaving the American shoreline behind. I knew we would be picking up a maritime contact for our transit across the pond but wasn't expecting a merchant ship.

We executed a FRIES (Fast Rope Insertion Extraction System), or rapid roping, onto the deck of an MSC (Military Sealift Command) vessel, which is a merchant ship to all intents and purposes but is actually owned and manned by the US Navy. There was a whole fleet of them in Diego Garcia when I was out there on ops so it was of no real surprise. They are usually filled to bursting with all manner of shit, from tanks to ration packs and everything in between. It was going to be a cruise to us and a safe one, all very relaxed and with all the comforts of home. Nothing dramatic really apart from getting on board her. I guess the idea was that no one knew we were there, no dockyard workers had seen us or our kit go aboard and the manifest was all but normal cargo and merchant mariners bound for Norway, completely kosher. Six days later we arrived in Bodo, Norway.

We were really against the clock now. We had a 2,190km journey to get from Bodo to Yaroslavl. That translates into a 30-hour drive, give or take. You can't fly direct – it's a three-stop connecting journey by plane and 13.5 hours if you're lucky – so not much to be gained when you add all the waiting time. Besides, we didn't want to be clocked in on a flight manifest, come up on a computer somewhere or turn on the Russian security systems to our presence, plus we had a passenger to bring back with us. Stealth was paramount. Now, as crazy as it all sounded at the time and the distance involved, you might be forgiven for thinking there were easier ways to do this. Norway, Sweden and Finland were easy transient and cooperational countries for us and our crossing into Russia would be via Raate on the Finnish and Russian border. Somewhat historical, as this was the road where the Russians fought the Finns in 1939/1940 to try and cut Finland in half.

However, Keith and I would make a more discreet unnoticed use of the road and border crossing.

That was the only real obstacle, getting over the Russian border unobserved. We would be able to proceed to Raate near the Russian border, pick up on the intel and the contacts that Keith had gained, then, utilising their assistance, get visas and border permits so we would be legally able to enter Russia in a suitably untraceable manner. A big security risk to the West was criminal organisations run by Afghans living in Central Europe who illegally transported Iranians and Afghans into the EU via Turkey and Greece, now redirecting them via Russia with only a need to arrange legitimate or fake border permits to get them into the EU through Finland. Finland has a 1,340km border with Russia and is one of the longest external borders of both the EU and the passport-free Schengen area. This was why we had planned this route, this was why Keith was with me; he knew the smugglers, the people traffickers, this was his side of the coin, the Iranian side, the terrorist side. Our enemy was the ticket to complete our mission. Fucking great when you think about it, how we used the fucking terrorists to our own advantage before closing them down. That's one of the cool buzzes you get from working intelligence, it's much more powerful than a bullet if you can wield it. We intended to get a return ticket across the border with our new fake identities.

Our backup plan and less preferred option was to veer off Route 9125 into the hills along a track to the River Lahtipuro, taking us into Lake Raatejärvi across the lake – the border into Russia – pick up transport somehow on the other side and off we go. Fucking very clever if we could pull that off; all a bit too fucking crazy but doable if we had to. Option 1 was all hinging on my new partner coming up with the goods, the Iranian contacts on the Finnish side of the border, to get us the border permits allowing passage across into Russia. This was why the Steering Group operated at levels above the system. There was no link between either us, the people smugglers, Finland or Russia. Lone operators make the unthinkable possible by operating at the most discreet levels of engagement. We could get entrenched into the other side, enabling us to achieve what no government or military force could contemplate without creating a diplomatic crisis. Putting the two of us together was a stroke of genius on Marcus's part, if we pulled this lot off. Two separate intelligence operatives bringing together two very different strands of work against terrorism, government corruption, arms dealing and the like, to achieve a goal the opposition didn't even know was in play let alone how deeply aware we were of their operations. Keith had the lead in this and explained how we would pick up the passes and a guide into Russia.

Keith and I departed the ship in Bodo very early hours and quickly procured a Volvo estate for our drive, nothing dramatic, a blue 240GL estate, a sort of non-interesting type vehicle. I suppose you need to understand that as N1 operatives we had what is called NOC, or non-official cover; this, in simplistic terms, is intelligence work undertaken under assumed identities of private sector industry. It has the financial assistance of the government but is totally untraceable. Companies would provide to the British Government assumed identity cards, false employment papers, and assumed addresses upon which passports could be arranged for an undisclosed sum of money. There are people, companies, organisations and individuals (often ex-armed forces) that are sympathetic to the Crown and who make NOC possible. It helps the operative gain access to overseas' bank accounts, money, credit cards and official documents such as driving licences, etc., etc. For us guys on the ground it was often a lifesaver and a quick exit route back home if things went to shit. This is the espionage side of the job and it relies on good relationships often born out of those conversations that never take place in hotel bars or over a round of golf where everyone seems to do rather well out of the final handshake. Trigger pulling, no matter how necessary, I always felt really belonged to the UKSF and the regular army; our role in my mind was just to identify the real targets.

The car suited our needs very well, and we headed off into the country, quiet at first then later a little chatter. I've always believed that if you can stand being with someone in a car for more than a few hours and enjoy a comfortable silence as well as any conversation offered then you're gonna get along anywhere. We talked about the Steering Group, laughed and shared pain about the training, how we had survived with all the mental training and torture, all the bullshit and how we fucking actually loved the job, how we loved being ghosts. We took the piss out of the Steering Group and our support team members, a series of character assassinations picking up on all the little mannerisms of our fellow colleagues. In between conversations we would sit in silence reflecting on those conversations, often bursting out with a random isolated laugh or smile. We put the radio on to listen to any local news to fill the gaps. The drive was boring and if I'm honest it was what we wanted. We had the passports and documents ready for the border with Sweden and Finland and weren't expecting any dramas. I took the first stint from Bodo to the Swedish border. It took us about four and a half hours and we didn't see much, just the road ahead, conditions were okay, some snow but nothing to get upset about, not enough to put the chains on. Fucking car heater wasn't great and the washer kept freezing up. We relaxed into the journey, stopping for petrol, remaining discreet but focused. I think the first leg of our drive was mostly beneficial in that it allowed us to settle into the task at hand and get our thoughts in the right place. I had to get Keith to go over the whole Iranian exchange thing over and over, and it took some time for the penny to drop on why we were taking a guide over the border with us when I was perfectly capable of navigating across Russia.

We were carrying small arms and other kit that might not be too favourable should we get stopped at a border crossing. We had stripped back all our kit to the very bare necessities. Thankfully, the borders before Russia were of no concern, as at the very worst we could re-route any awkward border officers to a prearranged contact in each country who would tackle any local issues before we went into Russia, but the whole intent, the whole point, was to pass unnoticed. It was all unnecessary concern; we passed into Finland barely saying hello to the border officers at the crossing and were accompanied by logging trucks and heavy lift transporters going about their daily business. Tiredness sets in as it does on all long car journeys, a fatigue that sees you prodding your driver as he does the nodding dog. It's a fight against boredom and monotony, the endless gentle vibration of the car over the snow-covered tarmac, accompanied by a straight and uneventful road, a lapse of concentration then a swerve as you wake up, endlessly winding down the windows and closing them up again.

Keith took the wheel from Olhava to Suomussalmi, a further three hours or so. Arriving into Suomussalmi, Finland we needed to take a break, get cleaned up, and Keith needed to contact the Iranian traffickers. We just couldn't use our papers for the Russian crossing, we needed only to be traceable back to a non-entity, a ghost or at best the Iranians, because to kidnap a Russian and make him disappear completely needed us to disappear equally as well. For any trail to lead to us or the UK would be a disaster; it all needed to lead to a complete dead end or someone quite different, and that was the intention. If the Russian intelligence services picked up on Anatoly leaving the Iron Curtain it should be because he was taken by Iranians, as this would help the West's cause in Syria, Iraq and the wider Middle Eastern political quagmire for peace. Iran kidnapping a Russian scientist would silently shift the balance in the alliances being played out in Syria. Well, that was how Keith and I had analysed the way things were being played out. However, if all went to plan then Anatoly should cease to exist before we made the return trip and the trail for that accident sent in a different direction. All yet to be played for.

Suomussalmi is a small town, pleasant enough, on the edge of Lake Niskanselka and the River Jalonuoma, only 45 minutes away from the border. All very picturesque. The drive had taken us through endless forests and beautiful landscapes which made the whole mission thing feel sort of unreal or false. It's these kinds of nonsensical parts of my work that made me feel dangerously at ease with what we were actually undertaking. The fact we were about to, in essence, kidnap a lead scientist and nuclear engineer from the Soviet Union and take him to the UK wasn't even really in my mind. At the time it actually only felt like I was taking Keith to meet my old friend Anatoly in Russia on some sort of fucked-up holiday. Perhaps this was my way of rationalising the entire event, keeping it compartmentalised into an easy to do, perfectly legal trip or something – a coping mechanism, not allowing my thoughts to turn it all into mission impossible or something equally as ridiculous. We entered town and found we had a good choice of food outlets, even a couple of burger joints, and pubs that we barely resisted. We needed to find a motel, make some calls and set up the border crossing. We did a couple of circuits and caught sight of a few notices of local inns and hotels.

We found a small motel next to the Jalonuoma River. Nice spot to rest up, the hotel was clean, quiet and hidden away. It had a spa and a good menu. We checked in for the night and paid upfront, saying we were businessmen from a company called Wooltech, which was our cover story, and would be leaving early in the morning. Keith was on the phone making contact with his people in Turkey who were to pass on our contact number to those in Raate by whatever comms circuit those guys employed. It was a sit and wait situation, which I wasn't happy with. We needed to pick up Anatoly on a specific day, and the fucking clock wouldn't wait for some fuckwit to give us a forged or otherwise acquired permit to get over the border. Keith was well aware of my impatience and the fact I had a deadline but remained confident in his fellow smugglers. Option two was looking more likely to come into play after a few hours of pacing the room.

I ended up leaving Keith by the phone. I fucked off for a swim and a steam in the spa. Fucking amazing what you do when the pressure comes on. Drop the lot and go chill out. I took an hour in the spa and got a hot meal, bringing a plate back to the room for Keith who was asleep in the chair, sidearm in his lap. I made a brew then crashed on the bed and set the alarm for 3am; if we hadn't heard back by then it wasn't happening and we couldn't wait, we would need to make other arrangements. Out like a light. Next, I'm woken up by Keith snoring his fucking head off. The phone rang precisely at the same moment I threw a cushion at him, and Keith was engaged immediately in conversation by the voice on the other end. I could pick up some details, return trip, passage to Russia, onward passage back to Turkey. One passenger out and onward passage to Turkey, three returns. Lots of timings and places covered, which Keith was busy writing down, then the receiver was slammed down. Keith stood up then turned to me and said, "We are on, mate!" No time to explain, we were up and off in the car.

Keith was driving and we had a deadline to meet the Iranians 10 miles or so before the crossing, at an outcrop in the forest outside Raate. It was all suddenly a mindfuck. We were less than 35 minutes away from the meeting point, no fucking around now, I've got my seat belt off and I'm rummaging in the bags for a weapon. I'm armed now and I pass Keith his Glock; he smiles, takes it but doesn't say anything.

"How fucking safe is it, Keith? Can we trust them?"

Keith just laughs and pushes on. I stay silent for the rest of the drive; it's his show now, to be fair, and it beats swimming across a fucking lake! The road is icy, a few swerves and manoeuvres by Keith, but he's in control, awake and alert. Lights are on full beam, making the snow feel thicker than it actually is. Wasn't expecting this kind of meet, but here we are, driving to meet some Iranian people smugglers in order to get a border pass and new ID. Only 20 mins later we are taking a right turn down a track to Honkajarventie, or something like that, and then into a cut-out in the forest. Track is bumpy as hell and the old car's back springs are creaking away like an old stagecoach. Wheels spin in some dirt where a truck has been, stuck now, feel the undercarriage scrape the earth below, some revving of the engine, reverse, forward, reverse, and finally forward, then we see it. There's a truck waiting. It's the kind of setting you see in a WW2 movie where the back of the truck canopy is lifted and you all get mown down by a machine gun, or you simply get out of your car and are taken to pre-dug graves, shot and buried. My safety is off and I'm ready for a fucking firefight with whoever the fuck this lot are, not to mention that we are only about 10km from the border. Patrols would be out.

No fucking caution or fuck all, Keith is out the car and straight up to the cab of the truck and bangs on the cab door; two guys jump out and they each embrace Keith in turn. Keith calls me over in Farsi and I respond and go meet the party. Four guys, all Middle Eastern, Iranian, twitchy as fuck really but pleased to see Keith. Seems like this was all like a family reunion or something. Lots of excitement on their side as money and papers are exchanged and we are guided round the back of the truck to greet our 'guide' over the border. The deal was we would get return border papers for three if we would help get this guy back to either Turkey or Kazakhstan. Keith is smiling now and checks that all the documents match for our crossing into Russia and the return. Keith looks up after about 10 mins and says he's happy. No problems, the papers are well established and already approved for this morning's crossing. The conversation then turns to the issues regarding getting our guide back to Iran through Russia direct or via Turkey. Keith is calm and collected as he begins to explain the camel train organised to get him back.

It's all smiles and the guys sling their AK47s and offer a drink and a smoke. I take the smoke and we stand there in the freezing cold as Keith catches up with old friends and people back in Tehran. They all looked like they have been sleeping rough, unshaven, scraggy hair, grubby and in tatty clothing, but are more than happy to boast how lucrative business has been. From what I gathered they had managed to get over 250 people successfully over the border in the last 12 months. Small firms like car washes, barber shops, taxi companies, etc., etc., set up in Norway, Finland, Germany, mainly Germany, and the UK by immigrants made the process easier and almost legit by the way they were speaking. It was just bizarre to hear them talking as though it was all perfectly within their rights to get whoever wanted passage from the Middle East into these countries. The price ranged from around €500 to €3,000 depending on the value of the passengers. Wankers, the lot of them.

I was spending most of my time and effort looking out into the forest, more concerned about border patrols than all the niceties being talked about at the truck. One of the Iranian guys eventually came over to me and said, "Don't worry, boss, our guys are following the border patrols and they're 20km west of us." They were organised, you had to give them that. I could relax a little.

Back at the hotel I rearranged the car and made space for our 'guide'. So here we were with a fucking 16-hour journey ahead of us, a dodgy Iranian border guide into Russia and a bootload of kit. We got up about 5.30am, handed in the keys and set off for the border opening at 6am. Keith seemed okay with our guide, now calling himself Taylan, and was looking well pleased with himself hitching a ride he believed we would take him all the way to Turkey. Keith and I decided to call him Taylor just to fucking wind him up.

We hit the border with Russia and there's already a queue. It's better this way, it slows things down, there's time to breathe and take in what may be against us. Besides, the guards just want to clear the early morning backlog and get back into the warm. We approach the checkpoint real casually.

The checkpoint is completely floodlit, with some of the lights deliberately aimed at blinding the driver. Wires lead out of the compound power source to the forest where signalling fences are no doubt set up. Keith drives up to the gates and is waved on to a stand by a small portaloo-looking cabin passing through a chicane of barriers before coming to a standstill. As soon as the car is stationary it is encircled by armed guards instantaneously. The guards are dressed in those camouflage tunics, some with oversize hats and others with the black ushanka hats with amazing hammer and sickle cap badges, all with semi-automatic weapons. They're not really guards but NKVD (People's Commissariat for Internal Affairs) border troops linked to the KGB in some instances. Mirrors are run under the car and it all seems very routine.

The Iranians were well aware of all Soviet security measures and had endless intercepted documents to better enable their smuggling operations. The security methods employed mirrored the same as on the Iranian-Russian border. Sometimes they wouldn't cross where they ought to and had other passing places along the fence lines.

The barrier is down and Keith winds down the window to greet the approaching guard. I get a tap on the window. I wind it down, fucking freezing as air engulfs the car's entire interior cabin. I say good morning in Russian to the guard on my side, who is very young. He peers in and ignores me. White skin like office A4 copier paper and red as fuck eyes shivering under his tunic. No need to open the boot as he can see into the back of the estate. He gets around to the rear driver's side and sees our friend Taylor sitting there with a big stupid grin on his boat race. That's it, I nearly shit my fucking pants as Taylor and the fucking guard start talking, something about a promise to bring him back some chocolate or some shit. Then Taylor is out the car and in the back rummaging through the bags and produces a package he hands to the guard. Seems like our friend Taylor does this fucking crossing every week; not for much longer, I'm thinking to myself.

For fuck's sake, the senior guard sees all the fucking around and is now laughing with Taylor but at the same time encouraging him to get back in the car. I can see that this has caught the attention of the guards in the main building across the other side of the checkpoint. The tension is there, I'm fucking pissed, but at the same time it all makes the encounter more normal if that is at all possible. The senior guard hands the papers to the guy in the cabin who stamps them, hands them back and the barrier is raised. Keith gently drives away, and then I see them in the wing mirror opening the chocolate and heading back to the main building. We pass around a corner in the road and all just fucking piss ourselves laughing.

"Fucking wanker, Taylor, you're a fucking wanker."

"It's okay, it's okay, I know all the guards."

Taylor has no idea what a wanker is but hands me a cigarette, laughing all the same. Keith floors the accelerator. Now the drive to Yaroslavl, 1,300 fucking kilometres, or 800 miles in old money.

Now, it sounds fucking crazy but many guys in the military think nothing of driving from say a Royal Marines base in Plymouth to Aberdeen, some 600 miles, just for the weekend, having less than 48 hours at home then turning around and heading back to camp. It's called being a weekend warrior. I'd often see cars on the A38 late Sunday night/early hours Monday morning heading back to Plymouth doing 100mph, with Guz or bust, written in the back window accompanied by a flag, beret or hat – this back then sometimes signalled to the police we were servicemen and they would leave us alone. It worked on a few occasions to our advantage; we had a jam sandwich up the back end for about 10 minutes, then he flashed us and dropped away. However, we were stopped once and the copper just pulled us over to say, "Keep it below a ton, boys!" Usually the cars had four guys occupying them, matelots or marines, three asleep and the fourth barely awake at the wheel. The idea being they/we would split the fuel cost four ways or have a driver roster for the time they are based in the UK. It was a pain to be the driver because you had to go around dropping people off at their homes on the Friday and then do the rounds to collect them all again on the Sunday night which could add a good few hours on to the journey. The real fucker was when one of your team decided to go down the pub Sunday night before the drive back, have a few sherbets, and need a piss stop every fucking hour. Whenever I did the driving in the early days, I would have a cut-off Fanta bottle in the back for them to piss in; I never stopped for anyone. Not just because it was annoying, but it was N1 protocol.

This drive was just that, a very long way to Yaroslavl, passing through Kaleval'skiy National Park, then through Kostomuksha, a small town, before coming to the milestone junction with Route E105 South. We stopped to fill up with petrol at 'РОСНЕФТЬ АЗС №14832', stretched our legs briefly and allowed Taylor to take a piss! Then we pushed on past Lake Onega and on to Vologda, which is like a miniature Moscow. It's known for the Vologda Kremlin and the 16th-century St Sophia Cathedral which is similar in looks to the churches in Red Square. This town signalled that we were getting relatively close. I was genuinely getting excited, I had that funny sick feeling, nerves I think, but only because I was so keen to see Anatoly again. It had been some time since we were able to enjoy any time together, and my mind wandered back to Moscow as I looked out the window and daydreamed of all those wonderful months we had spent together free from all the world's troubles and demands, a bubble in the world of hard truths and reality. Our relationship would be different now.

We were ahead of schedule and had plenty of time to get our shit together. It was dark about 10pm. I drove the last stretch as far as Lyubim and later pulled up to a row of old houses just before the cottage. I asked Keith to stay with the car, checked our comms worked and said I would come back for him, and to keep Taylor out of fucking sight until I knew all was clear. I got out the car and the road was slippery, puddles of rainwater frozen, cracking under my feet as I made my way over the road in the beam of the headlights, looking for something familiar. The skulls of beasts sat in a row on the rail outside one of the huts, illuminated by a lantern, unmistakable evidence of a hunter; this was Vadim's house I was sure. I signalled to Keith to kill the lights as I started walking up the road to the house.

About 10 minutes later I could see the house, the lights were on and lanterns placed strategically down the road. There was no smoke from the chimney into the night sky which felt unusual; there was more than one person in the house, no fire. I called for Keith to hide the car and approach from the west side to the log stacks.

I've got NV (night vision) on and can see pretty clearly. Keith comes out of the trees and joins me. We wait as silent as the dead. We sit and watch for about 10 minutes. Keith stays put as I go round the back to the kitchen door entrance. I can see inside now. Fuck, there's Cheesy!

I call Keith on the comms: "All clear. Bring up the car." I bang on the door, see Cheesy pull out his sidearm, but simultaneously he sees my stupid face looking at him through the window with my torch illuminating my grid in some kind of childish gesture – totally unprofessional. Cheesy lets me in and we just laugh at each other for a moment, then we embrace and ask stupid questions like "What you doing here?" and "Could have fucking shot ya, mate." Just bullshit. He slaps me about a bit and takes me into the main room.

"There he is," Cheesy proclaims, stepping aside to let me greet my friend. Anatoly just stands there wrapped in a blanket, crying, his white face and thick blond hair poking out the top of the blanket like an albino Eskimo or something. His breath is atomising from his mouth and nostrils into the cold room. He is smiling and laughing at the same time. A bear hug from my dear friend. So fucking emotional. We embrace, my friend and I, finally reunited once more. I hold on to him tightly as he tries to pull himself back together, neither of us really able to speak coherently. Anatoly, fuck, I'm with my friend. I couldn't believe I was with him again. He's looking well, he's put on a little weight, hair is longer than he usually has it from memory but as handsome as ever. He beckons me to the sofa and we sit together holding hands as he explains how fucking petrified he is, how everyone knows he's here on a holiday and has to be back at the research facility in three days. He's visibly shaking and a little irrational. The reality has set in that this is his defection.

"I'm here now. You're coming home with me this time. You're gonna be safe, don't worry."

Keith breaks up the party over comms. I direct him to come round the back in 10 minutes exactly with Taylor. I turn to Anatoly and tell him I have business with my friends before we depart for home and to stay in the main room whilst I, Cheesy and my friends get everything ready, and if he needs to get anything for his new life in the UK to get it. Now was the time to collect all his things. He had five minutes.

Cheesy and I go back into the kitchen, closing the door. Okay, Anatoly was all but ready for extraction, Keith and I would look after Anatoly now, we would take the responsibility. Cheesy would take over babysitting Taylor and would be using Anatoly's car for their onward journey together. Cheesy had that professional air about him, he was focused and time conscious, continuously checking his watch. I wouldn't learn the plan for Taylor or his fate until I got back to the UK. The entire team were assembled in country to see out the pantomime of Anatoly's death and to ensure it was played out using our friend Taylor as the decoy. Cheesy just wanted me to know everything had been carefully prepared and to fucking make sure that Anatoly made it to the UK undiscovered. Keith banged on the back door. Keith and Cheesy exchanged some papers and documents for Anatoly's trip to the West. I wished Cheesy all the best and gave him a hug and thanked him for ensuring my friend had made it this far. Cheesy smiled and was very open when he said that all this effort was definitely worth it, I had a good friend in Anatoly, and he was awesome and knew now why the Steering Group wanted this action. It was as though Cheesy were doing this as a favour to me personally.

Cheesy left the house first, picking up Taylor on his way past the Volvo before upgrading to the BMW, Anatoly's car. No need for the Iranian to see Anatoly; as far as Taylor was concerned this was just a driver and vehicle exchange at a safe house, a halfway point, perfectly normal in the underworld of people smuggling, and also perfect cover for Keith. Cheesy played the part beautifully and I have no doubt that during that long drive Taylor came to really like the man who was in fact probably going to kill him.

How bizarre to ride the lightning with your own assassin?

To journey in peace with your enemy,
A journey undertaken in trust.
To journey together, terrorist and Crown executioner,
A journey of corruption and purchased loyalties.

A journey to the place where even God has no light.
To journey in appeasement for those who desire power by
      might.
A journey to fulfil the promises of evil men.
To journey knowing the price of freedom and the cost of life.

A journey of destiny and majesty, as the light devours the
      night,
To journey and see the tent of night torn from sight.
A journey to dance the last ballet,
To journey riding the narcotic rush of the bullet.

A journey to the other side, where all seek freedom from
      this life.
To journey to virgins or the righteous, without prejudice or
      promise.

A journey that has no diadem and no remembrance.
To journey to the silent dark rows below the crows.

Keith and I gathered our shit together in an organised hurry as soon as we watched the rear lights of the BMW disappear into the woods. No time to lose, we got Anatoly to the car, managing to complete the turnaround in less than an hour. Anatoly was soon asleep in the back seat, no doubt exhausted from the loss of his patriotic fervour and the niggling betrayal that must now be chasing his every thought. I remember looking at him in the back seat – what a brave young man to defy such masters as he would have served. But just as Sarov looked ahead with confidence with all the young minds that remained there developing the world's foulest weaponry, the whole ideal of defection fitted the realities of the modern life and world in which we occupied. Change, capitalism, freedom and the right to choose that freedom and peace above all other things, only such freedom would satisfy the bravest of souls. How could such a gentle soul as Anatoly be involved in the development and delivery of mass destruction? How does anyone become involved in the machine of war? I would ask myself that question many, many times after I left the service. But for my part I believe I did the world a small service that day.

We didn't stop for nearly 10 hours and only because we were running on fumes. Keith and I had talked for hours about how attachment to families we had worked with had presented problems, for both the work we did and on a personal level. He too had very close relationships with families he had worked with in the Middle East, but never came as close as I to Anatoly. He envied my friend openly but in good spirit. His conclusion was to make the lives of all he met as happy as possible before the inevitable orders came, then to follow them without malice or any discontent towards those who issued them. I was lucky, I had found a way to save one of those people whose name was on a list, my friend, Anatoly.

The longer you worked for the Steering Group the easier it became to be detached from such relationships whilst maintaining the illusion of integration. I was pleased to have had so much time with Keith on that drive back into Europe. Not only did it give me time to talk with Keith but for him to meet and talk with Anatoly. It made a way for all three of us to understand the idiosyncrasies of our work, our lives and how it all entwined us so deeply in the tapestry of intelligence work, secret development projects and the whole world of national security. Enemies are just people with very different points of view that you feel the need to rebuke. Keith and I debated fervently all the issues of working with the Steering Group, and we did it in a healthy philosophical way. Not from a view to diminish or undermine our organisation but to better understand it; and yes, to confirm and seal our beliefs in all that we did for the organisation. I guess we needed to reaffirm with each other that what we were doing was right, because this was never going to be the end of things, rather the beginning. There was still a list to complete after bringing Anatoly home.

We refuelled at our checkpoint petrol station and then Anatoly talked all the way to the Russian border. He was scared, talking endlessly, which sort of took our minds off the border crossing that awaited us. It was all just gibberish about Sarov, the nuclear research centre and how it had changed, how one-third of those employed by the institute where he worked were people under 35, young scientists and engineers, closely guarded and monitored, the most sought-after minds in the world, he proudly explained. But then, falling into depression, he exhaled his malcontent with being so isolated from friendship and family. He explained that the mission was to sustain the reliability of Russian nuclear weapons, what he'd been working on, the problems of nuclear spectroscopy and nuclear structure and why he had to leave. We listened intently, both of us reminding him he no longer needed to worry about it, and he would be able to unload everything when we got home, make new friends and be free. We needed to press upon him that he was going home. This was a one-way ticket, there was no return option ever going to be offered. Keith and I completed the drive back to Finland from Yaroslavl in just under 19 hours straight. We were fucked, totally fucked. The tension, the excitement, the realisation of what we had just undertaken was fucking way too big to take in. We had made it back into Europe. We took Anatoly to the hotel in Suomussalmi, allowed him a swim and a few hours in the spa, got cleaned up and fucking crashed, Keith and I taking turns watching out for our prize.

Now, I don't fully know the details of how the boys delivered the 'Tragedy of Anatoly but from what I learned it was the most perfectly executed fake accident of a Russian scientist in history. You won't find any story of it in the Google archives and I doubt very much any of it will be released out of the government archives for many, many years to come, if at all. What exactly happened on the Murom Bridge over the Oka River I simply don't know. What little I did learn was that Cheesy delivered 'Taylor' to the Iranians on that bridge at an agreed time. They, the 'terrorists', having no idea who Taylor was (thinking he was Anatoly), were waiting on the opposite end of the bridge when Anatoly's car arrived on scene for the exchange. There it was, a cash for persons exchange on the Murom Bridge. Well, that's what it looked like.

Cheesy calmly got out of the BMW and took Taylor up to just beyond the halfway point, to the waiting ensemble, with a hood over his head, took the case (of money supposedly) and ran back off the bridge. But just as the deal was completed someone happened to execute a perfect sniper shot and kill poor Taylor just at the very second he got into one of the waiting cars. Chaos ensued with rapid fire coming from the BMW side of the bridge. A controlled explosion of the BMW rendered the bridge unpassable, adding to the confusion, possibly Baz's work. Then chaos and confusion as the receiving party dispersed in full retreat, their withdrawal incredibly well protected (by UKSF perhaps?).

Somehow the Russian military had been present, made aware somehow; maybe the KGB was given a heads-up by someone from the FBI or CIA, who knows. But the main group of Iranians/terrorists managed to get away because the Russians couldn't pursue them – an unpassable bridge and pinned down by heavy sniper cover. All that was left outside that wrecked vehicle was a dead pair of Iranians. No Anatoly. Anatoly had been taken by the Iranians, he'd gotten into the escape vehicle. There was nothing ever uncovered except Iranian bodies, Anatoly's burnt-out wrecked car, a terrorist's car stolen from Armenia and a whole lot of classified paper-work, maps, plans and correspondence from Iranian official departments authorising the removal of Anatoly Pavlovich back to Iran. How that was all left in that vehicle was a mystery, but of course none of that information was true, and there was nothing, not even a whisper, of our involvement.

I'm sure Moscow had many theories and suspicions, but I do remember that relationships remained very strong between Iran and Russia despite this possible setback to their nuclear and weapons programmes. Rather than to try and open up arguments over the loss of an engineer and scientist, Moscow maintained and opened up new avenues for cooperation with Iran for both increased arms dealing and nuclear technology, especially for the Iranian Bushehr nuclear reactor programme. I still can't believe they didn't suspect a third party; maybe we really were good at the shit we did, or were they playing a longer game? No one will probably ever know. The arms dealing had always been big, but perhaps not as corrupt or on such a scale as Moscow thought. I think it was all a bigger political move by Moscow because Tehran had previously not sided with fellow Muslims in the first Chechen War (1994-96) and wanted their continued support for territorial integrity of the Russian Federation. Who knows, but as far as the West was concerned those relationships must have been upset to one degree or another and that was enough. For us the politics was a distant game we never fully understood, but as the implements of government we did sometimes wonder as to the reasons why.

Keith, Anatoly and I got back to Plymouth thanks to the Royal Navy and a taxi ride on a lovely big British submarine with a miserable fucking CO. Brown and Marcus were aboard our ride home a T boat from Plymouth, and I left Anatoly with them in Plymouth to go on to the doughnut for the debriefing. Anatoly was expecting this, I had briefed him on the journey through Finland to be ready for a bit of an interrogation, but equally tried to instill in him that the people he would meet were my friends and the ones who allowed him to come over at great risk. I parted company with the group in Plymouth and headed to Canada for a break in Nova Scotia. Fucking crazy, I was probably less than 10 miles from home but the entire team was to assemble in Nova Scotia before picking up *Cavalier* for the ride back home. A decompression period out of sight, for me to be separated from Anatoly for a while, and a check to see if our tails were clean. We had to be off grid completely for a while; besides, we were all pretty knackered.

The Steering Group

Chapter 12

Kuznyechik

I arrived in Canada relieved to be finally off grid. We had taken a painfully slow military flight out of Brize to Greenwood Air Force Base Nova Scotia. The flight wasn't exactly business class but I'd managed to catch some zzzs crashed out in some cargo netting. Fuck, what a reunion; the Steering Group – well, Marcus – had arranged for a country house to be made available about 40 minutes outside Halifax just for the team. It was an unofficial celebration. We got utterly smashed. There was a lot of catching up to do and it was awesome to introduce Keith to everyone. We had been sealed now, no one was ever going to be able to black cat this last fucking op; it had been a rush for us all, especially after the long build-up to actually deploying, yet simultaneously a sort of anti-climax in so much as there hadn't been any high-octane moments to reflect on, not for me, maybe for the SF boys who had done the hard yards at the bridge.

Besides being individually debriefed by the Steering Group's self-appointed 'gestapo', as we aptly named them, we pissed up, partied, cooked, BBQd and ate meals together and generally fucked around for two weeks. There was a pool, sauna and Jacuzzi which we all made full use of. Our friendships were solid, so unbreakable now, safe in the history of our own self-made legacy. It was like a big family holiday, a royal gathering of the Steering Group's finest. The SF boys made sure they got in as much abuse and piss-taking of us N1 intelligence operatives as they could, all the usual shit, but we knew we couldn't have pulled it all off if it hadn't been for their efforts, and vice versa. No doubt the Steering Group would be able to showcase this joint venture to gain funding for future ops. But for this short time all everyone was focused on was taking a breath and enjoying the undeniable success of the team's planning, efforts and hard work.

One particularly memorable evening of that standdown was a gathering of all the clans, N1, SF, the Steering Group inner circle, and the dustmen, who flew in for a few nights to join us before we re-joined *Cavalier*. I think the dustmen are more covert than us actual operatives; they're like a group of Tasmanian devils, roaming around the planet cleaning up any carnage and removing any traces of the actual perpetrators and seemingly never getting involved. As I remember it, we had all gathered together for drinks in the main living area, which was all open-plan, encompassing the kitchen which was a huge open space, with plenty of sofas around the periphery, a massive island surrounded by bar stools and a log burner in the snug area of the room which was also home to the snooker table. Keith was playing the guitar, singing and taking the piss with a lot with substituted lyrics and the odd one-liner to make fun of anyone he could. He was a fucking *bon oeuf*. He was always the life and soul of a party, fucking typical southern shandy drinking southerner, drank way too much for me and loved all the drinking games. I can remember all their faces, each and every one, relaxed and confirmed in themselves after a success rivalled by no other. Happy faces. It was my family, a very close family to which I felt a warm belonging to all my brothers in arms. It was what I had sought all my life.

Cdr Brown and Marcus made their way around the room talking to everyone, shaking hands, laughing and joking. It was so cool to see them in a different light, and such a pleasant change to see them both so relaxed, relaxed probably for the first time since I had known them, and it was authentic, not some bullshit 'happy to see you' nonsense. This awesome brotherhood was my reason to continue on for one last push to clear the list with Keith. We all knew the next assignment was in the post, to finish the list and put the whole Russian file in the archives along with Keith's portfolio of Middle Eastern entanglements, but for that brief time in Canada we were content and happy to celebrate this milestone. Success celebrated amongst such company and friends was emotional. Both Keith and I always got in a real emotional mess with each other, I don't know quite why but we did. Cheesy always attempted to engage as a pissed-up counsellor of some sort, trying to make everything make sense to absolutely no avail. Cheesy was my prosthetic, without him I wouldn't have made it this far, and the congeniality between the three of us had grown and was undeniable. I do think that from the outside we may have looked a bit weird, but I couldn't give a fuck. When you've worked together and alone as we had, there is no poison strong enough to kill the bond.

I think we all needed time to process our work, and this downtime was what everyone desperately needed. Not only to be debriefed, but for each of us to celebrate and vent frustrations with each other after way too much to drink. What we were taking for granted was, we had made it back alive and unscathed. I was truly thankful for that as it could have been a very different outcome for many different reasons. These thoughts of survival were clearly manifested through drunkenness, with outbursts of emotions, anger, just standing crying (Keith did that a lot when we were together), sometimes fighting between ourselves, piss-taking and sudden fierce arguments, all extinguished quickly within the love of the brotherhood. It was a coming to terms with all the things we had gone through together, a reckoning of all we had achieved and what had yet to come.

Strangely, I do remember feeling that we were all getting older, Baz in particular looked brittle, battle-hardened, but Cheesy still looked like a fucking teenager and acted like one too! I had been with this team on and off at this point in my career for 10 years or more. How time had passed. Some of the team had kids now, had married then divorced, and we had each endured all the normal things in life on top of our military lives. It was all relative and apparent, but separate if that makes sense. I know I lived a double life but, talking to the boys, their lives were a bigger mess than mine in some cases. We all were living a dual life of some kind, our lives at home being short and sometimes very false, trying to pretend we were all normal and our life at work, real, raw, demanding and unforgiving but so rewarding. None of us really knew how to translate our work life in to something normal when we were at home. We worked for those we loved at home, yearned to be with them, but as soon as we were reunited we all wanted to be back together in our team, the second family – it's fucked up. What can I say? For our partners it felt like we were having an affair.

Getting back to the UK from Canada was a cruise – we had to take in just a few port visits and some fucking around on the ship whilst being sheep-dipped one last time by the Steering Group before we could all be finally released. It was all a welcome change of pace. Some of the SF guys flew off at Gibraltar for leave after the Atlantic crossing ahead of the ship but would re-join us later. I flew off by helo separately and then homeward bound, transiting Madrid for some leave, a break to seek that reassurance from Anna that nothing really changes much when you go away. I had only been away maybe five months, in which time it had taken just under a month's work to complete the op with Keith. Remarkable when I think about it and look back. It all felt so unreal and distant so soon after getting home. The drug of being active wears off quickly, and there is no substitute drug for that heightened activity in the area of the brain that processes the fear – the amygdala – it lasts for a while then dissipates. However, I think the team and I were now beginning to see the adverse and long-term effects of our work, and that drug we all loved so much wasn't the same, it was mutating. It wouldn't dissipate so quickly anymore and was bringing a new and more complex fight to each of us, in our private lives and when we were alone.

I spent time at home with Anna. We had a great time, trying to put all things military behind me before we took off for an amazing holiday to the Seychelles. It was what we needed, to escape life for a short while and explore some beautiful islands, a break in the routine for the pair of us. We flew direct on Monarch I think, fucking shit, and the hotel wasn't much better. Well, it was okay, a three-star hotel on the beach. We hired a car and toured the main island before getting bored and started venturing further afield. We visited an island called Moyenne owned by a crazy guy named Brendon Grimshaw, a former newspaper editor from Dewsbury. He actually died in 2012 so I'm pleased to have met him. He had a great story to tell. He had travelled the world and ended up buying this island believing he would find pirate treasure with his friend 'Man Friday' – you might recognise that name. So, rather than follow all the other tourists wandering around the island like sheep, I grabbed Anna and we banged on the door to his shack. He welcomed us in and signed a copy of his book over a pleasant conversation and a cup of tea.

This holiday, although really great, would be the last time I did anything less than five star. Both Anna and I were getting a taste for travel and the good life. I'd become a fucking snob really. I had programmed my mind that if I were to continue doing this work for the Steering Group until my time was spent in the military, then I would afford myself every luxury I could. I spent my money, the bank's money and loaded up the credit cards. Fuck saving, I might never see retirement, a thought that was massively reinforced after the death of my parents. I didn't give a fuck anyway, I had developed a need and a taste to live more in this life. I think I started to believe I was on someone else's list, and it would only be a matter of time. I still look out the window to this day at 3am, down the street looking for strange cars, anything amiss. Constantly on watch all day every day. Looking over my shoulder for any sign that I may be a target. Ridiculous really because I know they will never be that clumsy.

Back home I got drunk a few times and just enjoyed being at home in Anna's company. It was strange to be at home doing relatively nothing and attending to domestic stuff – it makes you feel like you've suddenly been made redundant, sacked, out of work, or just useless. This then grows until it makes you apprehensive or anxious about getting back to work. From nowhere weird thoughts enter your mind with a need to prove to yourself that you're still capable of making it at work. I began doubting my own abilities and fearing the possibility I'd become subjected to an inevitable skill fade eroding my abilities. The longer I remained on leave the less use I would be to the team on my return. It ate away at me as I slowly yearned to get back to the team and the job, yet at the same time I wanted leave to last forever and just be fucking lazy, to stay in bed and mope about the house. But no matter what I did, I always reverted to thoughts about getting back out and amongst it. What a mindfuck. So I had to keep busy, anything to stop my mind wandering off.

I occupied my time with Anna and did shit like decorate the house and do the garden, go out on trips and explore Cornwall. I loved to organise everything, then that became briefings to the wife, and then all excursions executed like a fucking op, insisting on everything being done to a timeframe, always early for everything and impatient to get things done or organised. Packing to go away for the weekend was like an equipment check, everything packed perfectly and even lists made. Then the itinerary became a tight schedule that couldn't be broken, destroying any chance of enjoying a journey or holiday. For fuck's sake, the military routines changed every aspect of my life and metastasised its way into everything I did on the outside. It becomes so fucking annoying to yourself and those close to you. I don't know anyone who hasn't been in the military who turns up 10 minutes early for every appointment and sets off with three possible routes and a backup plan for any eventuality, and that's just to get the weekly shop.

However, I found time on leave to focus on a trip for my dad to come out to the ship, to fly out and meet me aboard the *Cavalier* in Stavanger, Norway. He was going to accompany me back on a 'Dads at Sea' thing the navy does occasionally. It turned out to be the best thing I had ever done for my father. He flew out and spent nearly a week with me aboard the *Cavalier* before going home and finding out less than a year later that he had terminal cancer.

What a fucking bummer. Sometimes success is completely blotted out by tragedy when you least expect it.

At the time he didn't know, either that or he knew but didn't let on, because he threw himself into that short trip to Norway and the return voyage home like nothing he'd done before. I think it was like he was living his childhood dream of joining the navy or something. One dream come true to be at sea on a warship. To live a little dream before he died. He became part of the crew. I got him some navy uniforms, overalls and No. 8s to fit him so he could blend in with everyone. He fucking loved it. He kept watches in the SCC (ship's control centre), fired the ship's guns, took helicopter rides and threw himself into getting fucking shitfaced in the SNCOs' mess in the evenings (which was the best mess on board). The mess had an amazing bar built by the Tetley Brewery, and it was like being in a floating local pub. My dad was at that bar every night after scran for G&Ts. He loved all the bar and mess games and wasn't shy in doing all that was asked of him by the mess members. A sort of military initiation took place on the first night, making Dad so happy. I'd never seen my dad that fucking happy ever. He suffered every night from indigestion and heartburn something terrible, but got up and had a full English every morning and did it all again the next day. I think he ate about a kilo of Rennie tablets to keep it all down. He was the 'Daddy' and everyone loved having him aboard because he mucked in. He helped the crew clean the ship, run watches, operate machinery, steer the ship, help the chefs peel spuds, and got involved with everything. It was as though he knew this was his last ever chance to have a bit of fun and be truly free. I think he had a strength in him I will never have. Brave bastard, I think he knew he was dead but decided to laugh death in the face and have another fucking cigarette.

We spent a lot of time smoking cigarettes and drinking coffee in my office and in the chippy's shop (shipwright's shop) during that time together. He never asked any direct questions but I know he knew I was different now. His boy was all grown up and firmly tied in to the military. The guys spent time with him both individually and as a group. I let him draw his own conclusions from all the attention he received from the team, plus all the additional activities he was allowed to participate in that weren't really for family members. Even the captain sent tea and cakes to the workshop and joined us for a natter one afternoon. Fuck, he had a great time. I only wish I could have told him all the things I had achieved, my time in Moscow and all that shit. The Anatoly assignment success had got me my next promotion, but he never got to see me awarded this, he never got to know all the things I had done, good or bad. I wanted, and still want, him to know I made it to the top twice, in military intelligence and again in civilian life after the service.

After that trip back from Norway with my dad, life was a mess. I was based in the nuclear repair facility workshops in Plymouth, working towards a qualification in nuclear welding, and a G35 course, something to do with specialist pipework manufacture. I was occasionally accompanied by Anatoly in the workshops as he was wanting to experiment with different manufacturing processes and manipulation techniques. It was very strained at first because he wasn't allowed to spend too much time with me in Plymouth and was always taken away after a few hours, leaving me to guess exactly what he was trying to achieve. Occasionally I would go and spend time with him at the weekends, but it wasn't as often as he needed. He was being kept under a very tight regime, limiting his freedom and what he could do in his spare time. Sometimes Keith would ride along with me to see him at his quarters, and we always ended up in the pub despite Anatoly being under what was effectively house arrest. I think Anatoly was kicking up a fuss to fully oversee and work with myself and the engineers in the nuclear repair facility on the construction of a high-pressure cooling system for one of his projects. It wouldn't be too much longer before we were back together full-time, but I understood his impatience; he was getting upset at being isolated, and the Steering Group was not giving much leeway. The flipside of the coin was that I got to spend my weekends with Anna, which more than compensated.

Despite all the strain, Anatoly had been working well with the teams from the Steering Group, both in Wales and at the doughnut. Eventually we got to spend more and more time together. It wasn't long before we both endured that special but inevitable time in conversation together coming to terms with the realities of what had passed before us, between us, and to what all his family had done to destroy itself by delving so deep into the world of arms trading and the abuse of his position in Sarov. But the sword went deeper, deep into our relationship, deep into the realms of betrayal and sacrifice and all the pain that it brought to us both. We had known each other a lot longer than just the defection assignment; we had used each other, one for a mission, the other to escape. He admitted he had worked on plans to relocate to the UK, so he had used me and his family as much as I had exploited him. The more we discussed things the clearer it became, the more transparent it was that we were both very alike and had in fact become closer than family because of what we had endured from when we were both just boys out for some adventure. How fucked up all that innocence felt now.

From those first days when I had arrived in Moscow and explained my hardships to him and Evgeny regarding my childhood, we became bonded together; he knew what it was like to be abandoned and traded over. He too had seen a friend kill himself because of the pressure or the shame and guilt life trades with us. Anatoly understood the torment of being sent away from family so early in life and then to see what remained removed from his life prematurely. His childhood had been an abandonment of love to the requirements of the state, discarded only to become a human investment for future profit and gain disguised as an education spawned out of love. Even those who loved him had not seen his pain at being separated, and that was enough for Anatoly to have no feeling towards those who may remain alive behind the curtain. We both shared this pain of separation and loneliness. We were both sure that his mother was no longer alive. We had no proof or evidence but both knew how the authorities operated, and after the Bosnia shooting there would have been a clean-up, especially after his disappearance.

He became even closer to me as a friend whilst I endured the three months of hell watching my father die from oesophageal cancer and then my mother just a few months later. My mother was riddled with so much cancer the doctors couldn't determine the primary source. She had been dying slowly but unknowingly of cancer for years, but more acutely whilst she had attended to her husband's suffering with the same fucked-up sneaky bastard disease. Anatoly, having lost his own family, understood all my pain but allowed me the guilt of it, and to remind me my parents had died naturally, not by the bullet. To share pain is to share life and that is what we had always done, even when we sat together all those years ago in Moscow knowing what the future would bring.

Anatoly and I were both truly lost in our own worlds and now both orphans to its malice.

My family totally imploded after my parents' deaths. Fascinating now, looking back, because so much time has passed and the pain has numbed. The story, very briefly, is that my father's aunt was a wealthy woman, and she died and left all the money and her entire estate to him, or should I say he was the only relative, so inherited it all. He was given eight weeks to live literally about 24 hours after finding out that for the first time in his life he had some money coming his way. I remember his reaction: "I'll be the richest man in the fucking graveyard!" He never got to see a penny of that money. Fucking bummer. He'd never really had any money, never been on an overseas holiday with the family, always struggling to put food on the table and always scraping up fag butts to make a smoke. But whatever he did have he gave to his children.

There were a few very amusing incidents in the midst of all the suffering. Anna, my sister, brothers and I had to go to my father's aunt's house to clear out all the valuables before the house clearance people came in and got the property ready to be sold. We hired a long-wheelbase Ford Transit van and zoomed up the motorway to the property. It was a very large old Victorian house with big old gates that opened up onto a long sweeping driveway around a pond to the front entrance. It was quite a grand old house, in which my father's aunt only really occupied a few rooms upstairs in a kind of apartment-like arrangement, leaving many rooms in a kind of historical stasis. We plundered each room like thieves who had been let loose in a bank vault. Every drawer and item of clothing had money in it and there were hidden treasures in just about every room. We filled that Transit van to the point where the wheels were scraping the arches, bags of swag in the back and cries of laughter all the way back to our parents' bungalow where we took stock of our fortunes like pirates returning to their lair. I think we needed to find a release amongst all the pain we had endured.

Now, whilst all this shit was going on, we, the siblings, had to try and get time away from work, etc. to be with Mum and Dad, look after them whilst they remained alive and see it all through to the eventual funerals. The pressure was immense. The pain was sheer torment, for all of us. My sister nearly gave up her job to live with our parents whilst my older brother and I exhausted all the goodwill of the armed forces' compassionate systems getting time off. Whilst I, and no doubt he, was endlessly being recalled to go out to the Middle East on ops, in the middle was my younger brother, poor bastard, who was trying to organise his wedding... fucking ridiculous, but that's life and cancer, they don't mix no matter how hard you try to shake it up.

A number of times Anna came up from Cornwall and stayed with me at my parents' place whilst I took my turn looking after Dad. I saw him go from about 12 stone to 5 stone, the cancer eating him whilst it suffocated and starved him at the same time. I remember carrying him upstairs to bed in my arms one

426

night, just a shell of a body, lighter than a small child, whilst I on the other hand felt so heavy with sorrow. He eventually ended up on a morphine pump, which our local GP turned up a few notches just before he passed. It was a merciful act. My poor mother ended up in a hospice just weeks after the funeral. She died alone and I'll never forgive myself for not being there no matter how volatile our relationship had been. I was fucking working, conforming to the fucking machine of life, busy ensuring the end of a stranger's life in a foreign land whilst my own life was in ruin and my loving mother passed away alone and I never got to say goodbye.

My younger brother's wedding took place shortly after it had all concluded. It was more of a wake than a wedding. Miserable affair, no one to blame or anything. It was all done really well, but I think we were all still in shock, and to not have our parents at the church was just a big fat reminder that they were dead. There remains a lot of tension between me and my siblings, but after carefully examining the past none of us have truly allowed ourselves the time to grieve. We have never talked about our loss, let alone about the actual events, or the lives we have been left with or the secrets of our inner struggles. We remain in pain and all alone in it. We should have come closer together after all the shit we went through; maybe we will in time or maybe we will each take our sorrows to the grave ourselves.

I received my share of the inheritance a short time later thanks to the efforts of my sister, who we all hassled to death to speed up the process of probate. We just didn't care, we wanted our money; yeah, we all got greedy, not understanding how painful it must have been for her to deal with all the legalities whilst the three of us were asking every week how much longer it would take. To be fair, the money passed relatively quickly from my dad to my mum and within six months on to us, the four children – my two brothers, my sister and me. Money in the bank – fucking dangerous, it wouldn't stay there for long.

With thoughts that I was on some kind of terrorist's hit list or at the top of a want list somewhere behind the Kremlin, I wasn't keen on saving any of it. Besides, my parents had never done anything in their lives apart from look after the four children. I wanted to go and do all the things they didn't have a chance to, either before I became too old or was suddenly crossed off a list. This was made more apparent after the 9/11 attacks in America. We embarked on a series of holidays, no expense spared. A cruise on the *QE2*, New Zealand, Singapore – Raffles hotel, Hong Kong, staying in The Peninsula, a safari in Africa, five-star Quinta in Madeira and business class flights. We were millionaires if only for a brief time. This, coupled with a new kitchen, bathroom, UPVC windows and a central heating system to replace those shocking storage heaters, and a new car, saw all the money disappear and then some, ending up with a credit card bill the size of a small nation's deficit! I don't regret it, not one bit. Anna and I lived life and have always lived way outside our means because I refuse to go to the grave saying, "I wish I'd…"

Time passes as it always does and is the best healer and cover-up artist, which allows us as humans to move on even if we just pretend to be okay. I was soon back into the old routines. Anatoly and I continued seeing each other as much as we could before being reunited at the navy's nuclear repair facilities and submarine bases. There were three subs in refit or build in the yards that he would be involved with, and I was to accompany him, or vice versa depending on your viewpoint. I headed up an engineering department for the naval overseers, and Anatoly was plunged into the design and change team, or A&As (additions and alterations), for the various submarine project groups. He had brought with him not only his engineering and scientific expertise but an endless compendium of plans, drawings, documents and manuals which he'd obviously been working on in my absence. 'They' had kept him very busy.

The keys to the detailed technical information he had brought with him had all been encrypted in the Kuznyechik cipher methodology. Kuznyechik means 'grasshopper', and basically Anatoly had used the grasshopper methodology to transmit the 'keys' to solutions and algorithms regarding nuclear synthesis and future reactor asymptotic neutronics to both me and the Steering Group in our endless correspondence. These keys opened and resolved calculations and other difficulties in Anatoly's research. It made me laugh that all the brains at the doughnut hadn't spotted any of the coding, which I relayed sarcastically through Cdr Brown. Brown retorted to say it was even more remarkable that the new FSB's counterintelligence directorate hadn't uncovered it either.

The remarkable and bizarre outcome of this discovery, as Marcus later tried to explain to me, was that Anatoly had reversed the encrypted correspondence to further re-code the 'S' boxes in a secondary layer of 'P' boxes back to the original input bits in the 'S' boxes prior and following correspondence packages. Basically, a code within a code within a code, which is like, to quote a phrase, 'a riddle within Enigma'. You had to have all the emails and letters to put the jigsaw together because of the depth and complexity of the code. I didn't understand a word of what Marcus explained to me or the significance of Anatoly's research but tried to look impressed and interested. This was how Anatoly had set himself up to be a bigger catch than the Steering Group had ever imagined. I think from the day he revealed his hand in the doughnut to the Steering Group he had firmly secured his future. He had shown his cards and his terms and they were most agreeable.

Anatoly later told me that this had been his insurance plan all along, either to satisfy the wolves here in the UK on his arrival or to quieten the now FSB and SVR (former KGB) in so much that he could have threatened to decode or use the correspondence as a bargaining chip. His ability to unveil such technical advancements to the British, if they had discovered his intentions, would have been a significant bargaining point. This would have been the ace up his sleeve. From that time on everyone who knew Anatoly called him the 'Grasshopper'. Fuck, it was all way beyond my skill set to say the least. Nevertheless, Anatoly was very gracious towards me and my limited intellect in this his field of expertise, and although never revealing too much he and I enjoyed long technical conversations which were really his way of thinking aloud to resolve technical issues he was working on whilst blowing my mind as we both got drunk with a good bottle of fine red wine.

I spent nearly 18 months with Anatoly at various sites around the country, and he took on the name of Anthony but I never used that name. I enjoyed our time together away from the pressures of the Steering Group. He must have impressed a lot of people whilst making his changes to those subs; the only reason I know that is because of the number of visits and functions he attended, some of which I accompanied him on. They were all very serious and usually held in the offices of one of the nuclear sites or a posh hotel out of town somewhere. I don't know much at all about the projects he really worked on; he was good at appearing loyal to his new masters and keeping himself to himself. He usually worked away from everyone else but was always surrounded by a few people eager to learn from him, as he really was a genius in his field. I don't suppose he found it all too different to his life working in Sarov.

From what little I got to know, and most of what I learned was after a great deal of drink so can't be relied upon, he was the brains behind a new generation of nuclear reactors. Anatoly was the architect and engineer of a new hybrid of reactor that sat between the developments of the British PWR1 reactors and the American S9G (submarine ninth generation) pressurised nuclear reactors. He oversaw their construction, the fuel purification development, a highly enriched uranium, almost 99% enriched, the neutron shielding and the cooling systems with advanced inhibitors. Anatoly poured his every waking hour into his work. I think it helped him come to terms with his new life. I guess it was just something very familiar and what he had been used to. It was just another day at the office for him I guess; well, that's what we all wanted for him in some way or another.

Anatoly had all but finished his work with the subs and was set to move into a role involving nuclear warheads. I don't really know because he never told me much other than he wanted me to accompany him to his next assignment. So, he started dragging it out in order to spend more time with me at the sub bases, which slowed things down. The Steering Group had other projects for him to work on, more complex projects no doubt. I sometimes worked with him. I was out of my depth with him all the time, but it was noticed that he always seemed to deliver his projects quicker when I was around. I was linked to the project management teams for the surface platforms that were in build; it was a great trade-off as it enabled us both to be kept together, keeping both our identities and purposes perfectly secret. My main job, that sat underneath the daily grind of the RN, was with Anatoly, to really ensure his transition into his new life took hold, be a familiar face and a friend in a strange place, ensuring the Crown's investment settled and bedded into his new identity. All the UK nuclear sub refit and build locations are the end-of-the-line kind of places, perfect for any issues to be calmly dealt with, and little or no secondary damage to worry about.

It wasn't long before Anthony was mixing more with me and the crews of the sub building and refit projects; he helped us out both technically and with all the after-work drinking. I remember on one such night we had all been out on the town but it was too late to get a Joe Baxi so we decided to head back into the nuclear site and sleep under our desks rather than appear late for work. However, we ended up getting asked by the officer commanding the nuclear site why we worked so late and started so early. Security had informed him of unusual pass activity into the yard and the nuclear sites. We couldn't deny it as you had to swipe your personal ID to get in the gates, which recorded your every movement. We were commended for all our efforts and commitments to the job! What bullshit. We later bribed the security guys to at least turn off the cameras, as we painfully tried to navigate the security turnstiles pissed out of our heads, and cease reporting our early returns to the base CO. It only cost us a case of beer and 100 cigarettes each week. There was a real core group of us who had formed a friendship circle around Anatoly and who would later go on to the Middle East with me and the teams.

Anatoly became very engaged with my friends Taff and Steve, who had obviously clicked on to the fact that we were very different, and their suspicions were confirmed by the arrival of Keith who came to us just before our last op to the Middle East. They didn't interfere or cause us any problems, just enjoyed the fact we had a different agenda, and they wanted to be there to help in some way. Sounds weird, but having a few regular guys helped enormously with our life on the subs but also in helping Anatoly feel normal. They really were a bad influence on the alcohol consumption side of things but fucking great friends to Anatoly. I had gotten myself into a world of shit with the navy guys who lurked around one of the bases, fucking desk drivers. They had no idea of my real purpose in the secure sites and it went against the grain that both Anatoly and I were supposed to keep a low profile, but we were always getting into bother with the regular RN officers who couldn't get their heads around being told what to do, in so much as Anatoly and I were basically untouchable. No matter what fuck-ups we made or how rowdy we had been in a local pub, a call from London usually did the trick in our favour, but the Steering Group was slowly becoming less tolerant of our misadventures.

When we weren't working or pissing it up with the build crews of the subs, we spent a lot of time together either drinking by ourselves or hidden away in our accommodations talking of the past and the future, just as brothers. We both had small houses allocated to us in the local areas, which allowed for some comfort and a bit of normality in the fucked-up world in which we were now living. Anatoly was actually fucking lonely and only wanted to be in my company all the time. I think he was becoming more and more of a recluse as time passed on. To help, I'd take him out just to go shopping, visit the supermarket, go to the pub, eat in a restaurant and go for a walk in the National Parks. He especially loved those hikes. It was then we could really talk and be alone. It was all a freedom he hadn't experienced, a freedom to say and be anything he wanted. He too feared the future.

He loved having my company; he'd never been allowed friends in Sarov, always isolated in his work, hidden away from life and being watched all the time. So I guess he probably became a little too dependent on my being close all the time. I found this to be especially the case after my long weekends away at home with Anna. I'd return back to my digs to find Anatoly waiting for me, depressed off his face, or fucking shitfaced slumped in my doorway. I'd have to clean him up, which was a fucking nightmare as he'd always fucking shit himself and somehow get it everywhere. What can I say, I fucking loved him as my brother so I'd play fucking nurse and take care of it all. I was also painfully conscious that I'd been the architect of his situation and the assassin of his family, so a deep feeling of loyalty and duty to him lay beneath that love – because he was all my fault, all of my making. I had turned my childhood friend from Russia into an orphan, an alcoholic and a very depressed young man.

I usually disappeared back to Cornwall at the weekends and left Anatoly to his own devices. It was a great routine for me and I usually got four days at home every other weekend which was great for Anna. Fucking crazy times as we had moved to the South Coast to be closer together and now I found myself driving the five hours' commute every fucking weekend up to Cumbria or nine hours to Faslane. It was on the return to Scotland late one Sunday evening – I had dropped off a few colleagues at their houses then returned to my housing assignment, opened the door and found Anatoly dead in my bath full of blood. I had given him a key a few weeks earlier. Fucking fuck, fucker! I was in a mess. I didn't know how to react really; I couldn't call the police or an ambulance, I needed to get hold of Marcus. I called Keith and he arranged for the Steering Group to send round the dustmen, along with Cheesy to get me the fuck out of that house so the team could take care of Anatoly's body and the mess.

I had pulled him out of that bath after trying to resuscitate him. I just sat there on the floor wet through with him in my arms, stroking his blond blood-stained hair. I don't know how long I sat there sobbing uncontrollably until Cheesy and Keith ripped me away from him. I was so fucking angry, we had a fight – well, an attempted one – before Keith had me pinned to the deck. Cheesy took me and Keith away to a place out in the back of beyond, isolated and away from the world, to deal with it. I never turned up for work that week, which was okay – we just drank ourselves into oblivion. We couldn't believe what had happened, it was a fucking disaster. All that effort, the planning and the heartache I went through, all the talks and conversations I had had with him. I splurged it all out to Keith and Cheesy who simply helped me into an alcoholic coma. What a waste of almost my entire life, my childhood friend, the struggles we went through, the people we'd had to please, the fight to survive, all now lost. What was the point of it all? Now Anatoly was truly no longer an issue for the Steering Group or the Russians, he was as dead as he was supposed to be. What a complete waste of everything.

There are places in this life you can descend into that are dark, lonely and utterly depressing, places where you become a ghost in your own life. I had found this place. You have to fight the demons you harbour, they are masters of deception and lies, and for a time they were winning in my life. Their ability to trap you in a dark place surpasses all understanding. You feed them with your guilt and your helplessness in your grief-stricken drunkenness. The only antidote is found in those who can understand pain and loss. Anna knew pain – she had lost her mother at an early age. The pain is always there but to share it is a relief, a vent from within the pressurised anger of the heart. There is always light but it's often hidden by the heavy blankets you throw over it. Having lost both my parents and now Anatoly, I was in a bad place. There wasn't the bullshit option of going and seeing a shrink; I didn't want to face up to my inner demons, I wanted to escape them. Anna had always been the secret strength, the power behind the man. She lay hidden often many thousands of miles away but always believed in me. When shit went south, I had to find a way back to the surface, a way to remind myself there was someone else in my life who was worth living for, be that from war, a mission, an assignment, or the grief and state of mind I would never recover from. I admitted to Anna some years later that suicide had been on my mind at this time, and still creeps in to offer a way out to this day. Although tempting and no matter how depressed off my face I now become, she is why I'm still here.

I went to Anatoly's funeral, a small affair near the doughnut. Nothing special, just a gathering of people. There were those who had worked so hard to save him, those who had used him and those who had profited and benefited from him. He was cremated and his ashes went to Marcus. What a fucking waste. Time to move on. As Plato said: "Only the dead have seen the end of war."

From out of the ashes, they say – well, that's probably bullshit, but Keith and I worked together on a support vessel project as engineers and were now getting along really well with Taff and Tony. Keith never left my side. Marcus joined, took over command of the taskforce and brought in all the teams. Everything changed, including the bullshit naval overseeing officers who'd never seen a gun fired in action let alone been on the receiving end of one. They were all replaced. Marcus brought in an elite core of officers and crew and surrounded himself with key players, including Brown. It was fucking great to have them all back together. This was the final assignment. We put our heads down and did the prep, the hard yards before we deployed for work-up, then we would be off to face that fucking demon in the Middle East.

It was now time to finish the list and for me to leave the Steering Group and Foxtrot Oscar to retirement. First it was back to the briefing rooms and a repeat exercise, only this time it was totally focused on the remainder of the list and Keith's intel. London, the bunker, Poole then deployment. This time would be different – we were angry, more focused.

Chapter 13

The Derelict

This was to be my final deployment to the Middle East and it came after a long time away from the team whilst I had been working with Anatoly on the sub projects. Looking after Anatoly until his death, coupled with the loss of both my parents, had made for a difficult and extended period of absence from the more complex world of the Steering Group. Now it was time to get straight back into the saddle with the team, who were ready, expectant, battle ready and current, as they had no doubt been busy and involved in other ops whilst I had been the babysitter for Anatoly. Fuck, I was afraid I had lost the edge, succumbed to the inevitable, a skill fade that might become apparent and sneak out to betray me when I was least prepared. I could tell they were totally up for this next deployment, there was a buzz, whereas I was apprehensive, nervous about making a mistake but equally determined to finish what I had started.

Keith had become a lifeline after Anatoly, almost a crutch for me to lean on, and I suspected he knew of my fears. He took care of it by continually asking questions and repeating procedures built into his own OCD methodology of prepared-ness, which passed unnoticed because we were always check-ing and rechecking kit anyway, a habit that would follow us into old age no doubt. I knew he was okay with my period of insecurity; it was as though he saw his own future in me, needing to know that whatever happened in his life, he could return also, so he tried to keep me in my comfort zone whilst I upped my game and got back up to speed. Keith had become a great fit into my old team; he was their new plaything but had yet to prove himself in multi-threat scenarios. He lacked that respect from the team at this time so we had a trade-off: he would ease me back into live ops whilst he broke his cherry in the field. We were all set to be deployed to the Middle East – ALL IN. This deployment would bring closure for the Steering Group's list, removal of the Middle Eastern cell dealing in arms and technical information from Russia, whilst Keith would get to clean up the remnants of his past life in Iran.

Trying to understand this innovative role I had been assigned by the Steering Group with Keith was nothing short of remarkable after the whole Russian campaign. It was like I had been amalgamated into some sort of compromised unit, my work dovetailing into Keith's domain of Middle Eastern operations, which now, looking back, must have been planned but was not something I had ever anticipated. But beyond everything I was becoming more and more lost in trying to find my real self and 'my' life again, whatever that was supposed to be. My life felt in disarray professionally but was now overthrown by emotions drawn out from my relationship with Anna, who had become so central to everything I wanted in life. It's a strange thing love, sometimes you have to be apart from it to truly appreciate it, and sometimes it hurts so bad you wonder what the hell it's all about and want nothing to do with it. But always, every human seeks it, yearns for it and those who are lucky enough to have tasted it would trade anything to get it back should it ever be lost to them. I had fallen deeply in love with Anna, of that there was no doubt in my mind. However, my thoughts often turned to Anatoly, whose family had simply been erased from the book of life following the orders issued to satisfy the appetites of bigger wolves. My masters and my architects had left Anatoly alone in life, allowed to live, if only for a short time, but ultimately unable to cope with being alone. My dear friend was safe now, free from life's troubles and no longer afraid for the future. I remain honoured to have known him. He was a true and loyal friend and for that at least I am eternally grateful.

Looking back, I know Cdr Brown realised what he had found in the boy all those years earlier and his little bet must have paid off handsomely with those who gathered in heavy cigar-clouded, leather armchair filled rooms where the hands of the righteous never get dirty, rooms where whispers of dirty deeds are muttered under pungent brandy laden breaths, conjuring devious conspiracies, faces hidden behind large newspapers, big egos and political careers. I had begun to feel I had become the weapon of choice in the Steering Group's toolbox, a responsibility I didn't want anymore but at the same time strangely enjoyed. I had been carefully crafted under supervision, from being bed-shaped and broken as a boy in to a merciless assassin with the ability to be nameless and perfectly unattached to anything that could become an embarrassment to the Crown. I had exceeded all expectations, taking a childhood friend from pen pal to defection with no apparent regard for his or my own safety, not to mention our families'. I guess it was what I had always wanted. To be wanted, needed but simultaneously unattached from the responsibility and accountability of my actions, keeping business simple, allowing maximum autonomy on my part but kept on an extendable lead from London. Yes, I enjoyed being important, valued and needed despite the nature of my work, which was really starting to make me feel more and more angry and resentful. This made opening up to Anna so very difficult and still does. Sometimes life is too complicated to explain and the worst events in our lives are best left to suffer the silence only found in the grave.

I stood on the upper deck of the *Essex* daydreaming, feeling the ship's vibrations through my feet, and as always found myself drifting in thoughts back to the *Atlantic Star*, and this immediately made me ready for a new adventure. As we left the wall, all ties to the UK were released as the ropes fell into the water like sleeping snakes, only to be hauled taught and heaved back aboard the support ship's decks. We were slowly dragged out of our berth by the tugs, aptly named *Forceful* and *Powerful*, then sailed through Plymouth Sound with four small landing craft following us like signets following their mother. The landing craft were to be recovered later in deeper water, initiating the start of the work-up and training packages we must endure as we made our way en route to the Gulf. I remember my last moments being up top on the aft sponson waving to Anna from the flight deck. Well, I was pretty sure it was Anna, hard to tell from such a distance, a distant figure that was standing on the banks of Mt Edgcumbe, alone and apart from the other families waving to a shrinking tower block of cold grey steel with so many amputated souls aboard.

Souls lost to the Crown, the service and to the inevitability of change. Change within themselves, changes to their families, deaths and births, marriages, birthdays, and all manner of celebrations and bereavements to be lost to the slow and unrecoverable passage of the ship throughout its time away. Such is the consequence and irretrievable cost of all military deployments. Torn from their families, all who would return home after this deployment would age and become changed. Some would change as much as day is from night, others just enough to start a conversation which would be in private, hidden and silent to the world, an admission of a change to a loved one, but an admission never to be spoken of again. But for some men on this ship they would become unseasonably matured, moulded and misshapen from their previously sun-casted shadows to grow into darker more deformed silhouettes, silhouettes that would lurk in their minds waiting for a traumatic remembrance of their experiences yet to pass.

Before going below decks I waved to Anna one last time. This moment, this image, now branded into my mind was going to be the only key I would hold on to, a key to get back from the darkness and shadows that were set to consume my mind in the months ahead. Descending into the bowels of the ship I started the process of trying to forget, to forget about life with Anna and mentally switch everything over to mission mode in order to just get on with it, I suppose. To put love behind me, focus on the job and return home alive and to that planned exit from the Steering Group. I am sure each man has his own coping mechanisms for the separation from loved ones beset by the anxiety of the mission to come. However, an exit plan from all the complexities, the mental terrorism and paranoia that now surrounded me was becoming my third and fourth level mental escape. I could start to feel the end approaching, it was in the post. I knew this had to be my last deployment. I wasn't the boy I had once been, the once brave young soul, brave enough to venture into the shadows without any regard for the consequences. I had awoken and I was very aware of what I was now doing; it wasn't a game and I had to fight to survive this time.

This far into the system you get tired and adopt OCD traits on top of everything else because you slowly become fearful of making a mistake or forgetting a minor detail that could jeopardise the mission or the lives of your team members. I had become a prolific checker, always checking everything was functional, operational, serviceable and ready for immediate deployment. But it had spilled over into my personal life too. Anna had noticed me checking the front door was locked four or five times before we drove away to get shopping, returning to check the cooker, the upstairs windows, the washing machine, whatever. It's funny sometimes but equally a fucking nightmare to live with. I took time with Cheesy and Keith to discuss it. Apart from all the piss-taking it wasn't anything new to them as all the team had started to develop little interesting and weird personality traits. We let it be a point of fun rather than read too much into things. The trouble is, such things had started to play on my mind, and once you allow a thought to formulate in your mind it stays there for a very long time. Thoughts such as fear or uncertainty are especially dangerous if you let them set up camp in the dark alleyways of the mind. There they will stay until they have poisoned the entire world in which you pretend to live, all truths questioned, doubts exacerbated, strengths questioned and weaknesses exposed. That is why the team was so important – they were the only ones who could ever understand a conversation of this kind and keep it truly confidential whilst being fully supportive and above all keeping you functional.

I had decided in my mind whilst alone on the upper deck that this deployment was going to be different. In my mind, now that Anatoly was gone, out of the picture and no longer part of the team, so to speak, I didn't really care too much for how the rest of the list was completed, nor was I too upset at the lads being so keen to get some trigger time. These boys were different to me, they really were the best operators, hard motherfuckers, whereas I think at this point I had become tame by comparison. I remember sitting in my office at the stern and watching Plymouth slowly disappear into the silhouette of the Devon and Cornwall coast, hoping this would be my very last trip away and already yearning for hearth and home. I had to make it my last trip. Whatever it took, the team and I were going to remove all the ink from the Steering Group's list. I was tired. My mental cloud was at full capacity. There was no need for all that training now, there was no deceptions or layers of lies to fill my mind or time, this was simply a kill mission. No deception, no lies, no agendas or false friendships, just find the targets and get the hell out of there. The control layers in my mind were now all personal and more complex. It was time to start thinking about looking out for the team and bringing them all home, and less about the list.

I sat with Cheesy and Keith the many evenings we spent at sea and we had a laugh as we pretended how much we were looking forward to getting back in theatre, in the 'zone'. Cheesy hadn't so much changed as developed into a more complicated person to understand. There was some new anger in Cheesy that I hadn't seen before. In our time apart, he had metamorphosised into a colder but more focused and sharpened SF operator. He had a short temper that I had never seen before. Perhaps shit had gone wrong in that last assignment I hadn't witnessed. Maybe I was seeing the same strain, the same cracks in Cheesy as I was experiencing myself. Maybe we were all just getting a little older, a little more battle hardened. Perhaps we were all a little more tired than we cared to admit, more conscious of what we were involved in and the risks. The risks of what we did as intelligence and SF operators that were of no consequence to us previously and were so easily dismissed in the past, now seemed heavy and upon us in full force; like a yolk that was slowing us down, we seemed to be running through mud at times as we made our preparations. As the chaos man in our team we were gonna need a few diversions to pull off a full degloving of the remaining list members and the other targeted groups. Cheesy just sat back and smiled and simply said, "Hey, it's gonna be a sweet ride so enjoy it." I knew after he said this that he had reached the end; the lack of concern for his or anyone's life meant that he was dangerous, still reliable, a machine, but a percentage of unpredictability had entered into him that would either be advantageous or disastrous when the time came.

Back to routine. The Andrew is great at routine, and it was great that I was sailing with Marcus as the conductor of this new orchestra. I took the time that first evening to call on Marcus in his staterooms to discuss my requirements for the upcoming ops. Talking with Marcus alone was not like a military planning meeting, we just gently discussed what we both needed to do and how we both should leave sufficient flex in our planning for the unknown. Marcus was kind of gentle in his conversations about the brutalities he expected; for example, he would look at a map or point at a known terrorist bunker on a satellite image and simply say something like:

"Do you think your team could possibly make that go away if we put you close enough?"

No need to discuss details, or what was needed, just the giving out of a blank cheque of authorisation to do whatever was needed. It made things simple; we didn't need the argument of politics, cost, time or resources, just a simple green light to execute a mission with no prejudice. It was the same deal when Marcus passed me my sealed orders and simply remarked, "Good man," as he winked and passed me an envelope. We both knew what was required and the orders just made it official. Insertion into the Middle East would be easy enough to achieve and Marcus being Marcus had already drawn up plan A, plan B, C through to Z in order to ensure we got a clean insertion and extraction. The initial design was to enter Jordan at Aqaba on a pre-planned diplomatic visit for the ship, so there would be very little prep required. We would simply join the crew for some sightseeing in Aqaba then slip away into Israel, hopefully picking up the trail of the various targets and the arms dealers in the hope that we the hunters didn't become the hunted. I had arranged for my old friend Owen to meet us at Petra, from where we would plan a rendezvous with Israeli special forces as our navigational support team and acting dustmen for the first phase of our mission.

We enjoyed the cruise through the Med and passed through the Suez without any causes for concern, no unwanted onlookers or anything of that nature. The Suez is a dangerous place in so much as you're just a great big sitting target on a canal that would have made great world news if we or any other ship were attacked. Such an event has the potential to stop all or most of the world's trade by sea should some of our friends decide to try to sink a ship mid-canal. I have been through the Suez a number of times and the same routine is exercised by the navy. About a quarter of the crew are allowed to go off and visit the pyramids on a sightseeing tour whilst the rest of us sit with the ship as she joins a convoy through to the Bitter Lakes and on to the Red Sea. I remember seeing a ship I was once on making the transit as I raced alongside her on the canalside road in a Range Rover. The ship sailed along the canal but gave the illusion she was gliding majestically over the sand. The first time you see such things really makes you take a moment of pause to fully digest the magnitude of man's abilities to engineer solutions to insurmountable problems. It always makes a good photograph, and it's a cool photo to show people back home.

As always, the ship would allow some souvenir traders aboard for the Suez transit, and so the Gully Gully Man who did the same shit magic trick every time was aboard, to the amusement of all the Suez transit virgin sailors. Although a tense time for the command, it was pretty much a period of downtime for the crew and the RM detachment, who lazed around sunbathing next to the somewhat overdressed gun crews. We took up anchorage in the Bitter Lakes before the convoys passed each other; there is usually two southbound convoys and a northbound convoy each day and the transit takes about 12 to 14 hours. We completed our transit, recovered all crew aboard and headed south through the Gulf of Suez before making our turn north east into the Gulf of Aqaba.

I had the same feeling every time I turned up towards Aqaba – it feels like you're on your own for real. You leave the convoys, doesn't matter that they're merchant ships, it just feels like you're leaving behind your friends and the safety of the civilised world. I guess it's like leaving the herd or something like that. It's not to say that the entire Middle East is uncivilised, but there is definitely a mental switch that takes place in your mind. It's a switch to a different way of thinking, your behaviour changes, the mood darkens, everyone gets serious. Deploying to the Middle East on a mission is problematic at best, and when you arrive it's barren, totally inhospitable and everyone who knows you're there wants to take a shot at you; they don't really want you there at all. Well, that's how it felt as an intelligence alien aboard a British warship. When you enter the Middle East you're the infidel, and if you're caught as a spy or an SF operative the least you can hope for is to be branded with that name on your face or forehead. The alternative is possibly to be filmed at your beheading, wearing some orange overalls or some shit like that. Fuck that.

To be fair, amidst all the negatives there is also an almost romantic notion of adventure and mystery when you enter into this world, which teases the mind into a state of euphoric expectancy. Behind the veil of war there is something strangely beautiful and almost secret about the Middle East. Deep in its hidden culture and society the people can be unexpectedly friendly and genuinely caring in some very bizarre and unnatural circumstances. To share a simple meal in the desert or a coffee and dates under a sheet of corrugated iron and simply smile and enjoy the shade with your potential enemy is remarkably unexpected, but it happens.

I acknowledge that the missions I embarked upon were intensely serious and dangerous even though at the time they didn't feel anything other than routine, but it's the whole culture change that makes it different. It is the images of war sown into everyday lives that makes it so remarkably interesting and alien to our Western eyes. To see so many bullet-strewn buildings, so many limbless people attending to ruins of homes as if nothing were untoward simply switches your mind over from the normality you thought was normal to a normality that is war. It is best described by Yehuda Amichai, an Israeli poet, to whom I was introduced by an Israeli special forces guy who carried a little poetry book with him everywhere he went. He always gave a recital before we set off on whatever we were about to do. I recall these words...

"Always beside ruined houses and iron girders twisted like the arms of the slain, you find someone who is sweeping the paved path or tending the little garden"

These very words for me conjure up all the images I have tried to capture on camera and now in words, but these words portray it better than a thousand pictures. How bizarre that such few words tell a thousand pictures... This makes all the insensible mess make sense, as everything in the Middle East is upside down or back to front to our eyes. I think you have to be born there to understand it all, because to our eyes it's just a big fuck-up. I guess people just get on with their lives amidst all the chaos; why should they change their way of life just because tanks are driving through the streets? Or perhaps they have seen so many invaders come and go they just don't give a shit anymore. Maybe the West will finally grow tired of the Middle East after the oil runs out or we have all gone electric.

We berthed in Aqaba against a heavily guarded concrete pier, each end barricaded with shipping containers making for a robust chicane-type access route to the ship. The team disembarked with some of the crew and the RM detachment into a rather luxurious Jordanian military owned coach, a sightseeing trip for the crew to Petra, a gift from the Jordanian Government. I love Jordan, I don't know why – my first confirmed kill for the Steering Group perhaps, the hospitality, the food, I don't know what it is exactly, it just has a trance-like effect on me. Oman is similar. I think it has something to do with the people, more genuinely real people, no disguises or masks, they are open to conversation, quick to help, always generous and genuinely interested in you as a person. Of course, all this works against your previously made misconceptions and can be a lure into a false sense of security as we were never there to make friends, or be tourists, so no matter how genuine the people we met, we were nothing other than suspicious.

The marines were our escort out to Petra and did the usual bomb search on the coach before we loaded it with all our kit. A real sense of the moment came upon me as we soaked up the last luxury and comfort those deep coach seats could offer us. I was pleased that all the brawn of the marine commandos were our support to get us out; they had split up between my team in the coach and a couple of 4x4 Toyota Land Cruisers off the ship. It was like being on a holiday tour bus as we set off with some of the ship's company out into the moonscape of the desert. I was uncomfortable being in that fucking coach, a fucking sitting target winding its way through the barren hills, no end to the number of hijacking points that could have brought the mission to an early finish. I sat with Cheesy, who was also becoming twitchy as we tried to relax despite me wanting the team to be off the coach much earlier than at Petra, but Cheesy was happy to stay in the comfort and cool of the air-conditioned coach for just a little longer.

I sat back and tried to relax, impatiently taking in the scenery, my head against the glass, staring into the emptiness, my mind wandering back to that trip to the detention facility when I was a boy, how things change as life passes you by. I remember my mind wandering in and out of previous ops, Anna, home and the desire to bring it all to a conclusion. The coach rumbled along the winding road carved through the desert as though it had been made with a snow plough.

Amongst the desert debris and the jagged sandstone and granite rock mountain formations, odd groups of people headed off into the desert in different directions laden with either their belongings or goods for trade in distant villages. We were skirting the outskirts of the Wadi Rum as we headed north towards Petra, the light ever changing the colour of the sand and the rock formations as the coach changed direction, with the empty road giving a satisfying feeling of being alone. However, as we drew in closer to the hills the jagged peaks stood over us, making for a perfect ambush scenario. I was perhaps overreacting but was sure a firefight was about to kick off. I hated not being the aggressor, I needed to be in control of our insertion from the start, and it all felt too easy for us to be hit whilst riding along as though we were fucking tourists with no real purpose in this place.

On arrival at Petra we eventually separated from the RM detachment and the crew from the ship, who went off sightseeing the ancient city. You'll remember it from the film *Indiana Jones and the Temple of Doom*. From what I saw it's an amazing place. We took possession of the Land Cruisers and doubled back, checking our tail. We headed south and rendezvoused with Owen, Israeli SF operators and two members of the Israeli intelligence service (Mossad) who would see us through into Israel. We had a prearranged rendezvous at 30°01'22.7"N 35°29'04.7"E just west of Abu Al-Luson. It was a strange encounter. The team was in high spirits, and I was so very pleased to see Owen, fucking crazy streak of American piss that he had become! Fuck... all those memories of the previous ops and of course our time as children in that fucking detention centre – we had a lot to catch up on. It's really fucking strange how the tapestry of life can bring people back together again and again in the most unlikely places and for the most unusual reasons.

We gathered around the leeward side of one of the Land Cruisers and sat in the sand to catch up on the intel Mossad and Owen had pulled together, the Israeli SF covering our position. Owen's secret came out: he was working for the CIA with Mossad. That just made Keith and I fall around laughing. It made perfect sense of course! Couldn't believe it, Owen, CIA of all things. Well, it made working together much easier. Keith was keen to interrogate the information Mossad had on his targets and their crossover involvement with our arms dealers who had headed inland from Haifa. The Mossad guys were Avner and Shmuel, who we called Samuel which really annoyed the shit out of him. Talking with Avner was like having a chat with a friendly doctor about how to care for a baby or something equally as pleasant, despite the conversation mainly revolving around the subject of killing terrorists. He listened very intently, never interrupted and always carefully formulated any answer he gave you with a happy smile after a pregnant pause taken for his time to think. He looked like he was related to Cheesy in some fucked-up way which I just had to point out to Cheesy, who gave me the finger. Shmuel was different, black hair shaved very short revealing a huge semi-circular scar in his scalp, and he always interrupted anything you said with a question, or to ask if you were sure. He would be Baz's opposite number in so much as he was not someone you'd pick a fight with in a hurry. They were both very well informed and at the top of their game. They knew all the team as well as Keith and I. The intelligence world is a small community and allies get to know the players on their side of the coin. Reputations can be quietly significant to all involved. I'm not sure if we should have felt honoured that they knew us or concerned; either way, I was pleased to use them as a guide to get us started.

The conversation focused mainly on the whereabouts of specific names, which fortunately or unfortunately brought into play various other groups all sides were interested in following or eradicating. It was going to be a joint effort. We needed to head up to Jerusalem for our first engagement with

Keith's target cell before they made the crossing into Lebanon or Syria. The intention would be to just rattle a cage and see in which direction all the rats ran. Mossad would ensure we didn't venture into other ops they were conducting, to avoid any crossfire, but additionally to make our job there legal, if that's the correct term for what we were embarking on.

It's fair to say the next few weeks were just us doing the hard yards tracking down the trail of the arms dealers and terrorists. Getting behind the scenes takes time and, even though we had live intel from reliable sources, terrorists just don't come out to play when you want them to. Although it has to be said they can be careless with their movements and their identities, but what the terrorist doesn't expect is for SF and intelligence teams from the West to get down in the dirt and move at the same speed as them. Drones, hard intel, photos, bank accounts, global CCTV footage, airline intel and telephone lists all help piece the crumbs together but it's not enough. Understanding the target, the culture and the enemy's life story is what allowed us to get into their backyard and fuck their shit up.

Just a simple thing in your enemy's culture, such as understanding how they got their name; for example, in the Middle East a man's name will derive from his father and his forefathers, so tracing people becomes simpler (providing the name is genuine). If we could get into a family then pressure points could be used to get us to our target. We didn't need direct intel, just an entry point, a person, a place or a website, a frequently used restaurant, whatever, anything. I had learned this because of my time in Russia, my family connections, the years spent with the customers of the arms traders incognito; it was all training on the job back then, the Steering Group had known it, and now it was my bread and butter. Keith had done the same, spent time in Iran, done the hard yards living within a family getting under the skin of the people traffickers who had led him to the terrorists we were now targeting. It made us completely unpredictable, more deadly than the people we were targeting because we operated at a level both above them and below them. That's why they developed the sleeper cells in the West, to grow the terrorist in and amongst the crop, a weed that goes undetected until it's either pulled by us motherfuckers or it kills the surrounding plants in a self-detonation, another true phasmid of modern warfare.

We exited west into Israel and followed what is now called the Pentagon Tour. It got the name because the route that we developed was so successful. It became the standard route for following known terrorist groups, arms dealers, people traffickers and anyone else looking to conduct their dirty business. It's now a common route well-trodden by coalition special forces coordinated by the Pentagon (Washington), who would initiate a 'tour' either clockwise or anti-clockwise in consultation with other nations. It involves a route from Jordan into Israel, Jerusalem to Beirut, then east into Syria and down through Iraq to Bagdad and onto Basra before going waterborne through the Gulf round to Aden and finally across to Djibouti. I have no doubt that after our 'tour' there were many who followed, some taking in interesting detours, like Iran, Yemen, Afghanistan, Pakistan and Somalia, as the need arose.

Aden was and remains the wild west of the Middle East and nothing can prepare a person for it. It is a place of utter chaos and disorder. Terrorism, kidnapping, inner conflict, landmines littered everywhere and complete civil unrest being the norm. Seeing an execution on the street wouldn't raise an eyebrow from any local passers-by. The strangest thing is, you must be seen to have a sidearm – the pistol is the symbol of a leader, and the holder is somehow less likely to get hit... well, not first! Yemen has decayed into another fighting ground between the Iran-backed Houthi rebels and the Saudi-led coalitions, another example of 'your enemy today will be your friend tomorrow who will help kill your old friend from yesterday' – what a fucking mess. I think a lot of our time following intel and the terrorists felt worthless and frustrating as we always seemed to be getting further away from what was most definitely getting nearer. At times in my days spent in pursuit, I got depressed at the continuous steps back I had to make in order to move forward. It's never a clean fight, it's a labyrinth, a hall of mirrors, endless boredom followed by split seconds of lightning strike action. A firefight was the ultimate release of frustration and a way to actually get some sort of weird satisfaction from the thought that I could make a difference and I was succeeding. A firefight would pull me closer to my team, release anger and yet push normality still further out of reach.

We arrived on the outskirts of Jerusalem some 10 days later. Jerusalem is absolutely fascinating in a different way. It's a place of worship and conflict simultaneously coexisting alongside each other. Since Suleiman the Magnificent to the present day, I don't think there will have been a single day when someone hasn't thought of attacking this city. I don't pretend to know the city's entire history, but from what little I could glean from our friends from Mossad it had been captured and recaptured 44 times and attacked 52 times! I, however, would liken it to a scene from Tatooine in *Star Wars*, equally as dangerous and unpredictable with as many different cultures and religions walking the streets as there were aliens in the film. The two operatives from Mossad had a list of safe houses the arms dealers were known to have used. They gave us the intel, addresses, photographs of the traders and more importantly their customers and all their last-known meeting points, telephone calls, the whole package. My attention was drawn to a familiar name, a name on our list: Nasser Tamei (Yugoslavian arms dealer). We set about rattling a cage at an address on the outskirts of the city.

For self-explanatory reasons the bad guys always like to try and cloak themselves in society and as such always seem to find a nice quiet residential area in which to do business, and this was no exception. We went with Mossad as far as the San Simon residential district before we left them smoking cigarettes in the Toyota Land Cruiser as we went on foot towards the target address on Rav Ashi Street. We didn't have the luxury of time or the patience to undertake a slow surveillance operation, we went in on trust, on second-hand intel from Mossad (not something we would have relayed to the Steering Group in a hurry). We had parked the vehicles some distance away, the SF guys going to the rear of the building and Mossad later positioning themselves in the apartments across the road to observe. The area was calm, quiet, very little traffic, just the sound of kids playing in the apartment gardens walled off from the street. The flats were relatively modern, all low-rise, three to five storeys high and clustered along the estate road littered with ageing cars and refuse collection bins. The flats were all similar in design and construction, sandstone-coloured brickwork, with A/C units bolted randomly on the outside fascias, humming in the warm breeze as the occasional resident leaned out of their apartment windows to hang washing on makeshift lines.

This was my target but Keith was I/C for this op and we just casually went up to the apartment's lower ground floor access gate, which was open, up to the building's main entrance and pressed the intercom for apartment 5. Mossad had indicated that this building was only in use by maybe 10 families, all usually working, so we shouldn't encounter any innocent civilians. We expected two people, Nasser and an unknown, in our target apartment. We waited patiently for a few moments then a crackled and somewhat tired voice echoed through the intercom. Keith gave a name and the buzzer released the lock into the building. The lift was out of action so we ascended the stairs, cold air greeting us from the air conditioning, our eyes blinded slightly as the interior was dark by comparison to the Jerusalem sunshine outside. We paused on the first-floor landing to adjust our vision.

Our hearts were pounding as we ascended the final stairs and banged on the apartment door – no CCTV, the locks released, then Keith went into action. Nasser was on the floor and pinned down within a second, and I casually stepped around the struggle to see if we had company. A kettle was boiling, only one cup, two different cigarette brands in the ashtray, maps, and soldering equipment on the kitchen table still smoking, various tools left holding rolled-up maps stretched over the table, and two unmade beds. Hugh and Smudge quietly entered the apartment whilst Cheesy, Baz and Hugh kept a vigilant eye on the street, its approaches and the surrounding apartments. Keith, however, was immediately into Nasser, who what when where, nice calm voice but his knife going ever so slowly into Nasser's ear. It wasn't a loud uncontrolled vicious interrogation or anything dramatic, but an effective pantomime of show-and-tell encouraged by the very real prospect of a messy death. I think as the blood came from the side of Nasser's head, running down his face into his eye and mouth, he would have begun to know how deep and how serious the injury he was receiving was about to become. The talking became a whisper of exchanges, almost a polite conversation, before Keith released him, hauling him up onto a chair. Haifa, mortar attack on a coalition warship. The SF guys were out the door.

This first round of show-and-tell wasn't exactly what we were seeking and only confirmed that Nasser had been working with multiple groups as a trader or middle man at best. Giving up small but good intel immediately is a useful tactic during interrogation if it's sufficient enough to appease the interro-gators. It wasn't what we were seeking and we knew this line of conversation was a diversion, a valuable segment of information enough to keep us interested, but Nasser had totally underestimated our intentions, purpose and our depth of knowledge of the terrorist activities he was involved in. We had just over five hours to take this guy apart before the team came back from Haifa. I started a deep search of the rooms, looking for any intel, phones, notes, maps, receipts in clothing, photos of family and friends – everything was a clue. What I found that was more interesting than anything else was protective clothing, Russian respirators and NBCD equipment packed away in large rucksacks, exactly the same shit we had used in Drobeta. The maps didn't give it all away in an instant, but the missing chemicals (or another shipment) from Romania – Drobeta (Operation RIAR) – were definitely on the move, perhaps making their way to Iraq from Lebanon. It wasn't that long before they would reach their intended destination. Time was no longer on our side and we needed to wrap things up with this encounter and step things up. The invasion of Iraq was now fully underway.

Keith had entered into new and more persuasive discussions with our captive. Questions regarding BZ, Substance 78/ EA-2277/US Army code EA-2277 NATO code BZ/Soviet code Substance 78. We watched his reactions, his ability to hide the truth diminishing second by second; it was obvious to us that he knew he had finally been uncovered. Information began to flow now that he was submerged in this, his own personal tempest of an interrogation, and information flowed right up to the point of his last breath. Information that wasn't perfect, but enough, enough to get us moving forward. The information from Nasser enabled us to be on our way and head into Iraq. We had well and truly rattled a cage in Jerusalem and now needed the eye in the sky to locate a convoy headed east out of either Israel, Lebanon or Syria into Iraq.

As for the mortar threat which the team had deployed to neutralise, they found two six-mortar arrangements welded into the back of a delivery vehicle and taken up to the roof of a multi-storey car park near the docks in Haifa – the intention being to launch an unprecedented attack on a visiting frigate. It was a very crude arrangement and had there been no intervention on our part it could have been a very effective weapon and made headline news, feeding the terrorist propaganda machine. However, the outcome was somewhat different. Having eliminated not only the threat of the mortar attack but also Rolando Hernandez (the missing accomplice to Nasser, our South American arms dealer – probably the source of the US chemical weapons), a name on our original list, plus four terrorists known to Mossad, the diversion of resources had proved to be incredibly worthwhile. We were now embarking on a hunt for the convoys and a shoot-to-kill mission for Leon Antunovich, Otto Meiser and Keith's terrorist cell all headed into Iraq with WMD(b) – weapons of mass destruction (biological). The dots were being joined up – arms dealers, Russian suppliers on old routes and the terrorists, coupled with the demand for weapons and war brewing again in the Middle East.

There was to be no let-up in our pace, we didn't have time for a stand-down or anything like that. We had to be on the move as we needed to expedite all our efforts to meet the needs of the op that was unfolding before us. With our newly acquired knowledge we had gained a small advantage on the terrorists; we now needed to keep up with everything that was unfolding in real time. New intel, and a success already under our belts, bolstered everyone's ego as we departed from our Israeli friends to push north and east in the 4x4 Toyotas. Smudge and Hugh were on the laptops sifting all the satellite and drone intel of all movements out of our sector, as well as deciphering the maps from the apartment. It was as though I were destined to spend half my life racing across barren landscapes in search of people on kill lists! Not such a bad thing as the banter between us usually passed the time very quickly. Piss-taking is a military form of humour that goes beyond anything that is socially acceptable in an office or any civilised workplace. There's nothing much off limits and no one is exempt, it's just another glue in the building blocks of strong friendships that will outlast time. It gives courage and strength to the team no matter how diminished the light becomes.

Leaving Israel, we took Route 40 back over into Jordan and on to Amman, where we had to part ways, as two possible targets had been identified. A new shipment arriving at Beirut had been identified, and a convoy heading east into Iraq had been seen crossing the border some 24 hours earlier. Owen, Keith, Cheesy, Smudge and I would race on to catch up with the Iraq convoy whilst the rest of the team headed north into Lebanon. Lebanon is a different game, home to a different breed of asshole; this terrorist cell which Keith had been monitoring was part of an Iranian effort to form a collective variety of militant Lebanese Shia groups into a unified organisation. It acted as a representation for Iran in the ongoing Iran–Israel Cold War. The conflict is bound in the political struggle of Iranian leadership against Israel and its declared aim is to dissolve the Jewish state, with the counter-aim of Israel to prevent nuclear weapons being acquired by Iran. This is where old intelligence of mine from the Moscow days identified Asad as the successor to his father Mohammed Al Zidjali, picking up the pieces after we completed Operation RIAR. Mossad had identified him residing in Beirut. The technical information from Russia may still have been flowing through a new generation after Eric, Alex and Anatoly, but we had no idea who was now supplying it. I was keen to enforce that I would need to ID Asad if Baz, Pierre or Hugh thought they had found him in Lebanon.

We were soon on Route 10 in Iraq and on our way to Rutbah. We would have a brief resting point and resupply at Rutbah as the city had been occupied by the Americans in an attempt to curb insurgent and criminal activity. The Yanks had constructed an eight-foot dirt berm along the city's perimeter, ensuring insurgents could no longer freely travel in and out of the city, which had been a breeding ground for smugglers and foreign fighters making their way into Iraq for years. There was a safe American compound in which we could take refuge for a pair of hours. Rutbah is a strategic location for insurgents and smugglers alike, since it is located astride two main supply routes – one from Jordan, and one from Syria. Exit through Rutbah and travel east, and the supply routes lead to the heart of the Sunni Triangle – Ar Ramadi, Al Fallujah and Baghdad. This terrorist smugglers' route was the very route we were travelling on and it was fucking exciting. Rutbah, unfortunately for its occupants, was strategically placed and very convenient for smugglers, terrorists and insurgents to operate in and out of, but now, with only three ways into and out of the city (through heavily armed US checkpoints), this made this activity all but redundant. There was an airport which was also of strategic importance and one of our escape-to-freedom options should shit go south. We were often of the mindset that we the hunters may actually become the hunted ourselves along this route. No travellers along this route would be safe or immune to an attack, even if to just rob them of their vehicles and their contents.

We arrived in the US compound and I met the commanding officer, a quiet very relaxed officer, not your typical Yank. We got supplies, cleaned up and had a hot meal before we convened in the command shelter, which was a converted shipping container. Arriving at the American base we must have looked like a group of armed homeless people, scruffy, dressed in pirate rig (a mix of local civilian clothing and our own kit), very tired, unshaven and just dirty I guess. We looked anything other than professional soldiers/intelligence operatives, but to an extent that was very deliberate. American bases offer everything a good hotel can: good food, a bed, hot shower and a laundry service! We took full advantage of all that we could. Americans are great, have all the kit but no idea how to use it properly. To be fair, they just gave us everything we asked for and more. It was good to just sit and enjoy different conversation with the regular soldiers and eat scran, which we took outside at picnic tables like you see outside pubs and in beer gardens. They were living a joyless and thankless life within the confines of the city barricades and their compound. They spent endless days at checkpoints waiting for an insurgent to just walk up to them and blow them up, or a child to hand them an IED pretending to offer a gift. No doubt they all had many stories to tell, but most wore them on their faces, tired and raw with the hallmarks of being policemen at war in a country that hated its freedom as much as it did its previous oppression.

In the American HQ we sat and studied intel on all passing traffic and aerial reconnaissance that the American support units had gathered. At the same time we took advantage of the comms cell and reported in our progress to the Steering Group and Marcus. We gained their permission to make calls home, which came as a surprise and a welcome morale boost. It didn't matter where or what bullshit we said to our loved ones regarding what we were doing or what lies we made up, it was just important to have that call and feel the warmth of home transmitted down a telephone wire by a loving voice. Like all things, people don't appreciate what they have until it's taken from them, and the freedom to talk to your loved ones is a big take when you've signed up for the work we did for the Steering Group, or any serviceman for that matter. We were gaining on our target convoy so we didn't spend the night; we left at dusk keen to gain some ground and catch up with the convoy, hungry now after many weeks to fully engage and get the job done.

Now, believe it or not all humans, including terrorists, get sloppy and follow the same old routines and routes where possible. They get comfortable and complacent at times; that's not to say we should ever underestimate them. To not get lazy is a discipline and requires effort, a lot of effort, especially for us in the intelligence service never mind the terrorists. Changing such things as routes and stopping points becomes very difficult, especially if time pressures or other options become too costly or just plain inconvenient. That's why our friends the Americans had built that fucking great big pile of dirt around the city of Rutbah. Not so much to protect the people within it, but more to fuck up all the travel plans, routes, layovers and resting places of all the dirty smugglers, terrorists and arms traffickers who needed to get from Jordan or Syria into Iraq. Simple piles of dirt were fucking all their shit up, and costing them time and money. This had made it easy for us to use drone and satellite imagery to spot genuine traders passing through Rutbah because they would go through the checkpoints, fill up with fuel within the city and get supplies or food before heading back out into the desert. Vehicles that by-passed the city were more likely to be up to no good and, watching satellite imagery of traffic movements, they stood out like a shit in a pint glass, because there's fuck all out in the desert for 400km after Rutbah! So why wouldn't they come through the city? Well, despite all things it narrowed our search down dramatically.

Our time in Rutbah had been very valuable, we had learned a lot from the Americans, and from Owen who had been out on the streets in Rutbah pretending to be a haulage salesman or some such shit. If you wanted to send freight bound for anywhere south of Bagdad that you didn't want to drive through a US military checkpoint then it was best to send it by boat, and most illegal cargos were being transported between Bagdad and Basra in this manner on shallow-draught boats on the Euphrates and on the Basra Canal. We knew that Basra was the end destination for our cargo because Keith already had hard intel first-hand from his Iranian days that Basra was a warehousing and staging point for terrorist activity as well as a pick-up/drop-off point for people smuggling. Basra Port was the terrorist equivalent of one of Amazon's main distribution centres. Everything of serious value could be tracked moving through Basra, especially shipments to and from Iran. We were on our way, and some hours later we received comms from Baz that our cargo wasn't bio weapons but explosives headed to the oil platforms in the Northern Arabian Gulf, whilst they were awaiting a shipment in Beirut that was possibly the WOMD(b) we had been searching for.

Our journey skirted Bagdad and we were all geared up psychologically and physically ready for a firefight, each of us surveying every passing car or person standing on the roadside, fearful of an IED or roadside attack. Nothing materialised but the sights we saw were nothing short of astounding. From the open wastelands littered with the debris of annihilated escaping convoys, to the still-occupied cars and houses of outlying villages where burnt and charred bodies remained still waiting to be rested from this life, led us on to the result of mass bombing campaigns closer to the city and death on a larger scale being revealed to us. There we witnessed the utter destruction of outlying towns, bridges and roadways. We ourselves often had to veer off the highway to get around a crater or a busted tank disassembled from overzealous expenditure of ordnance. The smell of fuel oil, smoke and death scorched into the very dust and sand we now breathed. It was a sick smell that coated your lips and your tongue; a drink of water wouldn't ever wash that taste away but simply stretch its stench to the back of your throat. It was a taste that, when ingested, combined with the sights and smells of the undertakings of men at war that stained not only everything on the outside but on the inside of your mind and your very soul. These images are saved into your brain's hard drive for repeated viewing much later, when you thought you had forgotten.

I have never experienced such a combination of emotions. This was different to Bosnia. Emotions that should never be combined, as different as oil is from water. Forbidden amalgamations, yet strangely interfaced into combinations defined by expressions of an almost forbidden survival seen in the faces of those who passed us by. Fear with joy, compassion with hatred, I became irritated but understanding of all the sights, forcing me to look again and again into the liberated eyes of the homeless, the desperate, the hungry and the angry. To see into the eyes of your enemy walking in the dirt barefoot and to feel hopelessness on their behalf, yet fear them because trust has long since diminished into lawlessness through the terror of war – this made each and every person both your liberated friend and your hidden terrorist assailant all at the same time.

We were silent for most of that drive, only passing information to each other regarding possible targets. A woman with a heavy basket or a shaped charge? A man pushing a moped, or an IED? A donkey pulling a cart or an explosive device? Everyone was a potential target. Yet simultaneously people were cheering and welcoming the uniformed American soldiers, no doubt shitting themselves every time they were approached by the genuinely innocent and the suicide bomber intent on their destruction.

Many hours later I remember arriving at Basra Port. After Bagdad and the wastelands in between, we approached with caution. Smoke trails streamed across the horizon, fires from explosions or bombing from coalition forces, no one interested in extinguishing such fires, no one caring. I think these fires served as a reminder that the fires of hatred had in fact been re-lit. New enemies trod the bloodstained ground where old foes lay dead or abandoned after their ill-fated campaigns or escape attempts. The sky was saddened and dark with the tears of what everyone wanted to be the break of a new day and freedom of a new nation. What hopes these people once had must have been in turmoil and disarray as the change and metamorphosis of democracy took its chance to convince simple people they were in safer hands. I don't think the people I saw or encountered had hope in any form, or maybe they did. Someone once said you have to keep breaking hearts to open them. Maybe that was what the West was trying to do, open their hearts to democracy. My mind wandered in and out of such thoughts the entire time we were on that road as I witnessed the cost of freedom being paid for mile after mile after mile.

Basra is like any other port really – the cargo berths busy with loading and offloading full of eager swarms of people keen to complete their tasks and release the hulks back to the sea from whence they came. Here the ships were old and tired, stained yellow and brown from years in service with no care for their husbandry, no pride in the work they undertook, just a means to an end. The warehouses formed a natural blockade from the main road, and the endless activity to and from them distracted me. Man and machine each moving containers and loose cargo from place to place, any one of them our target. The hum of activity felt normal and comforting to me, almost a reassurance that I was safe in some obscure way, a reminder of the walks with my dad along the docks in Newcastle, asking to go aboard random ships for a chat and a smoke. Now, I knew what we were looking for wouldn't be on an IMO-registered vessel but on a dhow, an unregulated mode of shipping, because they are considered to be historical vessels and as such exempt from international regulations and so never inspected and never normally stopped, overlooked as being insignificant or unimportant. Such vessels transport all manner of cargos to countries bordering the Arabian Gulf, everything from camels to weapons and everything in between.

We set to work as a team to find out what had passed through the port and where. We went door to door through the port, before becoming more forceful, looking into manifests and cargo movements and the like, not caring for the complaints of local officials who we simply brushed aside in their own offices. Keith adopted a fierce and aggressive approach with absolutely no interaction with any of the port workers, whereas Owen was offering bribes and cash for information. We eventually ended up in a deserted warehouse that we had been directed to by some stevedores and ran into some US soldiers fucking around playing basketball – the warehouse was empty because it was being cleaned after housing DGs (dangerous goods). The Americans had seen a lot of munitions and stores being unloaded from US supply ships and from road trains, for onward distribution to bases out in the desert. No doubt a lot of supplies were being moved legitimately, but in my experience the more normal and the more obvious things looked, the more likely something was amiss. I was getting agitated in the heat. We were close but not close enough, and my gut feeling was that our cargo had already been deployed.

After a lot of fucking around and dead-end investigations and interrogations, we established that a pair of dhows had been seen leaving the city heading slowly south just an hour or so ahead of us. We set up a comms link with the Steering Group. We needed to get out on the water. It would have been a near on impossible task to identify and target a specific dhow from the air. Brown came back to me to give directions to a deserted Iraqi naval base, the maritime academy at Al-Dawoodi, where there was a possibility that a serviceable vessel which had been abandoned may be of some use to us. We left the port and the team soon commandeered an old Iraqi patrol boat at the academy berth. Now we were hard against the clock as we were sure now that the intent for the explosives was for the destruction of the oil platforms in the NAG, especially the ABOT (Al Basrah Oil Terminal) oil platform, which for some technical reason could never stop pumping.

The ABOT platform usually fed a minimum of two supertankers to keep the flow at a controllable pressure. The oil flowed 24/7 and it wasn't unusual to see four tankers slowly sinking with the weight of oil being delivered at this platform. It was a fucking miracle the whole thing hadn't collapsed into the sea years ago but the rust was still holding it together with the help of some crazy engineers and a handful of Iraqi soldiers to protect it.

Dhows laden with explosives were the preferred method to wreak havoc on oil platforms, merchant shipping and coalition warships – they were cheap, hard to follow, hard to detect and were fucking everywhere pretending to be local fishing vessels. But our superiors back in London were getting very nervous about the possible strike against the ABOT oil platform, which supplied something like 15% of the world's oil at the time, or so I was led to believe. By us tracking this supply route we were also beginning to fully understand the supply of ordnance to various settlements and munition dumps along the Euphrates, the scale of which hadn't been fully realised. This distribution network was where explosives would be either distributed inland from Basra or loaded onto fishing dhows or smaller faster dhows, completing the supply chain to the end user. This was the new order of how we the intelligence service operated with SF all over the world: to react, prioritise and adapt to unfolding live intelligence on the back of a main operation at short notice. Well, I guess that's the political way of saying make it up as you go along but make sure you don't fuck up.

We had been successfully following old and new intel to track and understand our terrorist friends' organisations through the whole fucking stink trail that spanned Eastern Europe, Jordan, Israel, Syria and Iraq, uncovering supply routes, terrorist and government links and the relationships between different groups to try and eliminate the threat against the supply of oil, and no less importantly our primary objective: to stop the flow of arms into the underworld of the Middle East, Iran and into the Death Triangle. We wanted to put a full stop to the demand and the entire supply chain. The Death Triangle (not to be confused with the Triangle of Death – Baghdad) is an imaginary area between Iraq, Pakistan and Somalia. Dhows were hard to track especially in open waters; they didn't have an AIS (automatic identification system) or a heat plume that could be tracked by satellite and could easily transport arms and weapons relatively undetected. Our Arabian friends had made use of old fishing dhows that were now simply floating phasmids – they all looked like innocent fishermen or traders but beneath the decks were far more deadly cargos bound for terrorist cells or the side of a coalition warship but if possible an oil platform in order to get the biggest headlines in Western newsrooms.

We needed to get the boat at Al-Dawoodi up and running, and quickly. It was an ageing patrol boat that had been part of the ICDF (Iraqi Coastal Defence Force) but had been laid up by a Task Force 58 commander some months earlier. Cheesy undertook an in-depth check for sabotaged equipment and traps before we set to work. Keith and I were down below getting the engines turned over and ready to fire up. It was a mess, a fucking oil bath of a bilge in which sat two aged diesel engines, but they were free to turn and we had fuel and battery power. There were some glitches with the control cables, which had been cut, and the steering gear was anything but ready to go. Alarm systems were all to shit and not reflecting the true state of the engine systems but who the fuck cared about that? Water strainers were found blocked and leaking but were quick fixes. Owen looked like a spare prick at a wedding, typical American. He didn't know whether to help Keith and me in the engine bay or help Smudge and Cheesy up in the wheelhouse before getting the deck guns ready. It was a complete pot mess of a boat, but once we had ditched everything off that was of no use to us and got our shit together, we were starting to look like we knew what we were doing. It was a fucking shitshow really but a great demonstration of our abilities as a team.

We intended on getting the boat down to Um Qasr before heading out into open waters in pursuit of our target. We had a team brief once we thought we were ready to try firing her up. There were two recognised routes down to Um Qasr and we decided to turn right out of the academy and then right again, south down the Euphrates. None of us were sure if the Basra Canal was open or if it had locks; additionally, we were not sure of the boat's draught to navigate the Euphrates or which route the cargo may have taken. We would have to decide which way around Bubiyan and Warbah islands we would navigate. The coin was flipped and we were all set to take the clockwise route. We gathered in the wheelhouse as Keith went below and fired up the diesels – a long set of coughing and choking before we had a plume of black smoke pouring out the side exhausts. Smudge climbed up on top of the wheelhouse to place a CIP (combat identification plate), taken from one of the 4x4s, on the roof just in case of any air activity, then control was passed from local to the wheelhouse and we left the wall, pouring out smoke and oil as Keith pumped out the oil and waterlogged engine bay. We were vibrating like mad and the steering was as sloppy as fuck as we bounced from bank to bank down the Qamat Ali Canal.

We took up defensive positions for river passage; going downriver on an Iraqi patrol boat was nothing short of military stupidity. The fucking boat was just a bullet magnet for any passing tribesman or, worse, a target for a more serious adversary. I was sitting with Keith between the two main diesel engines, Keith forward and me aft near the steering gear compartment hatch, behind which Cheesy was hidden. We had all doors and hatches sealed for the transit. It was like being in a steel coffin. It was about 50 degrees down that engine room with sweat dripping down your back and soaking you through within minutes. A fucking uncomfortable steel sweatbox, to say the least. It's strange how in such uncomfortable surroundings you can actually sleep. The usual routine would be to get a bail of rags and make a makeshift bed on the plates, moulding the rags to the shape of your head to help act as ear defenders – that would have been a luxury on this trip.

Smudge was up in the wheelhouse and acting as coxswain for this trip. Throttle was at max chat as we approached the rivermouth, then eased down as he took us into the 'navigable' channel. There was no chatter aboard just a silent expectation as the engine continued to roar and whistle as Smudge zigzagged and altered speed to make us as unpredictable as possible to any possible incoming fire. Each time the boat manoeuvred from one side of the channel to the other, the bilge water would rush across the hull releasing that sickening oil and stagnant water smell that chokes your throat, making shit smell nice. Poor old Smudge was having a hell of a job driving the boat, trying to miss all the endless debris from air strikes and other half-sunken boats. We had no idea if the river would be clear for a passage all the way to the open sea. Bridges were our biggest fear because if they had collapsed, blocking the river, we would be completely fucked, making us an easy target, but also if they remained intact, giving opportunities to be attacked from above as we passed under them. But things eased down after a while and soon Keith, Cheesy and I were almost asleep, allowing for the noises, vibrations, smells and control system lights and alarms to seamlessly blend into whatever dream we were trying to have in order to get some rest.

We were woken by a scream of "ALARM!" from Smudge from the wheelhouse a split second before an RPG hit the bank in front of us. Heavy incoming fire through the wheelhouse windows, with Smudge now unable to safely steer, we were destined for the west bank. We hit the bank as explosions so deafening merged into a single continuous din, making everything suddenly become silent as my eardrums were plunged into a blunt buzz of tinnitus, making all other sounds obsolete. We had to get out on deck and return fire. No time to think as Keith and I tried to climb up into the wheelhouse. Smudge was trying to turn the boat and pull it off the bank, full throttle astern on the starboard engine and wheel hard over now. I could feel the boat bouncing and the screws hitting the mud as Smudge desperately tried to get us off the bank, one engine then both screaming as he pulled the throttle levers back fully whilst trying to free the arse end by taking the rudder from hard over to hard over and back.

We were in a shit mess. Owen was on deck and releasing as much suppressing fire as he could towards the entanglement of wreckage, fishing dhows and boulders from where the RPG had originated. Multiple crack crack cracks of AK 47 gunfire, ricochets everywhere and that hammer-to-metal sound as the bullets hit the hull and pierced the superstructure. Keith was up with his assault rifle and giving covering fire for Owen as they tried to repel a boarding force. Smudge was ripped to shreds with all the glass and continuous splinters being burst into the wheelhouse, one eye fucked from shards of glass that had hit him in the face. I took a brief look around to assess our situation. We had driven straight into the dhows we had been fucking chasing and were transporting our cargo. No Cheesy, just screams from below.

I returned to the engine bay and steering compartment to see if Cheesy was okay. He was trapped by a twisted girder through his leg, and badly positioned under the deck plates that had all lifted. We must have hit a mine or hit the bottom real hard, forcing up the structure. The engine bay was fully smoked out, rancid acidic fumes now filling the entire engine compartment with that hot glycol-scented mist spraying out from one of the header tank sight glasses. Everything was hot and steam was billowing from the port condenser, creating a hot fog mixing with the glycol which was possibly suppressing a fire or explosion. Cheesy's leg was fucked, and water was coming in to the boat from the burst sea inlets and strainers and was rising fast. Fuck, fuck fuck. Cheesy was in and out of consciousness, water level rising.

Water level rising.

Leg stuck, water level rising.

His leg was completely penetrated by the support strut and welded back into the hull in a twisted mess. He kept looking at me. Now the water was up to his chest. I stumbled through into the engine bay, grabbed a toolkit and emptied it out over the steering block. I had to hack his leg off. I put a tourniquet of electrical wire and a hammer handle around his thigh and proceeded to hack through his leg, through the open wound and through his bone with a hacksaw. The entire bilge was red with blood now, and he was drowning. Screaming and then gobbling water, drowning, and bleeding out at the same time. It was fucking hopeless. I held his head up as best I could and watched his life pass from his eyes. Cheesy was gone. Hell was above and below me and I had to let him go.

Gunfire intensified on deck which was then silenced. The only sounds now were screams of pain, shouts for help in both English and Arabic. I remember hearing boots pounding the deck above – they had boarded the boat. My hearing was still fucked; everything sounded dull, as though I were underwater. Smudge was screaming, engaging in hand-to-hand now. I was up on the wheelhouse, it was a fucking free-for-all – two guys on Smudge, rolling around in all the glass and debris, with Keith pinned down on the deck half in and half out the wheelhouse door. I emptied my Glock into the guys on top of Smudge but a grenade went off. All three bounced. I was unconscious now. I don't remember anything from this point. It just went black. For me the struggle was over.

I awoke on the bank of the river, wet through and my head resting in Keith's lap. He was badly messed up. I looked up, and he just looked down at me and said, "It's all over, mate, just need a minute." We were like two disabled and disorientated drunkards. Couldn't stand up, I tried and there was no way, and Keith just sat bewildered and dazed. We both had suffered head injuries but Keith was way worse than me. I just needed time to get my shit back in one sock. I think we must have stayed there on the riverbank watching the debris float by for about an hour or so. I just lay there with my head in his lap as he sat and moaned and twitched around in and out of consciousness sometimes long enough to crack a joke about going twos up on my missus and the like. We were in a real fucked-up mess, but we needed to get away from the boat and this site. I managed to get up. Smudge was dead in the wheelhouse still, Owen lay dead on the bow of the boat and Cheesy was gone as well, the images of his death clinging to me like heavy fuel oil to my clothes. I was crying, the saltwater washing a clean patch on either side of my face. There was nothing to salvage here, the patrol boat was a derelict void now of both mechanical and human life. We had to thin out from this site before others arrived to investigate what had happened here; and besides, we were sending smoke signals about a mile up into the air.

I was conscious we had to move on and get out of this place but undertook a quick investigation of the settlement and the dhows into which we had stumbled. The dhows were loaded to the gunwales with explosives, but it looked like they had encountered engine trouble and eventually engine failure, forcing them to pull over to the bank and attempt to make repairs. Engine parts and tools lay strewn across the deck. Seeing an official patrol boat must have freaked them out and triggered the engagement. I gathered up some supplies, first-aid kit from one of the bergens to patch Keith up, water, assault rifle and my sniper rifle. All comms were fucked. We had to walk out of that place, and quickly.

I got Keith up and we started walking. Now, I cannot remember where exactly we were, or for how long we walked. We walked all day and all night and into the next morning, or was it through the night into the next morning, I can't exactly remember. I was exhausted and Keith was getting desperate. We were definitely in a hostile zone and needed to stay out of sight if at all possible. We managed to find a bit of shade and shelter in a half-finished dwelling in the middle of nowhere. We had no food left and only a little water. I was looking at Keith and knew we were in trouble – he didn't look good. Shit, we were well and truly in the shit. I caught sight of a dust plume in the distance – a vehicle was approaching us. This was our opportunity. I loaded the sniper rifle and took up position behind the wall of the dwelling. I wiped my sight and focused in on the target. It was an SUV of some description, one driver no passengers. I checked my sights, verified the distance and calmly took aim, putting the driver's head in the crosshairs. No, I didn't pull that trigger, I don't know why to this day. As the vehicle came closer and closer, I just stood up and walked into its path holding up my hand in a stopping gesture.

Now, shit happens in strange ways when you really don't expect it to happen. The guy, a local tribesman, pulled up the truck maybe 20ft from me and calmly got out of the vehicle. I tried communicating with him but neither of us spoke the same dialect, or language for that matter. He just stood and looked at me, and I at him. There was silence and a good two minutes passed as we both thought how best to come out of this situation alive. He was in a plain light-brown thobe, no headdress, short hair, greying beard and darkly tanned. He eventually beckoned me to his truck. He could see I had my hand on the trigger of my sidearm. Then Keith stood up from behind the wall. The guy was startled but didn't react badly. There was a long pause, and again he gestured to me to get into his vehicle. I rode shotgun in that SUV for four hours with my pistol in his side before he dropped me and Keith off at an American base. I remember that ride, fucking on edge the entire way, yet happy to share a cigarette with this unknown man, our saviour, before he sped off again into the desert.

We walked, well struggled, up to the entry point of the base, already having attracted the Americans' attention by just falling out of the SUV. They were on high alert, probably thinking we were suicide bombers or something, and a single shot was fired into the air. Orders were yelled at us from a handheld megaphone from a watchtower to halt, drop our weapons, take off our clothes and lie face down in the sand. We both lay there half fucking naked as a squad of overzealous troops came over, tie-wrapped our hands behind our backs and dragged us into a holding area. Now, for ops like we were on, personal ID and anything that could identify us must be left behind in case you ended up in the wrong hands, so it took some time before we were able to prove our ID and eventually get re-clothed and seen to medically. It wasn't a pleasant experience sitting half naked in a stress position under the heat of the day without water for maybe two hours, but I guess they were really nervous, or had probably had a recent attack that had claimed one of their own. Keith keeled over at one point and attracted some unnecessary aggression from our guards, but he just took it as did I because there was no negotiating anything when in this situation and we both knew it.

However long it took it didn't matter, as soon as clearance was established everything changed. We suddenly became very welcome and very well looked after. Keith was taken away to get fixed up and I became the centre of attention in the command centre. I passed all intel through the Americans to London to formalise a joint operation with central command in Iraq. Basra was entirely a British Forces operation whose mission was to secure the entire city. Until now there had been no need to keep the Americans updated with SF missions in this sector but this was now a joint mission as the oil platforms were high-value assets outside of any one coalition member's realm. I tried to give as much detail as I could as to the location of the patrol boat and the dhows. They were super sharp and keen to retrieve the explosives and had already initiated their own operations regarding oil platform protection measures following their own intel and recent terrorist activity in the NAG. That day was quite something – from being shot at, blown up and surviving a desert hike, to later witnessing the US central command undertake a full reconnaissance mission to find the patrol boat and the dhows, utilising drones and a P-3C Orion. British ground forces were deployed to the site of our firefight to find that the dhows had been abandoned in exchange for the patrol boat which had disappeared. My team members' bodies were recovered, but I never saw them again. They were flown home to England out of Bagdad. I never got to see them leave Iraq. Even now I'm not sure how I would have handled that.

War doesn't stop because something has gone to shit, it keeps moving forward relentlessly and without any regard for those who fall. Strangely, for some time it didn't feel like anyone had actually died, just felt like they had been deployed elsewhere. A coping mechanism perhaps, denial for sure, I wouldn't accept Cheesy's death for a long time to come and I knew it. I can remember watching all the imagery coming in as the P-3C Orion was re-tasked to find the patrol boat. The CIP was a fucking bonus in helping us identify that heap of shit out in the middle of a soup of dhows and small craft. I sat with the base commander in a blacked-out section of the command

and communications bunker, a three-tiered arrangement with probably about 30 screens displaying live footage, CCTV, statistics and satellite imagery all eagerly watched and reported on by young enthusiastic American service men and women to the watch commander. All those young men and women dressed in out-of-the-packet desert gear that had probably just arrived that week and never seen the light of day. A resentment crept into my mind as I watched them play their computer games, observing the engagement site with absolutely no respect or compassion. I wanted to tell them that this was where my friends had fought and died.

About an hour later the patrol boat was located and eyes turned to me as I confirmed its authenticity, the same patrol boat we had taken into a firefight at the engagement site and our ID plate code still in place – stupid of the terrorists not to check for an ID tag. Then all the information was relayed to an AC-130 gunship from the 4th Special Operations Squadron which targeted the boat some 298 miles south east of Bagdad, off the Al-Faw Peninsula. It was quite something to watch that gunship take out the patrol boat, almost like watching a video game, so I could forgive those young soldiers, and once it was gone there was a round of applause as if it were a gameshow, then a brief moment of relief before everyone was back into fighting the war, albeit an electronic war. Their war didn't include close-quarter engagements, no actual loss of life, no screams, no emotions, no fear or adrenalin, just images of people who could be anyone anywhere, images that were not husbands, fathers, sons or relatives, just images on a screen, sometimes in black and white, sometimes in colour and some-times marked for elimination.

Transpiring from all the drone, P-3C Orion and satellite imagery was a remarkable unfolding of activity that could be followed, traced and interpreted. Heightened activity out of Basra had identified the source and the lair of the terrorist groups that had taken the patrol boat. They had been captured on camera in large numbers deploying from an address in Basra immediately following our riverside engagement. They had obviously been informed of our engagement with members of their group and deployed immediately in support and to retrieve the explosives, before then retreating back to Basra. This was the most important intel we could have possibly hoped for and all just by accident, an engine failure on a dhow, our chance encounter with them, pulling the entire terrorist group out of hiding, revealing their home base. It was an extraordinary fuck-up on their part – to risk heading out to recover that cargo gave away everything. Over the next few days we watched in amazement the traffic going in and out of that building, both in real time and from historical recordings which confirmed undoubtedly we had found terrorist HQ. An air strike was arranged and just a few days later was executed by US fighter jets. In one strike overnight two US F-15E Strike Eagles, using laser-guided munitions, destroyed a building where 200 paramilitary members were confirmed to be in hiding, including everyone on Keith's list. British ground forces were able to confirm on site all that the Steering Group had hoped for. All that remained now was to locate Asad in Beirut.

Keith and I remained on base for a week or so. I think we were both trying to come to terms with the last few months and the engagement on the river. Nothing seemed normal anymore and the whole series of events started to surface more and more in our thoughts and how we behaved and interacted, not only between ourselves but with everyone who came across our paths. We withdrew away from everyone on the base into a self-imposed isolation, which served us well as we tried to process all the anger and frustration we each carried and shared so heavily now. We were closer than ever as friends and only felt able to face each day if we were together the entire time. There was no room for outsiders in this isolated mourning we had created, which pissed people off. We got drunk often and were becoming an unwelcome upset in the mess, the dining area and amongst all ranks. It went on for a little while longer until we managed to get a ride on a helo out to the *Essex* in the Gulf. I don't think the base could have tolerated us for too much longer. We had outstayed our welcome and there was no longer any room at the inn for past warriors or washed-up, burnt-out members of an organisation no one really knew or cared about. All that was visible to those young eyes that looked upon us was two angry British servicemen who didn't want to engage in any way with the base activities except to get drunk and close the door to all who knocked on it.

We got on that helicopter with all our baggage, emotional and psychological, the remains of an elite team heading home, knowing the closer we got to home the further away from it we would be.

The Steering Group

Chapter 14

Brotherhood

Leaving the American base and our trail of emotional debris behind was a good move because we both needed to get back amongst the people who could go some way to understanding us and actually deal with our fucked-up mindset. Being around people who haven't experienced a traumatic experience just made me more resentful and upset. It's like telling a cancer patient you understand how they feel when actually how the fuck could you possibly ever understand anything about cancer unless you've endured it and survived, or at least lost a family member to the disease? I naively thought cancer was a disease for 'other' people until both my parents died from it, but before that loss in my life I couldn't have even come close to getting to grips with the sheer enormity of pain, loss and suffering that that disease unleashes on its victims and families.

We were soon on the approach to the support ship. Looking out through the sun-hazed window, I could see all the oil slicks and all the debris of war in the otherwise beautiful blue waters of the Gulf, a small reminder that all was not well in the world and man's greed was taking its toll on all living things. Helicopter flights over water still fascinate me, it's the searching for the tiny dot on the radar, the speck on the horizon, searching for a platform on which to land. Every time I had to fly out to a ship or platform it always felt as though the helicopter was too big to land on the tiny flight deck that substituted for an airport landing site. But land we did and it felt great to see all things British once more. We got out of the helo and went into the hangar to be greeted by the ship's staff, eager to carry our shit and escort us through the ship to our accommodations. They all sort of knew who we were, and by the look of Keith and I they could have been forgiven for thinking the very worst of us. Walking down the passageways was a comforting experience, everything clean and polished, crew members rushing past, smiling and saying good morning and such shit, radios on in offices, the smell of the galley and the engine spaces combining to give that perfume only a ship could give. It felt safe. It felt good to be back aboard.

It was surreal to be back on board, like checking into a five-star hotel. I would be living in luxury after what we had been used to and it all felt as if nothing had happened, as no one knew what we had endured. No one knew what we had been involved with and no one really cared, which was good mostly as I desperately needed to keep a low profile, but at the same time I found the lack of interest annoying. I had a 20-minute hot shower despite the water rationing aboard the ship, fish and fucking chips in the mess cos it was Friday, and then off to my cabin and a pusser's navy bunk to crash out on. That first night back on board was so very strange, the sounds of the ship keeping me awake and yet taking me on a gentle journey to a sleep I hadn't been able to enjoy for such a long time – the breeze of the air conditioning being pumped through my little punkah louvre, cooling me as I lay under the crisply ironed sheets fresh back from the Chinese laundry, and my head on top of two pusser's pillows, all accompanied by the echoing chorus and vibration of the ship all busy at work outside my cabin door. I must have passed out for about 72 hours, no word of a lie.

When I finally managed to drag my ass out of that cabin I spent many evenings with Marcus and Keith, debriefing the entire op, sometimes just in person alone with Marcus, but sometimes with video links back to London and the Pentagon to discuss future ops that would build on the successes of our campaign. But Marcus wanted to just talk through what had happened aboard that patrol boat – long conversations that we needed to have, the justifications, the need, the pain and the regret of everything. Keith and I would often take those conversations to the SNCOs' bar to drown them and then take ourselves to places I never want to go again at the bottom of a second bottle of whisky. The SNCOs' bar was much more tolerant of us drinking ourselves into a coma, and between us we drank, cried and talked it all through. Sometimes we were joined by some really fucking decent guys who were the senior engineers aboard who liked nothing more than to get smashed with Keith and me. The mess president turned a blind eye so long as we were gone before he had breakfast in the morning. We would play drinking games, often ending up with stupid injuries like carpet burns on our faces, burnt lips from ignited cocktails and occasionally a black eye when the play-fighting turned real. The brotherhood between Keith and I was indescribable, and we would go on as brothers until the day I left the service. He still serves to this day.

But no matter how hard we played in that mess there are wounds you cannot see that will never be healed because there will always be a scab that gets scratched off occasionally, revealing the rawness that festers underneath. Now, there is nothing I can say about Cheesy, Smudge or Owen, it's just a no-go area. What can anyone say about lost friends, comrades or brothers, my brothers in arms? I loved them all. It's a tragedy of irreparable loss, but a loss that will remain with me forever, lingering in my mind together with the smells and the chaos of that day. All the plans that were made between us are now lost to the past and to that encounter on the river. There is no future with them now, the brotherhood lost, except to see their faces at night when dreams don't linger but give way to endless episodes of paranoia and fear – the fear of never being forgiven for what happened and what we did or didn't do. Thoughts that come in the small hours of the morning that we must be on a counter list, a kill list from a country's intelligence cell or some other scumbag organisation we pissed off or all but wiped out, leaving me to be always looking out the window, always looking behind to see who is in my shadow, always afraid of new people who proclaim their innocent interest in me as a person.

The *Essex* arrived in Dubai for an SMP (self maintenance period). I got off the ship and rushed over to the Madinat Jumeirah hotel complex on the beach in Dubai. Anna had flown out to meet me. It was very touch and go if the ship would ever be able to dock in the current political and complex climate of the Middle East, or if I would be allowed any R&R. There had been some very serious correspondence between the Steering Group and Marcus about keeping Keith and me on board, out of sight, but both Marcus and Brown knew how important a few days with family would be. Anna and I just kept hoping that we could be reunited, one week it being all on, the next calling it all off, only to call again to say get on the plane. But here I was finally in Dubai, Anna already at the hotel waiting for me.

I remember arriving at this luxury resort, unlike anything I had experienced. Totally surreal, I arrived dirty and tired into a reception area that was nothing short of palatial. I sat down in a huge sofa and was given hot towels to wipe my grubby face and hands which were soon clutching a glass of ice-cold champagne. Fuck, less than 72 hours ago I had been in a war zone, and here in this place people were on fucking holiday as though nothing were happening, as if no one cared for all the fucking shit service men and women were sacrificing just hours away. I was approached by a waiter and told there had been a problem with the booking and my wife wanted to discuss it with me before I could check in properly. My mind wasn't really focused on any details, just the need to crash out, but I was escorted to an abra (small boat) and whisked away through the hotel canal network to a villa where Anna awaited my arrival. Our original booking in one of the main buildings with a sea view was no longer available but we had been offered an upgrade to a garden villa (with our own butler). Anna thought I would be mad not getting the sea view, but fuck I was more than happy with that upgrade – a private villa away from everyone and a private pool! After where I had been for the past few months a youth hostel would have been amazing enough.

We had a brilliant holiday, emotional at times but amazing in every way a reunion of lovers should be, but I remember just crying in Anna's arms one evening as we sat in the enormous bathtub in our villa. The realisation struck home of what had happened, what I had just walked away from. It was a crazy delayed reaction maybe, I'm not sure, but I remember just not being able to control my emotions. A James Blunt tune had come on to the radio in the room, and the words just brought it all home. Powerless to hold it in, Anna began to see the first widening cracks in my hardened façade, the render of a false strength falling away revealing the real me, tired, scared and utterly fatigued from the endless demands of the Steering Group to complete their list regardless of the price. Their orders demanding satisfaction as if in payment now for the opportunity that was afforded to me, that eager boy so many years ago. There was never going to be an exit clause this far in to the system, the machine wanted to see a conclusion to its business that it had sought for so long. The scared boy looking to belong was now in debt to the machine and I knew it. I knew the price, the price was my piece of mind or my life; the investment must return its loyalty and return the dividend. I knew then as I know now that there would never be any going back, no redaction of my life's events; the story had been written and lived out and could never be re-written or edited to make good all that had gone wrong or change any of the outcomes. I had nowhere to take my anger for what had happened on that patrol boat, so I had to bury it and bottle it to be stored away and preserved, still raw and septic, waiting to be set free on the fool who would open the lid sometime in the future.

I wasn't sure where life would take me from that point on, but what I was sure about was making the most of my time with Anna on that holiday. The here and now was important; fuck tomorrow, it may never come. We ate and drank in all the finest restaurants, including a night at a Gordon Ramsay restaurant in town which was honestly shit compared with some of the other on-site restaurants. But the cherry on the cake was a meal in the Burj Al Arab. We had a golf cart pick us up from the villa and drive us over to the Burj. I've got to say it's all a bit garish inside, overcooked opulence trying to be regal or elegant but failing massively because it's so modern and lacks the great history of the finest hotels of the world like the Peninsula in Hong Kong or Raffles in Singapore, the Waldorf or even the Savoy in London. I think it could have been done more tastefully but it wasn't and that left it begging to be acknowledged simply because of its self-proclamation of being a six-star hotel. We headed up to the Skyview Bar, which I have to say was pretty impressive, for a few cocktails. I ordered a French 75 which received a 'what the fuck' look from the barman, fucking useless bastard. Now, if this had been the Peninsula, they would have already known what I had wanted, had it ready and replied with my first name.

Nonetheless here we were together and happy, and my cares dropped away as we descended in a super-fast lift to sub-level 4 or something to board a submarine (simulator) and undertake a fake underwater ride to the restaurant. After the ride, the door of the sub opened whereupon we were greeted into the restaurant which was like something out of a Disney movie. Anna and I were escorted over to our table right next to the biggest aquarium outside of Europe, and we sat down to an extravagant meal of seafood discovery whilst watching divers attend to the fish and other sea life through the 30ft-high glass walls. I ordered oysters to start, which came on a bed of dry ice that was overly theatrical to say the least. Ice vapour poured off the plate to surround me at the table as though I were a pop star in a concert or something equally ridiculous. I consumed those oysters in a matter of seconds and they tasted smooth, cold and satisfying yet lightly salted and exciting to the palate. We both ordered a glass of Billecart Salmon Vintage Rosé champagne and then ordered a bottle of it, costing £300, to go with our main course of lobster. I didn't give a flying fuck! Dinner cost nearly £500, which is madness I know, but in my mind I was lucky to be there. I was celebrating life because just weeks earlier I might have been fucking shot dead on that patrol boat, so what the hell. Life is for living and I was with the only person who made my life worth living, worth continuing for. Anna was and is my life and the vehicle back to a normal quiet existence away from such thoughts and memories as that time on the river.

The holiday/R&R was soon over unfortunately, and we had made sure that we spent all the money we had saved up. I took Anna to Dubai airport to see her safely on her way home. I remember waving her off into the terminal and then just standing there in the heat of the Dubai sun, lost in thoughts, lost in memories of my time in Dubai with Anatoly – all those thoughts now superseded and overwritten by new memories of me and Anna enjoying life in Dubai. It was a paradoxical moment that would have been a dream not too long ago. I was mentally trying to prove to myself that there was hope, a way back, that it was possible to rewrite things. I stood there for maybe half an hour, wet through with sweat, before I finally got a taxi into town and ended up at the seamen's mission.

I was on a mission to get absolutely shitfaced and I succeeded with the help of the *Essex* crew who were there enjoying the cheap beer, the pool and the freedom to be as drunk as they liked. Work hard, play harder. The lads off the ship were good eggs. Matelots are fucking great drinkers, and once they're on the pop there's no stopping them or their stupidity after a skinful. I don't remember too much after the first few hours and awoke in my cabin aboard the *Essex* with a fucker of a headache and the realisation the ship was actually underway, homeward bound, back to Blighty, as the lads liked to say.

I was due to get back with the ship maybe two months later after decompressing, but as things turned out I had to fly home early from Barcelona to be with Anna as she had a health scare. It got me home early and I was fucking pleased to leave it all behind. I got home and everything was fine, it was all a false alarm, so I was able to enjoy being at home on leave with Anna. We enjoyed long walks on the beach in Cornwall and hikes on Dartmoor which was so cool as I have always enjoyed the open space Dartmoor offers. I didn't have much to do with the Steering Group for a while; all the debriefing had been done on the *Essex* so no need for any of that bullshit to interfere with this leave period which was classed as an extension of decompression. Besides, I don't think Keith or I were ready for much more than mincing around doing nothing, readjusting to a quieter life. Keith kept in touch with me and we both sort of returned to a life back in the UK that was weird in many ways. There were no reunions, no piss-ups, no brass band or parade, no one gave a fuck or knew what we had been though apart from us.

Life continued as though nothing had been going on in the Middle East. People back home were more worried about the cost of petrol and shit like that. Life was allowed to be strangely normal in England, so I guess I had to pretend and get on with it, live life again, bury it all and try to be 'normal', if only for Anna's sake. Some servicemen can't do it, and get into trouble down the pub, become alcoholics or just fail at being normal altogether and end up in prison. They're not bad people, it's society that wanted them to be bad in the first place and just don't know how to reverse the training and the experiences they have witnessed, let alone know what to do with them once they've done all the dirty work and returned home looking for a bit of support or just some understanding without feeling weak or showing any sort of failure. Just to be accepted and be normal again – it's hard for everyone, not just servicemen.

It wasn't too much longer before I was dragged back into the thick of it all. I had been out walking along the coast with Anna from Cawsand to Rame Head and back through farmland on a 12-mile walk which was one of our regular routes, oblivious to what had been unfolding out in the Middle East. We got home and sat down to dinner in front of the TV to be hit with the news about Lebanon. Fighting had broken out between Israel and Lebanon. Fuck, I was immediately transported back mentally to the Middle East. It was all over the news. There had been cross-border attacks into Israel and rockets fired into border towns as a diversion, whilst further missile attacks on Israeli forces had seen two soldiers killed and reports of others abducted into Lebanon. I was hoping it hadn't got anything to do with my last op with the boys. I hadn't heard back from Baz, Pierre or Hugh but that was normal, they always disappeared for months at a time, it was their thing, and I had tried so hard to distance myself. I hadn't heard from them, I didn't want to; I had isolated myself from them in a veil of guilt because of what had happened on that patrol boat. To face Baz after what had happened and explain everything would be too much. For me to have to justify my life over Cheesy's would be impossible to do and I didn't want to go over it all again.

Eventually the phone call came, the sound of inevitability ringing loudly and persistently in my own home. I was to get an RAF transport from Brize out to Cyprus before organising a way into Lebanon. Baz had finally poked the hornets' nest in Beirut and all hell had broken out; retaliations for acts no one had laid claim to were the results of my old team at the helm. They were claiming they had Asad pinned down in a small town on the Israeli boarder called Dhayra. A full evacuation of British citizens was already underway from Beirut, with multiple British warships being used as ferries from Beirut to Cyprus, so there was plenty of opportunity for me to get out there and see to it that Asad, the last name, was taken off the Steering Group's list. Fuck, it was the last thing I had expected but secretly knew it was inevitable. Anna drove me to Brize Norton where I got an RAF transport out to Cyprus.

I landed in Cyprus to be greeted by an empty arrivals hall and no onward travel arranged for me by the Steering Group. My instructions were clear: get to Beirut, meet the team, all haste. I had full authority to commandeer or utilise anything to get me there. I walked out of that arrivals terminal in Cyprus and casually walked down to the apron at the end of the terminal building where there were several helicopters and some transport planes. I caught sight of a friendly face fucking around loading a navy Lynx helo. A casual conversation between me and the pilot and I had a ride out to a frigate that was going into Beirut to pick up refugees. I had my taxi booked and we left that evening. I think it was a 10-hour crossing by sea from Beirut to Cyprus so the refugees didn't need too long aboard the navy transports. My pilot put me on the deck of a Type 22 frigate 10 miles off the coast before we went into Beirut bold as brass.

I wasn't confident in any way undertaking this final assignment, and my heart was in my mouth as I went up to the flight deck after being called over the ship's tannoy. Baz was there. Fuck. We looked at each other, and emotions rose in my mind and in my heart. He just stomped over that flight deck, grabbed me and gave me a bear hug as though he were one of the refugees meeting a loved one for the first time in years. He simply held me at arm's length and let me look at him for a few moments before he said that he knew it was no one's fault and he was pleased I had made it out. He held out his hand, a shovel of a hand, and said:

"Hey, we're still brothers, nothing breaks the bond, what is done is done. We all knew the risks, so stop being a dick and come and help me fucking kill this cunt Asad."

I laughed, gave that big fucker a hug and we fucked off down the gangway and off the ship into the town for one last dance. Keith and Hugh were waiting in a Mercedes truck behind the dock barricades, and as we drove out of that city we caught up with all the shit we had done since we were last together as a team. My stories of the patrol boat flowed like a river; I didn't hold back and I think they appreciated the truth, how fucked up it had been. No blame, no sarcasm, just the understanding I would only ever receive from my brothers. They knew, they had endured worse, they had heard of our struggles and were powerless to assist, dealing with their shit here in Lebanon, the team spread thin to deal with too many pieces of the Gulf War puzzle. We had all seen and done all that was required to complete this fucking list, and now it was Asad and his team who would reap the wrath of our losses, our frustrations and our finishing strokes to our masterpiece of intelligence work.

Of course, it would have been easier to just call in an air strike to a pinpointed target, but we needed a confirmed kill and not a newspaper headline declaring Israel had killed hundreds of innocent civilians. We had to be patient, calm, collected and methodical in our planning to ensure a clean kill and an uninterrupted unpublicised extraction. The satisfaction would be all ours knowing we had taken care of our business and remained anonymous. Of course, after we had concluded our mission I would, out of courtesy, you must understand, give my friends in Israel the photos, addresses and coordinates of all those they would want to engage with to conclude their business. Their methodology wouldn't be as subtle as ours and I knew Avner and Shmuel would want a little time to talk to a few of those who dwelled in that house in Dhayra. Their end would be something I would not want to witness or hear about.

The team had set up a surveillance operation diagonally opposite the house where Asad and fuck knows who else had set up their border town base. The comings and goings were frequent, with the team capturing everything on film. It was a typical scenario, the six of us against an entire legion of terrorist activity, but it was soon clear what was happening. The house was an HQ for satellite strike teams dotted along the Israeli border. It was hard for the guys to keep up a good reconnaissance of all the destinations and individuals but gradually we put together a family tree of all Asad's relatives, which included Iranian and Russian connections. This was a whole new set of people that the Steering Group would have to go to work on. Not in my time though, I was too close to the end of my career; active operatives never really go beyond 38 years old, only if they're in a sleeper or long-term mole position, which is usually the case if you're able to keep in a family or organisation in more of a non-combat role.

Keith and I set up our little camp amongst the others, Baz, Hugh, Pierre and some new guys Taff and Bomber (surname Mills – think WW2 RAF). It was a shit apartment, and I didn't leave it, not even for a single breath of fresh air. It was five rooms, all tired whitewashed walls, paint peeling off, only mattresses on the floor to sleep on, those super-cheap shit ones that you can fold in half and put in a suitcase if you want to. There was very little other furniture, just a big table and five chairs. The floor was carpeted in that hard-wearing blue industrial shit that was badly fitted throughout, even in the kitchen. Fucking kitchen looked like it had been used by drugged-up students, with pots and plates stacked high in the sink and the tap dripping over the top, creating a water feature effect through and over the pans and bowls. The dustmen would need to do a good job after we had left, far too many giveaway signs, including Yorkshire fucking tea boxes and Bisto gravy granule tins left lying around the place. Either that or I would need to ask Avner to just blow the fucking place up after we had vacated.

Some evenings it was generally quite entertaining watching one of the guys prepare a meal under a single light bulb hanging down in the kitchen, all of us trying not to take the piss. Lots of card games and fucking Uno, which is impossible to play quietly and shouldn't be played when all your opponents have loaded weapons pointed at you as you hand out a series of 'pick up 4's!!! It was a great couple of weeks just watching, observing and recording everything including the attacks against Israel. It wasn't too long before the green light was given by London to end the party and extract back to Cyprus. Keith and I would finish what we had started with a multi-hit sequence from the apartment and another building further down the street. We decided to execute our orders at the first available opportunity on a Tuesday morning because we were pretty sure this was when Asad greeted his Russian friends into the house.

Keith repositioned himself with Taff and Bomber on the rooftop of the other building whilst Baz covered my rear. I had my mattress on the table in the living room with the window open facing the front of the target building, sniper rifle rested on its tripod, Hugh with the search sight, heart beating, feeling the gentle breeze through the window as I shuffled a little to get absolutely comfortable.

Russians arrived, deep breath.

Simple operation coordinated over comms.

Asad outside with two companions.

Photos taken, recorded and transmitted.

Confirmation to execute over comms.

Permission granted.

First round away, recoil, the echo interrupted by Keith as he let off his first round.

Two targets down, rapid repeat fire, six down.

Pause, looked up at Baz, smiled, and then we were fucking out of there and on the road to pick up the next British ship out of Beirut.

I know what happened next because Avner confirmed the utter destruction of the entire building we were occupying as well as the house Asad had been using. He simply sent a communiqué to the Steering Group thanking us for all the presents we had sent him for his birthday. I was back home within a few weeks after a piss-up in Cyprus to celebrate the end of my career.

I spent the next year in Plymouth doing crap jobs in a pre-release draft. I spent most of my time doing what I wanted. I basically worked shifts on the gate and in the armoury: week of days, week off, week of nights, two weeks off. I enrolled into some serious education to keep my mind busy as I planned my exit into exile for 10 years to New Zealand. It's pretty standard shit. After working for the Steering Group you are encouraged to disappear somewhere safe – New Zealand, America, Canada or Australia; some operatives choose to go completely off grid into the depths of Africa or Thailand. I was keen on New Zealand and took Anna out there a few times trying to convince her this was a great move after the navy, and my retirement...

We moved out to New Zealand to begin our new lives together. It was a struggle at first to get settled but that was all part of the plan. I wasn't retiring, I was just getting started and was about to enter into a new role for the Steering Group outside of the combat world. It wouldn't be too long before I was flying around the world as a delegate, meeting all the right people in all the right places and conducting business on a much, much higher level. But that's a whole other story.

Brotherhood

I have heard it said that God uses our past to be of use in our future. I am attempting to use some of my past to be of some use in the here and now, with my time with you and those who get to meet me. There appear to be so many similarities between the stories of warriors and kings in the Bible and my military past, some I may be afraid to admit.

I think in life we meet many people who cross our path but few become our friends. From what I've seen, God wants us to have brotherhood and fellowship gathered for a common purpose, his purpose. If we are together then we are strong, divided we are weak. Just like my time in the military. I was only strong when I had my team around me. We can't be an army unless we have brotherhood with each other and be close as true friends. I have heard of the love of God and what that is supposed to mean to believers, and it sounds like something I really want. I think it was a kind of love I had for the boys in my unit and my teams.

I have had the privilege to lead men and I think there are many similarities between the military and the Church, be that a temple, a mosque or your friend's house. In the military we would have a commander in chief. Jesus is sort of my commander in chief now. I guess the military would have generals or combat commanders like God has angels and saints – it's a parallel organisational tree.

Apparently, our common purpose in life is to do God's will and spread the good news. I'm not sure about that, I have a selfish quest right now which is to just feel some peace in my life. But I understand following a good leader, and Jesus seems to be a good choice after the realities life has shown me. I feel we need to be united in friendship, and through this love of God we all might find our peace or the love we all so desperately seek to do this life together. It matters not what race, religion or country you are from, we are all brothers under God, whatever name you may call him.

I struggle sometimes and need a point in the right direction. I'm guessing that others are struggling too. But to follow a commander or leader, we need many things from them, or qualities we can relate to or simply want; honour, respect, loyalty and integrity.

Honour – I think we need to be thankful for the gifts God gives us and those around us. I'm just thankful to be here, pleased to be alive I guess. If you do not love someone you do not honour them. Let's honour each other as brothers. Love binds us together to achieve the impossible. My past has shown that if we create bonds they are hard to be broken. I loved my friends to the end. I want to find that love and honour again. I'm thinking this isn't a bad thing and maybe God would like this.

Respect – I commanded respect from men, and they followed me, but we can show respect through our love of each other. His Unfailing Love, Psalm 51.

Loyalty – I want to be loyal to my God – I do not want him to abandon me, or for me to abandon him. Deuteronomy 31:6 says: The Lord your God is the one who goes with you, he will not leave you or forsake you.

Integrity – To be honest and trustworthy with God and each other. I've chosen to try as hard as I can to be honest and trustworthy. I've lied heaps to fit in but it never worked. I've pretended to be someone else but it's just impossible to keep up.

To understand what brotherhood is we need to understand what a friend is and what sets that apart from just mere acquaintances. A friend is supposed to be someone we have an intimate association with and is a favoured companion. I guess as believers in God we should look to Jesus to be that person, but we need to show each other that same closeness because life is damn tough.

To share the pain of loss and the joy of birth or marriage with an equal zeal. If I am to be part of his army, of his Church, then I need to trust people again, and eventually I guess care for you even when it feels impossible, even when we are betrayed or in pain ourselves.

Do you have a companion, a friend who will walk with you through all that life throws at you?

Psalm 68:6 says: God places the lonely in families. Who is your family?

My friends and my best friend followed me into battle and we fought together. They followed me because they believed. We stood together because we loved each other with all our hearts, we had shared brotherhood together, intimate friendship through fun times and hard times, through laughter and sorrow.

My best friend took the pain for me on that day; he saved my life. He was badly hurt but his love for me was greater than the pain he endured.

John 15:13: Greater love has no one than this: to lay down one's life for one's friends.

I had very nearly lost all hope, I was lost and in trouble, but my friend stayed with me... HE DID NOT LEAVE ME. He stayed with me wounded and in pain, he held me in his arms and loved me when all things looked to be over. He held on to me when I had given up. We must be able to do this for one another in everyday life. Look after your brothers and your sisters.

God can help us in our struggles, by us being together. We can help each other, through our lives and to find a way with God. It matters not who we are or where we came from.

When you are in pain, trouble or simply alone, do not abandon each other – draw closer and you will reap rewards, for we will be seen to have loved our friends above ourselves.

Allah is with those who are in service to others.

You shall love your neighbour as yourself. There is no other commandment greater than this.

Hurt not others in ways you yourself would find hurtful.

He who saves a life saves the world entire.

That which is unfavourable to us, do not do that to others.

The Steering Group

References

Chapter 2   Film – The Stanford Prison Experiment. 2015 – (mention only) Coup d'etat Films / Sandbar Pictures / Abandon Pictures

Chapter 2   Film – Karate Kid – 1984 Columbia Pictures (mention only)

Chapter 3   Film – Monty Python – The Meaning of Life 1983. Celandine Films / The Monty Python Partnership / Universal Pictures

                  "John Cleese ends up shouting at himself as the sgt major marching up and down the parade ground on his own"

Chapter 4   Russian toast – the story of the wolf – Original Source unknown to me at the time of writing this book. Reference found to a source in 'Pravda' author Evgeniya Petrova. I cannot determine if this is the original author.

Chapter 5   Film – Titanic 1998. Twentieth Century Fox / Paramount Pictures / Lightstorm Entertainment - Leonardo DiCaprio

                  "like a thousand knives stabbing you all over"

Chapter 5   Military Jokes –References found online at Upjoke.com / Filing Cabinet .com and many others. Original author not known at the time of writing this book.

Chapter 7   Mention of Cauchy's integral formula 1840– Augustin- Louis Cauchy 1789 to 1857

Chapter 8   Film – We Were Soldiers – 2002 Icon Entertainment Ltd / Studio Canal - Mel Gibson – mention only

Chapter 12   Winston Churchill, PM 1939

"a riddle within Enigma"

Chapter 12   Plato, Philosopher 428BC or 424BC

"Only the dead have seen the end of war"

Chapter 13   Yehuda Amichai, Poet 1924 to 2000 (Israeli Poet)

"Always beside ruined houses and iron girders twisted like the arms of the slain, you find someone who is sweeping the paved path or tending the little garden"

Lightning Source UK Ltd.
Milton Keynes UK
UKHW010708310821
389774UK00001B/163

9 781839 752063